NEW YORK TIMES #

JACK GATLAND

THE
LIONHEART
CURSE

Hooded Man
MEDIA
INSPIRATION ● PRODUCTION ● PUBLICATION

Published by Hooded Man Media.

First Edition: January 2022

PRAISE FOR JACK GATLAND

'This is one of those books that will keep you up past your bedtime, as each chapter lures you into reading just one more.'

'This book was excellent! A great plot which kept you guessing until the end.'

'Couldn't put it down, fast paced with twists and turns.'

'The story was captivating, good plot, twists you never saw and really likeable characters. Can't wait for the next one!'

'I got sucked into this book from the very first page, thoroughly enjoyed it, can't wait for the next one.'

'Totally addictive. Thoroughly recommend.'

'Moves at a fast pace and carries you along with it.'

'Just couldn't put this book down, from the first page to the last one it kept you wondering what would happen next.'

Before LETTER FROM THE DEAD...
There was

LIQUIDATE
THE PROFITS

Learn the story of what *really* happened to DI Declan Walsh,
while at Mile End!

An EXCLUSIVE PREQUEL, completely free to anyone who
joins the Declan Walsh Reader's Club!

Join at www.subscribepage.com/jackgatland

Also by Jack Gatland

For Mum, who inspired me to write.

For Tracy, who inspires me to write.

1

MEAN TIME

As Professor Richard Evans walked out of Cutty Sark Docklands Light Railway station, he knew for a fact that someone dangerous was following him.

Turning right, eyes set directly in front as he walked towards Greenwich Church Street, Richard tried to look back at the man through the windows of the shops to his left, catching glimpses as he did so. A shaven-headed brute, over six-feet tall in a black bomber jacket, with dark blue jeans over what looked like army boots and a telltale bulge under the jacket, maybe caused by a gun hanging there, if you believed movies. Richard looked towards the open plaza that surrounded the hundred-year-old tea clipper known as the Cutty Sark, wondering whether he should make a run for it; but he knew if he did, then the man would easily catch him...

Or worse.

He'd known there was a 'ghost' following him since he'd left Fleet Street earlier that day, but to be honest, Richard had hoped to lose them when he entered the maze of pedestrian tunnels that connected into Bank Underground Station.

However, as he arrived at West India Quay, Richard knew he'd failed.

He didn't know for sure why the man was following him, but he had a good idea. He'd been with him since Temple Inn, one of the four Inns of Court in London and so it was probably connected with the meeting Richard had just finished, one that necessitated an immediate visit to one of London's Hawksmoor churches.

A visit that simply couldn't happen if he was being followed.

Richard slowed as he passed the entrance to Greenwich Market, a portico of pale brown pillars that flanked a cobbled pedestrian pathway. Taking a deep breath, Richard prepared himself. He wasn't unfit, but the years in academia hadn't been kind, and his sixty-seven-year-old frame was as flabby, weak and prone to mild asthma as the next professor. Richard knew he wouldn't be able to outrun this man; the boots alone meant his shadow was probably ex-army, and therefore far fitter than Richard could ever be.

No, Richard had to out-think the man, to get some distance, even for a few moments, to do what he needed to do, before they eventually caught him.

As the bald-headed man took a call on his phone, briefly looking away from his quarry, Richard used this to his advantage, slipping quickly through the entrance of the recently refurbished Admiral Hardy pub, walking through the main bar and exiting out the back entrance into the busy thoroughfare of Greenwich Market, desperate to put some distance between him and his pursuer.

The Market was a natural plaza built within the surrounding buildings; a modern, metal framed glass roof that let in the natural light of the day, shining onto the stalls that rented space underneath, each selling goods from street food, all the way to handmade leather bags and twelve-inch vinyl records cut into novelty silhouette clocks. Usually this was a bustling indoor arena and Richard had hoped the crowd might hide him as he entered, but it was nearing the end of the day, and many of the stalls were closing up, packing their stock away as he hurried past.

He paused at a still open stall, a variety of football team postcards for sale on the table. A particular team photo caught his eye and, without pausing he picked up two copies from the lady behind the table, tossing a ten pound note down as payment and leaving before she could find the change, placing first-class stamps onto each from a pack in his wallet as he continued walking. Then, moving to the middle of the plaza, turning and briskly walking down the wider entrance of Durnford Street, Richard pulled a pen out from his inside jacket pocket and, resting against a wall beside an artisan French bistro, quickly began writing on both postcards, addressing each one. Unfortunately he could see no postbox nearby, so he placed both in his pocket and moved on once more, planning to find a place to post them as soon as he was safe from his follower.

Emerging from the market entrance onto Greenwich Church Street, he turned to face the imposing white presence of St Alfege Church, the reason for his Greenwich visit.

Unfortunately, in front of him, standing beside a large black limousine was the bald-headed shadow.

'Professor Evans,' the man called out, his accent slightly European, opening the door to reveal the limo's back seats, 'my employer would like a word with you.'

Nodding dumbly and aware that the chase was over,

Richard reluctantly allowed the man to manhandle him into the limo, the door shutting behind him.

Settling into one of the plush, leather back seats, he looked at the man sitting opposite.

Dressed in a simple black suit with a white dress shirt unbuttoned at the collar and spotless brown brogues completing the ensemble, Martin Shrewsbury exuded *money* as he sipped at a glass of whisky, his pale blue eyes never wavering from Richard's face.

He placed the glass on a small wooden side table attached to the side of the limo.

'You can proceed, Cyrus,' he said.

The bald-headed man, now in the front passenger seat, muttered to the driver of the limo and it pulled slowly out into the Greenwich traffic, as Shrewsbury turned his attention back to Richard.

Like a shark considering dinner, Richard thought to himself as he glanced out of the window, watching Greenwich pass by, trying not to look his captor in the face. Not that it was an unattractive face; over the years, Richard had found that his tastes moved more towards men than women, especially a bearded look on a man, someone a little stockier; it was simply the fact that this was a face that Richard knew well from a dozen magazine articles, news interviews, even talk shows. It was a boyish face, belying the middle-aged man behind it, and Richard didn't want to mentally link that face to kidnap, theft or possibly worse to come.

Martin Shrewsbury was a tech magnate right-wing poster boy; a proponent of ultra-nationalism and one of the richest 'alt-right' activists in England. Probably Europe, too, if you really looked hard into the details. With his good looks and neatly trimmed salt and pepper hair, Shrewsbury was quoted by the British news outlets as the 'acceptable face' of passive racism in the United Kingdom, while constantly claiming in press conferences and interviews he was nothing like the man 'portrayed by the leftist media.'

'I'm sorry about all of this cloak and dagger business, Professor,' Shrewsbury's smile was meant to disarm his opponent, but it did the complete opposite.

'There's a dozen bars in Greenwich. You couldn't just meet me?' Richard replied, the fury in his tone clear. 'Or perhaps back in Fleet Street when your goon first followed me?'

Shrewsbury shrugged.

'You have to understand that I have a lot of enemies, looking to attack me at their first opportunity. All of this? It becomes second nature.'

'But surely, they're just people on the Internet, not some kind of vast terrorist organisation?' Richard snapped in response. 'I mean, I know you *do* so love the term 'Antifa'.'

'*Everyone's* a person on the Internet these days,' Shrewsbury replied, 'that doesn't mean they're not insane enough to attack you with a weapon. Antifa is exactly what it says it is; Anti-Fascists. And people who are anti-fascism can be pretty violent.'

'Oh, I agree.' Richard smiled. 'I think we called them the Allied Forces during the Second World War.'

'I'm no Nazi.' Shrewsbury shifted in his seat. 'I'm a scapegoat for many people who can't find the true face of racism and look for the next best thing. Please, have a drink.'

He picked up a tumbler, already filled with whisky, offering it to Richard.

'It's a Balvenie forty-year-old malt scotch,' he explained as he waited, hand still held out. 'It goes for five grand a bottle these days. Incredibly rare. I believe the more recent Balvenies, however, are your drink of choice?'

'You mean the cheaper ones,' Richard reluctantly took the glass. He didn't want to drink with the man facing him, but the chance to sample such a classic whisky was too much to turn away from. There was a subtle aftertaste to it, as he felt the familiar kick of the whisky slide down his throat.

Sipping his own drink, Martin Shrewsbury leaned forward, steepling his fingers together as he faced the old academic.

'Let's skip the small talk and be blunt about things, Professor,' he started. 'I asked you into my limo for a single reason and I apologise that it was necessary to force the point, but I wish to ask you a question that is your area of expertise, a question I've not only asked you before, but also paid you to answer.'

'You paid without asking if I wanted your blood money.'

'*Everyone* wants the money,' Shrewsbury sighed. 'That you took it and ran, tells me more about you than me. So, as I've paid for the bloody information, tell me... what do you know about King Richard's gold?'

'Seriously? You follow me across London to ask about that?' Richard sat back in the seat. Street chases and strange car rides weren't his forte, but a question like this was far more his cup of tea. 'It's a myth, nothing more. King Richard's gold, the *Plantagenet* gold, no matter what you call it, it's just Anti-Tudor propaganda, created during the War of the Roses purely to convince people to fight for the Yorkist cause.'

'You don't believe it exists?'

'I don't think anyone does,' Richard sipped at his whisky. 'No proof of its existence was ever found, and when Henry Tudor defeated Richard The Third at Bosworth, it was nowhere to be seen, giving credence to the stories that it was nothing more than a fairy tale for gullible people.'

Richard smiled.

'You know, like you.'

'I don't care about battles,' Shrewsbury leaned back, rubbing at his eyes. 'Tell me of the *gold*.'

'Well, as I said, these are nothing but fairy tales, told to children—'

'*Then tell me like I'm a child!*' Shrewsbury slammed his fist on the side table, his glass tumbling to the floor of the limousine at the force of the impact.

Richard swallowed hard, suddenly recalling the man's reputation for violence.

'OK, let me rephrase that,' he answered softly. 'The stories talk about Crusader gold, booty looted from the Middle East and brought back by Richard the Lionheart. Treasure that was then taken into the care of William Marshall, Richard's most trusted supporter and the Knights Templar, because Richard was buggering off again. Silly bastard lived for fighting in other countries. Anyway, after Richard's death, William was supposed to give the gold to Prince John, but the Prince and William hated each other, so William refused, only telling John's son Henry of it when he became Henry the Third.'

Shrewsbury stared out of the car window at the passing shop fronts. Looking out of the same window, Richard could see that they were heading south, towards Deptford Bridge.

'So, what happened after that?'

'Well, nothing. It became this mythical gold that was apparently worth millions, billions, even. Every Plantagenet king was supposed to have passed the secret of the gold to his successor before he died.'

'So where do you believe it is now?'

Richard shrugged.

'It's in a room with Excalibur, Hercules' golden belt and all the other magical items of story. Even if its location had been passed down, and even if the Plantagenets had known its location after Richard the Second's death, Edward the Fourth would have told his son, not Richard the Third.'

'The prince in the tower?'

'One of them, yes.'

'So what, Richard locked him up until he told him the location? That didn't really end well for either of them,' Shrewsbury nodded silently, as if mulling over the story.

For several seconds, the car was silent before he spoke again.

'What if someone *found it?*'

Richard couldn't stop the chuckle that came out.

'Then I would say they were both the luckiest and the unluckiest person in the world.'

'Why?'

'Because the gold was legendary. Its apparent wealth in gold and jewels was *El Dorado, Cibola* and the other cities of gold all mixed into one. If it was worth millions almost a thousand years ago, it'd be worth trillions now. You could clear America's whole national debt with one payment. However, that much gold inserted back into the global economy would destabilise and destroy it instantly. In one swift move, they'd kill every currency on the planet.'

Shrewsbury nodded again, his eyes locking onto Richard.

'With that much money behind me, I could do anything, command everything. Control Europe by *divine right.*'

He smiled a dark, vicious smile, filled with hate and venom.

'Divine *white*.'

Richard Evans stared at the man in front of him, every hope that the press had maligned him now gone forever. Martin Shrewsbury wasn't how the media had portrayed. He was worse.

'No.'

Richard's voice trembled as he spoke.

'No?'

Richard nodded.

'Why would I help you?' he asked. 'What could I possibly want from this?'

'Apart from the money I've already given you?'

'Research grants never get used for what they're supposed to,' Richard smiled. 'Get used to it. Oh, and thank you for your donation.'

'What about the academic regard you'd get for your discovery?' Shrewsbury suggested. 'Make your peers regret they ever doubted you. I'd even make an endowment in your name, something to really stick it to them.'

'All your solutions are based on money,' Richard shook his head. 'Pay the problem to make it go away.'

'Money solves all problems,' Shrewsbury shrugged. 'And anyone who doesn't believe that is letting themselves be led to the eventual slaughter by capitalist politicians with selfish agendas.'

'And yours aren't?' Richard shook his head at this. 'No, I'm sorry, but I won't help you find money to fund your hate groups and your growing number of alt-white terrorists.'

'But you don't know what I want.'

'I think I do,' Richard sat back, a sweat now across his brow. 'You want the Sunne Dial. The code wheel from Doctor

John Dee's personal adaptation of the *Steganographica*. You think it'll help. It won't.'

'Then you won't mind giving it to me then,' Shrewsbury held his hand out, as if expecting Richard to have it in his pockets. 'I know you found a note about its location at a church in Antwerp last month. A little birdie told me just this week that you're still rooting around, hunting for it.'

Richard shifted nervously in his chair.

'I don't have the note anymore—'

Richard didn't expect the backhanded slap, knocking him backwards into the chair, moisture glinting upon his bloodied lip, and Shrewsbury now leaning menacingly over the academic.

'Don't lie to me!' he screamed.

'There you are,' Richard replied calmly. 'There's the man I've read about. Did you really think I hadn't seen the people following me over the last few weeks?'

Thrown off balance by this response, Shrewsbury's confidence suddenly evaporated, replaced by a horrified realisation.

'What did you do?' he asked carefully.

Richard sat back up, his spine straighter than it was before, as a grim and stark determination set in.

'You'll never know. And more importantly, your little Nazi shitwit friends won't ever know either.'

'Then let's make a different deal. Something a little more personal,' Shrewsbury showed the now empty whisky tumbler in Richard's hand. 'Your life for the note. I placed a nerve toxin in the drink. You should start to feel the effects by now. Increased temperature, nausea...'

Richard *was* feeling sick now, an uncertain sensation in

his stomach. And there had been an aftertaste that he'd ignored.

'You give me the note, or tell me what was on it, and I give you the antidote.'

Slowly reaching for the door's handle, Richard forced a smile. The lights ahead were red, and the limo was slowing beside a busy bus stop.

'I'm sorry, Mister Shrewsbury, but your threats aren't really that scary,' he replied. 'I've researched into death all my academic career. It's an old friend of mine.'

'Nobody's that friendly with death.'

'They are when they have terminal bowel cancer.'

And with that Richard pulled hard at the door handle, opening it before the driver could lock it, and quickly stepped out onto the pavement, slamming the door shut behind him and moving back into the bus stop queue, mingling with the surrounding people. As the lights turned green, he watched the limousine pause for a moment, and then continue on. Martin Shrewsbury wisely didn't want to be seen chasing after an academic on a Deptford street, and he sure as hell wasn't going to return to give Richard the antidote to whatever poison now coursed through his body.

With no time to lose, Richard stumbled towards Deptford Methodist Church. He could already feel his heart racing and didn't know how long he had left. A hundred yards to the east was a postbox, and Richard headed towards it. Reaching into his inside pocket, Richard pulled out the two postcards, placing them into the slot with a small smile of triumph. This completed, Richard lurched away, staggering down Macmillan Street for a further fifty yards before it turned to the right.

St. Nicholas's Church had first been built in the fourteenth century, but the building that loomed above him was built in the seventeenth, shortly before the parish of Deptford was split in two. Richard made his way slowly through the main entrance, a pair of brick pillars holding up an ornate, black, wrought-iron gate. As he did so, he looked at the two stone 'skull and crossbones' statues that guarded both sides of the gate. Although skulls and crossed bones were a common feature of graveyards, in Elizabethan times this had also been a naval church; the docks where Francis Drake moored the original *Golden Hind* were nearby, and Richard liked to imagine that some of the other English privateers who had attended church here, perhaps even Captain Morgan himself had seen these statues and created the 'Jolly Roger' because of them. However, they were nothing more than a chilling reminder of Richard's imminent future and, as he walked slowly into the churchyard, now leaning against a tree beside the path, Richard collapsed onto his knees, before struggling back up and gasping with effort as he continued around the large, red brick and stone church, lurching now towards its North wall.

This is so unfair, he thought to himself; *I was almost there.*

On the North wall, beside a tree and half covered in ivy, was a simple marble plaque:

NEAR THIS SPOT LIE THE MORTAL REMAINS OF
CHRISTOPHER MARLOWE
WHO MET HIS UNTIMELY DEATH IN DEPTFORD ON MAY
30TH 1593
Cut is the branch that might have grown full straight...
Doctor Faustus

Falling to the ground in front of it, his strength almost

gone as the toxin took its toll, Richard stared weakly up at the inscription. Scrabbling around in the dirt, he found two small sticks, no more than five inches in length. Laying them across each other, he made an 'X' on the floor before finally leaning against the brickwork of the wall.

'Ah, Kit...' he whispered to the plaque. 'If only I knew whether I was right. That's not too much to ask for, is it?'

The only response was the wind in the trees as Professor Richard Evans, staring blankly into the air, lay lifeless beside the wall.

———

2

SHAKESPEARE'S MISTER

DAMIAN LUCAS KNEW SOMETHING WAS WRONG AS HE WATCHED the other diners at the restaurant, but he didn't know what it was.

Gathering his thoughts, he leaned back and rubbed his eyes before examining his three dinner companions; Pierre LeFleur and Joanne Kendal, Acquisitions Consultants for *Taymaster Industries* and Max Larridge, a well-known 'fixer' for the seedier side of the academic world. Pierre was resplendent in a teal Ted Baker three-piece suit, his greying hair cut to a trendy Shoreditch style, while Joanne wore what looked like a more subdued Ralph Lauren, her hair pulled back tight into a bun. Max Larridge, however, was the polar opposite, in a pair of black Levis, a dark blue shirt and a black Superdry denim jacket, his brown curly hair left tousled. Damian himself was wearing a navy Hermes two piece with a tailored black dress shirt underneath. With the suit worth a couple of grand alone, it was a lot of money's worth of clothing for one man to wear.

'Where was I?' he asked.

Joanne leaned forwards.

'You were telling us about the manuscript, Crown Prince.'

Damian nodded, forcing a smile.

'Of course,' he replied. 'So, I don't claim to be any authority...'

'You can say that again,' a voice in his ear muttered. Damian tapped at it irritably.

'Something the matter?' Pierre looked concerned.

Forcing a smile, Damian indicated the earpiece inside the ear canal.

'I've been deaf in my left ear since I was five, Mister LeFleur,' he explained. 'I therefore wear a device to assist with hearing. But sometimes, the how do you say, the radio waves...'

'The frequency?'

'Ah yes, the *frequency* slips sometimes and I suddenly have voices in my ear, like buzzing bees.'

'Oh, that's nice,' the voice muttered again.

'No fear though, I'm sure it will stop very soon,' Damian smiled a winning smile.

'I can stop right now,' the voice snapped. 'I'll just shut up and you can do this on your bloody own.'

Damian went to reply softly, but paused as he saw the waiter returning to the table, Damian's card in his hand and a worried expression on his face. As Damian had offered that card to pay for this very expensive meal moments earlier, this was equally worrying.

'The waiter returns,' he muttered to himself. The voice in his ear was silent as the waiter stopped at the table.

'Mister Von Ludwig...'

'*Crown Prince* Von Ludwig,' Damian corrected him with all the force he could muster. 'What is the problem?'

'Your card. They declined it.'

Damian waved a hand dismissively. 'Nonsense. Try it again.'

'We did.'

Damian reached for his cell phone.

'There is some issue here. Let me speak to my personal banker.'

'It's fine,' Pierre interceded, reaching into his jacket. 'Let us cover this—'

'No,' Damian rose now, phone to his ear. 'You are my guests. This is my issue.'

He looked at the waiter.

'Stay,' he commanded as he walked away from the table.

'What the hell are you playing at?' he hissed into the phone, while really speaking to the mysterious voice in his ear.

'I don't know, I'm checking into it right now,' Damian could almost hear the voice of Andy Holdman frowning as he spoke.

'If this is a prank, it's not funny,' hissed Damian, his accent suddenly more working class than it was a minute earlier. 'The debit card's not going through.'

'Yeah. There's no money in the account.'

'What? We had enough in there to cover the dinner.'

'Someone removed it.'

'You *what?*' Damian looked back to the table, forcing a smile as he mimed a 'talking' motion with his other hand. 'Who could do that?'

'My guess is the Russians,' Andy replied.

Damian groaned.

'What can we do about it?' he asked. 'I have people waiting here.'

'I'm re-routing the last transfer,' the voice of Andy continued. 'it was only five minutes ago, so it hasn't cleared...'

Damian looked around the restaurant. It wasn't a cheap one; it wasn't even an expensive one; it was a restaurant where the *ultra-rich* ate, a stylish, marble walled chrome travesty of a dining experience, with reservations made weeks in advance and more Michelin stars on the wall than were in the sky. With the wine they'd ordered alongside it, the small lunch that he'd just offered to pay for was coming in at just under a grand before the tip, and someone out there was trying to stop him from paying that.

A someone that was likely to want him killed, or at the least hurt really bad.

Damian's eyes fell on a man at the bar in a slim fitting black suit, engrossed as he read something on his phone. Although there was nothing out of the ordinary here, something tweaked at the back of Damian's consciousness as he returned to the call.

'Feel free to take your time.'

'Yeah, I was planning to,' Andy's voice wasn't as sarcastic as his response warranted, and Damian wondered for a moment whether he actually was.

'Right. The card has money again.'

'Did you get the money back?'

'No, I transferred next month's rent payment to you in,' Andy replied. 'I'm guessing if this goes wrong, we'll be in prison by the time it's due, and I'll pay you in cigarettes. Just get Max to send us the cut ASAP.'

Damian looked at the man in the suit again, suddenly realising what was nagging him. The man was still reading something on his phone, but at no point had he swiped on the screen to scroll the text up, or move the page on. For someone to read the same static page for that long seemed incredibly out of the ordinary.

And the only out of the ordinary thing here was Damian, or rather Crown Prince Ludwig.

'Shit.'

'I promise you, the money's there—'

'No,' Damian turned the other way, hiding his face from the suited man. 'I think the Russians have found me. There's a guy here reading a phone, but it seems more of a prop than a source of reading material, if you know what I mean?'

'Get out now.'

'I'm too close right now, and we've already had lunch,' Damian replied. 'I'll get out when I can. But just in case, keep an eye on the dark net.'

'I love it when people say that,' Andy mocked. 'Like it's some kind of Twitter or Facebook where we can read all the posts.'

'Am I wrong?'

'Shut up and do your thing.'

Ignoring the jibe, Damian walked back to the table.

'My personal banker tells me we have no problems,' he said to the waiter, 'it is therefore your machine. Try again.'

Reluctantly, the waiter reinserted the card, passing it to Damian to type in the four-digit pin code. This time, however, the card was approved on the screen, and with a singular smirk, Damian took the card back from the waiter and sat down.

'As I said, your machine was to blame, making me look like a fool in front of my very important guests,' he said. 'I expect a bottle of expensive wine to be brought to the table, free of charge for the inconvenience and embarrassment you have caused me.'

The waiter nodded.

'Of course, Crown Prince.'

Damian stared at the waiter. The waiter stared back.

'Now.'

With a jerk of realisation, the waiter scurried away as Damian looked back at the three waiting faces, now back in character.

'Where were we?'

'The manuscript,' once more Joanne leaned forward.

'Of course,' Damian dropped his voice, leaning in to meet the others. By doing this, he knew they would naturally lean in to listen, joining Joanne as they subconsciously became part of the story themselves, and therefore more invested in the lie he was about to tell. 'So, tell me. What do you know about Shakespeare's lost play?'

'You mean *Cardenio?*' Pierre's eyes widened as he spoke. 'Attributed to Shakespeare and John Fletcher in a Stationer's Register in 1653 by Humphrey Moseley.'

Shakespeare's rumoured lost play *The History of Cardenio* was a unicorn among literary scholars; believed to be a story taken from Cervantes' 1605 novel *Don Quixote*, and expanded into a barely performed play by both Fletcher and Shakespeare ten years later. Damian had counted on them knowing this, as he hadn't known until Andy had explained it to him.

Twice.

'Moseley was a liar, though,' Joanne argued. 'He was known for using Shakespeare's name to sell things. The play probably never even existed.'

'No, because The King's Men performed it in 1613, while Fletcher and Shakespeare worked together on *Henry the Eighth* and *Two Noble Kinsmen*, so there's every chance that it existed,' Pierre looked angrily at his contemporary, and for a moment Damian thought that a fight was about to break out. You could never tell with literary academics, or acquisition experts.

'And what if something *did* exist?' Damian interrupted, letting the words sink in with his guests before he reached down to a smart slim briefcase, gold clasps over smooth black leather, pulling it up to the table and opening it. 'What if a page, the first scene of the first act, written in Shakespeare's own hand...'

'*With annotations by Fletcher,*' the voice in his ear added.

'With annotations by Fletcher beside it was to be found?'

Now both Pierre and Joanne looked at each other.

'It would be priceless.' Joanne said.

'Definitive proof.' Pierre agreed.

Damian carefully removed a sheet of clear plastic, a single parchment page held within, the words written upon it scratchy and hard to read. But at the top, they could see clearly the title of the play.

The History of Cardenio.

'I believe the British Library has the only known example of Shakespeare's handwriting in its archives, yes?' he asked. 'Then, as Taymaster Industries is a patron of the British Library, you'll be able to borrow the book to examine the piece, and compare the lines written within it against this.'

There was a moment of silence as the two consultants stared at the parchment, while Max drank from his wine-glass, as if hiding a smile.

'If this is genuine, how did you get it?' Joanne looked up from the parchment suspiciously. 'And why only this page?'

'Ah, and therein lies the story,' Damian smiled. 'Apparently this page was left in the library of King Ferdinand the Second and lost during the Thirty Years War. It was only in recent years that we learnt that this singular sheet of parchment, removed from Prague before the Second World War began and brought to our small, northern European Province...'

He smiled, apologetically.

'Well, that it was *so important.*'

Pierre and Joanne made appreciative 'umm' noises as they continued to examine the parchment. If real, something like this was utterly priceless in the right hands and the winner of the pissing contest to beat all pissing contests, displayed for all to see in their head office. Damian could almost see the thoughts running through their minds; the delight at the anger their closest rivals would feel, and the respect that they would finally be given both professionally and academically once Taymaster revealed this find to the world.

Quietly, Damian waited patiently for them to finish their examination. This was the important part, as the parchment, like 'Crown Prince Ludwig', was nothing more than a forgery and a lie, albeit a good one at that. But a romantic story of a lost scrap of history, almost forgotten in a world of war and poverty, was enough to paper over some of the obvious tears and rips in the tale. People bought items, but people paid more money for items with a legend attached. Just ask anyone who paid triple the asking price for 'love' diamonds, or anything with a romantic heritage.

'How much would you be looking for to sell this?' Pierre looked nervous as he spoke, mentally calculating such a cost. 'I mean, it's worth millions to the right person.'

'I do not sell it,' Damian replied. 'I give it to you. The Bard of Avon must be brought home to England. Perhaps I might receive a mention in an honours list, one day?'

This was the kicker. To not ask for a penny was the moment that everything clicked into place.

After all, why would someone spend all this time and effort to give something away?

'Um, Crown Prince?' Max now leaned forward, placing his wineglass down. 'That's not how things work here. For a start, I need my finder's fee for putting you all together.'

'Ah, true,' Damian allowed a conflicted expression to cross his face as he looked back at Pierre. 'I had promised Mister Larridge here an introduction fee of four thousand pounds. Perhaps you could provide this?'

'Of course we could,' the delight in Pierre's voice was evident. Max immediately handed him a card with some bank details on, and Pierre opened up an app on his smartphone, tapping the details in and paying the amount before anyone at the table could change their mind. Damian guessed that four thousand pounds was less than they spent on coffee in a month at Taymaster's fifteen storey head office in Canary Wharf.

Watching his own phone, Max nodded almost imperceptibly to Damian, who smiled.

'And perhaps as a goodwill gesture, your corporation could donate some funds to my favourite place in the world, the British Library?'

'We already do that,' Joanne spoke without looking up from the manuscript.

'Oh yes, I know. But libraries are very important, and I had heard that you had to drop your donation amount this past year.'

Pierre frowned, and Damian knew the businessman was

now wondering how much this 'additional donation' was going to be.

Again, this was a moment to be careful.

'Something that would give the library great joy, perhaps enable a modest showing in the Ritblat Gallery, nothing more. Shall we say twenty thousand pounds?'

Damian watched Pierre and Joanne look at each other. Twenty thousand pounds, plus the small finder's fee for possibly the greatest finds in recent history. As far as they were concerned, Crown Prince Ludwig was a bloody idiot, and they were about to become stupidly rich. They could inflate the purchase price to an easy million before they invoiced Taymaster, giving them just under half a million each in their soon to be hastily created secret offshore accounts; and even with that, it would still class them as heroes for their company.

The thought of it being a fake was completely gone from their minds.

'If this is impossible, I totally understand,' Damian said softly, 'I have a meeting with *The Globe* at—'

He stopped as Pierre held up a hand.

'No no, that's fine.'

'The Globe Theatre would have a stroke if we had this.' Joanne smiled.

'Screw them, imagine the *RSC*. They'd die on the bloody spot,' Pierre looked back to Damian. 'Oh, I think we can arrange this.'

'Good,' Damian took the parchment and placed it back into the briefcase, passing a business card over to Pierre. 'This has the account details of the British Library on it. Once you donate, you can have the manuscript. And the briefcase too, as a gift.'

As Pierre once more tapped numbers into his phone app, desperate to seal the deal before the idiot in front of him realised its true value, Damian glanced around the restaurant to see if the slim suited, possibly Russian man was still at the bar.

He was, and now he was staring back at him.

And, more importantly, a second, younger man, a vicious looking Asian dressed in the same style of suit, was next to him.

With a forced relaxation to his gait, Damian rose from his chair.

'I must use the washrooms,' he said apologetically. 'I will be back momentarily.'

The last lie of the day, he hoped. That the slim suited man was still watching as Damian made his way across the half-crowded restaurant to the side door meant there was no way in hell that he'd be returning here.

'Give me a back exit,' he whispered.

'Through the kitchen. Door's to the side of the toilets.'

Passing through the side door and entering the narrow, red walled corridor to the toilets, Damian picked up the pace, walking through a doorway marked 'Private' to the left and closing it quickly behind him. This done, he walked, almost running through the restaurant's busy kitchen, sidling through the confused chefs and kitchen staff. There was a slamming of a door behind him, and Damian glanced back to see the Asian man following at a sprint, grasping into his inside jacket pocket.

Damian didn't want to know what was in the jacket and, reaching out as he ran past the cook's counters, he grabbed a skillet pan, spinning around quickly to face his attacker, swinging it hard as he did so. It was a perfect move, and the pan slammed into the side of the attacker's head exactly on cue.

Staggering back, the man growled at Damian and charged at him.

Damian didn't have time to say anything as the two of them tumbled into a chef counter, the now bleeding and angry Asian man grabbing at Damian's throat, trying to squeeze the life out of the conman. Looking for anything that he could use as a weapon with one hand while trying to pull the hands away with the other, Damian grabbed an open spice jar of chilli powder and slammed it into the Asian man's face. As his attacker fell back, clutching at his eyes, Damian grabbed another pan, this time a heavy iron pot, and smacked it down with force onto the back of the Asian man's head.

As his attacker collapsed unconscious to the floor, Damian dropped the pan as he knelt, his own eyes watering from the chilli dust he'd inhaled, opening the jacket to see what he'd been reaching for.

'Ah shit. It's a gun.'

'Russians.'

'I'm not sure. They don't usually have Asians working for them.'

'Is he Asian, or is he Mongolian?'

'How the hell do I know?'

'You could ask him?'

'Yeah, I think I'll ignore that. The other guy's still in the restaurant.'

Damian looked around.

'I'm out of here,' he said as he took the gun and tossed it into a pot of boiling water, heading off towards a fire exit that led him into the alley beside the restaurant.

Now outside, Damian chose the lesser of two evils. To go right would bring him out to the front of the restaurant, and he'd be seen through the large bay windows by either his dinner companions or the slim suited man; which would make the whole escape pointless. So, Damian turned left and, no longer pretending to be anything more than a well-dressed, scared man in his early twenties, started off down the alley at a sprint.

Behind him he heard the door to the restaurant kitchen crash open again amidst shouts from within, and he didn't need to look back to know either the slim, suited man, his Asian friend or perhaps both followed his route through the restaurant and had emerged into the alley behind him. But Damian had enough advantage to gain some distance, and by the time whoever it was following him left the alley, the fake Crown Prince was nowhere to be seen.

In fact, Damian was almost beside them, currently crouched on the floor of a black cab only five-feet away from the pavement, non-moving and stuck in traffic. The floor was sticky and wet with mud and dirt left by shoes of previous passengers, and Damian carefully held himself so not one part of his incredibly expensive trousers brushed against it.

The driver, watching ahead, spoke quietly.

'Looks like a big balding bastard, that one.'

'I didn't know she was his girlfriend,' Damian lied, still wiping at his streaming eyes. 'He's gonna kill me if he sees me.'

There was a jerk as the cab continued on, as Damian held the seat to stop himself tumbling backwards onto the sticky floor.

'Nah, he's walking the other way now,' the driver said, and Damian risked a peek through the back window to see the slim, suited man angrily walking in the other direction. Rising from the cab's floor and sitting back onto the seat, Damian breathed out a sigh of relief, chuckling to himself for a moment, before the paranoia set in. He had escaped from his pursuer, and that was good. But what wasn't good was that he still didn't know the man's identity, or why he wanted Damian.

Had they found the con out? Was it the Russians? The police, perhaps?

No, the police wouldn't have guns. And even if it had been, there was nothing linking Damian to anything illegal. He hadn't tried to sell the fake parchment, and had instead offered it for nothing, a donation the only request. And the donation wasn't in any way connected to him, either; the British Library was a large and respected institution, after all.

He'd called himself 'Crown Prince' yet had never officially claimed the title, and even the bank account was a business account with the name 'Damian Lucas trading as Crown Prince Ludwig', ensuring the 'company name' of *Crown Prince Ludwig* was on the debit card. And Max, an old friend from University could simply claim that he too was conned, an unaware participant in something he thought was an elaborate academic game between friends, while quietly covering the cost of the dinner back to Damian with another grand attached to cover expenses, over two thousand pounds in profit for effectively an hour's work.

No, the only thing Damian had truly done today was convince Taymaster Industries to donate twenty thousand pounds from their purchase account to the British Library, and that was because they'd recently reduced their own yearly donation by the same amount, causing a valuable display to go elsewhere.

If Taymaster Industries learnt the piece was fake, there was no way they'd admit it to the world. Instead, they'd quietly remove Pierre and Joanne, who by that point would have a nice nest egg from the upselling of the manuscript to fall back on.

Looking out of the window of the cab, Damian noticed they were heading past Holborn station.

'Actually, drop me off here, please,' he said, passing a ten-pound note through the hole in the glass and hopping out of the cab.

Now on the Kingsway, Damian stretched, smiled, and for the first time in a while relaxed.

His phone pinged with a message from Max saying that the money had gone through, and Damian texted back that the Crown Prince, overcome with joy at the return of this piece of history to its home had been called elsewhere, but everyone should enjoy the expensive complimentary wine that was soon to arrive. Once done, Damian logged onto his own account on his phone, using the app to transfer the money that Max had just deposited so Andy could immediately place his rent payment back into Damian's mortgage account. The account of 'Crown Prince Ludwig' would now lie dormant and empty. There was no point in closing the account; these things often created warning bells within banks, so it was easier to simply forget it for the moment, and use it only if they ever gave Crown Prince Ludwig an encore.

He was so engrossed in this that he hadn't noticed the van pull up near him, nor did he notice a large Russian man, easily seven feet in height and half as wide, a wiry brillo pad of steel grey hair on his head and cheeks calmly walk over to him.

'Hello, Damian,' said the large Russian man.

Damian looked up at his name. And as his face paled and his insides turned to water, he weakly forced a smile.

'Is that Pietr?' Andy's voice was terrified. 'Oh crap, that's Pietr!'

'Hello, Pietr,' Damian said, his voice croaking, 'fancy meeting you here.'

'Yes, funny,' Pietr Babistov wasn't smiling. 'Come, get in the van, please.'

'Do I have to?' Damian looked around, hoping for the first time to find a police officer nearby.

There was nobody.

Just Pietr.

Who now smiled.

'I think so, yes.' Pietr showed the empty seat beside him in the van again. 'My mistress wants to speak to you.'

There was no place to run. No place to hide.

The Russians had found Damian Lucas, and he was well and truly screwed.

3

CONCRETE SHOES

THE JOURNEY IN THE VAN DIDN'T TAKE LONG, AND DAMIAN estimated that they'd travelled East from Holborn, through the city. He would have asked Pietr, but the tall, muscled beast of a man sat stock still beside him, and Damian didn't really want to interrupt whatever thoughts the Russian had.

Around Eastcheap, the van turned into a building site, one of the many city skyscrapers that were being built across London, and Damian felt another wave of fear. It was a well-known story that the Kray twins took their enemies to building sites in East London, usually motorways that were under construction, to then bury them in concrete, deep within the foundations of the supports.

'Can you say where you are?' the voice of Andy was soft in his ear, as if too scared to speak loudly in case the Russians overheard. Pietr now looked over to Damian, smiling, and for the first time on that journey, he wondered how the Russians had found him so easily.

'Nice suit,' Pietr said conversationally. 'Looks expensive. Maybe you have come into money, yes?'

'It's a loaner,' Damian replied, showing the tag still attached to the inside. 'I'm taking it back today.'

'Ah, so you must keep it clean or you will have to pay...' Pietr looked at the tag and whistled. 'Such money!'

'It's a con job,' Damian continued. 'I know I said that I'd stop them, but I needed to find the money for you, and this was a way to do it.'

The van stopped beside a large concrete mixer, and Pietr opened the door as he spoke.

'Ah, so the suit is to help us gain back our money?'

'Of course!' Damian mocked horror that the large, terrifying Russian could think anything else, as he followed him out into the building site.

'Not a good con job.'

'How do you mean?'

'We empty your account,' Pietr said matter-of-factly. 'Barely a thousand pounds. Not worth our time.'

'You could always give it back.'

Pietr laughed at this as they continued into the building site.

The first thing Damian noted was that it was empty. The building was half finished, and it was a weekday, but the construction crew were strangely absent.

'Day off?' he asked. Pietr shrugged.

'Private meeting,' he said, pointing to an SUV parked across the open space. Damian already knew who was in it.

'Do you want me to call the police?'

Before Damian could reply though, Pietr shook his head.

'Tell your fat friend that doing this would be a stupid thing,' he said.

'Oh damn,' Andy whispered, realising, as Damian had already worked out, that Pietr was listening in.

'How?' Damian asked.

'We hack your earbud,' Pietr said, tapping Damian's ear, and then showing a similar bud in his own. 'This is how we found you. Your fat friend does not change it from time you sell us Anton Chekov's lost manuscript. Or the Stanislavski play. Or the map to the Amber Room. We follow you from restaurant, listening to everything.'

'*I can explain--*' Andy spluttered, but then there was a terrible screeching sound, and with a wince of pain, Damian had to pull the bud out of his ear.

Seeing this, Pietr nodded.

'We jam transmission. Fat friend now deaf.'

Damian looked from Pietr back to the SUV across the building site courtyard, as the door now opened and a middle-aged, strikingly beautiful woman wearing an expensive fur coat over jeans and a faded *Manic Street Preachers* T-shirt emerged. Slowly, she picked her way across the terrain, ensuring that her expensive black shoes picked up the minimum of brick and mortar dust. Eventually, she stood only a couple of feet away from Damian, watching him silently, as if deciding what to do next.

In the end, she spoke.

'Hello, Mister Zhivago. Or rather, Mister Lucas.'

Damian forced a smile, while internally screaming. This beautiful woman was Isabella Vladimov, the Godmother of the London Russian Mafia. Seeing her here wasn't a moment of happiness.

'Miss Vladimov,' he blurted. 'I was just saying to Pietr how I've missed you guys.'

'Do you miss the money you took from us?' Isabella's face was emotionless. Damian wondered if she ever played poker.

'Now wait a moment,' he said, looking around the

construction site, noting the lack of witnesses and the large number of armed Russians now watching him with barely concealed hatred. 'I conned you, yes, that's true. But I didn't take the money. Well, not all of it.'

'We gave you eighty thousand pounds,' Isabella replied.

'True, but I needed that for a special event,' Damian explained. 'You see—'

'We know. You send much of it to Moscow museum to pay for Gorsky exhibit. That is why you are still alive.'

Isabella nodded to the side, where a large concrete mixing truck was started by one of her goons, the mixer slowly turning. Next to it was a hole in the ground.

'This will change soon.'

Damian couldn't help himself. He took an involuntary step back, bumping into Pietr, standing immobile behind him.

'So what,' he asked, his bravado hiding his abject terror. 'You intend to shoot me, dump me in a hole and cover me in concrete?'

'Foundation needs to be finished,' Isabella smiled darkly. 'But who said anything about wasting a bullet on you before you are thrown down the hole?'

The thought of an impending fate of drowning in concrete was not a happy one.

'Give me a week,' Damian replied. 'Seven days. I'll get you your money.'

'With interest.'

'How much interest?'

Isabella considered for a moment. 'Let us say thirty percent.'

'How about ten?'

'I think thirty is better word.'

Damian tried to think of something else to say, to find some way to continue the conversation before he had to choose. He knew if Isabella Vladimov wanted, she could have him thrown into the hole without a second thought, the concrete poured onto him, drowning his screams. Nobody would find his body. Just like the Krays' victims, he'd be encased in stone for years. Centuries even.

Even Andy wouldn't know where he was.

Damian hissed to himself.

'Twenty,' he countered. 'That's truly the highest I can go. And you can keep the grand you took from me today.'

The courtyard was silent. Even the cars on the road outside seemed to have stopped.

Isabella Vladimov thought for a minute, and then nodded.

'Twenty,' she agreed. 'Seven days. A hundred thousand pounds in total.'

'Hold on,' Damian argued. 'Twenty percent brings it to ninety-six.'

'Yes,' Isabella smiled darkly. 'But you made us chase you, so I round it up.'

Damian nodded with the confident smile of a man who thought this was easily achievable, but inside he shook with utter terror.

That was a small mortgage. And he had to find it in a week.

Isabella nodded to herself, turned away from Damian, and once more carefully walked back to the SUV. Nobody spoke as it drove out of the construction site. Turning off the mixer, the remaining Russians got back into the van until only Pietr remained beside Damian.

'Mixer was empty anyway,' Pietr smiled. 'You cry like child.'

'Hey,' Damian asked as a thought came to him. 'You were watching me at the restaurant, right? Were they your guys at the bar?'

Pietr shook his head.

'No, we were in van.'

Damian felt a second chill. *The men in the restaurant weren't from the Russians.* That meant that someone else was looking for him.

'Well, this was fun. Great talk,' he said, forcing a smile. 'We should do this more often.'

'We will do it in seven days,' Pietr said. 'oh, before I forget—'

The Russian grabbed Damian's jacket with one hand, bunching the material where Damian's left shoulder and arm met, and yanked hard, tearing the fabric with a sickening ripping noise.

'Oh, you bastard!' Damian moaned, looking at the torn shoulder. There was no way he could return the suit now.

'That is for making us follow you,' Pietr said, turning and walking back to the van. 'For being dick. And for making me walk in brick dust.'

He climbed into the van, closing the door behind him as it drove off at speed, churning up more dust as it did so.

As it drove off, Damian placed the earbud back into his ear.

'Did you get that?' he asked.

There was no reply.

Damian shrugged as he removed the earbud. The chances were that the earlier feedback had probably burned out the earbud's battery. And so, patting his torn shoulder back into a semblance of neatness, Damian left the construction site, taking one last, fearful look at the concrete mixer.

Would he be returning here in a week?

I₸ was rush hour before DAMIAN made it to an underground station, and by the time he arrived back at his Hackney apartment all thoughts of the Russians, concrete mixers and the strange, armed men in the restaurant were almost gone, replaced by various 'get rich quick' schemes to make a hundred grand in a week.

Which was a shame, as it meant that, as he entered his apartment through the front door, his guard was down as a man behind it, grabbed his arms with ease, and frogmarched him into the living room. Tall, stocky and well defined, the man wore his dark hair and beard short, and for a moment Damian thought he was somehow connected to the suited man he'd fought in the restaurant kitchens. The man wasn't suited, though, wearing jeans and a leather jacket, and Damian had already had his meeting with the Russians, so this was something new.

Damian didn't think he was police, but the thought of it being something else, something yet unthought of gave him images of covert agencies and the possibility of being thrown into an unnamed cell, never seen again, and he had to shake the image away, pulling back a sense of indignant and outrage as he allowed himself to be walked down the corridor to the living room door.

After all, as far as he knew, they had nothing on him, and he could still bluff his way out of whatever this situation was.

'What the hell's this?' Damian exclaimed as he entered. Small, with a bay window to the north, the room was wallpapered in a dark green floral print with a sand coloured carpet and white ceiling. On the wall were three movie posters; the first three *Indiana Jones* films. Beside the window was a pine dining table, currently working double duty as a computer desk, two monitors and a wireless keyboard and half covered by a random selection of bills, statements, and printed out Wikipedia pages.

Opposite this wall was a small flat screen television on a cabinet, a battered and well used PlayStation PS4 neatly tucked away underneath. In the middle was a three-seater sofa, once more in a floral pattern, with a small black coffee table in front of it.

Currently sitting on the sofa, quiet and terrified, was Andy, still dressed in his pyjamas and dressing gown, his black curly hair wild and unwashed.

Damian pressed on with the 'outrage' aspect of his new bluff.

'Where's your warrant to do this?' he asked, looking around at the man behind him, now releasing Damian's arms and stepping back. With no response given Damian went to ask again, to demand that he leave—but paused as a young woman walked in from the kitchen, a dark smile on her lips. The sort of *'gotcha, sonny'* smile that didn't bode well for things.

She was mid-to-late-twenties, long brown hair pulled into a ponytail. Her suit was sensible, but the white blouse gave it a little more of a feminine touch. Slim and about an inch shorter than Damian, she still bore the appearance of someone who could kick the living hell out of him if she so desired.

'Damian Lucas,' she said, a statement rather than a question. 'Or would you prefer Crown Prince Ludwig?'

Damian forced a smile. *Busted.*

'And you are...?'

The woman pulled out a small, black leather flip wallet, opening it up to show a warrant card on one side and a metallic police badge on the other.

'Katherine Turner, SO14.'

Damian almost held his hands out for the handcuffs. Police was bad enough. Police Special Operations was even worse.

'Look, it's all a big mistake, I promise you. I didn't know that the parchment—'

'Oh, don't worry, we don't give a crap about your little deal with Taymaster,' Katherine interrupted. 'They've been trying to get out of paying their promised dues for years. I personally wanted to see the British Library exhibit they cancelled.'

The response was unexpected, and now Damian mentally reassessed Katherine once more. She wasn't the cool, calm police officer she portrayed externally. There was something different with her, as if she was as unused to the uniform she wore, as he had been in his once-worth-a-couple-of-thousand-pounds suit. Silently, he waited for her to make the first move in whatever game they were now playing.

'You used to be a student of Professor Richard Evans?' she asked.

This was a question that Damian wasn't expecting.

'Professor Evans?' He repeated slowly, trying again to reevaluate the conversation's direction. 'What about him?'

'He was found dead two days ago in St Nicholas's Church,' Katherine replied. 'Heart attack.'

Now it was Andy's turn to jump as he looked around from his place on the sofa.

'I never knew him,' he explained earnestly. 'I only know

Damian in passing. Could I... Would it be possible to grab some clothes?'

'Who did it?' Damian's tone had turned cold. Evans may have been to blame for Damian's expulsion from University, but he had always been a good professor and for many years before that he'd been a good friend to Damian's family, even if he was one that had an almost Quixotic level of dream chasing—like Damian's dad.

'We're still checking into that one,' Katherine replied. 'But we believe that before he died, he sent you something by post, something that would have arrived by now.'

Damian looked at Andy, who shook his head.

'I tried to tell them, but they won't listen,' he said. 'Nothing's arrived from anyone. Unless you count Amazon Prime, and I needed those items for... research.'

'Professor Evans hasn't spoken to me in years,' Damian said, 'and he sure as hell hasn't sent me anything. Have a good look around, but I'm sure you've already done that.'

Katherine nodded.

'We have,' she admitted, 'and you seem to be clean.'

She looked around the room once more, and the facade seemed to drop again.

'Look, if anything arrives, please let us know.'

Damian went to reply in the affirmative, subconsciously falling into full charm offensive, but he paused, glancing at the bearded agent, frowning as a thought crossed his mind.

'Why does SO14 care about an academic?' He asked. 'Isn't that *Royal Protectorate?*'

'I think we're done here,' Katherine put the ID swiftly back into her jacket pocket with one hand while passing a business card with a single telephone number on it to him with the other. 'Here's my number.'

'Thanks, but I've had a messy break up recently, and I'm really not that sure if I'm up to dating again,' Damian smiled as he took the card. Katherine looked like she wanted to punch him.

'Just call us when it arrives, Mister Lucas.'

'I will when you answer my question,' Damian continued. 'What does Royal Protectorate have on Richard Evans?'

Without replying, Katherine motioned to the other agent to follow her out of the apartment, leaving Andy and Damian finally alone.

Damian waited in case they came back.

They didn't.

'Bloody hell, mate, I thought we were toast,' Andy said, falling back onto the sofa. 'I fair crapped myself there!'

'I thought it was the guy in the restaurant, when he grabbed me,' Damian sat down on a small wooden office chair beside the table doubling as a computer desk, the adrenaline in his system finally subsiding, his heart beating like a drum.

'Wasn't it?'

'No,' Damian leaned back. 'Which means *three* groups now seem to know all about me.'

'They turned up just as Pietr killed the feed,' Andy explained, picking up a small fidget cube from the coffee table and frantically pressing buttons on it as he tried to relax. 'There was no way I could warn you.'

'You could have texted.'

'They took the phone.' Andy looked up, suddenly realising. 'Why aren't you dead? Isabella Vladimov? Why aren't you in landfill or under a bridge?'

'I promised to pay the money back in a week.'

'Eighty grand? How the hell do we do that?'

'She gave me a week to find the money plus interest,' Damian replied. 'And it's a hundred grand now.'

'Oh, that was nice of them,' Andy sighed.

'Did they have a warrant to search?' Damian didn't enjoy being on the back foot.

'It all happened so fast,' Andy explained. 'Pietr caught you, I lost the feed, those guys knocked at the door. I thought it was a two-front attack. They were in and looking around before I could gather my thoughts—'

The knocking at the door made them both jump. Rising and grabbing a baseball bat from the side of the table, Damian made his way tentatively to the door, expecting Katherine and SO14 to have returned for more questioning, or Isabella and her Russians turning up for round two. However, opening it, he found Mrs. Hamilton, his small and portly, elderly next-door neighbour on the doorstep, pushing her bifocals up her nose to see him clearly.

'I'm sorry for the noise,' he started, trying to head off whatever complaint she had, 'it's really not what it looks like.'

'Oh, I don't care about all that,' Mrs Hamilton held up a postcard. 'this came for you earlier today. Got delivered through my door by accident.'

She pointed down the stairs.

'I didn't know if they were a drugs raid, so I thought I'd wait until they were gone.'

'Drugs raid?' Damian looked at Mrs. Hamilton in surprise. She leaned closer, as if worried that the walls themselves would pass on her words to the authorities.

'The people before you? Had some kind of greenhouse hidden behind a fake wall in the second bedroom. Grew their own product, if you know what I mean. Police were here every other week, half the time to buy.'

She sniffed.

'Nice kids, though. And Christ, they made good weed.'

Damian fought the urge to laugh.

'No, nothing so exciting, I'm afraid. But thanks for this.'

He took the postcard from her, looking at the address written on it, immediately recognising the sprawling hand of Richard Evans. With Mrs Hamilton already gone, probably to sample whatever remained of his predecessor's supplies, Damian returned to his apartment, examining the postcard. On it was an image of the Manchester City football team. Turning it over, Damian read the message Richard had written to him.

Among books, pirate treasure leads to Satan's step

'Is that...' Andy started, his face paling as Damian entered the living room. Looking up at his flat mate, still in his pyjamas, Damian nodded.

'Yeah, this is what they wanted. It was literally pure chance they didn't get it.'

Reading over the strange paragraph once more, he passed it to Andy to examine.

'I thought Professor Evans hated you?' Andy asked as he read the message. Andy had been Damian's roommate while working on his computer science degree, and he knew well of the issues between Damian and the University.

'He did,' Damian replied. 'And I deserved it. If Evans hadn't kicked me out, God knows where I'd have fallen.'

'A Hackney flat, conning multinational corporations out of promised grant money held back from libraries and museums, while making next to nothing for it?'

Damian grinned.

'Don't belittle what I do,' he said, 'it keeps me warm at...'

He trailed off as he stared at the message, snatching the postcard back from Andy.

'Oh no,' he muttered as he placed it onto the table as if it was a poisonous snake, 'I know what this is.'

'Go on then.' Andy looked over at it. 'Because I haven't a bloody clue.'

'Evans spent years looking for this. Reckoned it was in a Catholic shrine somewhere in Belgium,' Damian paused as if he was in two minds on what he was about to do, before picking the postcard back up, turning it over again and examining the picture. 'it's a code, a riddle that leads to a great secret.'

'Yeah? Is it by chance a secret that makes enough to pay off the Russians?' Andy had relaxed a little more now, leaning back into his seat on the sofa. 'I like those sorts of secrets.'

Damian didn't take his eyes off the postcard on the table.

'How does a vast quantity of Plantagenet gold, lost since Richard the Third do?'

Andy stared silently at Damian for a minute.

'Yeah, that sounds doable,' he eventually said. 'So how does this code work?'

Damian looked out of the window, down at the street below, as if scared that the police officer with the pretty female boss would come back at any moment and demand the answer. He looked back at Andy.

'I don't have a clue,' he admitted. 'I never bothered listening when dad talked about it.'

'In layman's terms, then?'

'It's a treasure map. One that's centuries old.'

'So, I'd better put some trousers on then?' Andy rose, as if expecting to begin immediately on whatever financially rewarding quest Damian was about to lead him on. Damian, however, stared back down at the message on the card, part of him wanting to burn it, to throw it away and forget all about the bloody thing, while another part was goading him, encouraging to fall down the rabbit hole.

'Yeah, that'd be a plan,' he said. 'You won't be allowed in the library like that.'

'Which one?' Andy was already rummaging around a dirty pile of washing hidden underneath the computer desk, looking for a mostly clean pair of jeans. 'British Library? Hackney Central?'

'Oh, there's only one we can go to get an answer about this.' Damian replied, pointing at the postcard, and the football team.

'Manchester?' Andy's face dropped at the news. 'I hate that place.'

'It's where the library is, so we have to go. Or I could go, and you could stay here.'

Andy shook his head.

'Be serious,' he said, 'You might know what Evans meant, but I've always been the brains in this operation. So when do we go?'

'Not yet,' Damian replied, 'I have something to do first.'

Because first, Damian had to go to Deptford and learn the truth about what really happened to Professor Richard Evans.

4

A MURDER IN DEPTFORD

Though they'd parted ways angrily, Richard Evans had been more than a professor to Damian; he was a family connection. He had been a friend of Damian's father for years, and Damian remembered several childhood moments with Richard who, even then, had been obsessing over lost gold and conspiracies. In fact, it was this familial connection that had placed Damian, a so-so student, about to fail his A' Levels, into a University in the first place.

He might have ended his relationship with Professor Evans on bad terms; being expelled does that to you, but he'd always held a soft spot for the man. However, with the arrival of one postcard, Richard Evans' obsession now continued even past the grave.

It was cloudy as Damian visited St. Nicholas's Church; a breezy day with the slightest hint of rain promised as he entered through the main gate, passing between the two skulls that guarded the entrance, walking quietly through the churchyard, the church on his left side as he approached the north wall. It wasn't his first time here; in fact, he'd been to see Marlowe's plaque many times throughout the years, even though he was one of the people who believed that Marlowe had faked his own death before being brought up on *Heresy* charges. Once he reached the edge of the lawn, the path swerving sharply to the left, following the corner of the church and continuing along the right of it, Damian stared across the clearing to the half visible wall among the wild foliage, directly at Marlowe's memorial plaque.

The blue and white police 'incident' tape was visible here, flapping in the gentle wind, still attached to the bushes around the Marlowe plaque, most likely the location of Richard's body while they'd examined the area. However, with nobody to stop him, Damian crossed to the edge of the grass, stepping amongst the bushes and looking down at the dirt beneath the plaque.

There was no footprint, no 'Sherlock Holmes' style clue that would immediately give away what happened. If you didn't know that a man had died here recently, the police tape fluttering listlessly could have meant anything. Damian knelt for a closer look, brushing aside some of the fallen leaves to check the ground for anything other than police footprints, noting that two of the sticks had been placed into an 'X' under the plaque. It could have been random, two twigs kicked together by a copper's scuffed gait, but the sticks were exactly ninety degrees apart, and dead centre where they met. There was no way this was a random placing, though Damian assumed that the police most likely did this once the body was removed, in order to show where it had been.

'Sorry, Richard,' Damian muttered to himself, 'I should have been here for you.'

A phrase he'd told SO14 the day before came to mind. *Professor Evans hasn't spoken to me in years,* was factually correct, and Damian had omitted nothing from that statement, but it wasn't completely true. Richard had tried to call Damian about a month earlier, but Damian had been out of the country after the Chekov scam on the Russians, his phone turned off. When he returned to the UK, he'd found a rambling voicemail on his phone from Richard, saying that he'd found something in Europe and he was *absolutely certain that this was it, that this was the one*; Damian hadn't bothered to return the call. He was sure that in the week between the message and Damian's return, Richard Evans would have learnt whatever clue he now had in his possession meant absolutely nothing, as usual. This wasn't the first time Damian had received such a call or message from Richard over the years.

However, now Damian wasn't so sure.

Getting up, he brushed the dirt off his knees, stepping back onto the lawn, staring at the plaque and the 'X' underneath; it still felt a little strange to see an 'x marks the spot' in a church graveyard so well connected to English pirates. However, if anything had been left, the police would have surely taken it.

Because of this, the next stop was Deptford Command Unit on Amersham Vale, a half-a-mile walk away where, claiming the technically truthful title of *family friend* and *old student*, Damian could gain further information about the last hours of Richard Evans from the officer in charge of the case.

To say that Detective Inspector Warren, a wiry mouse of a man in his late thirties, his blond hair slicked back over an obviously receding bald spot, was skeptical of any foul play was an understatement. Sitting at his overflowing desk and facing Damian, on a chair to the side of it, the pile of additional paperwork that had been resting upon it moments earlier now added to the towering mass, the detective passed a sheet of notes across with disdain, giving Damian the immediate impression that DI Warren would prefer to be doing anything other than this.

'As you can see, Professor Evans used his Oyster Card to exit Temple Tube Station at half-past one in the afternoon, and then again to enter at Bank just after four pm,' Warren explained. 'We believe that this was a major cause of his heart attack.'

"How do you mean?' Damian looked up from the paper. Warren shrugged.

'When we checked the card, there'd been no buses used on it in between the two journeys, so the chances are that he'd walked from Temple to Bank,' Warren explained. 'That's a mile and a half. Guy of Evan's age and state of health, that much exercise could have triggered—'

'What do you mean, state of health?'

Warren paused, surprised.

'I thought you knew,' he replied, his attitude softening for the first time. 'Professor Evans had terminal bowel cancer.'

'We hadn't spoken for a while,' Damian said softly.

Warren nodded, the prickliness now lessened.

'Well, the average person would walk that in twenty, thirty minutes, allowing for traffic or pedestrians. A slow walk could go up to forty-five minutes. Professor Evans was out of the stations for two and a half hours, so that gave him at least an hour somewhere in between.'

'That's a slow walk, not something that triggers a heart attack.'

Warren shrugged. 'That's as maybe, but we can only go on the data we have. He walked, he had a heart attack.'

Damian nodded. There were only a couple of reasons Richard had travelled to Temple. Probably Temple Church, or the Inns of Court. Richard seemed to spend much of his waking time in the Inner and Middle Temples, constantly hunting for clues to a mystery that nobody seemed to care about.

'And then?'

'Well, from Bank, he'd travelled to Cutty Sark Station on the DLR line, and a lady in Greenwich Market claimed that he'd bought two postcards from her. She remembered him because they were two for a pound, but he'd paid with a tenner. She said that he was nervous, didn't even wait for change.'

'And you still think this was an accident?'

Warren's face darkened. 'There's no circumstantial evidence to prove anything, Mister Lucas. And the coroner stated that Mister Evans died of heart failure.'

Damian continued to read the paperwork. 'What's this about a limousine?'

'Well, ten minutes after the incident in the market, Richard apparently got out of a limousine in Deptford. Witnesses saw him walk towards St. Nicholas's church. From there, we think he made his way to the church plaque and then died against a back wall.'

'Do you know anything more about this limousine?'

Warren shook his head. 'Probably someone he knew, giving Professor Evans a lift.'

Damian understood why Warren wanted this to be a simple, straight-forward case, but there was still something about this that screamed out at him that things were very wrong.

Warren coughed.

'What was your connection again?' he asked.

'Family friend,' Damian repeated. He could see that Warren was considering showing him something, possibly evidence.

'He helped me on my forensics course,' he lied.

'Forensics?'

'Criminal,' Damian smiled, hoping Warren wouldn't want to see proof. 'I want to be a forensics officer when I leave Uni.'

Warren looked back at the file, as if making a decision based on this new information.

'I know it's a bit grim, but if it helps ease these concerns about Professor Evans' death, we do have a photo taken at the scene,' Warren passed over a black-and-white photo of Richard Evans, taken where he died. 'We wouldn't usually show these, but as you're in training so to speak...' he trailed off as Damian took the photo, looking at Richard. He looked peaceful, almost at rest. Back against the wall, one hand rested on his chest, while his left hand was placed on the ground, almost as if pointing.

Damian looked closer at the image. The finger *was* pointing. And Damian could see what Richard was pointing at; the two sticks that Damian had seen, still placed in an 'X'.

Placed before the police had arrived. X marks the spot. Was this the pirate treasure Richard had meant?

'Thank you, this helps,' Damian replied, passing the paperwork back and rising from the chair. 'I'll let you get on with things.'

With Warren grateful for Damian's exit, Damian had thanked the detective inspector and left, his mind now buzzing. Richard had deliberately set those sticks, sending one last message before dying. And less than half an hour earlier, he'd bought, filled out, and sent a postcard to

Damian. This wasn't usual behaviour. There was something else going on here. The route from Temple to Bank involved Fleet Street and the Inns of Court. For there to be over two hours between uses of the Oyster card meant there was a very strong chance Richard had met with someone, most likely at the latter location. He had all the time in the world to send a postcard there, but he'd waited, sending it moments before he died, a message that led Damian to Manchester.

Walking from the Deptford Command Unit and now standing on the street, Damian pulled his phone out and googled the train times from Euston for that day. After seeing what he needed, he dialled a number.

'About bloody time,' the voice of Andy came through the receiver, 'I thought you'd gone AWOL.'

'Not yet,' Damian replied, 'but give me a couple of hours. I'm going to catch the 12.04 to Manchester.'

'You mean we're going to,' Andy replied, 'I'm your compadre. Your back up. And the person who actually knows stuff about history and all that.'

Damian smiled to himself, stepping out into the road and waving a black cab down as it approached.

'I suppose you have your uses,' he said. 'I'll meet you at Euston.'

'Done, compadre.'

'And stop saying compadre.'

'You got it, bro.'

Damian disconnected the call and entered the cab. Sitting back, he thought for a moment. He understood why Richard would go to Temple station; the Inns of Inner and Middle Temple Court were near there. But why go to Greenwich?

Maybe he did find something interesting in Europe.

'Where to, mate?' The cab driver waited patiently.

'London Bridge Station,' Damian replied, looking out of the window as the cab started its journey. Deptford was a place of death, and not just that of Christopher Marlowe. Damian was going to find out what happened to his onetime tutor and friend.

He just hoped that it didn't kill him, too.

5

NIGHT SCHOOL

It was raining when they finally arrived at Manchester Piccadilly Station, following a two-hour train journey from Euston. Walking out of the main entrance, exchanging chrome and steel architecture for dull grey skies, Damian pulled his collar up against it; the drizzle was light, and it was a fifteen-minute walk to their destination.

Clutching a plastic carrier bag holding a half-eaten cheese and ham Baguette beside a bottle of Coke Zero, Andy walked out behind him, nervously looking around the station entrance and back towards the exit barriers as he did so.

'What's the matter now?' Damian asked irritably. Ever since Andy had met him in Euston, he'd been constantly looking over his shoulder, as if expecting to be arrested at any moment. At the sound of Damian's voice, Andy's head snapped back around, as if caught daydreaming, or more likely, caught stealing something.

'I... I'm just worried, you know,' he replied, forcing a smile as he continued after Damian, also grimacing as he walked out into the Manchester weather. 'After what you told me about the death, the picture... I can't help thinking we're still being followed.'

He pulled out his phone, checking it briefly.

'Hey, here's a radical idea. What if we just caught the train back, and left this damn fool treasure hunt to others?' Andy's tone was almost pleading. 'We could get back late afternoon, grab something to eat in Euston? I mean, we haven't celebrated Taymaster's idiocy yet.'

Damian stopped, looking back at Andy.

'What happened to my compadre, my backup?' he asked.

'He realised that this isn't a movie and we could get seriously hurt here,' Andy reached into his carrier bag and pulled out his half-eaten baguette, continuing to eat it as they walked.

'Mate, I'm not stopping you going back, but I'm staying,' Damian said, trying to force a smile as he looked back at Andy. Damian didn't really want to be here either, but knowing that Andy was with him gave him a little more encouragement to see this through. 'I mean, I think I owe it to Richard to at least check out this one thing.'

Damian pulled out the postcard once more.

Among books, pirate treasure leads to Satan's step

Putting the postcard away, Damian started into the rain, turning towards the centre of town. Andy hurried to catch him, glancing once more at his phone, as if expecting some text message to have appeared in the seconds since the last time he checked.

'So, I've been thinking about why we've come here,' he eventually said as they headed towards the Arndale Centre.

'You couldn't have thought this during the two hour train ride here?'

'I was thinking then too, but now I'm discussing my thought process.'

'Fine,' Damian sighed. 'Go on.'

'You've come all the way here to visit a library, right? And let's be honest, if we're just talking the usual run-of-the-mill type library, you could find most things in London rather than travelling all the way up here, and we both have readers room access to the British Library, which has pretty much everything, anyway; although I don't think you've ever used yours.'

'Reading's overrated.'

'You're a philistine. So anyway, the question becomes whether there's a library in the city of Manchester worthy of us.'

'And is there?' Damian smiled as he replied. He knew very well Andy's love of libraries. He'd dragged Damian to enough of them over the years. Andy, in turn, smiled back, a triumphant grin on his face.

'Yeah. I reckon it has to be Chetham's Library. Oldest free public reference library in England, created in 1653 because of the will of Humphry Chetham.'

'Well, that's easy,' Damian responded. 'You can look that up on Wikipedia.'

'True,' Andy replied with a hint of pride, matching steps with Damian as he spoke, 'but Wikipedia doesn't mention that Humphry Chetham was a member of a secret society named *The School of Night*. I checked while we were on the train.'

Now it was Damian's turn to look surprised.

'Where did you hear that?' he asked, letting a car pass them as they crossed the road. 'I've heard of the School of Night, but never that Chetham was part of it.'

'Then you should have spent more time in your lectures, rather than screwing about.'

Damian stopped, looking at Andy.

'Seriously mate, what do you know about the School?' he asked. 'Because all I know was my dad and Richard Evans were obsessed by it, and that it was some kind of a drinking club for rich people.'

'Well, duh,' replied Andy, warming to the task. 'Primarily, it was a group of intelligent men and free thinkers, started by Henry Percy, the ninth Earl of Northumberland. People like Sir Francis Walsingham, Thomas Harriot, Walter Raleigh, Francis Drake, Christopher Marlowe and Doctor John Dee.'

'As I just said, a bunch of high-ranking toffs had a drinking club,' Damian flipped a finger at a Mercedes as it sped past, narrowly missing him as they crossed the road leading to Piccadilly Gardens.

'They weren't just toffs, these men were the voices in the ear of Queen Elizabeth,' Andy replied. 'And it's widely believed that the school was created in the late 1580s for one reason only; to make damn sure Elizabeth's legacy continued.'

'How?' Damian laughed. 'I might not be the historical whizz that you are, but if I recall correctly, I don't think she had any kids.'

'That's lineage'. By her 'legacy', I think it was more a case of stopping certain others from taking it,' Andy argued. 'In particular James the Sixth of Scotland.'

'That worked well.'

'I never said they were a successful society,' Andy chuckled as they walked along Market Street. 'Dee died penniless. Walsingham died of what we would now call bowel cancer, Drake of dysentery. Marlowe was killed in a knife fight. In fact, by the time James came into his birthright as King of Scotland and England, only Percy, Raleigh, and Harriot were still in favour at court, and they soon imprisoned both Percy and Raleigh for trying to overthrow James.'

Damian turned to Andy.

'So apart from Harriot, they all had bad endings,' he said. 'But what about Humphry Chetham? He seems to have done well.'

'Well, perhaps the society didn't die? Maybe it went *super*-secret?'

Damian paused as an old memory suddenly came to him, something his father had once said when Damian was just a child.

'My dad mentioned that John Dee tutored the young Humphry Chetham. I suppose it's possible that Dee spoke of the School of Night during these sessions?'

'Dee knew Chetham!' Andy clapped his hands together as if this was the answer to everything. 'There you go then! Six degrees of Kevin Bacon! Or in this case, I suppose Francis Bacon.'

By now they had turned down Corporation Street, the Arndale still to their right and the yellow steel of the platform of Exchange Street's tram stop to their left. Coming up in front of them was the Printworks, a stone, six-story building on the corner of Corporation Street and Withy Grove. Once one of the largest newspaper print houses in Europe, the Printworks had since become one of Manchester's more popular entertainment centres, with restaurant and cinema logos emblazoned on its side next to a giant LED screen. Damian ignored the spectacle, however, turning across the road, allowing a tram to pass before heading towards a grassy clearing, the route leading past the

National Football Museum and into Manchester's Cathedral Gardens.

'So, how do we get in?' Andy asked. Damian thought for a moment.

'We could just walk in,' he suggested. 'They do public visits.'

'Yeah, but I'm assuming you're gonna want some alone time in one of the rooms,' Andy replied, already working through the problem. 'That involves getting rid of people.'

'We could do the diplomat scam?'

Andy shook his head. 'You'd need the ID.'

'I still have the debit card saying I'm Crown Prince Ludwig in my pocket,' Damian mused. 'Perhaps I could use that?'

'On a cold read against a security guard or librarian? They'll want to see a passport, and we never bothered with that.'

Damian paused, pulling out his phone.

'And you mocked me for checking mine,' Andy muttered.

Damian ignored him, dialling a number and holding the phone to his ear.

'We didn't need a passport for Ludwig, because we front loaded the scam before we even started contacting Taymaster,' he said as he waited for the phone to connect, 'and because of that, they already believed who I was before I even entered the room. If we can find a way to—oh hi!' his attention returned to the phone as he spoke to the person on the other end.

'Yes, I hope you can help me. This is Luke Fairclough from human resources,' Damian spoke with a casual tone, barely skipping a beat as he moved from lie to half-truth. 'Who am I speaking to? Oh, hello Clive... Clive Walters.

Great. Don't worry, nobody's being fired, it's just that mainte-nance is running a phone check today and they've been coming up with some non-answering extensions. Worried they're not going through, so can you tell me who's off sick in your department today?'

Damian pulled out a notepad, jotting down a couple of names as the voice on the other end spoke.

'And which department is Susan—oh, she's the director of press relations? And how long has she been... Oh, well, send her my congratulations. Boy or girl?'

Andy marvelled at the way Damian pulled name after name from Clive. By the end of a call that lasted less than three minutes, he had half a dozen names on his notepad.

'And this helps because?' he asked. Damian grinned.

'Oh ye of little faith,' he replied, pointing across the green, indicating a large, red-brick building. 'Come on, we're there now.'

And with that, he strode purposely across the gardens towards the entrance. Risking one last look around, as if still expecting to be followed, Andy reluctantly followed.

CHETHAM'S LIBRARY MAY HAVE CLAIMED TO BE THE OLDEST public library in the English-speaking world, but the only way to get into the building was to pass through a security checkpoint.

As Damian and Andy walked up to the gate, a black, wrought-iron piece that blocked a gap between two red brick buildings, a black sign with gold writing proclaiming 'CHETHAM'S LIBRARY' upon it, Damian spied the security window a little into the courtyard on the right. Tapping Andy on the arm and motioning for him to follow, he walked up to the window and waited patiently, the face of a man who not only expected to be allowed in but also one who expected the guard to know exactly why he should be allowed in.

Slowly, finally recognising that someone was there, the guard looked up from his newspaper. Portly and balding, a black fleece jumper with 'CHETHAM' on it over a pale blue shirt and black tie, this was a man who obviously preferred the more sedentary art of security rather than one that involved high activity.

'Can I help?' he asked with the tone of voice of someone who really wanted the answer to be *no*. Damian put on his best smile.

'I certainly hope so! I'm Damian, this is my cameraman, Andy. We're here for the VR shoot in the library today.'

'VR shoot?' The security guard wasn't expecting that as an answer. Damian nodded.

'Virtual reality. As in putting on one of those headset things and looking around as if you're really there.'

'It's all the rage,' Andy added.

'My son's got one,' the guard muttered. 'sits in the chair for hours at a time with it on.'

'I'm sure it's a good look for him,' Damian grinned.

'He looks like an idiot.'

Damian forced the smile to stay on his face.

'Well anyway, the library's getting the three-sixty treatment, you see,' Damian continued, now relishing this new role. 'We're doing it next week, the full works, but today's the dress rehearsal, so to speak. Checking light ratios, sense angles, fluxing capacitors, that sort of thing.'

He turned to Andy.

'Do you have the thing?' he asked.

'Thing?' Andy froze.

'The cube,' Damian smiled. 'The VR thing.'

Realising what Damian meant, Andy pulled out a small black plastic cube from his pocket, only an inch and a half in diameter, covered in buttons and switches. Damian took the fidget cube and waved in front of the guard's face as Damian continued with his lie.

'Basically, in layman's terms, we put this on the floor in the middle of the room with a few of its friends in the corners; you know, like how a surround sound setup works, but for video? And then we let it do its thing while we grab a cuppa. It's all Bluetooth, from an app on a phone.'

He passed the cube back to Andy, who placed it back into his pocket.

'I don't know anything about this,' the guard replied, looking down at his sheet, looking a little flustered, 'Who gave you permission to do this?'

'If you just pick up the phone and call up Susan Clarke, she'll give you the go ahead,' Damian smiled. 'Big boss in the press department, I think? Anyway, she was the one who booked it for today. Last opportunity to do it before the 'you know', she said.'

Damian looked at Andy as if having a sudden thought.

'Wait, has she had the baby yet?' He asked. Andy, not sure where this was going, paused before nodding hesitantly.

'Maybe...?' he offered.

'Crap, that means she won't be in,' Damian continued, looking back to the guard, 'you'll have to use her mobile number to call her.'

The guard visibly swallowed. The last thing *he* wanted to do was call a woman who possibly gave birth a matter of days ago.

'If Susan said it was okay, then I'm sure it's okay,' he said, as if convincing himself. 'But I'll need to get someone to escort you—'

'Oh, that's fine,' Damian waved the suggestion away. 'Clive Walters is meeting us in what I believe he called the Medieval Building?'

Now this was a name that the guard knew and, happy to remove this complication from his day, he got them to sign a visitors log, passed them lanyards and, this done, waved them both past and into the courtyard.

'Yes, that's right, across the open area there and through the doors,' he said.

Nodding thanks, Damian and Andy walked past; but before they had moved more than five steps on, the guard emerged from the booth.

'Hey,' he said.

Damian paused, forcing a smile as he slowly turned around.

'Yes?'

The guard thought for a moment, watching Damian.

'Did she say if it was a boy or a girl?' He eventually asked.

'Oh yes, she did,' Damian said. 'A boy. She's named him Taliesin.'

'Taliesin?' The guard's eyes rose as he replied. Damian shrugged.

'After the famous bard. I know, I'd have picked an Alfie or a Louis, but she was adamant,' he held a finger to his nose. 'But keep it to yourself.'

The guard nodded as Damian and Andy continued into the building. As they moved out of sight, Andy glared at Damian.

'*Taliesin*? You know it'll be around the whole place by the end of the day.'

'I don't know,' Damian turned right, continuing down a corridor. 'He didn't strike me as a gossiper. And I like the name.'

'But it's not *his* name.'

'If a child's parents have no imagination, what fault is it of mine if I provide the popular vote with an alternative?'

'This isn't an election.'

'So you say.'

Andy pulled out his fidget cube.

'Ballsy move, showing him this,' he muttered, now clicking one switch nervously as they walked.

'Not really. Show someone a thing with buttons and dials, and they'll always be impressed, Andy. It's a simple fact of life.'

Damian continued on, a smile on his face.

Laughing, Andy followed.

———

6

LIBRARY FINES

DOING THEIR BEST NOT TO CALL ATTENTION TO THEMSELVES, Damian and Andy quickly walked across the car pack and into the Medieval part of the Library, a long, brick corridor lined with arched doors, littered with chairs and side tables.

'Don't see many books in this library,' Damian looked around as he spoke.

'They're upstairs,' Andy replied. 'They didn't want the books to be affected by rising damp or anything. I thought you said you'd been here before?'

'My dad's been here before,' Damian corrected. 'I never gave a damn about it.'

They carried on down the corridor, lit by glowing disc shaped lights embedded in the brickwork every six feet, towards what looked like a Tibetan prayer bell, easily four feet in height and held within a heavy frame made of dark wood, stationed like a guard beside a large wooden door.

Andy tapped the side of the bell. It made a dull, faint *dong* sound as he did so. Damian glanced around one more time to check if they were alone and, reassured that they were, he softly opened the door and entered.

The room was square and not very large. As Damian entered, he faced a small double window, the two panes criss-crossed with thin strips of lead. The wall to his left was paneled in a deep oak wood six feet high, with pale plaster finishing the three feet above it in a pattern that resembled leaves and flowers.

A pew-like bench ran along its length, while beside the window was an alcove, a small table and two benches set in front of a recessed window, with another window to the other side, almost where the wall cornered, with a small medieval globe, held in a tripod frame within the recess.

Mirroring it on the next wall were two more windows, placed either side of a wide, stone fireplace, with two small chairs placed either side, built differently to the other chairs placed against this wall. The last wall, leading to the door that they had just entered through, had no windows, just paintings of old, bearded men that hung against the deep oak panelling. On opposite corners, there were more carved wooden chairs to sit on.

There were three tables in the room; the first two had been placed in the middle to make a larger, square table, easily ten feet by ten feet in size. The other one was equally long, covered, and was to Damian's right, resting against the fourth wall of the room as he entered.

Finally, the ceiling was Tudor in design, dark panelled wood hidden behind the only modern-day finish in the room; a square neon-light metal frame held above the table by wires.

There was one more interesting thing about the ceiling though—it had four ornate wooden carvings, each one equidistant from each other, almost matching the corners of the table below it.

'Wow,' said Damian, genuinely in awe. 'Now this is a reading room.'

'It wasn't always,' Andy replied, walking into the room now, examining the walls as he did so. 'Before they made it into a part of the Library, it was the audit room in the Collegiate Church of Christ's College, Manchester.'

'So, accounts and stuff?' Damian now tapped at a panel in the wall, listening to see if its sound was hollower than the others. Deciding that it was the same as the one beside it, he moved on, tapping the next panel. Andy shook his head.

'Far from it. This was the Warden's office.'

'Wait, are you telling me...?' Damian trailed off as Andy looked back to him.

'Depends. I was going to say between 1595 and 1605, the Warden of the college was Doctor John Dee.'

'And this was where he met Chetham,' Damian smiled as he looked around the room, as if imagining himself there with the older Dee as he tutored the young Humphry Chetham.

Andy nodded at this.

'And this is where the gold is hidden, right?'

'No, this is where the *guide* to the treasure has to be hidden,' Damian corrected, looking up at the carvings now. 'There's not enough space to hide gold here, and I remember dad saying once that after Dee left, it was torn apart with people looking for all the magical gold he claimed to be making.'

'But he didn't actually make any.'

Damian shrugged, tapping some more wooden panels.

'You and I know that now, but back then, Dee was best

known for his alleged conversations with angels and trying to turn lead into gold.'

Andy started tapping on walls too. 'But he died penniless.'

'Exactly, and so after his death, people believed that the whole alchemy and talking to angels thing was a con.'

'And you'd know all about cons,' Andy wandered over to a chair by the large central table. 'Was it?'

'Who knows,' Damian replied. 'I mean, Dee was trying to convince people he could create gold from base metals but nothing ever came of it.'

'Seems pointless to claim you could make gold when you were penniless,' Andy turned the chair over. 'Especially if the only way that'd work was if you had the actual gold to show when finished. Huh, this chair is eighteenth century.'

'We're not here for the chairs,' Damian replied. 'As for the gold, technically, you're correct. But what if you went the other way, and use a con to explain gold you couldn't account for, that needed to have a way of existing?'

'So he was a con man?' Andy frowned. Damian went to reply, but then his eyes widened in sudden realisation.

'Jesus, John Dee was the first proper money launderer!'

'But it didn't work, did it?' Andy had his phone out again, tapping on it as he spoke.

'Doesn't mean I'm wrong,' Damian muttered, climbing up onto one of the two middle tables, pulling out a pocketknife, 'Maybe he was told to stop. Maybe something halted it after he laid the groundwork, but before he could start 'creating' the gold for whoever he was working for.'

Andy rose in horror as Damian chipped away at one carving with the blade of the knife.

'What in God's name are you doing?' he exclaimed. 'Are you mental? That's hundreds of years old!'

With his free hand, Damian tossed Andy the postcard.

'Look at it again,' he suggested. Andy did so, turning it over as he read the inscription once more.

'So it's Manchester City. I see how that made you come here. The line says libraries, and obviously this has to be the one. But Pirate treasure?'

Damian indicated the four carvings on the ceiling.

'Look. Four carvings, three of which have faces of various types and styles upon them, I'm assuming all in a style consistent with the first half of the fifteenth century, when the room was built, because why change them?'

'So before Dee arrived.'

'Exactly. However, the fourth, the one I'm currently picking plaster from, is nothing more than an elaborate X. If you're doing four engravings, why only do three, and then rush the final one?'

'Maybe whoever carved it got bored with faces?' Andy suggested.

'Perhaps,' Damian placed the pocketknife back into his jacket as he pulled at the engraved cross above him. 'Or maybe this was altered after they made the others, perhaps when Dee was here?'

'Why not the walls? The floorboards?'

Damian looked back at Andy.

'Think outside the box for a moment. What do pirates say about their treasure?'

'Yaarr, I have pirate booty?'

'More specific. Think *Treasure Island*.'

Andy considered this for a moment. 'X marks the spot?'

'Exactly. And when I visited Deptford, I had a look at the

place where Richard's body was found. On the ground were two sticks, perfectly laid at right angles to each other, as if Richard was leaving me an X when he died. He was aiming me directly at—'

He pulled once more at the carving and with a *click*, the cross moved out from the shape, still connected to the ceiling by a metal rod.

Damian tried turning it; there was no give in the rod to the right, but it turned to the left.

Turning it ninety degrees to the left and hearing another click, Damian pushed back upwards and slotted the cross back into place.

There was an audible clunk, and the cross came free in his hand.

'X marks the spot,' he whispered.

'You broke it!' Andy protested in horror. Climbing down from the table, Damian turned the cross over. On the other side, the wood was pale and sanded flat, with painted markings down each tine of the cross. At the tips of all four ends were four numbers.

6-0-4-1

'John Dee's last secret,' Damian whispered hoarsely.

'What does it mean?' Andy stared down at the cross as Damian placed it on the table.

'No idea,' Damian replied honestly. 'It's a code. And, before you ask me how to break it, check the postcard.'

'Satan's step?' Andy raised an eyebrow. 'Ol' Lucifer visit Manchester much?'

'Only the once, if you listen to legends,' walking across the room, Damian pulled the cover off the right-hand edge of the large side table, exposing a small, circular burn mark on the corner of the wood. 'Dee was believed to have burned a hole in the table while working on alchemical mixtures, but the local legend became that he summoned the Devil himself in an occult ritual, and the devil's hoof struck the table and left the mark.'

'Another story from your dad?'

'Richard, this time,' Damian slid under the table now, lying on the floor as he looked up at the underside.

'Can you see anything?' Andy couldn't help but stroke the burn mark, as if it was a lucky talisman.

'Actually yes,' Damian reached into his pocket, pulling out his phone and turning on its flash, holding it up to examine the table. 'There're four ratchets. Tiny ones, but I think it's a Tudor equivalent of a tumbler.'

'Try *6041*?'

'Already did,' Damian lay back against the wooden floor, thinking to himself.

'It doesn't have to be that,' he replied, moving back to the tumblers, 'it could be any of four lineal combinations, depending on where you start. So 0416, 4160, 1604...'

'Stop. Use that,' Andy's tone was both urgent and commanding as he stared down at his phone.

Damian paused, and then manipulated the tumblers now, moving them to new positions under the table.

There was a click, and a small, thin drawer appeared on the side of the tabletop. Damian clambered up to examine it, pulling a small wooden slide, only ten inches square and comprising two thin sheets of wood stuck together out.

'How did you know?' he asked.

'1604. The year Dee's wife Jane died,' Andy waved the phone at Damian. 'Wikipedia is my friend.'

Grinning at this, Damian now prised the two thin strips of wood apart, almost dropping them in shock as he did so.

'Oh man, this is it!' he exclaimed, gently prizing free a parchment wheel from the strips of wood.

It was divided into sixteen slices, each one split into four more sections, and each section covered in cryptic letters and images. Attached to it at the centre was a second piece, a sliding rule covered in numbers and runes that could move around the wheel.

'Richard spent years looking for this. The lost code wheel of the *Steganographica*,' Damian looked up from the sheet slowly. 'And it was here all along. He just needed the clue in Antwerp to find it.'

'Yeah, no idea what you're saying now, mate,' Andy was still examining the slim gap in the table.

'Richard used to talk about it all the time. Johannes Trithemius wrote the *Steganographica* in 1499,' Damian explained. 'They believed it to be a book about magic and showing how spirits could communicate over incredible distances. But around a hundred years later, a decryption key was published, showing that it was in fact a book of cyphers and codes.'

'Spy stuff?'

'Yeah. I think that's why it interested me as a kid. Tudor James Bond and all that,' Damian examined the piece of parchment now. 'The book was a legend, only seen but never bought. Dee tried to buy it in 1564 in Antwerp, but all he could do was pay someone a lot of money to borrow the manuscript for ten days.'

'What could he do in ten days?'

Damian smiled.

'He copied by hand the whole damn thing.'

Andy leaned back, running a hand through his hair. 'And gained himself some cool secret codes in the process.'

'Many people believe his books of magical script were actually codes, and that he was really a spy for Lord Walsingham,' Damian indicated the wheel. 'Years after Dee died, they claimed that nobody broke the codes because Dee and Walsingham created a 'master' code wheel of sorts so they could keep communicating. And although never seen, it was whispered of. They called it the Sunne Dial.'

'God, this is spy porn for you, isn't it?' Andy grimaced, picking up the cross, nervously passing it to Damian. 'Can it tell us what the things on the back of the cross say?'

'I think so,' Damian placed the cross down on the table as he grabbed a chair and pulled it over to sit on. 'With luck we might—'

'Oh, I think we're past the point of mights and maybes,' an unfamiliar voice spoke from beside the door, and Damian turned to see two men; one was a tall bald hulk of a man, currently pointing a Glock 17 pistol at him, but the other was a more famous face.

Martin Shrewsbury, the tech millionaire, a leather satchel over his shoulder.

'I'm sorry, Damian,' Andy stepped back as he spoke. 'I had no choice. They came to the apartment when you were in Deptford.'

Damian looked at Andy, sadness on his face.

'This is why you kept checking the phone,' he whispered. 'Why you kept looking around, as we came here.'

He then looked at Shrewsbury, anger in his eyes as realisation took over.

'You're the man in the limo, who spoke with Richard

Evans, maybe even killed him,' he stated as a fact more than as a question.

Shrewsbury nodded as he entered the room.

'I am. And if you don't do what your little friend says and translate the code, you'll most likely join him,' he replied.

7

NEW PLAYERS

DAMIAN STARED AT SHREWSBURY, NOW WALKING OVER TO SIT on one of the middle tables, staring up at the X shaped gap above his head.

'You made a hole,' Shrewsbury said, looking back at Damian. 'But then I hear you ruin a lot of things.'

'Funny man,' Damian snapped back. 'You shouldn't listen to people who say you're not. You're a regular laugh riot.'

Shrewsbury chuckled to himself and looked at Damian.

'I could just have you killed and translate the damn thing myself,' he suggested, 'if that's what you'd prefer?'

Damian kept his mouth shut at this, holding his anger in check.

'If I do this, you'll let us go?'

'I'll let *you* go,' Shrewsbury looked over at Andy, now beside the wall. 'He, however, has made his own arrangements with us.'

'I'll bet,' Damian glared at his housemate, who had the grace to turn away, avoiding Damian's accusatory expression, before turning back. 'Why?'

'Why what?'

'Why kill Richard Evans?'

There was a pause, and for a moment Damian wondered if Martin Shrewsbury would actually answer the question put to him.

'Honestly, he wasn't supposed to die,' he eventually replied, 'I didn't know he was terminal, or that he was going to decide to be some bloody hero martyr. It was mainly done to give him an incentive.'

'Join or die,' Damian muttered as he took the notepad offered to him by Cyrus, pulling a pen out of his own pocket and opening the pad on the table. He didn't want to translate the code on the wooden cross, but doing this meant that he didn't have to look anyone in the eye as he continued.

Shrewsbury smiled, a humourless, cold smile that didn't reach his eyes. It was as if he'd been taught the mannerism, but not the emotion behind it.

'No matter what you've heard about me, Mister Lucas, I'm not a monster.'

'You'd be surprised what I've heard about you,' Damian leant back from the table, 'Bigot, racist, Nazi—'

Cyrus brought the gun across Damian's temple, pistol-whipping him hard. Damian rocked back on the chair but caught himself before he fell, rubbing his bruised forehead, checking for blood.

'Truth hurts,' he hissed.

'Look, who gives a damn what Shrewsbury believes in? Just help him do this and we can go home, yeah?' standing by one of the windows, Andy looked nervous now, as if realising that the deal he'd made was going south right now. 'He'll pay us well for it.'

Andy pulled away from the window as he moved closer to Damian, the urgency in his voice clear.

'Think about it! No more needing to scam corporations to regain lost museum money, you can just give them it instead!'

'It was never about the money, Andy,' Damian shook his head sadly. 'It's the principle of the matter.'

'It was always about the money!' Andy argued. 'Corporate sponsorships! Money for the arts!'

'We took the battle to those wealthy pricks who believed that they could get what they want just by throwing money at things, and who could take back when they felt bored, no matter what they promised!' Damian was shouting now, as he glanced at Shrewsbury. 'Just like now!'

Shrewsbury made a small bow of acknowledgment. Damian looked back at Andy.

'Good to see you knew your price, though,' he muttered.

Andy's face darkened.

'It wasn't like that,' he replied.

'Did they threaten you? Did they hurt you?' Damian had turned from the table now, facing his friend. 'I'd understand if they did something like that. I really would.'

'No,' Andy admitted, 'they didn't threaten me at all. In fact, they were very persuasive.'

'You mean they offered to pay you,' Damian laughed. 'Bloody hell, if I'd known you were that cheap, I'd have done it myself.'

He rummaged around in his pockets.

'I'm sure I've got thirty pieces of silver around somewhere.'

'Do you have a hundred thousand?' Andy snapped. 'Because that's how much we have to find in a week if we want to stay alive!'

He pointed at Shrewsbury.

'I did this to cover our debt! The one that you created when you got greedy with the Russians! I did this to save you!'

Damian went to throw back a reply, but stopped himself. *Andy was correct.*

'You're right,' he whispered, turning back to the table.

Andy went to speak, as if to apologise himself, but Shrewsbury interrupted, clapping his hands to gain their attention.

'This is all great, but I'm bored now,' he said. 'Can you finish the translation please?'

'Oh, didn't I say?' Damian replied, leaning away from the table. 'I already finished it.'

Furious, Shrewsbury snatched the notebook away, reading it.

'It's a two-line riddle,' Damian explained, 'with each of the lines split over two of the tines of the wooden cross.'

'*Where doubles build up legacies, and marshalled forces hold,*' read Shrewsbury, '*The Yule King's hand upon the sea, the light provides the gold.*'

He tossed the notepad to the ground, furious.

'What gibberish is this?' he exclaimed. Damian shrugged.

'You asked for a translation,' he said, 'and so I gave you one. If you don't like it, have a go yourself.'

Shrewsbury walked away, mumbling the riddle to himself as Damian turned to Andy.

'You need to get out of here,' he said softly, 'because the chances are, we're not both gonna make it.'

Andy stared from Shrewsbury to Cyrus now, finally realising the deal he'd made had been the worst possible one to consider. He went to speak, to smooth things over with

Damian, but Shrewsbury turned, his eyes blazing with excitement.

'Temple Church!' he exclaimed. 'Evans had been in Temple Inn the day we spoke to him. It has to be there!'

'Yeah? Why?' Damian crossed his arms. 'Because every other conspiracy nut-job goes there?'

'*Where doubles build up legacies, and marshalled forces hold,*' Shrewsbury quoted, picking the notebook back up as he read the first line again. 'William Marshall was made a Knight's Templar upon his death and interred with his brother knights. The church is where his brothers, *marshalled forces,* hold ready, all buried beside him. And when it was built, the rounded part was designed to mimic the holiest place in the Templar's world, the circular Church of the Holy Sepulchre in Jerusalem. A double of a church, there to build the Templar legacy, where in the crypt *Marshall's forces hold ready.*'

'Well, it certainly sounds plausible,' Damian smiled, his tone mocking. 'But that's the joy of conspiracies.'

Shrewsbury stared at Damian before replying, as if trying to read Damian's thoughts on the riddle.

'You're saying it's not the church?' he asked.

Damian shrugged.

'I'm saying there are probably a dozen places in the country that could match that. We should look into other—'

'No. You're trying to lead me away from there, aren't you? You know I'm right,' Shrewsbury chuckled at this. 'Yes, I thought so. Lead me away, while you go find the gold for yourself. No, I don't think so. If it's at Temple Church, I'm willing to look.'

He tucked the Sunne Dial and the notebook into a satchel

before slinging it over his shoulder. Almost as an afterthought, he turned to his bodyguard.

'Cyrus, shoot him.'

'Wait!' Andy stepped forwards, his arms up. 'I told her I'd only help if there was no killing!'

'You're right,' Shrewsbury nodded, 'but frankly, we don't really need your help now anymore, do we?'

And with that statement made, Martin Shrewsbury turned and walked out of the room as Cyrus calmly shot Andy in the head.

8

HUNTED MAN

As Andy's body hit the floor, Damian was already moving, picking up the wooden cross and hurling it at Cyrus, the carving striking hard, drawing blood over his right eyebrow.

As Cyrus barked out in pain, the gun blindly turning towards its next target and firing wildly, Damian was already diving forward, his legs pumping hard as he charged into the bodyguard, grabbing at the gun. They struggled for a moment, the gun firing into the ceiling before Cyrus kneed Damian hard between the legs, sending him stumbling back to the door.

But before Cyrus could re-aim and fire, Damian was already running out of the room, pausing only to pull at the Tibetan bell as he passed, sending it crashing to the floor in front of the doorway, giving Damian a chance to run the hallway before Cyrus could follow. Martin Shrewsbury had already disappeared, and there was no way that the gunshots hadn't been heard and the police called. Damian just hoped that they wouldn't arrest him for Andy's murder.

Before he could run further, though, another bullet hit the plaster wall beside him, the explosion showering him with brick dust.

'That's enough,' hissed Cyrus, clambering over the bell, his gun still trained on the terrified Damian, 'you're a tricky bastard to kill, but needs must and all that—'

'You need me,' Damian said softly as he waited, stock still.

Cyrus paused.

'Why?'

'Because your boss is wrong,' Damian forced himself to relax, ignored the view of his friend's dead body in the next room, and stared calmly at the gunman. He'd conned his way out of dozens of situations. He could do this.

'You said that earlier.'

'And I was right then too,' Damian lowered his voice as he spoke, ensuring that Cyrus had to concentrate on hearing the words. This way he was considering fewer ways of killing Damian, and was slowly, unconsciously, leaning towards his target as he listened.

'Go on then,' Cyrus was relaxing. Damian tried to look just as relaxed, while bending his knees slightly, preparing to hurl himself forward.

'It's not the church. It's—*look out he has a gun!*'

The last part was aimed behind Cyrus and, as Cyrus spun to see who was behind him, Damian dived through one of the side doors on his right, slamming it behind him. Now alone in the corridor, Cyrus swore and started towards the door, but the faint sound of police sirens in the distance halted him. This was the problem with trying to kill someone in the centre of a city; the police were never that far away.

Pocketing the gun, Cyrus quickly and quietly slipped out of the door at the end of the corridor.

After a few seconds, the side door opened again, and Damian poked his head out nervously. Seeing the route was clear, he ran back to the Tibetan bell, clambering over it to re-enter the Warden's room, running across to Andy's body.

He was definitely dead. Damian had hoped that the bullet was glancing, or that it caught Andy in the shoulder, but the bullet wound was dead centre of Andy's forehead, his eyes still wide open and staring. Damian closed the eyes, glad that at least it'd been instantaneous.

Andy would never have seen it coming.

On the floor was Andy's phone, and Damian picked it up as he ran over to the 'Devil's hoof' table, picking up the discarded wooden cross. Tucking both into his jacket pocket, Damian turned to the door, to find armed police now entering, rifles aimed directly at him.

'On the ground! Now!'

'It's not what it looks like!' he said, immediately regretting it; the sort of thing a guilty person would say. The rifle muzzles waved towards him again and he complied, lying face down on the floor, his arms now behind his back. As the police secured the room, Damian felt his hands being cuffed together by an officer before he was unceremoniously pulled back to his feet.

'Where's the gun?' one officer screamed at him.

'It wasn't me!' Damian exclaimed in response. 'I didn't do it!'

'Search the room!' the officer started screaming at the other police in the area. 'He can't have hidden it well in the time he had.'

Now held between two armed officers, they dragged Damian to the door as the police moved him towards the exit.

'Get some SOCOs down here ASAP! Nobody moves the body—'

'His name was Andy,' Damian whispered.

The police ignored him as they dragged him into the courtyard, past the now-confused gate guard, and before he could protest any further, threw him into a police prisoner transport van. Scrambling back to his feet, he sat on a bench that ran along the side, looking out of the back of the van before the doors were closed. He had a clear view of the security entrance he'd entered only twenty minutes earlier.

And there, standing in silence, fury on her face, was Katherine Turner.

'Wait!' she shouted, storming towards the van. 'Get him out of there!'

'And who the hell are you?' the lead officer turned to face her, one hand still on his rifle as she flashed her warrant card.

'I'm SO14 and he's my asset,' she hissed in anger, pointing at Damian.

'Well, he's also a murder suspect and we're taking him in.'

Katherine stared long and hard at the officer, and even though he was twice her size and likely double her age, he squirmed under the gaze.

'Did you find the weapon?' she asked. 'I mean, if he shot someone, then the gun would still be there, right?'

'He had time to hide it.'

Katherine looked around in disbelief. 'Where? It's a bloody old dump of a building and he had less than a handful of minutes from gunshot to his arrest in the same room you found the body. That is, if what I heard on the radio is correct.'

The officer looked uncomfortable at this.

'There's panelling. He could have put it behind something.'

'Oh, I see,' mocked Katherine. 'Well, that makes it easy then, doesn't it? It's all sixteenth-and-seventeenth century wood and plaster in there, so grab a metal detector and have at it until you find something.'

She stepped forward, now nose to nose with the officer.

'Until then? He's coming with me.'

The lead officer, now unsure, looked at his partner.

'What's SO14?' he asked uncertainly.

'SO14 Royalty Protection Group is a component of the Metropolitan Police Service Protection Command,' Katherine explained slowly, as if repeating a well-spoken monologue. 'They protect the Royal Family and associated residences, and comprise several sections, namely Personal and Close protection, Residential Protection and Special Escort Group. SO14 also protects members of European Royal Families visiting the United Kingdom.'

'She's right, it is,' the second officer, seemingly more an expert on this, nodded.

'Is there much cop for that sort of work these days?' the lead officer muttered. 'I mean, Harry and Meghan have left for Canada and Prince Andrew's...'

He stopped at the stony expression on Katherine's face.

'Do I look like I'm having a holiday?' she asked.

'I should call this in,' the lead officer was still unsure about this. Katherine, in reply, shrugged.

'Go for it,' she said. 'But when the press get here and we're still arguing? You're the one taking responsibility.'

'So why is *he* important to you?' the second officer turned to face Damian, who kept completely still. 'I didn't see him at any Royal Weddings recently.'

'Get him out, and I'll show you.'

Reluctantly, the officer that threw Damian into the van now pulled him back out into the courtyard.

'Check his wallet,' Katherine said. 'No, actually, don't. I don't trust you to do it right, so let me.'

Reaching into Damian's back pocket, Katherine pulled out his wallet. Rifling through it, she pulled out a credit card, seemingly at random. With a dark expression on her face, she held it up to the lead officer.

'What does the name say?' she asked. The officer stared hard before speaking.

'Crown Prince Ludwig,' he replied. Damian had a flush of surprise at this, but fought to keep his expression straight.

'Now, let's play a game. Which two words do you think I give a shit about?' Katherine put the card back into the wallet.

'Crown?' the lead officer now looked sick.

'And?'

'Prince?'

'Exactly,' Katherine replied, now taking Damian from the officers. 'The Crown Prince here might be a suspect, but we can't let him be *seen* as one, understand? The diplomatic fallout would kill all of our jobs.'

The first officer paled at this. Katherine moved behind Damian, pulling out a key.

'So, I'm going to uncuff him—' she did this as she spoke, Damian rubbing his now free wrists, letting the blood return to them, '—and then I'm going to take him to my silver Audi over there. Publicly, he's nothing more than a tourist caught in the middle of this.'

'But we still need—' the second officer started, but Katherine cut him off mid-sentence with a raised finger.

'I'm not setting him free. I'm making sure the paparazzi

don't see him. We'll drive him to the station on Northampton Road, take him in through the back entrance and then everyone's happy, okay?'

The officers didn't know what to say to this; Katherine had already uncuffed Damian and was leading him away, effectively ending the conversation.

'Thanks?' the first one offered. Katherine ignored him, picking up the pace.

'They killed Andy,' Damian whispered.

'You're a goddamned idiot,' Katherine hissed as they reached the silver Audi. 'I told you to contact me when you heard anything.'

'You also told me—and those police over there—that you're SO14, Royal Protectorate, but that wouldn't bring you here,' Damian snapped back, opening the passenger door, 'so how about you cut the shit and just tell me what the hell's going on?'

By now they were sitting in the Audi as Katherine started the car, pausing only to pull a postcard out of her jacket, tossing it across to him.

'Recognise this?' she asked as she pulled the car out into the traffic, waving to the police cars that pulled back to let her through. Damian stared down at the image of Manchester City Football Club.

'You stole my postcard,' he muttered. 'Look on the back,' Katherine replied. Damian turned it over, but was surprised to find different writing to his own card on the reverse side. The addressee was *Katherine Turner*, and the message simply said:

Help him find it. And take him home.

'What's this supposed to mean?' Damian looked at

Katherine. 'Help who do what? Help me? Help Shrewsbury? And whose home?'

'Well, as I didn't leave you to the police or help Martin Shrewsbury kill you, which one do you think it is?' Katherine hissed as they turned south, away from Manchester.

'Who are you?' Damian turned his attention from the postcard now, staring in a mixture of suspicion and awe at his rescuer.

'All you need to know is that I'm a friend, and Richard sent me to look over you after he died,' she replied softly, turning the wheel, pulling into a smaller side road.

'You knew Richard?'

Katherine paused momentarily before replying.

'Enough to trust him and agree to any requests he made,' she looked back at Damian. 'Such as babysitting you. Fat lot of good that did, though.'

'What's that supposed to mean?' Damian turned to face her. 'I told you the truth in the apartment. The postcard arrived after you'd left.'

'And you took it straight to Martin bloody Shrewsbury,' Katherine hissed.

'That would have been Andy,' Damian whispered.

'Does he know where the next piece of the puzzle is?'

'Andy? No, he's—'

'Not him, for Christ's sake! *Shrewsbury!*' Katherine was getting angry as she spoke now. 'Did you wrap it up and put a bow on it before you gave him it?'

Damian pulled the wooden cross out from his pocket, staring down at it. 'I told him—'

He was thrown forward in the seat as Katherine slammed the brakes; the car skidding to a halt.

'*Are you kidding me?*' she shouted. 'You just *happened* to have this on you?'

'Everything happened so fast!' Damian replied. 'I didn't know if I'd need it, and then Andy... Oh God, Andy—'

Damian hurled the passenger door open and leaned out, puking into the gutter.

Closing the door and leaning back, he saw Katherine watching him with what looked like sympathy on her face, but at the same time Damian saw something different, a morbid curiosity, as if Katherine Turner had never seen someone react this way.

'Here,' she said, passing him a pack of mints.

'Let me guess, they help settle the stomach?'

'I don't know,' she replied, already gunning the engine. 'I gave them to you because your breath now smells of vomit.'

Damian gratefully took them as the Audi continued on.

'We've got about thirty minutes before the police realise I'm not taking you into custody, and we're about ten minutes behind Shrewsbury. So, there's a chance we can get to wherever he's going before—'

'He's going to the wrong place,' Damian leaned back against the seat, fighting more nausea. 'He thinks it's Temple Church, but it's not.'

'How do you know?'

Damian turned the cross over, showing Katherine the code. 'The cypher read as a two-line riddle. *Where doubles build up legacies, and marshalled forces hold, the Yule King's hand upon the sea, the light provides the gold.*'

'What does it mean?'

'No idea,' admitted Damian. 'But I remember something my dad told me years ago, that Temple Church was nothing but a long-standing joke in the quest community.'

'So where now, then?' Katherine looked to Damian as she drove. 'Because currently we're in a holding pattern.'

Damian thought about this for a moment.

'How long would it take us to get to Oxford?' he asked, eventually.

'A couple of hours at best,' Katherine replied as the car turned onto the motorway. 'Who are we seeing?'

'We're going to another library,' Damian replied. 'One my dad and Richard both visited regularly.'

'We can't go to the Bodleian Library,' protested Katherine. 'The whole place is covered with CCTV. You'd be arrested before you found whatever you're looking for in there.'

'Don't worry, we're going somewhere smaller,' Damian smiled. 'Lincoln College Library, housed in All Saints' Church.'

'Oh good, another bloody church,' muttered Katherine with absolutely no joy in her voice, as the car drove south towards Oxford.

9

LEGACY CARD

ON THE NORTH SIDE OF OXFORD'S BUSY HIGH STREET, ALL Saint's Church was a bold, baroque building with a spectacular spire rising above it. Walking from the south side of the street, Katherine couldn't help but marvel.

'And it's no longer a church?' she asked in surprise. 'Waste of a good church if you ask me.'

'Closed in the seventies,' Damian replied as they walked up to the door.

'Doesn't look that old.'

'The spire fell around 1700,' Damian placed a hand on the stone surrounding the entrance, feeling the age running through it. 'They rebuilt it about twenty years later. Nicholas Hawksmoor built the new spire, so the stories go.'

Katherine stopped walking for a moment. But Damian didn't notice this, or chose not to mention it as he continued into the library.

'Surely we need to be students to visit?' she asked.

Damian, smiling, pulled out a card from his wallet.

'Lincoln College Undergrad Damian Lucas at your service,' he said, flashing the card.

'I thought you failed university?'

'I didn't fail. I was kicked out.'

'To some, that's failing,' Katherine replied stubbornly. 'So I'm guessing that was made by you?'

'Not at all,' Damian walked up to the counter. 'My dad came here all the time. He used to love the chapel. And he was Lincoln College Alumni. Worked with Richard alongside several of the professors here, and in return he got a lifetime family pass, which meant that when I was old enough, I would have my own card to help with his research.'

He tapped the card on the desk to emphasise the point.

'Did having the card help?' Katherine looked around the library, once an ornate nave; the stone walls rose high above them, the windows long and narrow, while wooden book-shelves lined the sides in rows, modern tables and lights looking out of place in the middle. Damian, writing a book's name on a note and passing it to a librarian, smiled as he looked back.

'Not really, I haven't been here since dad died, and that was a while back.'

Katherine kept quiet, as did Damian. After around ten minutes, the librarian passed Damian a small leather-bound book from the back of the office and, taking Katherine with him he found a quiet corner to sit and examine it.

'What is it?' Katherine asked. Damian showed it to her.

'*A History of the Inns of Court and Chancery* by Robert Richard Pearce. Written in the mid-nineteenth century.'

'So, it's a guidebook?'

'More a 'tell-all' about Temple Inn,' he said, flicking

through it. 'Dad and Richard always talked about it. I pretty much know the name because of that.'

'You know the name but not the content,' Katherine muttered. 'We're risking everything for a book your dad might have looked at once.'

Damian pulled out a card from the front, showing how many times it had been taken from the shelves, and by whom.

'Look,' he said, pointing at the last name.

Richard Lucas, only a week earlier.

'So now what? Would he have left notes in the margin?'

'Unlikely,' Damian pulled out a note from his jacket, hastily written in the car, placing it beside the book.

Where doubles build up legacies, and marshalled forces hold, the Yule King's hand upon the sea, the light provides the gold.

'So go on then, what does this mean?' Katherine picked up the paper, reading it again. 'You're sure it's not Marshall?'

'It definitely doesn't mean Temple Church,' muttered Damian, flicking through the book's pages. 'Martin Shrewsbury believed the double referenced the fact that the church's round was built as a copy of another in Jerusalem, and that Marshalled Forces were the brother knights of William Marshall.'

'Sounds plausible,' Katherine mused, 'but the riddle says *where doubles build up legacies,* and the round in Temple Church was built when the Knights Templar were at their strongest. Their legacy had already been built by that point. And marshalled forces holding, if it had been dead knights, they would be waiting, or lying. 'Holding' infers standing to attention, ready for battle.'

Damian stared at Katherine for a moment. She smiled back.

'So where is it really aiming us at?' she asked. Damian shrugged, looking down at the book.

'I honestly don't know. It could be one of a dozen places. But I know it's not where Shrewsbury is heading.'

'You seem incredibly sure of yourself,' Katherine noted. 'Care to clue me in?'

'My dad,' Damian replied. 'Temple Church fascinated Richard, but my dad loved the Middle Temple. Well, before he died.'

'Oh. Sorry.'

'Sorry for what?'

'Their death,' Katherine said. 'It must have been hard on you.'

'How would you know that they both died?' Damian demanded.

'How about we keep you out of the police's hands for the moment?' changing the subject, Katherine went to continue, but saw that Damian had pulled out his phone and was now texting on it.

Grabbing it off him, she quickly opened it up, pulling out the sim card and snapping it. The sound made several students look up, glaring at the strange lady now holding a broken smartphone.

'What the hell!' Damian exclaimed.

'You're a murder suspect,' Katherine hissed, 'you're on the run. Now they know we're running, the first thing they will have done is ping your phone. They're probably on their way here right now, so you'll have to wait before you update Twitter or check your Instagram.'

'Fine,' Damian pulled out Andy's phone, quickly scrolling through the messages. This done, he then passed it to Katherine.

'Whose is this?' Katherine was already taking this second phone apart as she spoke.

'Andy's. When we arrived at Manchester, he mentioned Humphry Chetham being part of the School of Night. That's a group of freethinkers created back in Elizabethan times.'

'Okay, and this helps how?'

'It's not on Wikipedia, and it came out of nowhere. I think someone mentioned it to him. And he was texting a number I don't recognise, one that passed information on to Shrewsbury.'

'Why couldn't it be Shrewsbury himself?'

Damian shook his head.

'Nah, the guy I met struck me as someone who'd have others do his dirty work. Like the guy who killed Andy,' Damian smiled for the first time. 'Which means he'll need to play by the rules. Temple Church doesn't open until ten tomorrow morning. We have about eighteen hours before he does that. Plenty of time.'

'Any you know this how?'

'Hunch, based on a cold read when I met him.'

'I still don't know how you're so sure that it's not the church,' Katherine shook her head in disbelief as she placed the broken parts of phones into a waste bin.

Damian, still flicking through the book, paused, tapping a page with purpose.

'Here you go, I told you!' he exclaimed loudly, mouthing apologies at the students who now glared at him. 'Look at the first line. *Where doubles build up legacies.*'

Katherine read the page. 'In 1602, Shakespeare, then part of the Kings Men theatre troupe, performed his new play in the great hall of the Middle Temple. It was called *Twelfth Night*, and it dealt with the confusions surrounding a pair of shipwrecked twins, both mistaken for each other by the locals.'

She looked up, realising what she had read.

'Doubles. Of course.'

Damian grinned.

'Queen Elizabeth herself was at this performance, and the patronages that Shakespeare gained from her gave him fame and prosperity, ensuring his name would be forever known.'

Katherine smiled.

'The doubles of *Twelfth Night* literally built up his legacy. So whatever we're looking for, it's in the Middle Temple.'

'Possibly,' Damian closed the book, already rising, 'the problem with something like this is that you can fit anything to the riddle. We need a little more background intelligence.'

'And how do we do that?'

'Well, we're already in Oxford, so we're going to see an old friend of my dad's,' Damian replied. 'Someone who knew everything there was to know about secret societies.'

'You sure he can be trusted?' Katherine was skeptical.

'She, actually. And you'll love her. Real nut job,' replied Damian. 'Cambridge Professor, lives in Oxford. Professor of Lincoln College, actually. Name of Farringdon Gales.'

'Awesome,' Katherine replied, but Damian had the impression from her tone that this was actually the last thing she wanted to do right now. Either that, or she was annoyed they'd come to a library in Oxford just for one line of text before leaving.

'You okay?' he asked.

'Never better,' the tone was clipped, cold now. 'Where do we find her?'

Damian checked his watch.

'This time of day, she'll be in the Eagle and Child, grading papers with a pint.'

And with that, Damian and Katherine left the church-now-library, heading for the pub.

10

FARRINGDON GALES

IT WAS GONE SEVEN IN THE EVENING BY THE TIME THEY ARRIVED outside the Eagle and Child.

'We shouldn't be hanging around,' Katherine said, looking about the street as she spoke. 'We should just get out of here, find a place to lay low until we can get to Temple Inn. We don't even know if she can help.'

Damian shrugged.

'Frankly, she might not even be here,' he said, walking up to the pub's entrance and opening the door. 'Ladies first.'

Damian watched Katherine as she walked past him into the pub. He'd spent his post-university life conning people out of things, and he felt he had developed a pretty good radar for whether someone was lying, or hiding something.

And currently, Katherine was doing both.

Inside the pub, it was quiet, caught in the middle point between afternoon tourist visiting and evening student revelry. As they entered the main bar, bypassing a small room to the right that housed several chairs and tables around an ornate wooden fireplace, they walked down what was effectively a narrow, wooden-walled corridor with a bar along one side. There was a divider halfway down, no wider than a door on the left-hand side, to the sloping ceiling, it cut across to the right, above head height, creating a small archway into what was signposted as 'THE RABBIT ROOM'.

Here, a small selection of tables and chairs studded a room that was a mixture of oak panelling, pale plaster and covered with framed photos, notes and sketches of C.S Lewis and J.R.R Tolkien. And, in a corner to the right of a roaring wood fire, drinking a pint of cider, sat Farringdon Gales. 'Bloody hell,' she muttered as she saw Damian approaching, 'the prodigal bloody son returns, then.'

Dressed in a brown corduroy skirt and pale shirt under a slim fitting, grey jacket of Harris Tweed with a small, ornate red Templar cross pinned to the lapel, Farringdon looked every inch a country lady, even down to her silver hair cut into a neat, trim bob. Her face was etched with every heartache that life had given her, but her blue eyes sparkled with delight at the new arrival.

'Farringdon,' Damian smiled, embracing the now rising woman as if welcoming an aunt, or old friend, 'it's been too long.'

'And whose fault is that?' Farringdon replied, pulling away from the embrace and staring up and down at Damian. 'You're skinny. You need to eat.'

'Most likely,' Damian grinned as he showed Katherine. 'Farringdon, this is my friend Katherine. If you've got a few minutes, we have some questions we'd like to ask you.'

Farringdon stopped and examined Katherine for a moment. Katherine stood there, silently allowing this.

'You have as long as I take to drink the pint you're buying

me,' Farringdon said, sitting back down at the table. Damian nodded.

'Fair enough,' he said, looking at Katherine, sitting down facing Farringdon. 'Drink?'

'No,' Katherine replied.

Walking to the bar, Damian ordered another cider and a soft drink, watching a small television at the back of the bar as it showed highlights of a football match from earlier that day. Glancing back, he saw Katherine and Farringdon still silently measuring each other, as if waiting for the other to speak, and therefore lose whatever unspoken game they played.

Then, drinks purchased, he returned to the table, placing the pint glass in front of the elderly academic.

'To Richard,' she said solemnly, raising her glass. Damian followed suit. Taking a long draught from the glass, Farringdon set it down, facing Damian.

'I'm guessing this isn't a social visit sort of question?' she asked politely. Damian shook his head.

'I was hoping you could enlighten us with something,' he began, looking to Katherine briefly before continuing, 'I heard something today that I'd only heard once before, by you. About Humphry Chetham.'

Farringdon's eyes narrowed at this. 'I only ever mentioned him to your father, God rest his soul,' she replied. 'This is a School of Night question, isn't it?'

Damian nodded, his throat suddenly dry at the mention of the name.

'Well, it's good that you asked me here, in the room where Hobbits and Narnia were created!' Farringdon laughed. 'Where else is a fantasy story to be told?'

'Damian gave me the impression that you were quite the believer,' Katherine leaned back in her chair.

Farringdon nodded at this. 'Oh, it was real, all right,' she replied. 'But some stories related to it...'

She tailed off, waggling her hand as she did so, looking back at Damian.

'This is Evans, isn't it?' she asked. 'You're following his damned fool Quixotic quest to find that gold.'

'I am, but it might not be that Quixotic. When was the last time you spoke to him?'

Farringdon shrugged.

'I saw him about a week or so back,' she replied. 'He was at the church library. He told me he'd been in Antwerp for a few weeks.'

'Did he tell you what he'd found there?'

'No, but I could guess from the look in his eye. Did he tell you? I didn't think you were even on his radar these days?'

Damian ignored the comment. 'A phrase. *Among books, pirate treasure leads to Satan's step.* It led me to Chetham's Library... And this.'

Looking around to ensure that nobody was watching, Damian pulled out the wooden cross from his jacket pocket.

'You don't need to tell me what that is,' Farringdon took the cross from him, turning it around in her hand. 'I've seen it countless times before. But usually, it's attached to a ceiling.'

'Damian—' Katherine started, looking nervously around the bar.

'Richard Evans sent us to this,' Damian explained. 'He found something that showed that the cross was a clue to a bigger message.'

'I suppose this led to the cypher?' Farringdon asked.

Damian nodded.

'Until it was taken from me,' he replied. 'That's why we're in a bit of a hurry. The people who took the Sunne Dial are looking to use the gold for the wrong reasons.'

'If the gold truly exists, there's no *right reason* existing for that much money,' Farringdon placed the cross back on the table. 'So what do you need to know?'

'We're playing catch up,' Damian said. 'the people we're up against know more than we do. To get ahead of them before they win, I need to know what the real purpose of the School of Night was.'

Farringdon steepled her fingers together as she pondered this. 'Much of what I have is conspiracy and half-truth rumours,' she replied, taking a final draught of her cider. 'Easiest way to start is to ask what you know already.'

Damian thought about this for a second.

'Not a lot,' he admitted.

Farringdon nodded.

'Then let me start simply. People know the School of Night only because Shakespeare hinted at it in *Love's Labour's Lost*,' she started. 'They believed it was started by Henry Percy, the ninth Earl of Northumberland, to keep the legacy of Queen Elizabeth alive.'

Damian looked at Katherine as Farringdon spoke, but if she was getting something from this, she was giving nothing away.

'Percy was a survivor,' Farringdon continued, 'an ally of many conflicting causes. He set up this 'gentleman's drinking society' with Sir Francis Walsingham in 1588. They brought in similar mindsets; Christopher Marlowe, Sir Walter Raleigh, the poet George Chapman, translator Thomas Harriot, Sir Francis Drake and Doctor John Dee; all these men were rumoured to be members.'

'And that's literally about all I've heard of them,' Damian said. 'Apart from the fact that Marlowe was Walsingham's spy, and I now think Dee's attempts to turn base metals into gold were actually some kind of money laundering plan.'

Farringdon nodded.

'If we're going down that rabbit hole, I'll give you my personal conspiracy theory,' she started. 'Elizabeth needed money and fast for the upcoming war with Spain. Her gold reserves had always been low, after her father squandered away pretty much everything before he died. But, there was one reserve she hadn't tapped.'

'The Plantagenet gold,' Damian replied.

'Or rather 'alchemically created' gold by Dee,' Katherine finished the sentence. 'If the gold even exists, and she could get hold if it, this would be a perfect way to explain her sudden wealth.'

'Ideal way to hide it,' Farringdon smiled. 'However, it never happened.'

'How do you know?' asked Katherine.

'Because with that much gold, Elizabeth could have created a new Roman empire,' Farringdon replied, watching Damian with a wickedly mischievous expression on her face, as if waiting for him to catch up with what she was insinuating.

'Elizabeth wasn't a Plantagenet! She didn't know where the gold was!'

'I believe so,' Farringdon nodded. 'It's said around 1590, when Walsingham died, relations between Elizabeth and the School became confrontational. They'd always assisted her, but not given her everything, which was both contradictory and confusing for her. Elizabeth was approaching the end of her reign, she had no heir, and the School knew that the most likely candidate to replace her would be King James of Scotland. And none of them wanted to see that happen.'

Farringdon paused for a moment, picking up the tweed cap and passing it to Damian.

'Here, put that on,' she whispered.

Doing as she said, Damian looked back to the bar where, on the television, was a news item. Over a 'live' video of Chetham Library, a clear photo of Damian, taken from the CCTV, was displayed. Cap now on, Damian looked back at Farringdon.

'It seems they're gaining on you,' she whispered sadly.

'I didn't kill him,' Damian rose from his seat, but Farringdon placed her hand on his arm, halting him.

'They won't be looking for you here, as long as you keep a low profile,' she said, 'so sit, drink and let's finish this.'

Sitting back down, Damian looked at Katherine, noting that she'd already moved around the table so she could see the entire bar from where she sat, as if to prepare for a quick escape.

'So, the gold?' he asked.

'If you listen to mad old women in pubs, the gold has an unlikely ally in Sir Robert Dudley,' Farringdon continued, 'who somehow gains the information of its whereabouts. However, at this point Dudley is massively out of favour with Elizabeth. On his deathbed in 1588, he gives the location to Henry Percy, who served under him while fighting in the Netherlands.'

'And Henry Percy creates the School of Night the same year,' Katherine said, still watching the bar.

'Exactly. The School isn't set up to help Elizabeth, it's created for something else.'

'How does Dudley know where the money is?' Damian leaned forward now.

'Who knows? Maybe he learnt it from his grandfather,' Farringdon held Damian's gaze for a moment. 'But we're not talking about the Dudleys. We're talking about the School.'

'Here's where I get confused though,' mused Damian, 'as far as the history books say, the School is pretty much disbanded and dead within thirty years of its creation.'

'That's what they wanted you to believe,' Farringdon tapped the side of her nose. 'It went underground, and over the years, others joined. Dee brought in Chetham, who brought in Inigo Jones, who introduced Christopher Wren, who inducted Nicholas Hawksmoor, and on and on. They kept out of the spotlight throughout the Civil War and into the Restoration, but they were there.'

'So where are they now?' Damian was getting tired now, a small point at the back of his neck itching as if he felt that everyone in the bar was staring at him. 'I mean, surely we would have seen the money by now?'

Farringdon sighed, finishing the pint.

'From what I've learnt over many years rooting around in musty old books hidden away in archives, after Queen Anne's death in 1714 with no immediate heir, it's said that Hawksmoor went rogue and stole the gold. He altered the clues to its location, and never told a soul where it was.'

'Why would he do that?'

'He was unhappy that George the First had taken the throne over the London-born James Francis Stuart, thanks to a 1701 Act of Settlement that prohibited Catholics from ruling England. When the School of Night offered the gold to assist King George against the Stuart claim to the throne, leading to the Jacobite Revolution in 1715, they found it was gone.'

'So, this whole thing is pointless,' Damian picked up the cross, looking at it. 'Even if we translate Dee's cypher, it doesn't matter. Hawksmoor's altered the game.'

'Yes, but he still left clues, God knows why. And he would have most likely kept to Dee's cypher, as he truly believed that someone would follow him, someone who believed as he did. He wanted the gold to be found. Just not found by the wrong people.'

Katherine rose from the chair.

'Come on, it's time to go.'

'Is everything okay?' Damian saw Katherine was watching the barman, now on the phone and staring straight at them.

'We've overstayed our welcome,' she replied. Farringdon grabbed her hand, cupping it in her own.

'Take this,' she said, palming a car fob into it, 'look for the red Peugeot outside. It's a loaner from the University, not in my name. Nobody's looking for it.'

She pulled out a card with a single phone number on it.

'And if you need anything, just call me, okay?'

'Thank you,' Damian took the card and embraced Farringdon one more time, 'I owe you even more now.'

'Just solve the riddle, and keep me in the loop,' Farringdon replied, sitting back down, 'but also remember that the School didn't just hold the gold as its only secret. Look for where Marlowe went.'

Damian nodded, following Katherine out of the Rabbit Room and onto the streets of Oxford.

'Time to go,' Katherine clicked the fob, hearing a 'beep' from a nearby red car parked further down the street. They walked towards it, but both heard the faint sound of multiple police cars.

Katherine ran to the car. 'Come on!'

Already, the first of the police cars could be seen approaching from the other end of the street. Damian looked around, as if looking for an escape route.

'I can't,' he said eventually. 'If they see me get in, they'll chase us both.'

'And you think you can outrun cars?' Katherine stared at the rapidly approaching police cars coming from the north. Damian was already moving, running south across the road and towards Balliol College's gates.

'I know some shortcuts,' he said as he ran. 'Meet me at St Aldate's Saxon Church.'

And with that he was gone, and police cars now surrounded Katherine.

'Quick!' she shouted, pointing at Damian. 'He's the guy from the TV! He wanted a lift, but I said no!'

The officers who had left the cars now started off after Damian and Katherine entered Farringdon's car, trying to keep her breath stable.

Because all of Oxford's police were hunting Damian now.

11

FOX HUNT

As a child, Damian had spent many happy days in Oxford, exploring the side streets and learning the secret short cuts through the many colleges within its boundaries. That said, he had never expected to use them like this.

As he ran through Balliol College's still open gates, glancing at the Martyr's Monument to his right, he ran into the large courtyard garden flanked by college buildings. He knew that someone running wouldn't cause issue here, as students were always late for class, but a runner pursued by police was another matter. More importantly, the only exit was south, onto Broad Street, and the police would already be looking for a young man wearing a brown leather jacket and flat cap. He had to think cleverly.

Ducking to the right, he ran diagonally to the south-eastern corner, across the Croquet Lawn, aiming for the Master's Garden and the large Beech tree beside it. Pulling to a stop behind the tree, he turned to see that the police were only now gathering at the main gate, stopped by a steward asking why half a dozen uniformed men were trying to enter University grounds. Damian decided not to wait and slipped into the Master's Garden, but as he crossed, he could already hear police sirens ahead.

There was a coat on a bench to his left; the gardener's wet weather jacket, dark green with a hood. With no sign of the gardener, Damian pulled it on, rummaging through the pockets as he continued onward. A navy blue woollen hat was removed, replacing the flat cap, thrown into a bush. A pair of thick-rimmed glasses were in the inner pocket and Damian put them on, grateful that whoever owned these wasn't too blind. And now, bespectacled and clothed as a gardener, Damian ran to the gate beside the Chapel.

Which was locked.

Another rummage in the coat located a key that opened the gate, and Damian slipped through, locking it behind him. Then, walking swiftly across the Front Quad, he joined a queue of college students waiting to leave, their exit blocked by two officers, checking each of the male students as they left.

Damn.

With no option but to bluff it out, Damian marched past the students, straight up to the officers.

'You lookin' for a lad in a brown coat?' he asked, gruffing his voice up. The closest officer looked at him.

'You've seen him?' he asked. Damian tossed him the key.

'Locked him into the Master's Garden, over there,' he pointed. 'You're welcome.'

As the police swarmed past him and towards the Chapel, Damian headed through the gate, out onto Broad Street, crossing over and walking away from the college, already pulling off the glasses. The sounds of the sirens were fading now, but as Damian reached the junction of Turl Street and Market Street he heard yet another police car approaching, sirens still blaring, Not wanting to risk his new disguise, Damian turned into the Covered Market, making his way south. To the side was a joke shop and Damian on a spur of the moment walked in, picked up a cardboard sheet of five brown 'fake moustaches', placed a ten-pound note on the counter, and left before the assistant could see his face properly; the fact that Richard Evans had done something similar only a few days earlier was not lost on him.

Taking the more natural of the fake moustaches off the sheet and throwing the others into a bin, Damian pulled off the double-sided tape and affixed the moustache to his upper lip. It wasn't an identical match to the hair, but under the woollen cap no one would know. And now the woollen hat and moustache, alongside the waterproof jacket, transformed Damian into a completely different person. And, with his head down, and with a slow pace, and fighting the urge to run, Damian sauntered south through Oxford, even passing two police officers who gave him no notice.

For the first time in a while, he was alone and feeling safe. He had a momentary thought of turning away, leaving Katherine here and finding his own way to London; but after Andy...

Andy.

The memory of his friend's body lying dead on the floor of Chetham's Library slammed into Damian and he staggered for a moment, holding the edge of a stall to steady himself. Calming, he allowed the wave of nausea to pass, followed by a fresh wave; one of cold, hard anger. Anger at Martin

Shrewsbury, currently living the high life of a millionaire without a care in the world.

There was a payphone to the side of the door as he left, mostly ignored in a world of mobile phones. Pulling out a pound coin, Damian dialled a number.

'Hello?' Max Larridge answered.

'Max, I need a favour,' Damian said.

On the other end of the line, Max was silent for a moment.

'What happened to Andy?' he eventually asked. Damian winced. Of course Max had seen the news. Bloody well everyone would have seen the news by now.

'Big bald bastard shot him.'

'Russian?'

'No, Martin Shrewsbury's bodyguard.'

There was a whistle down the line.

'Jesus, Damian, you don't half pick them.'

Damian looked around. He could see market security approaching, but there was no need for concern in his current disguise.

'Yeah, you could say that,' he replied. 'I know you don't owe me anything, but I did just make you some money...'

'Go on, what do you need?'

'I need you to get a message to Isabella Vladimov.'

There was no sound on the other end of the line, but Damian could imagine the expressions Max was pulling right now.

'You sure about that? I mean, really sure about that?'

'I have to be,' Damian replied. 'Look, I'm onto something big, and there's a chance that I can pay her back the money I owe, plus a little extra.'

'She'll probably be overjoyed to hear that, but I can see her asking me what the catch is for this additional windfall.'

Damian thought for a moment, phrasing his reply carefully.

'Isabella Vladimov is known for a variety of illegal activities. I might... need use of them.'

'What sort of illegal activities?'

'That, I don't know yet. But Shrewsbury killed Andy, and he needs to pay,' Damian felt the anger rising in his voice and forced himself to relax, before he drew more attention to himself.

'You're not thinking of offing him?'

'Bloody hell, no!' Damian glanced around, as if scared someone had overheard Max. 'I need allies. People who can help me. I've got someone helping me right now, but I don't know what their own game is yet. I need alternate options.'

There was a pause as Max considered this.

'I'll do it for Andy, but only because I believe your story,' he said eventually. 'She probably won't go for it, but I suppose it's worth a try.'

'Thanks,' Damian said. 'I'll call you back tomorrow.'

And with the favour provided, he hung up the phone and left the Covered Market as quickly as he could.

Exiting onto the High Street and turning right, Damian slowly and carefully followed the road to the left, St Aldate's churchyard now visible as he did so. And, as he approached, he saw the red car parked down Pembroke Square, a nervous Katherine sitting in the driver's seat.

'Bloody hell!' she exclaimed as he entered. 'Where did you get all that?'

'Long story,' Damian said, looking around. 'Can we get out of here?'

Nodding, Katherine put the car into gear, turned left onto St Aldate's road and drove back down the High Street towards the A40 and London.

———

EVEN THOUGH IT WAS ONLY AN HOUR INTO CENTRAL LONDON, Katherine suggested they check into a motorway service motel for the night; the Inns of Court were often closed after dark, and the security at the entrances would be more alert than in the morning, when the first batch of tourists arrived. Once Katherine had registered, she brought Damian quietly inside, still wearing the hat and moustache. And, after Katherine agreed to walk over to the service station food court located across the car park and bring back a couple of bags of fried chicken pieces and chips, things didn't seem too bad.

When she returned to the room, however, she found Damian at the desk, examining the wooden cross and writing what looked like notes on a piece of hotel stationery.

'Found something else?' she asked, eating a chicken piece.

Damian shook his head.

'If we're going to chase after Shrewsbury, we're doing it with one distinct disadvantage,' he explained.

'They have the Sunne Dial, and we don't.'

'Which means they can translate any clues, and we can't.'

Katherine nodded as she wiped her mouth with a napkin. 'Yeah, I thought that might be the case. So, we're screwed then?'

'Well, let's hope Shrewsbury believes the same, because if

he does, then you're both wrong,' Damian turned from the notepad with a grin. 'We're back in the game.'

'How?' Katherine rose and walked to the desk. There, written on the notepad, were the letters A through to Z, and underneath nearly all of them was a cypher symbol.

'You've deciphered it already?' she asked.

'Do you know how Bletchley Park broke the Nazi codes?' Damian said, continuing before Katherine could answer. 'They found words that stayed the same, words that they could gain the cypher for.'

'Nazis put the same words in their messages? That's just sloppy.'

'No, it's actually quite understandable when you work out what the words were. Every Nazi message they intercepted had two encoded words at the end. The first was four letters, the second was six.'

Katherine thought for a moment.

'Heil Hitler.'

Damian nodded. 'With that, they knew six of the letters of the code, including E, one of the most commonly used ones. Eventually they could decipher entire notes. Well, until the Nazis changed the codes again.'

'And this helps us how?'

Damian held up the cross.

'Shrewsbury had me decipher this for him. '*Where doubles build up legacies, and marshalled forces hold, the Yule King's hand upon the sea, the light provides the gold.*' Knowing what letters matched where, I've checked them off against an alphabet.'

He put the cross down now, excitedly waving the notepad at Katherine.

'Only the letters J, Q, X and Z aren't used in this riddle. Which means we have over eighty percent of the letters needed. Add the fact that most of these won't be used anyway, and we've got a working cypher.'

He looked at the bed, seeing the bucket of food for the first time.

'Ah, dinner.'

As Damian attacked the chicken, Katherine checked out of the window.

'What did Farringdon mean when she said to look where Marlowe went, and why?'

'I'm honestly not sure,' Damian replied through half eaten chicken. 'All I can think is she means St Nicholas's Church; after all, that's where Richard made his 'X', right underneath Marlowe's plaque.'

'Yes, but Richard placing that isn't public knowledge,' Katherine argued, 'Where else could she have meant?'

Damian thought for a moment. 'Marlowe spent a lot of time travelling on behalf of Walsingham as his spy; at least half his years at University were spent in France, Italy or Spain. However, he was dead by 1593.'

He paused.

'If you believe the stories, anyway.'

'And you don't?'

Damian shrugged. 'Never did. Growing up near Canterbury, you can't get away from his stories.'

'Probably helps to have a history obsessed dad.'

'Not this time,' Damian reflected. 'We never spoke about him.'

He thought for a moment longer.

'Marlowe was about to be arrested on charges of *Heresy*,' he said. 'A few days later, and right before he was to be brought in for questioning, one where he was likely to give up some very sensitive secrets, he's murdered in a brawl in Deptford.'

'That's bad luck.'

'Well-timed bad luck, especially when you look closer at the event. Marlowe spent the day with three friends, drinking and playing backgammon. At some point Marlowe and a friend named Frizer fight, and Frizer stabs Marlowe in the eye, apparently in self-defence.'

'He kills him?'

'So it's claimed. And it's a crime they're all cleared of, following a small show trial. Interestingly, they were all men who had worked for Francis Walsingham at the same time as Marlowe.'

'What, Marlowe was executed?'

'That, or he faked his death,' Damian explained. 'There are no papers of any kind of the examination of the corpse, the Queen's coroner oversaw the case but didn't know Marlowe, and they buried the body the same day in St. Nicholas's church in an unmarked grave. For a man like Marlowe, with the skills and provisions given to him by Walsingham, it would have been easy to fake his murder and then travel somewhere far away.'

'He's your idol, isn't he?' Katherine smiled. 'A rogue that pulled the ultimate con?'

'I like the underdogs,' Damian shrugged.

Katherine nodded, and for a moment there was silence in the hotel room.

'So, Temple Inns,' she eventually spoke. 'You think that book was right?'

'Farringdon's list makes me more certain,' Damian finished a piece of chicken, wiping his mouth with a napkin. 'Raleigh, Drake, Walsingham, Wren, even Dudley were connected to the Inner Temple, and Percy's son Algernon, the only one to spend significant time with his father while imprisoned in the Tower of London was also a member of the Middle Temple.'

'Medieval Law School. Crazy to think that this is where the next clue is.'

Damian nodded.

'I just hope it's the last clue,' he replied.

12

TWINS AND LEGACIES

Martin Shrewsbury furiously stood outside Temple Church, Cyrus beside him as they waited amongst the morning crowd of tourists, impatiently waiting for the doors to open. It was nine-fifty in the morning, there were ten minutes left, and no matter how hard Shrewsbury banged upon the door, there was no response from inside.

Around the tree-edged courtyard within the Inns of Court the other tourists and visitors watched Shrewsbury with interest, many doing their best to inconspicuously film him or take photos on their phones. Shrewsbury gave up banging on the door and, with Cyrus following behind him, walked over to a statue in the middle of the courtyard; a tall plinth where, at the top, he could see the well-known image of two brother knights riding the same horse.

The Knights Templar.

Staring silently at a tourist until they reluctantly moved aside, he sat down on the seat beneath the plinth, glaring at the door, as if trying to will it to open with his anger alone.

'We've wasted a whole bloody night on this,' he grumbled. Cyrus, standing beside him, shrugged.

'You've waited this long, what's another few hours?'

'Everything,' snapped Shrewsbury. 'He's still out there somewhere, he's avoided the police for eighteen hours or so, but if he's captured, he could mention us. It'd cause issues. And I don't pay you to give pithy answers.'

'No, you don't,' muttered Cyrus.

'I pay you to get results.'

Cyrus looked at his boss, narrowing his eyes.

'Are you saying it's my fault?' he asked.

Shrewsbury shrugged.

'I seem to recall telling you to get rid of him. And let's face it, you didn't do a very good job of that.'

'Maybe I'll get another chance,' Cyrus replied, his face lightening at the thought.

———

ACROSS THE COURTYARD, WATCHING FROM BEHIND A PORTICO OF pillars, Damian turned back to Katherine with a smile.

'Told you he wouldn't be able to get in,' he said. Katherine looked at her watch.

'He will in about five minutes.'

'Won't do him any good,' Damian pulled her away from the courtyard. 'Come on, we've got places to be.'

He guided her through the leafy Elm Court and back down an arched, covered corridor that led back onto Middle Temple Lane, then across Fountain Court to a tall, wide red brick building, a large, deep set archway to a heavy wooden door in front of them, blocked by black railings, each with two Tudor roses with a golden lamb of God above them.

'Middle Temple Hall,' he said as they walked towards the gate. "Have you been here before?"

Katherine shook her head.

'Maybe a school trip when I was a kid, perhaps, but I think I'd remember it. How do we get in?'

'We don't,' Damian replied, pointing at a large wooden sign, white text on a black background outside the entrance that read HALL CLOSED TO THE PUBLIC. 'Only members of the Temple can enter.'

He stopped.

'You're not a member, are you?'

'Oh yeah, get birthday cards all the time,' mocked Katherine. 'You have a way in, right? Because we parked the car a long bloody way away.'

'You can't blame me for that. Parking south of the river wasn't my decision.'

'We can't let congestion charge cameras pick us up,' Katherine glared at Damian as he walked up the steps to the gate that covered the large wooden door. 'Southwark is just outside the line.'

She took another look around Fountain Court.

'So, how well do you know this place?'

'My dad used to bring me here as a kid,' Damian replied. 'So hopefully there might be a few familiar faces that can help us.'

Sighing, Katherine followed him into the Hall. To the left of the door as they entered was a small side room, with a chest high barrier blocking entrance to the small security cubicle behind it. Only large enough for a small workstation, computer and chair, the Middle Temple Hall's security would traditionally sit here, only moving from their post when required. Straight ahead was a corridor made up of names;

dark wooden walls with panels showing lists of members of
the Middle Temple, each with a particular year next to them,
running along the green carpeted hall in chronological order,
and lit only by a large, ornate lamp hanging by a chain, and
emblazoned with stained glass crests upon each of its eight
sides.

Ignoring the corridor ahead of him, Damian turned left
into the security office to see a suited guard already watching
him. Portly, with close cropped silver hair and a peppered
goatee, the guard stood, as if expecting some kind of
confrontation. Most likely, he was expecting them to be yet
another pair of tourists, hoping to get a look in the hall, even
though the sign outside was quite adamant on the subject.

'Can I help you?' he asked reluctantly. Damian grinned.

'I dunno, Mark. Can you?'

The guard paused for a moment, thrown by Damian's
obvious familiarity. Then, after staring hard at the man in
front of him, recognition flooded across the face.

'Robert's lad!' he exclaimed. 'Bloody hell, I haven't seen
you for donkey's years!'

Damian grasped Mark's outstretched hand, shaking it
warmly.

'It's good to see you,' Damian said with genuine sincerity.
'And yes, it's been a while.'

'I heard about your father. Terrible way to go,' Mark
replied. 'He was a good man.'

Damian looked back at Katherine.

'Mark's been a guard here for close to forty years.'

Mark now looked at Katherine, suspicion now upon his
face. 'Have we met before? I'm sure I've—'

Katherine pulled out her warrant card, showing it to him.

'No. Katherine Turner, SO14.'

'What's this about?' Mark turned back to Damian, trying to put all the pieces together as he did so. 'Richard Evans came by a few days back. I heard he died the same day. Now you appear with police.'

He looked to Katherine.

'Special police at that.'

Damian nodded.

'I'm here about the same thing as Richard,' he said. 'We're in a race against some bad people.'

'This the same treasure hunt that your father followed?' Mark shook his head. 'I'd hoped you had more sense.'

'Oh, believe me, I did,' Damian rummaged in his pocket, pulling out a notepad. Opening up a page, he showed it to Mark. 'But then I didn't have this before.'

Mark read the riddle written upon it.

'*Where doubles build up legacies, and marshalled forces hold, the Yule King's hand upon the sea, the light provides the gold.* So, I can see why you came here. The first bit is definitely us,' he said.

'We guessed the first part because of *Twelfth Night*,' Damian explained. 'But we weren't sure about the rest.'

'No, it's still definitely us.'

'The Marshalled forces?' Katherine seemed surprised. Mark grinned, an unusual sight on such an imposing guard as he walked past them.

'Let me show you something,' he said, nodding to another guard down the corridor to take over the booth, as he led both Damian and Katherine out of the security room and into the great hall.

The Great Hall of Middle Temple was over four hundred years old, a hundred feet long and over forty feet wide, with oak panelling covering the lower half of the walls leading to four large windows on each side, each with eight stained glass panels within, with a beautiful and ornate double-hammer beamed roof of blackened wood rising above them. In front of each window were the breastplates and helmets of a soldier, although no weapons were present.

Beneath them, the oak panels were covered with coats of arms; each one that of a Middle Temple Reader, always a senior barrister, three high and travelling along both sides of the hall, each with three rows of ornate text underneath giving their name, whether they were a Spring or Autumn Reader, and the year of their reading. They continued around to the panelled wall at the far end of the hall, above a slightly raised stage area and the famous 'bench table'.

Damian paused as he saw the stage. He'd been in here many times as a child, and even now, years later, the fact that he was in the room where Shakespeare once performed *Twelfth Night* for Queen Elizabeth the First still gave him cause to stop and marvel.

Above the stage and interspersed between the shields of the Readers were six paintings of varying large sizes. These were of Queen Elizabeth the First, Charles the First, an immense painting of Charles the Second, James the Second and, all in their coronation robes, William the Third, Queen Anne and George the First. With three royal crests and another stained-glass window at the top of the wall above them, it was as if centuries of divine rulers stared down upon the barristers as they ate below.

There were several long tables in the hall, and the lunch placings were being set out by waiting staff as Mark paused, pointing up at the breastplates.

'There's your marshalled forces,' he explained. 'There used to be busts of Caesar along the windows until the late eighteen hundreds. Then, for some reason, they replaced them with these from the armoury.'

'The armoury? Why would barristers need an armoury?' Katherine stared up at the armour.

'All the Inns of Court have armouries. If someone invaded these Inns of Court, it would be up to the Barristers of Middle and Inner Temple to repel them,' Mark explained. 'The armour was held in case of need during battle, but to my knowledge, they were never used. And back when it was first built, these breastplates lined the walls. We didn't have as many plaques on the wall back then.'

'Marshalled forces.' Katherine nodded. 'The literal term is to array for battle.'

'Okay, so we have the temple, and we have the forces, so who the hell is the Yule King?' Damian asked. 'And what's the 'sea' a euphemism for?'

'If it was a phonetic 'c', it could mean the cupboards.' Katherine mused as she looked around the hall, turning back to Damian, now staring at her in surprise.

'Come on, everyone knows that when a solicitor is called to the Bar, it means he or she is brought to one of the Temples of Court,' she continued. 'There they sign the members' book on a table called the 'cupboard.''

Mark nodded, pointing off to the left of the paintings, to a large wooden table against the wall in the corner of the great hall.

'That's the Middle Temple's cupboard over there,' he said. 'Legends state it used to be the door hatch of a famous ocean-going ship, The Golden Hind, brought here by Francis Drake himself.'

'Francis Drake?' Damian glanced at Katherine, who, seeing this, nodded.

'Another name we keep seeing,' she replied. 'Although we didn't know that Drake was a Middle Temple member?'

'He wasn't, and that's the curious bit,' Mark was walking back out of the hall by this point, and Damian and Katherine raced to catch up with him. 'Drake was an Inner Temple member. And at the time he donated the hatch, Inner and Middle Temples weren't the best of friends, as the Inner Temple had just screwed the Middle Temple out of a very lucrative land deal.'

Now back out in the corridor, Mark pointed up at the lamp. It was a large, eight-sided one, with each side a stained-glass image of a heraldic shield, held in place by thin lead wire that secured the small pieces of glass together, housed in an ornate gold casing, with stained glass red and white roses underneath.

'Drake also gave the Middle Temple this,' Mark said proudly. 'It's a ship's lamp also from The Golden Hind. It's not the original though, as that one was destroyed in the bombings of World War Two, but we had some incredibly detailed sketches of it, drawn about a hundred years earlier. The Temple was able to recreate an exact copy from the designs. Well, exact to the original, that is.'

'What do you mean?' Damian looked up at the lamp once more.

'I mean that over the centuries bits broke, and the glass was replaced by lead here and there. One architect even paid for repairs there and then when he broke a pane of glass back in the early seventeen hundreds.'

'You allow many architects into Middle Temple?' Katherine raised an eyebrow.

'No idea,' Mark shrugged. 'It was during the redesign of

the gardens, so I think there were probably a couple helping with the outer walls of the building.'

'So Drake, who wasn't a member of the Middle Temple, gave a lamp and a table to it,' Damian stared at the light, but he wasn't looking at it. 'Drake, who was a member of the School of Night.'

'*The Yule King's hand upon the sea, the light provides the gold,*' Katherine said, suddenly more animated than she had been for a while. 'The cupboard was a hatch from a ship. The sea would have hit it constantly. And, it's a 'C', so it's a double clue.'

'Only if Drake was the Yule King,' Damian commented.

Katherine looked back at the lamp.

'Okay, but even so, this has to be the lamp to provide gold of some kind,' she nodded to herself. 'We just need the Yule King's hand, now.'

Mark froze, as if suddenly realising something.

'You need to come with me,' he said with a sudden urgency, leading them quickly away from the entrance and down the corridor, deeper into the building. 'We need to check something.'

The something that Mark needed to check was in fact a display cabinet at the end of the corridor, leading into the Prince's Room, and built into the oak-panelled walls to the left as he entered it. Behind the glass, there was a small exhibit comprising a helmet, breastplate, and gauntlet.

'More armour?' Katherine peered at the breastplate. 'No, wait. There're designs etched into it. Some kind of ceremonial piece perhaps?'

Damian looked closer at the breastplate.

'It's etched steel,' he said. 'Antwerp did this sort of thing in the late sixteenth century.'

'Let me guess, you've forged similar?' Katherine mocked. As Damian made a face to protest his innocence, Mark frowned at this.

'It's not the armour you should look at, it's the owner,' he replied softly, looking around to ensure that he wasn't being overheard, now as much a part of this treasure hunt conspiracy as Damian and Katherine were. 'It was worn by Robert Dudley and given to the Middle Temple at the same time Drake gave the items from The Golden Hind.'

'Wasn't Dudley also an Inner Temple member?' Katherine examined the armour more intently now. 'Why were the Inner Temple members giving the Middle Temple such presents?'

'Nobody knows,' Mark replied. 'But the Yule King line made me think. What do you know about the *Christmas Revels of 1561?*'

'That there was a Christmas bash in 1561?' Damian rolled his eyes. 'Tudor lawyer knees up. Sounds spectacular.'

Mark ignored him. 'There was. The Inner Court named Dudley the Lord Governor of the Christmas revels. He was called the *King of Christmas.*'

'The Yule King,' Katherine chuckled. 'His gauntlet is right in front of us. The Yule King's hand.'

'So what does it all mean?' Mark looked questionably at Damian, who shrugged.

'I can answer that, but you're not gonna like it,' he said.

'Try me.'

'Well, we need to take down Drake's lantern, put it on the cupboard, shine a light through it and see what happens when we stick this gauntlet in front of it.'

Mark stared at Damian silently for a moment.

'You're serious,' he eventually concluded.

Damian nodded.

'Is there any way we can do this?'

Mark looked around, scratching his beard.

'There's a changeover at ten thirty, in about ten minutes. We could see if we could do something while that's happening.'

And this decided, they made plans to dismantle a lantern, open a glass case without anyone noticing, and steal a gauntlet.

13

THE YULE KING'S HAND

IT TOOK FIVE MINUTES TO GAIN THE KEY TO THE CASE THAT held the gauntlet, and the caretaker was unhappy that Mark wanted to unclip the lantern, but a wave of Katherine's warrant card made him reluctantly pass it across to Mark who, with Damian holding the gauntlet as carefully as he could, strode over to the far left corner of the hall and to the table made of The Golden Hind's hatch door. Removing the canvas covering, the security guard stared down at the wood surface.

Pitted and scratched, this table had endured hundreds of years of usage, and there were a dozen deep indentations and marks upon the surface.

'So where do we put it?' Mark asked.

Damian examined the base of the light, a jagged eight-sided stand. Looking back to the table, he ran his fingers lightly over the surface, stopping on the right-hand side.

'Here,' he indicated the wood, 'there're indentations that match the base.'

Gently and with great reverence, the stand was placed

onto the table, and the base fitted perfectly into the very faint slots.

'Will you look at that!' Mark exclaimed in amazement at this. 'There's no way that's coincidental.'

'Which way?' Katherine asked. As Damian looked at her, she showed the lamp on the table. 'Which of the eight sides goes where?'

'They would have put a candle inside the lamp, and the light would have streamed out across the desk,' Damian replied as he turned the lamp around in his hands. 'There would have to be a marker so that people knew.'

Katherine paused at a red cross on a white shield, a lamb carrying a flag upon its shoulder. Above it was a design of two roses; one red and one white.

'This one,' she whispered as Damian set the lamp.

'What's so special about that one?' Damian asked. Katherine smiled, but it was Mark that replied.

'It's the *Agnus Dei*, the Lamb of God. It's the emblem of the Middle Temple.'

'It's also a culmination of Knights Templar images, with both the Plantagenet and Tudor roses above it,' Katherine replied, placing the lantern in its correct position. 'Which, considering that the others are pretty dull in style, is a bit of a standout, wouldn't you say?'

'There're no candles in here,' Mark looked around. 'I might find a torch or something?'

'No need,' Damian held the gauntlet up to the window, staring carefully. 'There are little holes etched into the steel. Probably done after Dudley stopped wearing it, as it would weaken the gauntlet.'

He looked to Katherine.

'Can I borrow a phone? After all, you destroyed mine.'

Katherine pulled out her smartphone.

'Who are you calling?' she asked cautiously.

'I'm not,' Damian turned the gauntlet in his hands, examining it. 'Put the torch app on, or turn on the flash. Then put it into the lantern.'

'A fake candle,' Katherine nodded, turning on the flash and placing it into the lantern. Immediately, light splayed out across the table, a mixture of whites and reds, mainly from the bottom panes of the lantern. This done, she looked to Damian who, with a smile, laid the gauntlet down directly in front of the lantern, blocking the light.

But it didn't block *all* the light, as the small holes that Damian had seen now let light through, a pattern of small dots that now danced across the table. As they stared down at it, they could see that along the top of the table were two wavy lines, a luminous 'join the dots' of sorts. Under them, seemingly placed at random across the table, were other dots of light, lit through other holes in the gauntlet. However, one dot, half caught by light refracted through the red rose on the lamp, was the deepest red.

'What is it?' Mark asked in wonderment.

'I think it's a map,' Damian replied, pointing at the two wavy lines at the top of the table. 'That's the Thames, see? Look how it slaloms across the table like a snake.'

Katherine leaned forwards now, seeing this.

'If this is Millwall,' she said, pointing at a section where the river dropped south before returning upwards, 'then *that* dot is around Greenwich, *that* one looks like it could be the old palace there. And if that's correct, then the red dot is Deptford.'

'The others?'

'I'd need a map to work them out, but they're probably

there to throw people off the scent, or they're there because these were relevant locations back in the sixteenth century,' Damian stared at the red dot. *'Yule King's hand upon the sea, the light provides the gold.'*

'So it's at Deptford?' Katherine looked surprised. 'All this time running around and it's where Richard died?'

'X marks the spot.'

The voice was a new one, echoing across the hall, and Damian looked up to see Martin Shrewsbury walking towards them, Cyrus a few paces behind.

'You don't know us,' Damian muttered under his breath to Mark, but the guard was already moving.

'Sorry sir, but only Middle Temple members and their guests can enter during the day,' he said, blocking Shrewsbury's path.

'I have a dozen board members with access and another dozen solicitors on retainer,' the millionaire replied. 'I don't think it'd be a problem to get a lunch date, do you?'

'Well, you can come back at lunch then,' Mark was unmoving. Damian looked at the map one last time—

And then smiled.

'Let them see it,' he said, stepping back from the table. Katherine stared at him in silent shock as Martin Shrewsbury approached.

'I'm impressed at you,' Shrewsbury said as he faced Damian. 'I should have listened to you more, I feel.'

'Rather than shooting my friend?'

Shrewsbury sighed.

'Eggs and omelettes, boy, eggs and omelettes. Did you know we spent half an hour in that bloody church until we realised our error?'

'Should have listened to me,' Damian folded his arms. 'I

told you there were a dozen other places. And I recall I said that Temple Church was a place for conspiracy nut-jobs.'

He looked at Cyrus.

'I reckon you fitted in perfectly.'

'Yes, you did, and I didn't listen to you. Just like your father,' Shrewsbury muttered.

'You knew my dad?' Damian shook his head at this. 'No. He would never hang out with someone like you.'

Shrewsbury ignored this, looking over the table.

'And I see that you've worked out the other parts of the clue,' he looked at Mark and Katherine. 'And who are your new friends?'

'She's the tour guide for Middle Temple and he's a guard. They don't know what this all is, I conned them into helping me,' Damian pulled a wallet out of his pocket, his thumb over the photo, opening it briefly to show a warrant card.

Katherine's one.

'Told them I was Special Branch,' Damian explained, quickly closing it before Shrewsbury saw it properly. 'Seemed the quickest option.'

He noticed a moment of shock on Katherine's face as she realised he'd taken it from her, but she quickly masked it, glaring at him.

'You wanker,' she hissed. 'You said this was for a Royal visit.'

Shrewsbury looked back to Mark and Katherine.

'You shouldn't stay near this man,' he explained softly. 'Bad things always happen near him. People die.'

He looked at Damian.

'Friends and family—'

Damian couldn't stop himself. The punch came quickly and sat Shrewsbury onto the floor, rubbing his jaw. As Cyrus moved in, blocking Damian from attacking further, Shrewsbury clambered to his feet.

'That's the only one you get,' he said.

'That was for Andy,' Damian hissed.

Shrewsbury nodded.

'You shouldn't blame him for what he did, you know,' he replied. 'He did it for you.'

'And how did you work that out?' Damian pushed against Cyrus, fury powering him on.

'He knew you owed a hundred grand. He was desperate to find a way to pay it,' Shrewsbury walked back over to the table. 'You know, if you hadn't been so gung ho for conning people, proving the establishment to be frauds, you wouldn't have owed it.'

He looked at Damian, his voice lowering.

'And if you didn't owe it, he wouldn't have listened to our offer. It's amazing how many people get hurt or die because of your mistakes.'

Damian stared at Shrewsbury, the weight of the implication hitting him. *Andy wasn't killed by Cyrus. Sure, the gun was in his hand, but it was Damian who pulled the trigger. He just didn't know it.*

Shrewsbury looked back at the table.

'I suppose the gauntlet is the Yule King's hand, and the lamp is the light to find the gold? You have been busy,' he followed the light dots on the table. 'Glad I missed all the boring stuff.'

Cyrus showed a map image on his phone's screen.

'The red dot. It's St Nicholas's Church, in Deptford. Where the old man died.'

Shrewsbury grinned. 'Evans played us all, it seems.'

'Fat lot of good knowing this'll do for you,' Katherine

snapped back. 'The church was destroyed and rebuilt a hundred years after this message was left.'

Martin Shrewsbury paused for a moment, looking at Katherine, and Damian worried her outburst had revealed her as more than he'd said. But then he looked away.

'And yet no gold was discovered, which makes me believe they placed it somewhere safe under it. Or perhaps it leads to another clue. Marlowe's plaque perhaps?'

Shrewsbury looked around the hall as he spoke.

'You know, I thought this would be bigger.'

'So what, you're going to dig up the church grounds? Good luck with that,' Damian leaned back against the table as he spoke. It was Cyrus who replied.

'You've got a lot to learn about what millionaires can and cannot do,' he sneered. 'Mister Shrewsbury here can have a construction crew in there within a matter of hours.'

'You don't know where to start.'

'I've seen the photos of Evans too, Mister Lucas. I saw the 'X' that he left. I thought I'd go there and look if you didn't lead me anywhere exciting.'

'So what now, you going to shoot me again?' Damian looked at Cyrus, who was already reaching into his pocket. Instead of a gun, however, he pulled out his phone once more. Dialling a number, he put it to his ear.

'Police? I have just seen Damian Lucas. Yes, the guy who shot that man in Manchester. He's in Middle Temple Hall in London. That's the one. You'd better hurry.'

He disconnected the call and looked to Shrewsbury, who nodded.

'No killing this time,' he said. 'After all, if you're in prison, we'll know where to find you if we have any more questions.'

He pulled a business card out of his jacket pocket and passed it to Damian.

'When you get your one call, consider me an option.'

'I'd rather die,' Damian spat back.

'We tried that, remember? I don't think it took.'

Shrewsbury looked at Mark, still watching silently.

'Capturing this murderer? You might even get a promotion out of this,' he said, turning back to Katherine. 'I think I'll be seeing you again.'

And then, following Cyrus, he turned and left the Great Hall.

There was a moment of silence as Mark looked at Damian.

'You killed someone?'

'Shrewsbury did,' Damian replied, looking back at the lamp. 'And I'll make sure he pays for it, eventually. But don't worry about that right now. Before the police arrive, we need to solve something quickly.'

'Solve what? You just gave them the answer!' Katherine almost shouted this in her anger, but Damian shook his head.

'Remember what Farringdon said? Hawksmoor went rogue and moved the gold.'

'So?'

'So I think he changed the clue when he did so.'

He turned to Mark.

'You said an architect in the early seventeen hundreds broke the glass and paid for it to be fixed, right?'

'That's what the stories all say.'

Damian pointed at the base of the lamp.

'Would *that* have been around the area he broke?'

Mark moved closer, nodding as he finally understood.

'It would have been,' he replied. 'He put new glass in, and

it was this pane here.' He indicated a sliver of glass near the red Tudor rose. 'But the report I read said that there was an error, and the glass replaced inside was the wrong colour. It was green or blue, I think.'

Damian placed his finger over the piece of glass and looked at the table.

One dot had disappeared.

He removed his finger, and it reappeared once more.

'Greenwich,' Katherine said, as she watched the dot appear and disappear again. 'And if the glass had been changed to a green tint, then it would stand out as much as the red would.'

'Exactly,' Damian nodded. 'The gold may have been connected to Deptford by Drake and the others, but a century later Hawksmoor changed the clue to Greenwich, by breaking a single pane of glass.'

He pointed at one of the other dots beside the line of the Thames.

'And *this* dot, just south of where the Thames hits its peak could be the naval college, or rather the old palace, as it would have been back then. Which means the one we're looking for, to the west of this is St Alfege Church.'

'Which Hawksmoor rebuilt in the early eighteenth century, around the same time he had the falling out with the School of Night,' Katherine watched Damian for a moment. 'How can you be so sure of this?'

Damian tapped the red tinted light spot that represented Deptford.

'Richard left an 'X',' he said. 'Shrewsbury thinks it's because of 'x marks the spot', and even I thought that when I spoke to the police yesterday morning, I think it was the opposite. Richard was a University professor. He lived in a world of ticks and crosses.'

'You think that the 'X' meant *incorrect?* That's a hell of a hunch.'

'I know, but the more I think about it, the more I believe Richard wouldn't leave us a clue saying *'it's here'*, especially if he'd just escaped from Martin Shrewsbury.'

Damian looked at the edge of the table. Something caught the light, the slightest hint of a familiar shape.

'Hold on, look,' he exclaimed. 'There's another cypher here.'

He leaned closer to the table to examine it, rubbing gently against the wood with his index finger to check that it wasn't some kind of age mark. Stepping back, he pointed at a thin line of faint etchings on the side.

'These images look like the ones Dee had in Manchester, but they're cruder, rougher in design.'

'Maybe made in a hurry?' Katherine leaned in to look. 'Hawksmoor didn't want to be seen doing this. Maybe he did it at night, with limited light?'

'Could be,' Damian shrugged.

'Can you decipher it?' Katherine knelt beside the message, shining the torch from her phone on it.

Pulling out the sheet of paper with the homemade cypher on it, Damian worked through the letters, writing the answers down on the paper with a pen from the side of the table. After a couple of minutes, he leaned back, staring down at his hand.

'*Mr Stantons creature points the way,*' he said.

'No rhyme? Sounds like Hawksmoor wasn't into the riddles as much as Dee was. What does it mean?' Katherine looked back at him.

'No idea. I think to answer that, we'll need to work out who Mister Stanton is. Or was, even. And thanks to Hawksmoor's alterations to the lamp, we know where he might be found. St Alfege church, Greenwich.'

Damian picked up the gauntlet, kissing it.

'You beauty,' he whispered to it. Mark watched him cautiously, as if expecting him to take off with the gauntlet at any moment.

'You don't know where that's been,' Katherine muttered.

Damian went to reply, but something inside the gauntlet caught his eye. Grabbing Katherine's phone from within the lantern, he quickly took a photo of the inside of the gauntlet before passing it back to Mark.

'We need to leave,' he said as he started for the main entrance. 'Cyrus wasn't bluffing. With response times for London, the police—'

'Are already here,' Mark pointed at the stained-glass windows to the left of the main entrance, behind the breast-plates and leading out into Fountain Court, where red and blue lights were already seen flashing outside the building.

For the police, hunting the murderer Damian Lucas had arrived in force.

———

14

RUN THROUGH ROSES

DAMIAN LOOKED AROUND THE HALL, HOPING TO SEE AN EXIT but none presented itself.

'Is there another way out?' he asked urgently.

'I'm assuming you want one that doesn't pass the police?' Mark asked. Before Damian could answer, Katherine pushed aside a chair placed against the wall of plaques that faced them on the opposite wall of the annexe.

'Follow me,' she said, tapping a plaque.

WILLIELMUS WHITAKER, AR. LECTOR AUTUM, ANNO 1627

The words were written under a black shield of three white diamonds, a thick white line running horizontally through the middle of them, with two of the diamonds above and one left alone below. Damian was about to ask what Katherine meant, but then he realised what she was really showing. To the bottom right of the plaque, between this and the one below it was a small brass knob, only an inch in diameter; a well-hidden door, merging into the oak panelled, plaque covered wall around it.

Taking the brass knob and pulling the door open, Katherine revealed a spiral staircase leading down to a lower level. Entering through the door and taking the steps two at a time, Katherine led Damian to the bottom of the stairs, following the steps around to face a doorway leading to a large, white, external door.

'If we go through that, we're in the gardens,' she said, turning back to the stairs where Mark still stood. 'We can make it across them, climb over the railings and get out onto the embankment.'

'I'll close up behind you, leave the chair where it was,' Mark was already turning back towards the secret door at the top of the stairs. 'We don't usually allow visitors down here, and they won't realise it's a door before it's too late. I'll then send them off towards the church and see if I can give you some time.'

Damian grabbed his shoulder, halting him.

'I owe you,' he said as he shook Mark's hand before turning back to the white door, Katherine already moving off ahead of him.

'Just let me know how everything goes, right?' Mark smiled. 'I was always curious about what your father saw in all that stuff.'

'What, the gold?'

Mark shook his head.

'Nah, all the Perkin Warbeck conspiracies.'

And before Damian could reply, Mark was off, back up the stairs on a direct route to distract the police. Damian turned and ran back to Katherine.

'What was the photo for?' she asked as she opened the

door, exiting out into the Middle Temple Gardens, leading south towards the Thames. 'I know you're not the type for keepsakes.'

'There was etching on the inside of the gauntlet,' Damian said, pausing as he looked around the small courtyard that they had entered. 'Hold on. Do you know where we are?'

Katherine, already moving on, stopped and looked back to him.

'Yes, it's where the Wars of the Roses started, and it's all very exciting,' she said, grabbing him by the arm and pulling him away. 'Can we go now?'

'It's more than a location, it's history,' Damian protested as he followed Katherine across the grass, past the changing brickwork of the Plowden Buildings. 'Each side picked a rose, one red, one white, to show who they supported. Noblemen decided right there who they would fight for, who they would *die* for.'

'If you believe Shakespeare, that is,' Katherine replied as they continued towards the tree line around the edge of the garden.

There was a faint yapping from behind them, and they both looked to see a small brown fox-like dog, the size of a terrier, running towards them.

'Great,' hissed Katherine as she veered left, running up to a black, wrought-iron gate that bordered a road to the south. 'All we need is a bloody dog barking about and bringing the police after us!'

She shooed the dog away, but the dog kept yapping, and Damian saw with a sickening sensation that two police officers in fluorescent jackets were now looking over to them.

'*Oi!*' one of them shouted. 'Wait right there!'

As the police started running towards them, Katherine grabbed Damian by the arm.

'Give me back my bloody warrant card,' she hissed. Damian quickly slid it back into her pocket as she grabbed his arm, twisting it violently and sending him to his knees. The police slowed down as they saw this, one pulling out a taser device.

'Let go of the suspect, Ma'am,' the lead officer, a ginger haired, bearded man asked as calmly as he could.

'Don't taser me, I'm reaching into my pocket,' Katherine said, holding out her hand to show that it was empty, before reaching in and pulling out her warrant card. 'I'm SO14. We've been hunting this bastard since Manchester, but I dropped my cuffs while chasing him. Can I borrow one of yours?'

The bearded officer paused, looking at his colleague, who shrugged.

'Do we get the collar?' he asked cheekily. Katherine grinned.

'Tell you what, how about we share it?'

The two police officers smiled at this, nodding at each other. The bearded one passed his cuffs over to Katherine, who quickly cuffed Damian's hands behind his back, pulling him to his feet.

'I didn't do it,' Damian protested.

'Don't care, mate,' The lead police officer said, turning to Katherine. 'So how do you—'

He didn't get any further, as Katherine swung a haymaker of a right hook into his jaw, a punch so strong he fell to his knees, only to take a second hit to the face by Damian, shoulder charging as he slammed into the officer, the two of them sprawling out onto the ground.

The second police officer only had a moment to react, but by the time Katherine had turned to face him, he was already pulling out his small, yellow X26 stun gun taser. As he brought it up to aim at her, she moved in with a spinning kick, knocking it from his hand, but not moving quick enough to avoid his own punch, knocking her backwards. With a moment of clarity, the officer grabbed at his radio.

'Code thirty! Officer needs immediate—' He didn't get any further, as Damian, now uncuffed and holding the officer's fallen stun gun, had fired it point blank into him. He collapsed to the floor, twitching.

'Thanks,' Katherine said, hurrying to the officers and dragging the closest to the railings.

'How did you know I'd be able to pick my cuffs?' Damian asked. Katherine shrugged.

'Seemed like the sort of thing you'd be able to do,' she said, leaning the tasered officer into a sitting position before cuffing his right hand to the railings. Then, yanking the radio from its socket, she tossed it across the grass. 'That said, I thought you'd be faster.'

'Everyone's a bloody critic,' Damian muttered as he cuffed the bearded officer next to his partner. But before disconnecting the radio, he leaned in, pressing the side button.

'Code four, situation resolved,' he said quickly. 'Suspect seen escaping into the Strand.'

This done, he tore the radio out and tossed it over to its fellow radio on the grass.

'Of course you know police codes,' she said. 'Now what do we do?'

'Get the hell out of here before that bloody dog brings more police,' Damian turned to the wrought-iron gates, the other side of a series of iron railings. The gate was empty, and with the help of a lamppost, both Damian and Katherine could leap over the fence beside it, landing safely upon the cobbled pavement that led to the Temple Inn's south exit. Damian looked north, through an ornate white arch that looked up Middle Temple Lane, out to the front of Middle Temple hall, where he saw the faintest blue of police lights, and police officers heading away, towards the Strand, where they believed their suspect now ran. Katherine grabbed him by the arm once more, pulling him through the gates and onto the Victoria Embankment, slowing their pace to merge with the unsuspecting tourists and visitors walking down the street.

'You were saying about the gauntlet,' she continued as she led him away from the entrance, walking towards Blackfriars Bridge.

'Yeah. I think it has text etched in it, symbols that looked like the same cypher that the Sunne Dial used.'

'And Shrewsbury didn't get it either? Well, that's a bonus that can help us down the line,' Katherine looked behind to see if they were being followed. 'Could it be more clues by Hawksmoor?'

'No, they looked more refined, more like the ones left at Dee's,' Damian replied. 'I think these are earlier than Hawksmoor.'

Damian stopped, looking across the Thames as a sudden thought came to him.

'How did you know about the way out?' he asked.

'Can we discuss this later?'

'No,' Damian stood stock still, his arms folded. 'One minute you say you can't remember coming to Middle

Temple, and then the next you're showing me routes out of the place that only staff know.'

'There was a map of Middle Temple Hall in Mark's office,' Katherine explained. 'On the wall by the desk. It showed the stairs and the exit to the garden. And I always like a second exit out of any location. Now can we go?'

'And the garden? The Wars of the Roses?'

'Anyone who's seen *Henry the Sixth* knows that story.'

Damian knew she was lying. But at the same time the explanation was plausible and there was the slightest chance that he could also be paranoid. Katherine would have been standing guard while he examined Drake's table. There was every opportunity for her to have seen the secret door for what it was, and a simple glance out of the window beside it would have revealed the garden below.

But then again, there could have been another, darker reason. One which said that she was playing him, leading him down the path by the nose, taking him to slaughter.

Could she be the enemy as well?

The fact of the matter remained that Katherine Turner, for all her secrets and lies, was his only chance of not only escaping the police, but of solving this riddle and clearing his name.

He had to trust her. There was no other option here.

'Lead the way,' he eventually said, following Katherine as they continued over Blackfriars Bridge towards Southwark, out of the congestion zone and towards Farringdon Gale's stolen car.

15

PERKIN'S PRETENCE

DAMIAN SAT AT THE BISTRO'S TABLE AND PULLED HIS BASEBALL cap down over his face. The sun was shining so his sunglasses and cap weren't out of place, but he was feeling increasingly paranoid that any of the dozens of people passing the table or sitting nearby would recognise him as the Manchester murderer.

'We can't go inside,' Katherine said softly as she sipped at her coffee. 'There's no reason for someone to wear a cap and glasses in there. You'll stand out.'

'I know,' Damian replied sullenly, still fighting the urge to look around. 'Doesn't stop me thinking that everyone's looking at me.'

'Well, if you stop looking at them, maybe that'll help?' Katherine quipped as she passed over her smartphone. 'Maybe instead you could translate the cyphers that you found on the back of the gauntlet?'

Damian scrolled to the photo he had taken of the gauntlet and used his fingers on the screen to zoom in on the words. Even though they were faint, the illumination was good enough and Damian had no problem deciphering the zoomed in text onto a napkin beside his flat white coffee.

Eventually, he looked up from the napkin.

'So, what does it say?' Katherine asked.

'*Warbeck's crime creates a line that no one must deny, a marriage made and then betrayed can counter Cecil's lie. The Spanish Prize, who crown denies is finally outrun, the dead deceived must now retrieve and educate the sun.*'

'Warbeck's crime? This is the second time I've heard Perkin Warbeck's name connected to this,' Katherine thought for a moment, 'Mark said that your father knew the 'Perkin Warbeck' stuff. So, Perkin's also a link to the gold?'

'Actually, if you believe the rumours, he's more than that,' Damian re-read the napkin. 'The whole reason that Perkin Warbeck is in history is because he claimed to be one of the princes in the tower.'

'The ones that Richard the Third murdered to keep his stolen throne.'

'*Allegedly* murdered,' Daman retorted. 'And that's the problem. Remember, Henry was King because he won the crown claiming he was avenging an injustice. If Richard turned out *not* to be a horrible, child killing monster, then things might not have gone so well for the Tudors.'

Damian leaned back, thinking for a moment.

'Ten years after the deaths of the princes in the tower, Warbeck appeared out of nowhere, travelling across Europe, raising armies to take down the Tudors, claiming that he was in fact Prince Richard, the younger of the two princes, and had been smuggled to safety after his brother's death from illness in the tower.'

'And people believed him?'

'According to trial transcripts, he was incredibly persuasive. And more than that, he seemed to be very well informed on the subject,' Damian sipped at his coffee. 'After they caught him, at his trial, people who had known the young prince said they believed Warbeck was Richard, as he knew details only the young Prince could know. And this was a problem for the Tudors.'

'Because they'd said the whole war thing was to avenge dead Princes.'

'Exactly. Now if the avenged Prince turns up, you'd expect Henry Tudor to step aside, give him back his rightful throne. But kings don't do that.'

Katherine leaned back.

'This is all fine, but wasn't Perkin Warbeck supposed to have changed his story, a full one-hundred-and-eighty-degree swerve and confessed it was nothing but a lie? A couple of years later, around the end of 1499, he was then caught trying to escape London and so was executed? After that, the Tudors carried on as if nothing had happened.'

Damian watched Katherine for a moment.

'I didn't think you knew about this,' he said, mentally re-evaluating her once more. He knew she had a connection with Richard, but he also knew that if he asked her right now, it'd spook her and he might never know.

'I never said that. Did you hear me say that?' Katherine smiled. 'I never really understood though why he changed his story. Especially if he was the real Prince.'

'Most likely because Henry would have killed his family,' Damian shrugged. 'If Warbeck *is* Prince Richard, the nephew of Richard the Third and the true King of England, then for Henry to remove him—and believe me when I say that there was never a chance of Henry *not* doing that—he'd have to also take out Warbeck's wife and children. They were all in line to the throne, and therefore, they were threats. The Wars of the Roses would start up all over again. However, if Warbeck changed his story, and said that he wasn't the Prince...'

'Then there was no need for his children to be executed,' Katherine finished the sentence. 'So his crime was simply treason?'

'I suppose,' Damian mused. 'And it secured the Tudor line in the process. But there's more to the story.'

'There always is,' Katherine looked out across the road at the imposing white brickwork of St Alfege church.

Damian paused.

'So, do you know all this and you're just humouring me, or am I actually saying stuff that's new to you?'

Katherine smiled again.

'I won't know until you tell me.'

'Okay then. First off, the moment he said that he was an imposter, he was removed from the Tower and given rooms in Court. He was treated with respect as a lord. He even attended Royal banquets, something no prisoner would have been allowed to do. It was only an attempted escape two years into this that eventually caused his execution,' Damian shook his head. 'If he hadn't done that, he could have lived happily at court.'

'So why would Henry do this for a man that had legitimately fought against him?'

'Maybe Henry secretly believed him,' Damian held up his hand to stop Katherine's reply. 'Think about it. What if Warbeck was Prince Richard, smuggled out of the tower when his elder brother succumbed to a fatal illness? As such, he was, by divine right of succession, the true King of England, no matter what the Tudors said. When he returned to take his throne, if Henry believed his story he'd be unable to execute someone that could have been a prince by divine right.'

'So he placed Warbeck in Court. Keeping him close by.'

Damian nodded. 'But, when people asked questions about this; remember, Henry would have spent serious amounts of gold on Warbeck's housing, and this would have ruffled feathers in court, Henry changed the plan, moving him away from London, putting him under a very comfortable house arrest, and faking his death.'

'So not king, but not dead either.'

Damian nodded.

'It's believed that they sent him to live in the country house of Edmund Dudley, at the time one of Henry's lower level administrators, and eventually one of his financial advisors.'

Katherine almost dropped her coffee cup at this.

'Robert Dudley's *grandfather* spoke to him?'

Now it was Damian's turn to smile.

'So you don't know everything,' he said. Katherine blew a raspberry at him and leaned back.

'For someone who doesn't seem to care about history, you know a lot about this.'

'It's one of the few things I do know about,' Damian admitted. 'It's what destroyed my relationship with my dad.'

Katherine raised an eyebrow at this, but Damian shook his head.

'Another time.'

'So go on then. Tell me about Edmund Dudley.'

'Well, he was an absolute nobody in the court. A onetime Privy Council member who'd fallen from grace, who mysteriously rises to 'Speaker of the House' within a couple of years of this. And at this point, Henry's son and heir, Arthur, dies.'

'Everyone knows this bit,' Katherine chipped in. 'The future Henry the Eighth becomes next in line, but he's not trained for the role. All he does is drink, hunt and have sex.'

She paused.

'Pretty much what he does for his entire reign.'

'Exactly. He's nothing like the heir Henry senior wanted. And Henry senior believes that this is a punishment from God for killing Richard the Third at Bosworth, a war over a belief that Richard killed the princes, something that Henry now knows to be false. So, a decision is made, one to name Perkin Warbeck as an heir on Henry's the Seventh's deathbed, over his own son. There's even a whole conspiracy story that says that Henry senior signed a proclamation to this effect that was never released.'

'What happened to it?' Katherine leaned forward, as if caught up in the story. Damian sighed.

'You see? Look at you. You're already nine-tenths into believing this. Just like my bloody dad was.'

'Just finish the damn story,' Katherine finished her cup.

'Well, Henry's confessor was an ambitious priest named Wolsey.'

'Cardinal Wolsey?'

'Not at this point. Wolsey was told by Henry senior of his plans and was given the proclamation for safe keeping. However, Wolsey was also an ambitious man, and informed the *young* Henry of this. On the day that his father died, no proclamation was discovered. Henry was crowned Henry the Eighth, Wolsey became a Cardinal almost overnight and Edmund Dudley, Richard Empson and an 'unnamed man' are arrested and hanged the same day, for the crime of 'planning to raise arms against the new King after the old King's death.'

'Perkin dies?'

'We never know. But it's pretty much a certainty.'

'The proclamation?'

'Legends and lies, nothing more. Enough to destroy my relationship with my dad, anyway.'

'You never spoke to him again?'

'He died shortly after.'

Katherine stared at Damian for a moment.

'What happened to your parents?' she asked.

'I thought you knew?'

'Just that they died, nothing more.'

'Car accident,' Damian replied softly, his tone level and flat. 'Slammed into the back of a truck on the M25, killing my mum as well. Can we get out of here? I don't really want to talk about this anymore.'

'Sure,' Katherine waved to the waitress and placed a ten-pound note under the cup, showing it. 'Let's go see what Hawksmoor left us at the church.'

Damian nodded and rose from his chair, starting away from the bistro, already moving to cross the street.

Katherine hung back for a moment, watching him.

'I hope I'm not there when you learn the truth,' she muttered softly before following him, as he headed towards St Alfege Church, and the next clue to this treasure hunt.

16

TALLIS PLAYED HERE

Although facing out onto Greenwich, the entrance to St Alfege Church was actually at the rear of the building, beside a picturesque, tree-lined driveway.

Entering through the main doors, Katherine and Damian found themselves in a low-ceilinged portico area, a room to the left, a sales table in front of it festooned with brochures and flyers. They seemed to be the only two in the church, but after a couple of moments there was a noise in the side room, and a grey-haired, portly man emerged.

'Good day,' he said jovially. 'are you here for a tour?'

'Just looking around,' Katherine replied.

'Well, feel free to do so,' the man said, walking around the table to face them. 'Though there isn't much left of the original place. In 1941 we lost the roof and most of the Nave to the Luftwaffe when they bombed London.'

Damian walked out from under the portico and into the Nave of the church, looking around as he did so. The floor was made from large stone slabs, a warm, almost brown shade in colour, covering the whole floor and lined either side with enclosed wooden pews, extending to the white side-walls, half of which were under an upper balcony along both sides of the church, oak panelled railings blocking the view into the upper levels, and the arched windows that brought light into the church.

Exits to the North and South Vestibules were visible halfway down the church, while on the right-hand side of the Nave was a raised pulpit, a fierce looking wooden one under a canopy and with a sun design set into it. In the middle of the church hung a giant, five-level golden chandelier, lit with fake candles and topped with a golden dove.

At the end of the Nave were three rows of choir seating on either side of the East Vestibule. Here a giant, golden arch revealed an altar covered with a purple cloth, surrounded by beautifully carved wooden pillars, and topped with golden frescos plus a huge stained glass window of St Alfege kneeling before the Lord, surrounded by triumphant angels.

Either side of the East Vestibule, on the upper levels were two large, wooden plaques listing benefactions and, as Damian turned back round to look at the West entrance, where Katherine still spoke to the grey-haired man, Damian saw the stone baptismal font at the end of the walkway.

Above it, the church's pipe organ, an oak frame guarding it, loomed over the whole Nave. Damian noted that on the wood beneath the pipes of the organ there was the lion and unicorn 'royal seal' of the United Kingdom, created during the 1603 accession to the throne of King James the First; when the lion of England joined forces with the unicorn of Scotland.

However this carving was different from the usual depic-tions, first because the unicorn, rather than looking at the lion, was looking directly out into the church, staring out towards the altar; and second because the usual French motto written at the bottom, *Dieu et mon droit* - translated into 'God and my right', was instead *Semper Eadem*, 'Always the same'.

The motto of Elizabeth the First, not of James the First.

Katherine walked over to Damian, nodding back to the grey-haired man, who returned to his desk at the entrance.

'Dermot was very helpful for our treasure hunt,' she said.

'Who's Dermot?'

Katherine nodded at the man at the desk. 'He's the guide,' she said, 'and has pointed out what's left from Hawksmoor's time here.'

'Yeah,' Damian looked around once more. 'That's a worry for me, too. The bombings might have taken away any clues we have.'

'Well, the pulpit's original, and the older of the benefaction plaques is too.' Katherine started walking down the Nave, peering around. Irritated, Damian looked up at the two benefactions boards, noting again that a lion and unicorn topped each one, still showing the wrong monarch's Latin motto. The gold writing on the black background was clean, and writing on the bottom of the boards stated when they had been refurbished; they had restored the left-hand one in 1849, the right-hand one in 1953. Damian assumed they had both been restored in 1849, but that the bombing had damaged the latter, causing a *re*-restoration several years after the war ended. The dates of the benefactions were along the left of each board, with the fees down the right.

Damian ignored the left board; the dates on it were from 1704 until 1813, which meant that only the first two benefactions on it were of any use. However, the right-hand sideboard provided dates from 1558 until 1701 and, as he read down the list, he suddenly grabbed Katherine's shoulder.

'I've found Mister Stanton,' he whispered, pointing at the board, where it read:

1610. Wm STANTON, Gent, his house called the Unicorn, to the Church and Poor. Rent Per Annum, 12.00

'*Mr Stanton's creature points the way.* Well, it looks like his creature is a Unicorn,' mused Katherine. 'But which one? And how does it point the way?'

Damian looked back to the great seal hanging over the west entrance, and to the unicorn that now looked directly at him.

'The horn,' he said, now walking up to the seal and standing underneath it. 'I saw it earlier. Traditionally, the unicorn's horn is supposed to point to just above the lion facing it, but this one points east, out past the end of the church.'

Damian turned to Dermot, still at his counter.

'You wouldn't by chance have a map of London, would you?' he asked. 'A proper one that is, not something on the phone or a computer screen?'

Dermot thought for a moment.

'I think so, but we've not used it for a while,' he said as he walked back into the side room, emerging a moment later with a fold-out map. 'This do?

'Perfect,' Damian replied, opening up the map and spreading it out on the table. 'Do you have a ruler?'

As Dermot walked into the back room once more, Damian searched the map with his finger, eventually tapping it onto St Alfege Church, glancing to Katherine, now standing beside him.

'Right, so all the streets are slightly angled in a north-west direction, but Alfege is positioned almost straight centre on the map, which means each wall faces exactly north, south, east and west, in the style that most churches are,' he tapped the church again, on the western end. 'We're here, and the unicorn is pointing...'

He looked up, estimating the unicorn's view.

'Slightly to the left of centre of the stained glass. Which means, if the angle's right...'

He graciously took the ruler from Dermot, laying it on the map, tracing the imaginary line from the unicorn's horn out into Greenwich.

He didn't have to follow it far.

'The unicorn is pointing directly at the Naval College,' he whispered. 'Which back then was the Queen's House.'

'Yes, but that can't be right,' Katherine replied, double checking the line. 'Hawksmoor was never involved with that. Perhaps it points to something in here?'

'In here? Well, in that case, you're scuppered,' Dermot replied. 'Nothing really survived from the bombing. Even poor Thomas Tallis is lost from us.'

'Tallis?' Damian looked up. 'As in Thomas Tallis the Tudor composer?'

'The very same,' said Dermot. 'His body was buried here, but his remains are now scattered, lost to us after the bombing.'

He looked up at the ceiling, as if expecting to see Tallis smiling down at him.

'He was a wonder for sacred choral music, and even performed right here for Henry the Eighth and both Mary and Elizabeth during his time. There're stories that as a child Queen Elizabeth would ask to be brought to St Alfege to hear him play. This was very much a Royal chapel you see; it was the closest to the Palace of Placentia nearby in Greenwich. Henry the Eighth was baptised here, his sister Mary married here...'

Dermot leaned forwards.

'And if you believe the local legends, so did his *daughter*.'

There was a moment of silence as Damian took in what the elderly guide had just said.

'You're saying that Elizabeth the First is said to have married here?'

Dermot nodded.

'Local legend, of course,' he admitted. 'But I was told once that there used to be papers showing that Elizabeth and Robert Dudley secretly married here in a ceremony witnessed by only three people; William Cecil, John Dee and Thomas Tallis, who played the organ for the ceremony.'

'But why keep such a thing secret?' Damian leaned back, stretching as he looked around the church, trying to imagine an older, forgotten church. 'I mean, I've seen the films, and they show Robert Dudley was toxic at the time because of his wife's death, but still...'

'There were rumours of an illegitimate son of Elizabeth the First and Robert Dudley,' Dermot said, tapping the side of his nose. 'In 1587, the Spanish find a shipwrecked boat on their North coast. They arrest a man who instantly says that he's Arthur Dudley, the son of Elizabeth and Robert. The Spanish King believes him and allows Arthur to stay at court. A year later, it's claimed he's died. Nothing's ever mentioned again, and everyone says it was just Spanish lies.'

Damian looked down at the altar.

'Wait,' he whispered. 'What if he *was* their son, and they were married before he was born?'

Katherine nodded.

'Well, there was always talk among academics that Elizabeth was pregnant with Robert's child in 1561, and reports said her belly was visibly swollen. The palace claimed she was ill, and Elizabeth spent the rest of the year in Hampton Court while Robert Dudley...'

'In 1561, he was at Inner Court,' Damian continued. 'It's when he became *The Yule King*. That can't be a coincidence, that he did this right after his rumoured son was born?'

He looked back at Dermot.

'You don't know anything else about this, do you?' he asked.

Dermot shrugged.

'Well, it's all hearsay mind you, but Arthur Dudley claimed to the Spanish King that he had been taken from Hampton Court as a child, and kept safe, banned from leaving England no matter what. He'd said he'd even visited his father on his deathbed.'

'But they didn't legitimise him,' Katherine said. '*The Spanish Prize, who crown denies is finally outrun.*'

'You sound just like the fella who told me the tale!' Dermot laughed. 'He was just as batty as you both are.'

'Was his name Richard Evans?' Katherine asked.

Dermot shook his head.

'Oh no, we all know Richard. Lovely man, if a little eccentric. Been coming here for decades. No, I mean his friend. Came with him a while back, maybe five, six years ago. Anyway, he was an expert on the Dudleys or something, and he was the one who told me the story.'

'And you just believed it?' Katherine raised an eyebrow.

Dermot shook his head.

'Oh no, he had old diaries that talked about it. Very well researched.'

A sudden icy chill came over Damian, and he pulled out his wallet. Opening it up, he pulled a photo out and showed it to Dermot.

'Is this the man?' he asked.

Dermot took the photo, holding it to the light as he squinted for a moment.

'Yeah, that looks pretty much like him,' he replied, passing it back. 'How do you know him?'

'He's my dad,' Damian said slowly.

'Well, that's just amazing!' this genuinely impressed Dermot. 'When you see him next, say hello from me!'

'He died.'

'Oh,' Dermot's face fell, and then brightened. 'Well, I'll tell Richard when he comes back in! He'll—'

'Richard also died a few days ago,' Katherine interrupted.

Dermot stared at Katherine and Damian as if the world had suddenly collapsed around him. Rubbing at his forehead, he looked at the table.

'Guess the gold really is cursed then,' he muttered.

'What did you say?'

'That's what Richard was always looking for. Some lost gold. He never talked about unicorns like you two, but he'd come back, time and time again, as if *this* was the time he would magically work out what the next step was,' Dermot rubbed at his eye. 'Guess he'll never know, now.'

There was a moment of silence at this.

'If you're still interested in Hawksmoor, we've got a book on him,' Dermot offered, changing the subject. 'Well, it's more a church history.'

He picked up a black and white pamphlet, opening it up to show them.

'It's even got pictures of the church back in the thirties. Last one we have in stock, too.'

As he flicked through the pages, Damian paused on a double-page image of the interior of the church.

'When was this taken?' he asked. Dermot frowned as he peered down at it.

'I think mid-thirties perhaps, before the bombing—you can tell by the lack of a chandelier, as they put that up after,' he replied. 'Why?'

Damian pointed to the wood panelling next to the pulpit, directly over the passage to the South vestibule.

There, faint in the black-and-white image but clearly visible on the wood panelling, was the lion and unicorn seal.

'It was moved,' Damian whispered. 'It was originally on the south wall, facing north.'

Almost leaping from the desk, Damian ran to the middle of the church, standing directly under the lip of the balcony where the seal would have been. Facing north, and judging his angle by eye, he held his arm out straight, at a slight angle to the left.

'The Unicorn would have been facing that way,' he said as he marked the relevant window in his head. Running back to the map, he grabbed a pen.

'The seal would be here,' he marked a spot, almost mid-way along the south wall of the church, 'and the window is here,' he marked a second dot on the map. Grabbing the ruler, he measured it along the line.

'Anything?' Katherine leaned over. Damian shook his head.

'Not yet, but there has to be,' Damian extended the line, following it past Canary Wharf.

'There,' Katherine pointed to a church just south of Commercial road. 'St Anne's Limehouse.' It was directly to the right of the line.

'The line doesn't go through the church, though,' Damian replied. 'It goes to the left.'

'I know,' Katherine said. 'And I think that's exactly where it needs to be. To the left of St Anne's Church is Hawksmoor's Pyramid.'

'His what now?'

Katherine sighed.

'Didn't you learn anything in Art History? Hawksmoor rebuilt St Anne's Church after he rebuilt St Alfege, but he technically he didn't finish it. There was an eight-foot-high isosceles pyramid that was supposed to go onto the roof, but it never did. They left it in the churchyard.'

She tapped on the ruler.

'Right there.'

'So that's where we go next,' Damian nodded, folding up the map and passing it back to Dermot.

'Good luck, lad,' The elderly guide said. Damian smiled.

'It's probably another bloody wild goose chase,' Damian grinned as he and Katherine started towards the door. 'But thanks for help.'

Damian opened the double doors and walked into the courtyard behind the church, feeling the cool breeze upon his face—and stopped.

Facing him were a dozen police officers, several armed with Heckler and Koch MP5 carbines, all aimed at him. Two police cars and three vans, all with blue lights flashing parked across the grassy clearing, and as he looked to his right, Damian saw three more armed police emerging from the side of the church.

'*Damian Lucas! Get down on the ground!*'

Damian looked to Katherine, now emerging into the open behind him, her hands already rising into the air as the armed police swarmed in, surrounding them, and pushing Damian face-first into the cement step, cuffing his hands behind his back as they read him his rights. Brought back to his feet, his arms behind him, he saw Katherine, also cuffed, being led to a police car.

'Where are you taking her?' he asked the police officer behind him. The officer said nothing, instead pushing Damian forwards, aiming him towards another of the police cars across the green. As Damian looked back at the entrance of St Alfege, he saw Dermot at the door, watching the scene unfolding outside of his church with a look of growing sadness. Damian wondered if it had been Dermot that had called the police, or whether he'd been spotted in the bistro earlier. Either way, it didn't really matter anymore, as soon he'd be locked away in a cell and charged with Andy's murder.

And we were so close to finding the gold, Damian thought angrily as he was guided into the back seat. The door now shut behind him, Damian glanced across to the other police car, where Katherine stared dead ahead.

Leaning back against the seat, Damian shut his eyes. He was almost glad that he'd been captured. But then, it also meant that Martin Shrewsbury was likely to find the gold first.

And, as the police cars filed out of the church gardens, Damian suddenly felt terrified for the future.

17

INTERVIEWS

THE POLICE CAR HAD FOLLOWED THE A2 WESTWARD INTO Central London, and it was only when it drove down the Embankment towards Westminster and the Houses of Parliament that Damian realised he was being taken directly to New Scotland Yard itself, passing the three-sided NEW SCOTLAND YARD sign that rotated outside of the offices, turning right through large, wrought-iron gates, following the path between buildings and eventually pulling up in a gated car park beside the Broadway building.

'Why are we here?' he asked the two officers in the car's front.

'Orders,' one of them replied.

Damian sat back as the police car continued to a specified bay, leaving the car only when he was commanded to do so by the officers. The car park was almost empty, with only a couple of police vehicles in the bays nearby. However, as they walked him to a side entrance, Damian noticed another car had arrived, most likely the one that held Katherine.

Entering the building through the side entrance, they led

Damian up to a desk sergeant who, once Damian was uncuffed passed over a clear plastic tray, like the ones that airport security checkpoints used.

'Personal items in there, please.'

Slowly, Damian pulled items out of his pockets. There weren't that many, and Katherine had already thrown out his phone, but he noted a surprised expression on the sergeant's face when he removed the wooden cross from Chetham's Library from his outer jacket pocket, tossing it into the tray.

'You might want to send that back,' he said.

The sergeant took the cross, examining it as Damian was taken away from the desk and down a corridor. Halfway along there was a door to the left, marked *Interrogation Room 2*. The door was opened, and they led Damian inside.

Unlike American television shows, there was no full-length mirror on the wall, a double-sided screen where detectives could watch the interrogation. All the room had within it was a table and chairs, two on each side, a recording device on the end of the table, and a CCTV camera positioned on the wall in the room's corner. No windows, no pictures, just an uninspiring grey paint scheme on the walls.

Damian was guided towards a chair on the left-hand side of the table. Sitting down, he looked back to the officers escorting him.

'Why are we at Scotland Yard?' he asked again. 'Surely I should be taken back to Manchester? Or processed in Greenwich?'

'All we know is what we're told,' the lead officer replied. 'So shut up, sit down and wait for the officer in charge.'

'And who's that?' Damian asked, but the two officers left the room, the door locking behind them, and Damian was left alone once more.

Damian leaned back on the chair, weighing up his options. There weren't many. He was captured and soon to be arrested for the murder of his friend. Katherine was likely to be charged with being an accessory. But when Cyrus had chased after Damian in the Library, he'd taken the gun with him, as the original plan was to also shoot Damian.

Which meant that the murder weapon still hadn't been found.

Add to that the fact that the CCTV in the Library grounds had probably been doctored to make sure Shrewsbury wasn't seen, so there was a distinct lack of evidence here. All he had to do was hold his nerve, and hope to God that Katherine was doing the same in a different room.

He sat there for a while, but eventually the door opened, and two plain clothed detectives walked in. A man and a woman, the former was tall and wiry, and in his thirties. From the way he held himself, Damian decided he was probably a marathon or ultra-runner, hence the slim frame. Which might be a problem, as a man like that wasn't fussed about quick finishes, and would take his time, unlike DI Warren.

The other detective was a woman, short, only five feet four, curvy with short cropped hair and a grey suit that bore no sign of style whatsoever. In her arm was a bulky file, and her glasses were non-designer. This woman was all business, and someone who didn't care about appearances. Damian settled back. He was likely to be here a while. But he could do this; Shrewsbury was looking at the wrong church, and all Damian had to do was stay cool. The woman sat down facing Damian; the file slamming onto the table. The thin man sat beside her.

'I'm Detective Inspector Conlan, this is Detective

Constable Briggs,' she said, indicating her partner. She looked at the name on the file.

'Damian Christopher Lucas. You prefer to be called Damian?' she looked up, catching Damian's eye. 'Or Crown Prince Ludwig?'

Damian's expression didn't change, but behind the calm exterior, he felt liquid ice slide down his spine. This wasn't just a murder case. If they knew about his lies as Ludwig, they could know about everything. They'd probably searched the apartment. *What had he left behind?* No, there was nothing. Andy and Damian were always good about that. The forged Shakespeare manuscript had been finished weeks ago, the items used in the creation long gone. The ink used was still there, but who looks at ink? And they hadn't started another scam, so there was nothing else he could think of that could incriminate him.

Had the Russians said anything? Could he be linked to them and their network of crime?

There was of course that Taymaster might have pressed charges, although he didn't see that happening. To do that would reveal a chancer had scammed them, and the twenty grand they lost was way less than the resulting dip in share prices at such news. What if the police had pressured Pierre and Joanne to give him up, though? What if Max had told them his role as 'fixer' in the scam?

No. Damian realised Conlan was simply fishing. Calming himself, Damian frowned and leaned forward.

'I think you have something confused here, detective,' he replied calmly. 'I'm a sole trader, trading as 'Crown Prince Ludwig Industries'; it's not my name.'

'You sure about that?' Conlan placed the debit card on the

table, the one with *Crown Prince Ludwig* written on it. 'Because it looks to me like you're impersonating a Royal.'

'To do that, there would have to be a Royal to impersonate,' Damian replied with a smile. 'I work in antiques and rare books. The market I move in prefers a more 'elitist' style of clientele. It's nothing but middle-class branding. And if you've examined my apartment, you'll know that already.'

Conlan leaned back, nodding to Briggs who, moving across the table, clicked on the recording device.

'Detective Inspector Conlan and Detective Constable Briggs, interviewing Damian Christopher Lucas, at three twenty-five pm on the fifteenth of August.'

She looked at Damian.

'Why did you kill your flatmate?'

'Sorry?'

'Andrew Holdman. Why did you shoot and kill him in Chetham's Library?'

Damian stared back, all emotions stripped away.

'I didn't,' he replied. 'Martin Shrewsbury's bodyguard did.'

'Martin Shrewsbury?'

'Yes.'

'The tech magnate?'

'Yes,' Damian looked at Briggs. 'He also killed Richard Evans.'

There was a pause as Briggs and Conlan looked at each other. Damian knew this wasn't how they expected the interview to go.

'We're not here to talk about Richard Evans, we're here to talk to you about the murder of Andrew Holdman,' Conlan opened the file as she continued.

'Sorry, can I ask how I killed him?' Damian interrupted.

'He was shot at close range,' Conlan replied matter-of-factly.

'With what?' Damian challenged. 'I mean, I'm assuming you have the murder weapon, and you've matched my fingerprints on it or something before you accuse me of the murder, yeah?'

Damian paused, remembering that during the struggle with Cyrus, he *had* at one point grabbed the gun. His fingerprints *would* be on it.

Shit.

Conlan didn't notice this though, as she carried on.

'We're still looking for the gun that you hid.'

'Hid? Have you seen the place? Where can you hide it? You found me in the room where Andy was killed! I'd only got to the corridor outside, so there's not a great number of hiding places!'

Conlan ignored his outburst, reading through the notes.

'There was a Tibetan Prayer Bell pulled down in front of the door,' she read. 'Were you trying to barricade yourself in?'

'No, I was trying to slow Shrewsbury's bodyguard down. As I said, he's the one who shot Andy,' Damian looked back at Conlan. 'And he's the one who had the gun. *Has* the gun, still.'

'And you know this because?'

'Because I saw him this morning, and he had it on him.'

'And where did you see him?' Conlan asked, no change to the tone of her voice. Damian leaned back in the chair.

'Middle Temple Hall. He called the police on us.'

'Check that,' Conlan said to Briggs, who nodded and, rising from the chair, swiftly left the room.

'Listen, the girl you found with me,' Damian continued. 'She's nothing to do with this, I swear.'

'She helped you escape a crime scene,' Conlan replied coldly. 'I can't see how that makes her innocent.'

'She's SO14, Royal Protectorate,' Damian lied. 'I convinced her I was Crown Prince Ludwig, used the card that you showed me a minute ago. By the time she realised I was lying, she'd seen that I was telling the truth about the other stuff and agreed to help me.'

'Help you do what?'

'Stop Martin Shrewsbury.'

'Stop him doing what?'

'Gaining enough money to fund every far-right organisation in the world.'

Conlan stopped reading the file and looked up at Damian at this accusation. Damian nodded.

'I swear, detective. I'm telling you the truth.'

'And you claim she was SO14?'

'That's what she told me.'

Conlan nodded. 'We found the ID on her when she was arrested. But we checked. She's not registered with the Unit.'

Damian considered this. He'd always known that something was wrong there, but it looked like the con man had been truly conned.

Conlan leaned back, watching Damian for a moment.

'Interesting thing about the Royalty Protection Group,' she said. 'SO14 officers operate in plainclothes and are routinely armed with nine-millimetre Glock seventeen pistols. Can you guess what weapon killed Andrew Holdman?'

She didn't wait for a response; the question was entirely rhetorical.

'A nine-millimetre pistol, likely a Glock.'

'Katherine didn't kill Andy either.'

'Did Andrew and Katherine Turner know each other?'

'No.'

Conlan looked up from the files at this, as the door opened and Briggs returned to the room, closing the door behind him.

'You sure about that?' she asked. 'We have a witness, a...' she looked back to the file, reading the name.

'A Mrs Hamilton, that states that Katherine Turner was seen exiting your flat the day before Andrew Holdman was killed. And that it was Andrew who allowed her into the flat.'

Conlan looked back at Damian.

'Was she a client of yours, perhaps? Something more than a partner in crime? Connected to some of the criminal families you've dealt with in the past? Isabella Vladimov, perhaps?'

Damian's stomach flipped at the name.

'I don't know any Isabella Vladimov,' he whispered. Conlan raised an eyebrow at this.

'You sure? A couple of months back, she paid a rather substantial amount of money into a bank account owned by you.'

'Maybe Andy had worked with them. We did a lot of things together.'

Conlan nodded.

'You've been with Mister Holdman a long time,' she said, looking at her notes. 'But let's look at Miss Vladimov again. You know what her organisation's primary income is?'

She didn't wait for long, answering before Damian could reply.

'Drugs. In particular heroin and cocaine.'

She looked up at Damian.

'Why were you expelled from university again?'

Damian felt a lurch in his stomach. Conlan wasn't just a copper who wanted to know about a murder. She was digging deep.

'It was several things,' he replied sullenly. Conlan held up a piece of paper.

'You can say that again. I have them right here,' she said, looking down at it. 'Caught forging texts from the university library, changing your grades by cyber fraud, excessive drug abuse, drug dealing...'

She paused reading and looked at Damian.

'What drugs?'

'All of them,' Damian didn't lie. There was no point now.

'Cocaine?'

Damian nodded.

'For the record, the suspect has nodded agreement to the question,' Briggs spoke for the first time.

'So the very drugs that Isabella Vladimov sold.'

'I didn't know Isabella Vladimov then!' Damian was getting angry now. Conlan smiled.

'*Then*? So you admit to knowing her now?'

'You're twisting my words!' Damian took a sip of water, trying to calm himself. *He was making mistakes. Conlan was good.*

Calming himself, he looked back.

'I was missing lectures. My grades were slipping. I took cocaine to give myself an edge. But that led to other stuff. None of that led to Andy being shot by a facist millionaire!'

'Do you still take drugs?' Conlan watched Damian now as he shook his head.

'Coffee, a drink or two, nothing more. I've been clean for years.'

Conlan turned back to an earlier sheet of paper.

'Miss Turner. Was hers the number that Andrew Holdman was texting only minutes before his death?'

Damian leaned forward at this, surprised and relieved at the change of tactics here.

'He was texting Shrewsbury,' he replied. 'Telling him where to meet us.'

Conlan flipped through the pages of the file, pulling out a sheet of phone numbers. One of them was highlighted.

'And yet this number, the one he texted, isn't connected to Martin Shrewsbury, or Cyrus Novak, his personal assistant in any way.'

Damian looked at the sheet, reading the numbers; the last numbers that Andy had ever called, including three texts and a phone call made to an unknown mobile number.

'What did the texts say?' he asked.

'We're still waiting for those to be released,' Briggs admitted.

There was a silence as Conlan stared at Damian, as if weighing him up, working out what tactic to try next. It was almost like a chess master, considering their next move in a championship match.

'Things aren't looking good for you, Mister Lucas,' she eventually admitted. 'We have you at a crime scene where the dead body of your friend was. We have you accepting money from a Russian crime organisation, one who deals in the very drugs you've admitted you were addicted to, and even dealing at one time in your life. We have you evading capture with a woman holding a forged police warrant, while you yourself have traded under fake identities and forged items since university, where you were expelled for these same crimes. You were expelled by a Professor Richard Evans, who was found dead in a Deptford church, a church that you yourself visited after the event, and when told to halt in Oxford, you ran from the authorities.'

She leaned in.

'I'd suggest you work with us here, Damian. Because at the moment? You're utterly screwed and likely to spend the rest of your life in prison.'

Damian said nothing, watching Conlan as she leaned back. He knew she was right.

He just didn't know yet how to prove her wrong.

———

18

CALL MY BLUFF

DAMIAN LOOKED AROUND THE EMPTY ROOM, TRYING desperately to think up a plan. Conlan had found out a lot about him, and he'd found her incredibly hard to cold read. His only options were to confess or wait it out, call her bluff.

Conlan shifted, waiting for a response. Damian stared at her.

Come on, come on, give me a clue...

Conlan looked away, unable to meet Damian's eyes. After all she just said, she couldn't look him in the eye.

She's bluffing.

With a small nod to himself, he decided to try the latter of his two options.

'You have me at the scene of Andy's murder, but as a witness, not a suspect,' he started. 'There's no CCTV showing me killing Andy, nor is there a murder weapon. You won't believe that Martin Shrewsbury is the actual killer, even though I'm sure if you checked thoroughly, you'll see that his car was in Manchester at the time, and coincidentally he was at Middle Temple today when we were. He's chasing me, I'm in fear for my life and Katherine Turner, who I honestly assumed was a genuine police officer, was assisting me in proving my story.'

He leaned back.

'Show me a scrap of actual evidence that proves that I'm the killer or release me.'

Silence.

Conlan's lips tightened in anger, and Damian knew he had made the right choice. Conlan went to reply, but as she did so the door to the interrogation room burst open, and a suited man walked into the room with the arrogance of someone who expected to be allowed wherever he wanted.

'What the hell do you think you're doing?' Conlan asked, as the suited man walked to the table and turned off the tape. In response, the man simply pulled out a leather ID holder and showed it to her. Damian didn't see it, but Conlan's expression showed that she wasn't happy.

'Special Branch is upstairs,' she said.

'GCHQ has some questions for Mister Lucas,' the man replied. 'We'd like the room.'

He waited.

'Anytime you want to go,' he continued, showing the door.

Reluctantly, Conlan gathered up the files and, with a nod to Briggs, left the room, her partner following. The door now closed, the man walked to the corner of the room, where he pulled out a device and wirelessly disconnected the CCTV to the room.

They waited for a moment, and then the door opened. Through it walked Farringdon Gale, a leather folder under her arm.

'Looks like you're in a bit of trouble,' she said.

'What the utter hell?' Damian exclaimed. Farringdon ignored this, sitting down opposite Damian at the table.

'In fact, it looks like you're up to your neck in shit,' Farringdon said bluntly. 'That girl you're with, she's not police. Did they tell you that?'

'Yeah,' Damian looked at the suited man in the corner, now ignoring the conversation. 'But I can't work out why she bothered saying she was SO14. I mean, she could have said Special Branch, and I'd have believed her.'

He leaned back.

'But I'd rather talk about *this* than that.'

Farringdon nodded.

'We'll get to that in a minute,' she promised. 'However, the police have you on a variety of small cons, and this is enough to hold you for a couple of days. In that time, Martin Shrewsbury will have worked out why you were at St Alfege, and he'll work out the next clue. You found the clue, right?'

'I did,' Damian replied. 'It's Hawksmoor's pyramid.'

'Should have guessed. And you were arrested before you got there?'

'I didn't need to go there,' Damian said with a smile. 'I've been there before.'

Farringdon's eyebrows raised. 'You have?'

'Dad.'

'Of course.'

'Look,' Damian said, leaning back in the chair. 'I don't know what's going on, but unless you can get me out of here, there's no point talking any further.'

'I'm doing my best,' Farringdon replied. 'I have some sway here.'

'How? You're a college academic. How do you suddenly

appear with people who can clear out an interrogation room with a wave of an ID?'

Farringdon looked at the suited man, smiling.

'I'm currently petitioning for you to be given into my care,' she said.

'And how does that work?' Damian asked. 'Academic day release?'

'I'm wearing another hat,' Farringdon replied. 'One based in GCHQ.'

This was a surprise to Damian. In all the years he'd known Farringdon, a government spy was not a career he would have expected her to take.

'You're a spook?'

'More connected to a particular covert group,' Farringdon shook her head. 'One that has been around for several centuries, in fact.'

Damian let the words rattle around for a moment. He might not have been as fast on the take as Andy had been, but even he could see what Farringdon alluded to.

'The School of Night,' Damian whispered. 'That's why you knew so much.'

'By now you know the story,' Farringdon said. 'In the eighteenth century a rogue agent caused us a lot of hassle, but you're close to solving that particular mystery for us.'

'And my dad? Richard?'

'Knew of this,' Farringdon steepled her fingers together as she spoke. 'Your father was following an... alternate route... to Richard.'

'How do you know this?' Damian sat up at this news.

'Because he gave his notes to me for safekeeping,' Farringdon opened the leather folder, showing a stack of papers. Damian leaned back, buying a couple of seconds of valuable time as he tried to make sense of everything he'd just heard.

'What's next?' he asked.

'We place you under the auspice of *Domestic Counter-Terrorism*,' Farringdon explained. 'You help find what was stolen, and in the process stop Martin Shrewsbury.'

'And clear my name?'

'Of course.'

'And Katherine?'

'Not your problem anymore.'

'No,' Damian folded his arms. 'If I finish this, she does it with me. And she gets immunity.'

'You don't owe her anything,' Farringdon argued.

'She wouldn't have been arrested if it wasn't for me being hunted. Immunity.'

Farringdon considered this for a moment.

'Done,' she said. 'On the basis that you know what the next clue is.'

'That's simple,' Damian replied. 'There's only one thing that it can be. Hawksmoor's pyramid. What do you know about it?'

'Not much. Just that on one of the sides is a crest, a Unicorn and a Lion, and above it the words *The Wisdom of Solomon,*' Farringdon leaned in closer. 'You know what it means?'

'No,' Damian admitted. 'But my dad did. It'll be in his notes.'

'So look now,' Farringdon pushed the folder towards Damian, who shook his head.

'He would have written it in a code,' he lied. 'We had our own little cypher, and it'll take a while to work out. But if I'm doing this, I'm not doing it here. I need a night to work on this. A comfortable bed. A shower.'

He pulled at his clothes.

'I've been wearing these for two days now. I'd like a change of clothing.'

'You want to return to your apartment building?'

'If possible,' Damian nodded. 'I have other books there that can help me. If it makes you feel better, you can disconnect the Wi-Fi, take my computer away. Place a guard on the door, watch the windows, go wild. By tomorrow morning I should have something solid for you.'

Farringdon thought about this for a moment.

'The police wouldn't be clearing you if you left,' she replied. 'Any attempt to escape, to go after Shrewsbury yourself would just start the whole thing up all over again.'

'I'm aware of that. But one other thing. Katherine Turner comes with me.'

Farringdon nodded, her face expressionless. Damian wondered how she'd be playing poker against.

'We can do that,' she replied.

'She's not going to understand what's going on,' Damian said, now warming to this conversation. 'Let me speak to her, get her on our side. After all, she needs to tell me who she truly works for now. She could be a useful asset.'

Farringdon laughed.

'I think you'll find that Miss Turner knows a lot more than you realise about what's going on,' she said.

'Who is she?' Daman leaned forward. 'You know, don't you?'

'It'll take a few minutes to get this sorted, so I'll have her brought into your apartment when you arrive,' Farringdon ignored the question. And, before Damian could press her on this, she gathered up Damian's father's notes once more, rose from the chair, nodded to the suited man and left without another word. The suited man fiddled with his device again, and the red light on the CCTV returned on as he followed Farringdon out.

Now alone in the room, Damian paced around, trying to make sense of all the new data that had arrived in the last few minutes. Farringdon could have told him all of this the previous night in Oxford. Why didn't she? What was it about Katherine that had forced her to keep quiet?

Damian sat back down, considering the appearance of his father's notes. He'd never been to Hawksmoor's pyramid; he'd bluffed Farringdon to give him new information. And now he had it, he realised he had no idea what the *Wisdom of Solomon* was, or why it was important. Especially as every other clue had been connected to the Sunne Dial cypher, and this was clear as day.

It was a problem he had to solve—and he had about eighteen hours to do it.

19

A ROYAL SECRET

FARRINGDON WAS TRUE TO HER WORD. ONLY FIFTEEN MINUTES after she left the room, a police officer arrived at the door. Damian winced as he realised it was the bearded officer that Katherine had beaten earlier that day.

'Should you be up and about?' he asked. The officer stared at him coldly.

'Look, I'm sorry for what happened,' Damian continued. 'It was nothing personal, I swear.'

'You're free to go, sir,' the officer said, indicating the corridor behind him. 'If you'll follow me, I'll take you to your belongings.'

'Just like that?' Damian asked.

'Just like that, sir. Seems that justice doesn't exist for some people.'

The reluctant officer led Damian to the front desk, where the desk sergeant passed over Damian's possessions with a sullen expression. It was one thing to be told that they couldn't charge a suspect, but to have that suspect torn from their grasp was a true travesty of justice.

'Sorry,' Damian muttered as another officer walked over with the leather folder. Passing it to Damian without a word, he walked off. Opening it and looking inside, Damian saw he was now looking at a pile of papers and notebooks. His father's notebooks.

In the car park was a simple black Lexus, the rear door open. Farringdon stood beside it. She motioned for Damian to enter.

'Katherine?' Damian looked around.

Farringdon shook her head.

'She'll be arriving later,' she replied. 'I want you clear-headed when you read the papers.'

She looked at the driver's side where a vicious looking Asian man glared out at him.

'You can go with Mister Sun here. He'll keep you safe.'

Damian said nothing. He stared at Mister Sun. He recognised him.

This was the Asian man who attacked him in the restaurant's kitchen.

Damian looked at Farringdon.

'Problem?' she asked.

'We've met in the past,' Damian replied. 'And he sure as hell isn't police.'

'As we've established, neither am I,' Farringdon replied coldly. 'And if my agents work on other cases, that's nothing to do with me now, is it?'

'You're saying you didn't send him to try to kill me in a restaurant?'

Farringdon considered her words before answering.

'Let's just say at the time we didn't know how important you'd become, and he was there mainly to keep you out of trouble.'

'By killing me.'

'You're just overreacting. Maybe knowing what my agents are capable of will stop you trying anything foolish,' Farringdon shrugged as she looked around the car park. 'Once you arrive at your apartment, Mister Sun will enter with you. He will remove any communication devices you might have inside.'

'You mean he's the one who's going to tear out my phone and my Wi-Fi.'

'Pretty much,' Farringdon said as she walked away from Damian and the car. Sighing, Damian looked at Mister Sun, attempted a smile and entered the back seat, closing the door behind him.

'Sorry about the chilli powder, and you know, hitting you with a pan,' Damian said. 'You see, I thought you were working for the Russians.'

Without replying, Mister Sun reversed the car out of the parking bay and edged onto the Victoria Embankment, heading East towards Hackney.

'Good talk,' Damian muttered to himself, settling back into the seat. He knew the journey was likely to take a good hour or more, this now being rush hour. So, he opened up the leather folder beside him, pulling out some notes and examining them.

The last words written by Robert Edward Lucas.

The ghost of his father sat beside him in the car; letters, notes and notebooks covering years, decades, even of treasure hunting. Turning back to the notes, pulling a couple out at random and started to read.

He wasn't looking for anything connected to Hawksmoor's St Anne Pyramid, but he had wanted his father's notes for another reason. He hoped to find clues to what someone had etched into Robert Dudley's gauntlet back in Middle Temple Hall;

'*Warbeck's crime creates a line that no one must deny, a marriage made and then betrayed can counter Cecil's lie. The Spanish Prize, who crown denies is finally outrun, the dead deceived must now retrieve and educate the sun.*'

Back in St Alfege, Dermot had spoken to Damian's father, who had told him the story of Elizabeth and Robert Dudley marrying. Which possibly meant that he must have been researching it. But what was *Warbeck's crime?* He'd tried to escape captivity, but that didn't create any kind of line.

What kind of crime created a line?

They were now passing through Dalston, and the traffic was heavy. Damian continued to flick through the pages of the books, looking for words that might stand out. He was going through the third notebook when he stopped at a page, staring down at it.

$$P + E = J \; Ssx \; 04$$

At first, it made no sense, nothing more than additional codes to work out, but a couple of lines lower, Damian read something that cleared everything up.

E.D Speaker 04 Ldn

'Can I borrow your phone?' Damian asked. Mister Sun looked at him in the mirror.

'Why?'

'I need to look something up, and my books aren't here.'

Mister Sun thought about this.

'No.'

'Can you look something up then? Edmund Dudley. I'm sure he has a Wikipedia page.'

Mister Sun pulled his phone out, tapping on it. Eventually, he passed the phone over his shoulder to Damian.

'There,' he said. 'You try anything, and I'll break an arm.'

'Understood,' Damian was already reading through the Wikipedia page, trying to hide his smile. He had been right to check, and what he read corroborated what he remembered from half overheard conversations as a teenager. Edmund Dudley had been made Speaker of the Commons in 1504, and had moved to London the same year, leaving his new wife, Elizabeth, at the estate in Sussex until early 1505, unable to attend London because of her pregnancy. And in late 1504 she'd given birth to Edmund's son John, either at the estate in Sussex or in London.

E.D Speaker 04 Ldn meant *Edmund Dudley, Speaker, 1504, London.*

Damian read the code again, and something itched at the back of his mind. Edmund was in London for most of the year and had only returned to the Sussex house briefly throughout the seasons. Elizabeth had been left alone there, with only her servants to keep her company.

And, if the story that his father believed was true, Perkin Warbeck was also there, staying by order of the king.

Elizabeth was two decades years younger than the older Edmund, a lifetime in those days, and was only just twenty when she married him. Perkin would have been only five or six years older than her, another lost soul, seemingly banished to the estate. It was known that Warbeck was a charismatic man; he'd raised a loyal army based on nothing more than a rumour.

$$P + E = J \; Ssx \; 04$$

Perkin plus Elizabeth equaled John, in Sussex, 1504.

The crime that was spoken of, that Perkin had committed —could it be the crime of adultery?

Damian leaned back in the seat as he took in the situation's enormity. Elizabeth Dudley moved to London in 1505, and Perkin, unable to return anywhere near the court, would have been left to his own devices, until executed by Henry the Eighth. There was a chance that Edmund never knew who his son's true father was. Maybe nobody did.

No, someone did, because the clue had been left. *Warbeck's crime creates a line that no one must deny.* Perkin Warbeck's adulterous act created a new heir to the Plantagenet Line, although an illegitimate one. Through Perkin's supposed bloodline, John Dudley was now a Plantagenet. Which meant that, as his first-born heir, Robert Dudley, Perkin's *grandson,* would have been the next Plantagenet heir.

Robert Dudley, who married Queen Elizabeth in a secret ceremony in Greenwich. Who united the Tudor and Plantagenet lines within their only child, Arthur Dudley.

Damian put the notes away, running a hand through his hair as he considered this. Henry the Seventh's proclamation, legitimising Perkin would have been a Tudor equivalent to a nuclear bomb. Even decades after his death, a signed proclamation like this would cause a second Wars of the Roses. No wonder Robert Dudley acted like he did during his years in court, with such documented arrogance. If he somehow knew this, then he could have believed that Elizabeth was the pretender, and he was doing *her* the favour.

A marriage made and then betrayed can counter Cecil's lie.

According to the history books, Elizabeth never married.

Which means that if the marriage happened, someone had to have annulled it. And the person who did this would have been William Cecil, one of Elizabeth's advisors and Spymaster of the Elizabethan Court before Walsingham, even though he had reportedly attended the wedding. And when Elizabeth died, it was Robert Cecil, William's son and the new Spymaster who not only ignored the messages from Spain about Arthur Dudley, but who pushed for James of Scotland to take the throne.

The Cecils *knew*. And they lied about it.

Damian placed the folder to the side as he took a deep breath. He'd always believed his father and Richard to be fools hunting for 'pirate gold'. But this wasn't gold. This was a secret.

A secret that, if revealed to the world, could change every-thing, and in the process maybe even destroy the British Monarchy.

20

FAMILY LIES

DAMIAN LOOKED UP AS THE CAR PULLED UP OUTSIDE HIS apartment building. Grabbing the folder, he climbed out and followed Mister Sun up the stairs to his apartment.

As they approached the door, Mrs Hamilton opened her own door, staring out into the hallway. Damian didn't know how she did it; she must have been watching out of the window when he arrived.

'He didn't do it,' she hissed at Mister Sun. 'You should be ashamed of yourself. They were a lovely young couple.'

Mister Sun glared back at Mrs Hamilton, who stood her ground, looking at Damian.

'You all right?' she asked. Damian shrugged.

'I'll be better when they catch the real killer,' he replied.

Mister Sun coughed, and Damian nodded a thanks to Mrs Hamilton and followed the suited man into his own apartment.

The police had been there, that was clear. They'd turned the whole place over and it looked more like a burglary than a police investigation. Chairs were overturned, Andy's laptop had been removed, and the sofa's cushions torn to shreds, as if the police believed Damian had hidden something deep inside them. Within a couple of seconds, Mister Sun was already moving around the apartment, disconnecting and removing the router, unplugging the landline telephone, and winding the cable around both items as he checked the other rooms.

'Phones?'

'Thrown out of a car window.'

Mister Sun nodded, examining the rooms for a second time. Then, confident that the room was clean, he nodded to Damian and walked out of the apartment, shutting the door behind him.

Damian didn't follow; he knew there was only one exit out of the building, and that Mister Sun would watch it. Even if Damian went for the roof, there was no way to jump onto a neighbouring rooftop. This wasn't Gotham, and he sure as hell wasn't Batman. The only way he could escape would be to use the other skills he had.

Settling some cushions back onto the sofa to cover the gaping holes in it and resetting the coffee table to its rightful upright position, Damian sat down, placing the leather folder beside him, emptying it out onto the table, beginning to sort the papers into order. As he did so, a small black control pad by the television stopped him.

Andy's Playstation 4 controller.

It was a small thing, but suddenly a floodgate of emotion burst open, and Damian fell to his knees, sobbing uncontrollably. His best friend had been dead for two days now, and he'd not really had a moment to process it. He'd been too busy running from location to location, constantly on the run, constantly hunted, adrenaline spiking at every opportunity. But now, in the room he'd shared so many happy memories in—and more than a few arguments—it was simply too much.

After a minute or so, the wave dissipated, and Damian clambered up from the floor, wiping his eyes as he did so. He was tired, exhausted beyond belief. All he wanted to do was to climb into bed and hide from the world. But he knew this wasn't an option. He needed to find a way to stop Martin Shrewsbury. And the search for gold had now become three different searches;

To search for the location of the lost Plantagenet Gold, re-hidden by Nicholas Hawksmoor.

To search for any information as to the Plantagenet Line of Perkin Warbeck, last held with Arthur Dudley, believed murdered in Spain.

To search for a proclamation or scroll created by Henry the Seventh that legitimised everything above.

Currently, the last two items on this list were likely to be dead ends. Any proclamation would have been destroyed, and Dudley wasn't married when he arrived in Spain, nor did he have children. So, the gold was all that was left. And to find the gold, Damian had to convince Farringdon Gales and Martin Shrewsbury that it was in a completely different location than its correct hiding place.

Walking to the bathroom, Damian turned on the shower. A blast of hot water was exactly what he needed right now. New clothes and clean skin. And, as he stood there, washing away the dirt and sweat from the last two days, he allowed himself a moment of calm, to relax, to clear his mind and see whether he'd missed anything.

But all he could see when he closed his eyes was Andy, dead on the floor.

After the shower, Damian put on some fresh clothing, made himself a coffee, and sat back at the sofa. After a moment he rose, walking to the door to his apartment, opening it.

As he expected, Mister Sun wasn't there. There was, however, a new wireless camera attached to the wall, aimed directly at the door. Mister Sun could be anywhere within half a mile of the apartment, watching the screen. Damian went back in, grabbed a sheet of paper and, with a marker pen scrawled

I'm hungry. Order me a pizza. Deep Pan, anything goes but no anchovies on it.

Returning to the door, he held it up for a long minute, until he was pretty sure it'd been seen. Then, walking back into his apartment, he closed the door.

Damian had food in the kitchen, but this was a power play. He wanted to see how much they wanted to keep him happy, and how far they'd go to do this. And, this done, he returned to his father's notes.

As he had expected, they were massively disorganised. It was as if Robert Lucas had simply opened a book and hunted for space on a random page to write on, rather than keeping any type of linear form. Lines of text from plays by Marlowe and Shakespeare were written beside sketches of household plants. Occasional shopping lists were written on pages lined with names of Elizabethan sailors. Page after page, sheet after sheet, there were rough notes on a variety of different subjects, all items that, over the years, Robert Lucas had searched for. *The Francis Bacon Society's* notes on Marlowe's *Edward II.* A screenshot of the original 1592 printing of *Tamburlaine The Great*. The randomness was endless.

Now and then there was a note that started with *R.E:* and Damian assumed these were reminders either to tell Richard Evans something, or to write down something he said. One of these notes caught his eye, though. A simple note in the margin, nestled next to ingredients for making a figgy pudding, a traditional Christmas dish.

R.E: 1530 Wols gives Bonn scroll 4 insurance.

Damian walked across to his shelf and pulled down one of Andy's books on Tudor history. Flicking through it, he came to the page he wanted, marking down notes on a separate piece of paper as he read. In 1529, Cardinal Wolsey had fallen out of favour with Henry the Eighth, who'd been angry with Wolsey for being unable to annul his marriage to Catherine of Aragon. Because of this, Anne Boleyn, then Henry's mistress and the woman that Henry wanted to marry had spread lies and slander about Wolsey, saying that he was working with the Pope in Rome to stop them.

Wolsey was stripped of all titles and sent to his estates in York until further notice.

A year later, he was called from York to travel to London to answer charges of treason. The charges were ludicrous, basically Henry's usual way of removing troublesome issues. But it was a stressful journey and in November 1530 Cardinal Wolsey fell ill along the way, dying in Leicester, his faithful aide Edmund Bonner by his side. Which, based on the note, could be when a bombshell was revealed.

In 1530, Wolsey gave Bonner the scroll for insurance.

Of course, this could have been any scroll, but Richard

wouldn't have cared about any old thing. Could this mean that Wolsey had kept the proclamation for safe keeping for over ten years? Had he known that John Dudley was likely to be Perkin Warbeck's bastard son? And what of Edmund Bonner? Although a loyal servant of Henry the Eighth, it was under the Catholic Queen Mary years later that he became known as 'Bloody Bonner', executing non-Catholic heretics with glee.

Reading on through the pages, Damian saw Doctor John Dee had also been placed under house arrest in Bonner's care twenty-five years later in 1555, while under investigation by Mary's Catholic judges for *Heresy*, a charge that Dee had denied and eventually overturned. This had apparently created a strong friendship with Bonner in the process. Could Bonner have mentioned the proclamation then? Did Bonner know about the Dudley's connection? Dee had tutored both Robert and John Dudley in the previous three years. Had John Dee realised their importance and, learning of this scroll, taken it from Bonner and kept it safe somehow? It would certainly make sense as to why he would create the School of Night years later.

But Bonner's end wasn't a great one. When Elizabeth finally succeeded Mary, Bonner refused to renounce his Catholic beliefs, or apologise for the terrible acts he had performed for Mary and was arrested within days of Elizabeth's coronation in 1560.

Yet Bonner was never executed like the others; instead, he could visit other prisoners and pray with them, and passed away peacefully in Marshalsea prison shortly before his seventieth birthday.

Had Bonner staved off execution by bargaining with Elizabeth a scroll, one that showed Elizabeth that her current love had Royal

blood? Maybe gave it to her, through Dee to make sure Robert
Dudley never had the proof?

The doorbell went and Damian got up, walking over and opening it to find Katherine standing there, a pizza box in her hand.

'Your guy outside has a great sense of humour,' she said, a deadpan expression upon her face. 'He made me wait until the pizza guy turned up, just so I could be the one to deliver. Oh, and he said you don't need to send him love letters, as the camera has a microphone, and that he added extra anchovies for you, as he knows you love them.'

'Come in,' Damian moved aside so Katherine could enter, 'and put it on the side table.'

Katherine did as asked and then turned back to face Damian as he closed the door behind her.

'So, you've probably got questions,' she said. 'And I understand if you don't trust me.'

'Hi,' Damian said, holding out his hand to shake. 'I'm Damian Lucas. How about you tell me who you really are?'

Katherine took the hand, shaking it solemnly. 'I never lied to you,' she said. 'My name is Katherine Turner.'

'And the whole SO14 thing?'

'Technically the truth,' Katherine tried to force a smile, but it came out crooked, as if she was nervous about the response she was about to get and trying to disarm him with a friendly gesture. 'The fourteenth letter in the alphabet is the letter 'N', you see.'

'S.O.N. School of Night,' Damian nodded. 'You're saying that you're one of the mythical School of Night? Because if you're saying that, I have to say you're the second person to claim it today.'

'Farringdon,' Katherine nodded. 'I know.'

'This is why you were uncomfortable when you met her, wasn't it?' Damian walked over to the pizza box and opened it, taking a slice, picking off the anchovies. As angry as he was, he was also starving. 'She's your boss or something?'

'No,' Katherine's voice was bitter as she answered. 'If anything, she's a rival. A sworn enemy.'

'Really? You hid it well in Oxford.'

'I didn't know whose side you were truly on back there,' Katherine explained. 'I mean, come on, we escape a murder scene and the first place you go is to Farringdon?'

'We went to the library first—'

'Oh come on!' Katherine half laughed at this response. 'I was worried that I'd missed something, that you were in fact School of Night yourself.'

'So who's the actual School of Night then?'

Katherine shrugged. 'Technically, we're both correct. In the early eighteenth century, there was a splinter group that came out of the School of Night. Nicholas Hawksmoor himself started it.'

'I thought Hawksmoor was a member who was rogue and alone?'

'Not at the time. Back then, many of the younger members were unhappy with where the School was going. Some wanted to follow John Dee's belief of a 'British Empire', using the money to create this through maritime supremacy. Others wanted to use the gold to further the society's agenda, in a way becoming a behind the scenes political manipulator in the same way that the Knights Templar were, hundreds of years earlier,' she answered. 'And then of course there were the people, like Hawksmoor who believed that the Planta-genet gold should be used by the Plantagenets, that there was a true heir, and this was to hold aside for them, when they finally revealed themselves to the world. And when Nicholas Hawksmoor left, they followed.'

Katherine sighed.

'But the splinter group, although believing that they held the true heart of the School within them, didn't have the power within court circles that the older, more established members of the School did. And added to this, Hawksmoor never told anyone where he'd hidden the gold. They were forced to practice underground for centuries and eventually, they became smaller and smaller. Until now? It's just me.'

Damian almost laughed.

'Just you? What about the man that came with you last time you were here?'

'A friend from work,' Katherine admitted. 'I thought a show of force might get you on my side quicker than turning up alone.'

'What work?'

Katherine slumped a little. 'Well surprisingly, being a full time School of Night employee doesn't pay well. I had to take alternate employment to pay bills.'

Damian waited. Katherine sighed.

'I work in a call centre,' she admitted. 'I phone people up and offer them carpet cleaning.'

'Fulfilling?'

'It has its moments,' Katherine was getting angry. 'Can we move on now?'

'But if the gold is hidden, and your team are broke, how does the other school of Night still work?' Damian frowned. 'Surely *they* don't have the gold either?'

'They had decades, centuries even where the gold was in their possession,' Katherine explained. 'They had assets gained from this, finances they've used and grown. The problem is, that although they may have a few million in the background, the gold they lost is worth billions. Trillions, even, at current rates.'

Damian nodded at this. He understood greed very well.

'So it's been just you hunting the gold? For how long?'

'There was another, the one who inducted me,' she explained. 'But he... died recently.'

'Richard?' Damian was surprised at this, although he immediately realised it was the obvious choice, and explained a lot of questions he'd had over the years.

Katherine nodded.

'He was my granddad,' she said now, sitting down next to Damian and taking a slice of pizza. Damian stared at Katherine for a good few moments before replying.

'That's why you've been watching over me.'

'In part, yes. From childhood, I followed Richard around, his little helper. He showed me everything, taught me all that he knew,' she smiled. 'I even met you a few times as a kid, when you visited Richard with your father.'

Damian thought back to his childhood. 'There was a blonde girl...'

'I dyed it brown a few years back,' Katherine smiled. 'Anyway, when I was eighteen, I confronted Richard. I knew there was more to this quest than he was letting on. I'd also noted his particular fixation with your father.'

'Fixation?'

'Robert and Richard were the best of friends, but they often fell out, as academics do. Rather than give the argument time to dissipate, Richard would always be the first to apologise, take the blame for the row. It was almost like Richard was scared that your father would cut him out of his life, that he'd lose access to him.'

'Was Richard gay?' Damian frowned. 'I remember dad saying he was married at one point, but it didn't take?'

'He was bisexual, but that wasn't what was going on. This wasn't attraction, this was compulsion. And I confronted him about it one day. And that was the day he introduced me to the School of Night. Well, the *Portakabin* of Night.'

'All this time, all these moments, the Temple, the church, you just let me run ahead like I was the expert, when you already knew what we'd find,' Damian was getting angry now, rising off the sofa. 'You lied to me! You played me!'

'No, I swear,' Katherine grabbed his arm, bringing Damian back down to the seat. 'Hawksmoor never left his followers the treasure map, believing that divine inspiration would strike the chosen one.'

'You're kidding?'

Katherine shook her head.

'I guess you work on enough churches, you start to believe,' she said. 'Richard hunted for the gold for years as an individual.'

'But Farringdon and Richard were friends!' Damian exclaimed. 'Did she know?'

'Yes, and she didn't care. None of them did. Our School was a joke to them, and Richard was a modern day *Don Quixote*, chasing dreams as far as they were concerned. That was the level of disdain that they had. In fact, she frequently tried to get him to join her School. Partly to do with his research, but also because of his closeness to your father.'

'What is it about my bloody father!' Damian hurled his half-eaten slice of pizza across the room in anger. 'What was so special about him?'

Katherine stared at Damian for a moment.

'You really don't know?' she asked.

Damian shrugged, immediately regretting his outburst.

'He's the key to the whole damn thing,' Katherine said. 'It was your father who sold Martin Shrewsbury the first clue about the School of Night, through some bookseller in Henley-Upon Thames.'

At this, Damian paled.

'No.'

'Yes,' Katherine rose now, walking around the room as she spoke. 'No offence, but your father was an idiot. Picked the one thing that could aim people straight at this and threw it out into the world for a couple of grand.'

'He didn't do that,' Damian whispered.

'You sure? Because I seem to recall it kicked a massive wasp's nest. Granddad and your father didn't speak for months about it, especially as it was granddad who gave it to him.'

'I swear, I didn't know,' Damian leaned forward, fighting back the bile rising in his throat. 'It was years ago. I was a teenager.'

Katherine paused.

'What the hell are you talking about?'

'It was me. The sale. That is, I took the paper and sold it,' Damian looked up, tears running down his eyes as the full enormity of what he had done hit him. 'It's the whole reason me and dad never spoke again.'

He leaned back on the sofa, staring at the ceiling.

'I sold his work to fund my addiction. A Henley-Upon-Thames bookseller bought it, and it must have put my dad in his sights. Richard's death, hell, even Andy's death…'

'It's all my fault.'

21

STOLEN GOODS

KATHERINE STARED AT DAMIAN IN HORROR.

'You have ten seconds to tell me everything before I walk out of that door and never speak to you again,' she hissed. 'You caused my granddad's death?'

'In part, I suppose,' Damian replied, unable to look her in the eye. 'It was my first year at University. I was a mess. Drugs, drink, you name it. I'd spent my grant money in a term, and was one step away from flunking.'

'Still not getting to the part where you kill my granddad.'

'I came home over Christmas break,' Damian continued. 'I was broke, looking for something to help pay for the next fix. I... I stole from dad's wallet, mum's purse, negligible amounts, enough to pay a local dealer for some gear. But it was never enough. I knew I couldn't last on what I had, I needed to pay my debts.'

'What debts?' Katherine paused. 'Drug debts?'

Damian nodded.

'And the rest. Andy bailed me out of some of it, but I owed

a couple of grand. And then one night, I found some old papers in dad's favourite hiding place.'

'What sort of hiding place?'

'A secret one.'

'You broke into your father's office?' Katherine was incredulous. Damian nodded.

'Look, I'm not proud of what I did, okay? But I was an addict. I was looking for something to sell, to cover a couple of hits. And they were just left there, seven or eight of them. I couldn't help it, I took a couple and ran.'

'Do you even remember what they were?' Katherine's voice was icy.

'Pages from a book by a barely known Elizabethan poet named Heywood,' he replied. 'It was also the first forgery I ever did, as I had to create some kind of provenance for them.'

Katherine silently waited, so Damian continued. It was almost as if he couldn't stop himself now the cork had been removed.

'There was a guy in Henley-Upon-Thames my dad had dealt with, I knew he gave good prices. I took it to him. Made three grand off it. Later found he had sold to someone else for thirty. I remember being pissed that I'd undercut myself.'

'Martin Shrewsbury?'

'I don't know,' Damian said. 'All I know is that I came back and found dad in a rage. He knew what I'd done. He'd tried to buy them back, but they'd already gone. We fought that day; the worst we'd ever been. I grabbed my things and left, went back to University. I never spoke to him again. And then a year or so later he...'

Damian stopped, and Katherine nodded slowly at this, putting the pieces together.

'Shrewsbury bought the papers, learnt who sold them, and then went to your father,' she said. 'You know your father worked for Shrewsbury before his death, don't you?'

Damian shook his head, wide eyed. 'I never...'

'I don't know the full story,' Katherine continued. 'I just remember overhearing granddad on the phone, saying that Robert couldn't be trusted while he was in Shrewsbury's pocket.'

Damian thought back to earlier that day—had it truly still been that day—when he had faced Shrewsbury in Middle Temple.

'It's amazing how many people get hurt or die because of your mistakes.'

'He knew,' he muttered. 'From the start, he knew I was Robert's son. And he didn't care. He didn't say anything.'

Katherine sat beside Damian.

'You didn't kill anyone,' she whispered. 'If your father worked with Shrewsbury, it's because he chose to.'

'I should have got clean,' Damian replied. 'Instead, I went back to University and continued down the path I'd already started along. I couldn't go home, so I started finding other ways to make money. Forging old papers, hacking into systems and changing my grades... whatever it took. I always said that it was all to make the money to buy those papers back, to prove I wasn't a screwup. But then a year later...'

'The car crash?'

Damian nodded. 'Suddenly, I had everything. All left to me in the will. But the funny part? My dad changed the will. Everything was held in trust until I was thirty. I couldn't get anything. So I doubled down, on the forgeries, on the hacking... and on the drugs.'

'Until you were kicked out.'

'Until Richard couldn't take any more, and booted me out, yeah.'

Damian paused.

'You were going to say something about my dad?' he asked. 'before I went all emo on you?

Now it was Katherine's turn to look uncomfortable.

'I promise you, I've never held back from you about anything, except for one thing,' she said. 'In 1593, Christopher Marlowe was murdered in a tavern brawl.'

'We talked about this last night at the hotel,' Damian replied. 'You changed the subject.'

'I did, because I didn't feel that it was the right time to tell you something.'

'And now is the right time?'

'Well, now we're sharing everything, I thought it the right time, yeah,' Katherine shifted in her seat. 'In 1593, Marlowe dies. But as you said yesterday, the fight was most likely staged, Marlowe needed to escape *Heresy* charges, and nobody saw the body before they buried it.'

'I said that Marlowe survived.'

'And you were right. My granddad once told me that a prominent Marlowe scholar, your father, in fact, had worked out that days after this murder, Marlowe travelled to the Spanish court under a fake name, to confirm something that John Dee had seen while passing through the court four years earlier, in 1589, while on his way back to London. The son of Arthur Dudley.'

'Arthur Dudley was believed to die shortly after he arrived in Spain,' Damian argued. 'How did he gain a son?'

Katherine squirmed, as if uncomfortable at this.

'Well, the story goes that Philip of Spain, believing Arthur Dudley's story when he was captured, and believing that he had some serious leverage on the elder Elizabeth, immediately married him into the Spanish Court. It was a low-level lady of waiting whose name never made the history books, but it was enough to give him some level of comfort.'

'Marry into the court, make him an asset.'

'Exactly. A year later Dudley tried to escape home and was killed in the attempt, but he'd left behind a wife and a new-born child, maybe a year old by that time. And one that Dee saw when he passed through Spain.'

'And John Dee's seen enough Dudley children.'

Katherine nodded.

'Dee returns in late 1589 and tells Walsingham that Elizabeth's heir is dead, and her new heir is now a half-Spanish grandson. But by now Robert Dudley is dead, Elizabeth is old, and Robert Cecil has taken over his father's spy industry.'

'So how does this affect Marlowe?'

'A few years later, after Walsingham dies, Marlowe is accused of *Heresy*, something that would involve him likely being tortured for information. Knowing that he could give up even more valuable secrets, Marlowe's forced to run. He makes a deal with the School of Night, and in part Elizabeth herself. He 'dies' in the tavern brawl, a brawl where his body is never publicly seen, travels to Spain and takes charge of the young Dudley child, now about four years old, with the aim of eventually bringing him back to London under an assumed name. It's a short-term deal, to keep the child safe until the Queen acknowledges him. But it never happens. Whether it's because she's convinced not to, or because she has an issue about the Spanish side of the child's heritage, I don't know, but it simply never comes to pass.'

'And James of Scotland is made King by Thomas Cecil the

moment Elizabeth dies,' Damian mused. 'The son of Arthur Dudley fades into the background, Marlowe beside him.'

'Marlowe brought him up as his ward, so the legend says,' Katherine replied. 'And in turn he grew up, got married, had his own children, and the line continued down.'

Damian stared at Katherine.

'*Warbeck's crime creates a line that no one must deny, a marriage made and then betrayed can counter Cecil's lie.* Perkin has a child out of marriage, continuing the Plantagenet line. Elizabeth marries Robert Dudley, but William and Thomas make sure it's never revealed. *The Spanish Prize, who crown denies is finally outrun, the dead deceived must now retrieve and educate the sun.* Not sun, but *son*. The dead deceived is Marlowe, as he finds Arthur Dudley's child.'

Katherine nodded. Damian frowned.

'So why does Farringdon want me to follow Marlowe? What's this got to do with me?'

Katherine sighed. 'Haven't you got it yet?' she asked. 'The School of Night had one remit. To ensure the line of Elizabeth was kept safe, in order to hopefully return it to power one day. To watch over them. But also, to learn who the genuine members of the line are.'

She stared at Damian.

'Your father was possibly the only man in existence who knew who the true heir to the throne was. And as I just said, before he died, he was spending a lot of time with a tech magnate with a regal sounding name. Martin Shrewsbury, believed named after Richard of Shrewsbury.'

'Richard of what?" Frowned Damian.

Katherine leaned back.

'Didn't you know?' she asked, surprised. 'The Prince in the Tower was Richard of Shrewsbury, and because of this,

Martin Shrewsbury thinks he's therefore descended from the true King of England.'

Katherine shrugged.

'Of course, nobody knows,' she replied. 'Marlowe's new identity was never learnt. Shrewsbury hired your father to find him proof. Robert had been working on this for years by then, so he probably thought that some money for nothing thrown his way was a nice retirement fund of sorts. Maybe he was trying to get back the papers you'd sold. Either way, he never found the proof that Martin wanted, or if he did, he never told him. And then after his death, Martin moved onto another source.'

'Farringdon.'

'Possibly. I don't know. What I do know is this,' Katherine leaned forward. 'The Royal Family is tainted right now with sex scandals and members leaving in droves. Martin Shrewsbury is a villain, but he's a populist one. If he proves he's the true King of England and finds the Plantagenet gold, he'll evict the current crowd by popular vote and the alt-right will rise to power. He'll do better with one threat than Hitler did with a war.'

For the first time in a long while, Damian had no words.

22

FORGERY

'No,' Damian said. 'I can't believe it.'

'Shrewsbury or the lineage?'

'Either.'

'The latter is definitely true,' Katherine said. 'Your father knew of it. He'd been looking for the scroll for years, for proof that he wasn't just wasting his life.'

Damian frowned as he put pieces of the jigsaw together.

'What happened the day he died?' he asked.

Katherine paused, looking away for a moment.

'I don't know,' she replied. 'All I know is that he visited the other School of Night, so probably met with Farringdon Gales. There was an argument. He left.'

'And then later that day he died,' Damian's voice was flat and cold. 'How convenient.'

He rose, walking over to a side cabinet, pulling out a half-empty bottle of whisky.

'You sure that you should drink after hearing that?' Katherine asked.

Damian shrugged.

'Not often you get told your dad was helping a Nazi become the real heir to the throne, most likely because of your own screw up, and that there's nothing you can do about it,' he said. 'Especially with the people tasked with guarding it screwing you over.'

'What's that supposed to mean?' Katherine rose now, walking over to the cabinet and pouring her own glass of whisky.

'It means I'm sick of secrets.'

'From who? Me or them?'

'Take your pick,' Damian replied. 'You might have kept this from me, but Farringdon has her own secrets, too. The guy outside who gave you pizza? Tried to kill me right before we even met. And if he works for her...'

Now it was Katherine's turn to look shocked.

'Why was Farringdon trying to kill you?'

'Who knows, maybe she wasn't. Maybe I overreacted. Maybe he did,' he leaned back, looking to the ceiling. 'That said, she was also pretty much the only person Richard told about Antwerp.'

'If Shrewsbury was told, then surely that means she works for him?' snapped Katherine, pulling away. 'She killed my granddad. The bitch needs to pay for what she did.'

'And if I'm right, and she is, then she will, I promise you,' Damian replied. 'Either way, she hopes that I'll have a solution to Hawksmoor's clue by the morning. That I believe we'll be solving it together, but in reality she'll either pass it to her bosses, whoever they are, or maybe even go for it alone.'

He smiled.

'Instead, we'll be sending her on a wild goose chase to the north of England, while we escape.'

Katherine paused for a moment, watching Damian.

'Did Mister Sun come in with you?' She looked around the room. 'Could he have bugged the place?'

'I checked everywhere he went,' Damian replied carefully. 'I didn't see anything. And, I honestly don't think she classes me as a threat yet.'

'So why come here?'

'My forging supplies. Once I work out what to forge, that is. And I'll need some help while doing it.'

'What do you need?'

'An historical lie,' Damian admitted. 'It doesn't matter how good the forgery is if nobody believes the story. And if the story's good, then people will gloss over the fact that there could be unspoken questions in the forgery itself.'

Katherine considered this.

'Is that what you did with the Shakespeare forgery?'

'Let me guess. Andy told you?' Damian sighed. 'Bloody idiot. Yes, pretty much. He was the brains behind all that. He could get the historical facts to link up, you see. All I had was ink, paper and a lie.'

'And a forged Shakespeare signature that could beat authentication?'

Damian shook his head.

'Even that isn't as important these days. If they'd complained that the writing didn't look like Shakespeare's, I'd have just said that he never did the same signature twice, so why would his writing match? At the end of the day, if the paper and ink match, they believe simply because back then nobody would have forged his work.'

'Because he wasn't famous then.'

Damian stroked at his chin in thought.

'But with this, we need something small that, when

looked from a certain angle, leads someone on another jolly treasure hunt.'

'Castle Howard,' Katherine replied with a smile. 'Granddad spent years looking there. Convinced there was something worth checking, but it never came to pass. He always complained that he'd wasted the best years of his life there.'

'That could work.'

'No, Farringdon will never believe it. She saw Richard's failed attempts,' Katherine shook her head.

'He only failed because he didn't have the right clue,' Damian smiled. 'So, let's create something that'll make Farringdon and Shrewsbury believe in it.'

He paused.

'Of course, if there really is something there, we could send her ahead of us.'

'The Wisdom of Solomon?'

'I still don't know where it leads to,' Damian admitted. 'We could be accidentally sending them the right way.'

'It'd be nicer if we had more clues to the proper direction,' Katherine mused.

Damian sipped from the glass of whisky.

'We might,' he breathed. 'If we get away, I might know a place we can look.'

'Then let's get away. What'll we need?' Katherine was warming to the task as Damian gathered up another piece of pizza and ate it, ignoring the anchovies in his excitement.

'There's an eighteenth century book in my bedroom,' he said eventually. 'Swift's *A Modest Proposal*. We need that for a start. I can't mix the right inks without alerting Mister Sun out there, but I still have some left from the Shakespeare forgery and that'll only be fifty years out from the needed date, once I tinker with it.'

'Will that be picked up on?' Katherine was already walking into the bedroom as she spoke. Damian shouted out after her.

'I'm relying on the fact that they'll authenticate it by eye, and with a travel kit,' he replied. 'If she sends it for a full scan, it'll take days. And if she *is* thinking of going it alone, then there's a risk that others will find it while she waits. So, she'll go with an expert, most likely on the fly.'

He sighed, rubbing at his temple as he spoke into the air, the sounds of Katherine rummaging in the bedroom for the book now coming through the door.

'All I have to do is forge myself a Hawksmoor design in a couple of hours.'

Katherine was already returning from the bedroom, a thin, leather-bound book in her hands.

'What do we need from this?' She asked. Taking it from her, Damian opened the leather-bound book to the title page, grabbing a box cutter from the table as he did so. The third page was blank on both sides and, using the box cutter as he cut down the edge of the page closest to the centre of the book, Damian expertly sliced the page out, a straight vertical line that left no tearing. Katherine stared at him in shock.

'That's a first edition!' she exclaimed.

'It's also severely water damaged in the middle, so I got it for fifty pounds in a flea market.'

'Then why buy it?'

Damian grinned.

'I'm a forger. I need supplies, and you never know when you'll need something different.'

He held up the page.

'For fifty pounds I got this, an authentic sheet of paper from the 1730s,' he said. 'So when someone bothers to test the age of whatever I put on it, they'll find that the paper is the right time zone for the forgery. Add the inks, and they'll waive the fact that they're slightly off, date wise. It'll be old inks, or something wrong with the chemical mix that examined it.'

'The devil's in the details,' Katherine nodded. 'What else do you need from me?'

'Everything you can tell me about Castle Howard and the family that owned it. Why Richard was obsessed with it.'

Damian stopped as a new thought came to mind. Walking to the kitchen, he opened up the coffee tin, emptying it into the sink, turning on the tap to flush all signs of it away.

'What the hell are you doing now?' Katherine exclaimed. Damian walked back to the table, grabbing a piece of paper and writing on it.

'I'm being watched, and now so are you,' Damian carried on writing as he spoke. 'The CCTV outside the door stops us entering or leaving without Farringdon knowing about it. We can't get a message out, but at the same time we need to make some preparations.'

Damian finished writing on the paper and folded it.

'Conlan said that I was working with Isabella Vladimov. But I'd conned the Russians without knowing it was her. When I realised I owed her money, they upped the debt to a hundred grand.'

'Ouch.'

'Yeah. Anyway, when I was running in Oxford, I made a call from a payphone. I had a friend reach out to them, offering more if they helped me.'

'Did they agree?'

'No idea, I haven't spoken to my friend since. But if I can get this note to him, we can hope.'

Katherine nodded.

'But how do we get this out there?' she asked.

Damian picked up and waggled the coffee tin.

'We're out of coffee,' he said with a smile.

———

MISTER SUN WAS READING A BOOK AS THE IMAGE ON THE laptop screen flickered with movement. Looking over to the laptop, currently on the passenger seat and arranged to face him showed Katherine at the door, holding up the empty tin to the CCTV camera, giving the impression that she was looking out of the laptop screen, directly at Mister Sun.

'We're out of coffee,' she said, the words coming through the laptop speakers as a tinny, faint sound. 'We need to keep working. We need caffeination.'

On the screen, Katherine pointed to the door to the side.

'We're going to ask Mrs Hamilton for some. She knows Damian. Or, you can go down to the shops for us. Beep your horn twice if you'd rather do that.'

With that, Katherine listened for a moment and, not hearing Mister Sun beep his horn, mainly because the last thing he wanted to do was drive to a shop, taking his eye off the door for even a moment, she moved to the side and knocked on Mrs Hamilton's door. Mister Sun was annoyed at this, because the door was just off the edge of the screen, but the CCTV's view was enough that he could still see Katherine's back. The moment she moved out of sight, he'd move in.

The door opened, and Mrs Hamilton's voice could be heard.

'Oh, hello, you're that police lady, aren't you? Can I help you with anything?'

'I hope so,' Katherine replied. 'I'm with Damian next door, he's, um, helping us with a puzzle and we've run out of coffee. We were hoping we could borrow some?'

'I only have instant,' Mrs Hamilton's voice faded off as she entered into the apartment, returning a little while later later. 'Here you go. Tell him he owes me one in return.'

'I will do,' Katherine said, turning back to the camera and triumphantly showing a small glass jar of instant coffee to Mister Sun. And with that, she entered the apartment again, as both Damian's and Mrs Hamilton's doors closed.

Stability now resumed, Mister Sun went back to reading his book, an eye kept on the door shown on the centre of the screen. And when Mrs Hamilton left her apartment and walked down the stairs twenty minutes later, a piece of folded paper in her hands as she quickly and quietly exited the building, he barely noticed.

BACK IN THE APARTMENT, DAMIAN USED THE NEW COFFEE TO make two more mugs, passing one over to Katherine as he returned to his seat on the sofa.

'Do you think this'll work?' she asked, taking the mug from him and taking a sip before placing it on the table. Damian simply shrugged.

'I've never done something this quickly,' he admitted. 'If we're able to get everything ready, the cracks in the physical proof can be papered up by the legends about it.'

Katherine stared at Damian for a moment, not speaking. Noting this, Damian frowned.

'What?' he asked. 'Have I got pizza on me?'

'No, not at all,' Katherine replied, looking away. 'You just surprise me, that's all.'

'How so?'

Katherine shrugged. 'When I met you as a child, you always seemed bored with this. And over the years, your name came up now and then through my granddad. I knew you'd gone to University to learn under him, I knew about the expulsion, but Richard never hated you for it,' she continued. 'I think I'd gained this vision of you, this impression from what my granddad had told me. A spoilt boy with the world at his fingers who lucked his way into everything while I had to fight every step.'

'How do you mean?' Damian looked at Katherine now. She looked away, as if realising that she'd spoken too much.

'When Farringdon Gales doesn't like you, it's really hard to get into a good University,' she said. 'Every place I applied to rejected me. It's why I confronted my granddad, asked him why this woman who I'd met a handful of times in my life hated me so. He told me everything and then went to speak to her on my behalf. The next day I had an acceptance from Birmingham.'

'What in?'

'History.'

Damian nodded. He'd quietly guessed that one. 'You resented me for learning under Richard?'

'A little bit. Until they kicked you out. Then I felt a bit better, to be honest,' Katherine grinned. 'But I also knew that you'd probably get reinstated. And then you disappeared. It was only a few months back that I even saw that you were in town again. And of course, the first time I'm told to look for you, you're pretending to be the Crown Prince of an imaginary country.'

'And you were pretending to be a cop,' Damian countered. 'Is that what history graduates who work in call centres do these days?'

'In part,' Katherine admitted. 'It seemed the easiest way to get close.'

'You could have just said who you were,' Damian said. 'I would have trusted you.'

'Trust is a two-way street,' Katherine took another sip of the coffee. 'And the last time I heard about you, it was because you were a drug addict with a criminal past.'

'And now?' Damian looked at his watch. 'We're what, sixty hours plus since you broke into my apartment. Any additions to these opinions?'

'Yeah,' Katherine's voice was soft. 'I wish I'd gone your route. If anything, Andy might have been saved.'

She leaned back on the sofa.

'I'm so sick of this,' she muttered. 'You know, I've not had a proper holiday since I was twelve.'

Damian watched her for a moment.

'What about friends, family?'

My parents emigrated to Australia when I was eighteen,' Katherine replied. 'Richard Evans was my only other family here. And social life? I seem to recall what that was once.'

She looked at Damian, an impish smile on her face.

'Or were you subtly trying to see if I had a boyfriend?' she asked. Damian felt himself blushing as he shook his head.

'No, of course not,' he denied, but he knew this was a lie. He knew an attractive woman when he saw one. And Katherine Turner was stunning.

Katherine raised a hand.

'I was joking, I swear.'

'I guessed. And besides, being on the run while forging a document to stop a right wing Nazi from becoming King of England is probably not the best time to consider a new relationship.'

Katherine laughed.

'Yeah, there is that,' she agreed. Damian smiled and turned back to the forgery.

'Anything I can do?' Katherine asked.

'Yeah,' Damian replied as he leaned close to the paper, checking a blemish on it. 'Keep talking to me.'

'Why?'

'Because I like the sound of your voice. It's soothing.'

'Oh.'

Damian looked up to see Katherine look away, blushing slightly.

Maybe if we do survive this, I'll ask her to dinner, he thought.

But then, the chances of them surviving this weren't exactly very high.

23

THE PITCH

AT EXACTLY NINE O'CLOCK THE FOLLOWING MORNING, Farringdon Gales knocked on Damian's door, arriving with black-suited agents, possibly from Domestic Counter-Terrorism, or maybe the School of Night, who took down the CCTV camera on the stairs. As Damian opened it for them, a courtesy he appreciated as they probably had a key anyway, they found Katherine asleep, half slumped over the edge of the sofa, as Damian sat back down beside her and drank the last vestiges of his coffee.

'So?' Farringdon asked eagerly.

'I think I have something,' Damian replied as he leaned back against the sofa. 'There wasn't much in my dad's notes, but there were a couple of things.'

Farringdon walked over to a chair by the window, watching Damian intently as she sat down.

'Tell me,' she said. 'Was it the pyramid, the phrase or the seal that gave you the clue?'

'A bit of all of them, to be honest,' Damian said, opening

one of his father's notebooks and passing it to Farringdon. 'But I'm not sure what it leads to.'

The page Damian had given Farringdon to read was a random jumble of notes from three different years, all written on the page in different angles and colours, as if Robert Lucas had been trying to save paper by filling in every available space. Which, as far as Damian knew, he probably was.

But on the top right was a box, with small writing held within, written in faded blue pen.

Wisdom of Solomon = key of Solomon = 8 and pyramid
Note hidden curious collection – Apr 1740

'I don't remember seeing this before, but then I haven't had time to really go through these,' Farringdon passed the book back to Damian. 'What does it mean?'

Damian shrugged, giving the impression he had no idea. In fact, he knew exactly what it meant, as he'd written it himself into the notebook around four hours earlier.

'I think it means we need to go to the British Library,' he replied. 'There's a book there in the *Rare Books and Music* reading room that my dad would often look at when I was a kid. I think it might even be the last book he read in the British Library reading room before he died.'

'This 'curious collection'?' Farringdon shook her head. 'I don't recall it.'

'That's because it's not technically a book,' Damian explained.

'*The curious collection of original pictures, prints, drawings and books of Nicholas Hawksmoor,*' Katherine said, opening her eyes as she woke up. '*To be sold at Auction, at Mister Lambe's April 1740.* It's a sales brochure.'

'And you'd know this how?' Farringdon's distaste at Katherine's interruption was evident. In response, Katherine smiled.

'Because knowing Hawksmoor is what my granddad and I did best, in our little club that you hated so much.'

Farringdon ignored the jibe and looked back at Damian.

'All right, so your father visited the British Library and read this brochure several times. That doesn't mean there's anything spectacular waiting for us there, does it? We've all had books we've returned to, clues we've believed were right in front of our eyes until they weren't.'

'I understand that, but I think there could be a hidden note there, inside the book,' Damian continued. 'Either in the margins or hidden within the pages. Something to do with the key of Solomon, the number eight, and a pyramid. That's why my dad kept going back to it, and that's why he wrote it in the notebook.'

'And do we have an answer?' Farringdon asked.

'If you're including yourself in that, then no,' Katherine replied. 'However, *we* have an answer, thank you very much.'

'I think we can have Miss Turner leave now,' Farringdon said, looking to an agent beside her. 'If you could—'

'Take Kate away and I stop helping,' Damian interrupted. 'I don't give a damn that you don't like her. I like her, and I trust her a damn sight more than I trust you right now.'

Farringdon raised a hand to halt her agent.

'Then carry on, please,' she said.

Damian grabbed an old leather book off the coffee table, opening it up. From the cover, Farringdon could see that it was a list of stately homes and buildings, written sometime within the nineteenth century.

'Castle Howard, north of Yorkshire,' he continued. 'You've heard of it?'

'I know it,' she replied. 'What about it?'

'Well, first let me explain why I'm looking at this as the answer,' Damian explained. 'I think Hawksmoor's quote on the St Anne's Pyramid, *The Wisdom of Solomon* is actually connected to the *Key* of Solomon, a book that was believed to be King Solomon's Grimoire, but was actually a book of renaissance magic, most likely written in the fifteenth century, and owned at one time by John Dee.'

'I see where you're going with this,' Farringdon leaned forwards. 'Lord William Howard was one of the people that stole John Dee's library while he was abroad, or at least paid someone for several of the books to add to his own extensive collection.'

'Lord Howard was also a member of the School of Night,' Katherine muttered.

Damian leaned back, a smile on his face as he watched Farringdon's surprised expression.

'Briefly, that is,' he amended. 'He was the Earl of Northampton's son, and always blamed Dee for the events that led to his father's execution, something that built considerable animosity between the two academics.'

'And even though he had the right credentials, he was barred from becoming a member of the School by the request of Dee, mainly because of his connections to the Church of Rome,' Katherine continued, 'however he bought his way back into the society when he paid a ransom of ten thousand pounds to Elizabeth the First to regain his estates and his name, while Dee was stuck up in Manchester.'

'While Dee was out of favour with the court,' Farringdon replied, nodding. 'Yes, that makes sense. Dee wouldn't be able to monitor everything, Elizabeth was dying, everyone was looking for an exit strategy.'

She frowned, suspicious.

'But it doesn't explain why I've never seen his name in any records.'

'Because he wasn't there long enough to be put into any,' Katherine continued. 'When James was crowned King, Howard was a staunch follower and ally. Because of this, he believed he would quickly rise up the ranks of the School of Night.'

'But instead, with the other members against the new ruler, Howard was quietly left out of the School's planning, in fear he passed on any anti-James details.' Damian leaned back, a triumphant smile on his face, as if he'd just discovered the greatest secret in the world. Farringdon Gales, however, was not so believing in this tale.

'I've never heard this,' she replied cautiously.

'That's because when Dee returned from Manchester, he immediately expelled Howard. His membership was never made official,' Katherine chipped in. 'It was the last step in an unspoken hatred that had lasted for decades. And after both Howard and Dee's deaths, it still proved to be a bone of contention for years.'

Damian watched Farringdon as she took in the information. He could sense that they had reached the point where to go too far would result in them losing Farringdon. There was a point in every con where too much explanation killed the story. But at the same time, they needed it to build the world that the lie would come from. Damian leaned forward once more, lowering his voice a little as he continued.

It was time to pepper the food a little, and to get Farringdon Gales' taste buds really popping for their story.

'Now jump forward over a hundred years,' he said. 'Hawksmoor is moving the gold and has cut all ties with the School of Night, who he believes have sold out over the Stuarts' claim to the throne. He needs someone who hates the School as much as he does to help him create a place that nobody will find, but there aren't many around who would go to the extremes that he needs.'

'This is Charles, isn't it?' Farringdon's eyes glinted with excitement, and Damian knew he had her once more.

'Exactly. By chance, he comes across Charles Howard, the third Earl of Carlisle, and the great-grandson of William,' he continued. 'Charles knows what happened to his great-grandfather, had issue with it for years, and therefore 'commissions' Hawksmoor to create a mausoleum for William in the gardens of Castle Howard. It's never explained why such a thing was created, but Hawksmoor does what Charles asks and builds a pyramid, with eight towers set around it; two on each corner.'

Farringdon leaned forwards again, now completely taken by the story.

'Eight and a pyramid,' she said, echoing the made-up note Damian had shown her earlier.

Damian nodded.

'In the Key of Solomon, there's a line about created magical items. The *knife, sword, poniard, dagger, lance, wand* and *staff* are the first seven. The eighth item was always to be left open, as it would cover all other instruments of the magical art.'

'How do you know this?' Farringdon raised an eyebrow at Damian, who simply grinned.

'I was an initiate in a coven once,' he said. 'Not for long, but enough to learn the basics.'

Farringdon nodded at this. There was every chance that Damian could have learnt this during his teenage years. And by this point, she appeared completely sold on the secrets and lies that Damian and Katherine were telling her. She *wanted* to accept it. To accept it meant she was one step closer to reclaiming the gold that Nicholas Hawksmoor had stolen almost three hundred years earlier. Picking up the notebook and staring at the scrawled message once more, she frowned.

'So each of the towers represents an item? Do we need to find them? As in the items?'

Damian shrugged.

'To be honest, that's where I draw a blank,' he said.

Farringdon looked up at him, surprised.

'I expected better of you,' she chided. Damian straightened.

'I've done more in one night than my dad and Richard did in years,' he snapped. 'More than you, too. Give me some slack if I didn't give you everything in the space of six or seven hours.'

Farringdon nodded, a silent apology.

'And this is why you think the British Library has the next clue?' she asked.

Damian nodded.

'I think that's what Hawksmoor was trying to tell us, that we needed to go to the mausoleum on the Howard Estate and do something, but I don't know what. I think that whatever it is, the next clue is somewhere in the British Library, and is most likely a note in a sales brochure that gives us more details. Or notes in a margin, something that points the way. It was probably originally placed somewhere else, but over the years it found itself placed in a brochure selling off his items after his death, where my dad saw it. And of course, without the advantage of the journey that we've all taken that leads to this note, he never knew the importance of it.'

'We may never have found the gold, simply because Hawksmoor's last clue wasn't left in the correct location,' Katherine admitted.

'My dad didn't write more, because he didn't have any context, like we have now.'

'We should go to Limehouse,' Farringdon replied. 'We should check this pyramid.'

'We can do, but there's pictures of it all over the net,' Damian suggested.

'Perhaps there are scratched clues there too?'

'If they are, they're long gone,' Damian shook his head. 'Hawksmoor must have known this though. Only things he's etched into are wood, or metal. Nothing outside that's weathered by time and nature.'

'Apart from this mausoleum.'

'Inside a mausoleum,' Katherine added, and Damian was beginning to wonder if he'd pushed too hard. There were a lot of conflicting clues here, and there was an element that his father should have worked this out, no matter what additional new information Damian had.

That was the problem when spinning a story, he thought to himself. *You might think you've given enough, but the reader sometimes needs more.*

'Then we need to examine the book,' Farringdon nodded. 'We'll go today.'

'Not so fast,' Damian said, rising from the sofa and walking over to the kitchen, taking the time to slowly pour himself another coffee, allowing the tension in the room to increase. 'You have to know that Martin Shrewsbury will watch all locations. British Library, London Library, most of the museums...'

He trailed off.

'The moment we arrive, one of his lookouts will tell him. He'll know something's happened, and that we know more than we're letting on.'

'That makes us sound like amateurs,' Farringdon bristled. 'You think people would just tell him what our plans are?'

'Actually, yes,' Katherine said, leaning back against the sofa. 'You have a spy in your ranks. Someone told Shrewsbury what Richard Evans found in Antwerp.'

'And how do we know it's not you?' Farringdon flashed an angry glance back at Katherine, who simply stayed silent. 'After all, you seemed to turn up in Manchester very quickly after Shrewsbury was there. Almost as if you were meeting him.'

'I was sent by my granddad, just like Damian was.'

'Convenient.'

'Are you saying that I was connected to my granddad's death? Or to the people who committed his murder?' Katherine rose, the fury in her voice clear. Farringdon held up a hand to stop the conversation.

'Of course not,' she reluctantly responded, as Damian looked back from the kitchen, sipping at his coffee.

'When you two have finished, I have a plan,' he said. 'I have a friend who works at the British Library named Max Larridge. He's worked with me on a couple of things in the past—'

'You mean those scams you perform.' Farringdon interrupted. Damian, ignoring her, continued on.

'—so he knows how to keep a secret. If I ask him, he'll keep whatever we do quiet until his grave,' he walked back into the room. 'If you pass a message to Max from me, he can wrangle it so the pamphlet is ready and waiting for us in the *Rare Books* reading room when you arrive.'

Farringdon nodded.

'We can do that,' she replied. 'But it's when *we* arrive.'

'Oh no,' Damian sat back on the sofa, coffee in hand. 'I'm done with all this. It killed Andy and sent my dad into a lorry, and I really don't intend to follow the family tradition.'

'You don't understand,' Farringdon leaned forwards, taking the coffee mug from Damian's hand and placing it back onto the coffee table. 'You don't really get a choice in this. If something is in this pamphlet, what if there's another clue we must solve, another riddle to decipher? We might still need your expertise in finding the next location. You said it leads to the Howard mausoleum, but whereabouts in it? What if there's one more place to go before this finishes?'

'I don't think so,' Damian shook his head. 'This will be the last location, I'm sure of it. Howard gave Hawksmoor full rein to build the mausoleum. If it's anywhere, it's there.'

'Well then, we find it together,' Farringdon was already waving to her agents to leave the room. 'And then you'll be free to go, all charges against you dropped.'

'All charges against us *both*.' Damian countered. Farringdon paused at this, as if going to argue, but then reluctantly nodded.

'Of course,' she replied. 'Both of you go free. And Miss Turner is free to go on with her life, on the condition that she doesn't cause the School of Night any more problems.'

Damian looked at Katherine. They both knew this was unlikely, but as they were intending to welch on the deal too, it wasn't that much of a worry.

'You'll have no more issues from me,' Katherine replied.

Damian glared up at Farringdon, but he was silently punching the air. If he'd pushed too hard to go with her to the Library, there was every chance that Farringdon would have decided against it and left him and Katherine here, with only Mister Sun and his CCTV camera for company.

Now, he had a chance to truly put this plan into effect.

'Well then, let's go,' he said, rising from the chair with a smile. 'No time like the present. If someone can give me a phone, I can get Max to pull the pamphlet for our arrival.'

And with that, Damian and Katherine followed Farringdon Gales and her School of Night agents out of the flat and into waiting cars, before driving off towards the Euston Road, and the British Library.

24

READERS ROOM

Built in 1997 by John Laing PLC, the British Library was either a miracle of modern design, or an eyesore and insult to book lovers everywhere, depending on who you spoke to.

Damian was definitely within the first group; ever since he'd first come here he'd seen the magic of the place. He'd spent hours musing in the Ritblat Gallery, a dark, side room off the upper ground floor, sitting on one of the cushioned benches, surrounded by glass cabinets holding priceless works of art and soaking up the history in the room; whether it was Shakespeare's *First Folio,* Mary Queen of Scots' death warrant, original sheets of music by Wolfgang Amadeus Mozart or even lyrics to *Beatles* songs, written by John Lennon on the back of a Christmas card and nestled next to Ian Fleming's *James Bond* manuscript. There were even pieces of the parchment that held the *Gospel of John,* if you went in for that sort of thing.

However the library itself was as un-library like as you could imagine. Walking across the plaza towards the main entrance, Damian couldn't help but stop to stare once more at the enormous statue to his left, a giant, twelve foot brass figure of a naked man, sitting on a large wooden seat, bent forward and bound to the plinth by a length of metal banding across his lower spine, his brows furled in concentration as he examines a measurement he has made on the floor with a pair of dividers.

The statue was of Sir Isaac Newton—although he was never known to have attempted measurements in the nude—by the sculptor Eduardo Paolozzi, and named 'Newton, after Blake'. It drew inspiration from a William Blake print, drawn in 1795, of a naked Newton on a cliff edge, leaning forward as he sat to measure the ground; and the statue was created to honour the outstanding scientist.

Damian silently laughed at that, as Blake's original print was actually a criticism of Newton, because he had turned away from nature to work on science. But nobody else, apart from maybe Farringdon, had any clue whatsoever about this more subtle history, one of a bound, vulnerable man, trapped in a role that he couldn't escape from, yet was strangely good at.

A bit like me right now, he thought to himself as they arrived at the main entrance. Farringdon looked to the four agents that had joined them, including the always happy Mister Sun.

'They'll check bags, but they won't check your person,' she commented as they joined the line to enter the library. Damian wondered why she'd bothered to mention this to her agents, but then remembered Mister Sun's gun back in the restaurant's kitchen, what seemed like years earlier; they were probably armed, she was letting them know that there were no metal detectors present, and that there was a large probability that they wouldn't be frisked once inside the library.

Shame.

Only Damian and Farringdon had bags. Damian had a satchel filled with his father's notebooks, brought on the lie that 'they might be needed for research if they found another clue', while Farringdon had a small side messenger bag that held a variety of assorted pens and papers. Both were opened up as they entered, the guards giving these little more than a cursory glance using a small probing stick with a light on the end. Once they were through, Damian turned to see the agents also entering with no problem. Although he needed them out of the way, he was happier with them inside the library.

Far easier to contain when all hell broke loose later.

'Where's your friend?' Farringdon asked, looking around. To the left of them was the library shop and an entrance to a special exhibition. Across the lobby to the right was another small shop and a coffee counter, while in front of them were two sets of stairs, one leading up to the upper ground floor, the other down to the cloakrooms, with an information and ticket booth bridging between them.

Damian shrugged.

'I don't know,' he said. 'I mean, it's not like you allowed me to have a long conversation with him or anything. He's probably by the reading room.'

'Which one?' Farringdon frowned as she looked about. 'Rare Books? Or would it be in Maps and Antiquaries, with Hawksmoor's other works?'

'Rare books,' he replied.

Farringdon nodded.

'The Rare Books and Music reading room is on the first

floor,' she said, turning towards the escalator that led up to the upper ground floor, and the King's Library Tower, a four sided-column of glass and black brass, with shelves of books visible as you passed. It was the centrepiece of the museum, reaching six storeys high from floor to ceiling, and holding the *King's Library;* over sixty thousand books, and twenty thousand pamphlets collected by King George the Third, within. However, as she moved, Damian grabbed her arm to stop her.

'Come on, Farringdon, you know we can't go into the reading rooms like this,' he muttered, showing the bag. 'And when we enter the rooms, the security will check us over a damn sight more thoroughly than the guys on the door.'

Farringdon thought about this for a moment and then nodded, turning to the cloakrooms on the lower level. Glancing at Katherine, Damian followed her.

Here, a large, blue sign gave information about what could and couldn't be taken into the reading rooms, what was acceptable and what was banned. Visitors could then remove any banned items and place these in the cloakroom, while items that were permitted could be transferred to clear, plastic bags for ease of security, or carried on the person.

Yes, you needed a reader's pass to show on inspection as you entered the reading room. Yes, you were allowed pencils, and clean, dry hands were a necessity, as many of the books were ancient. Laptops and phones were allowed if you had the sound off, and cameras were permitted as long as you didn't use the flash. However, no pens or highlighters were allowed, no scissors could be used, no food, drink, bottled water or even gum could be taken inside the rooms, and more importantly coats, bags and umbrellas were specifically banned, most likely to stop people stealing rare books or parchments.

This meant that by the time they had finished, Farringdon and her men were bag-less and jacket-less, their weapons probably hidden away inside the jackets which were now hanging up in the cloakroom while Damian's satchel hung on hanger number '21' beside them.

'That's better,' Damian grinned. 'All friends together.'

Now ready for the reading room, Damian led the small group of people up to the first floor by the upper ground floor escalators and a small, spiral staircase to the left. Arriving at a walkway, a pine wood lined corridor led them to the doorway of the reading room itself. But before they could enter, Damian paused for a moment and looked down over the balcony to the lobby below.

Entering among the morning visitors, a cap over his head to hide his face was Martin Shrewsbury, Cyrus walking in behind him.

'What the hell is he doing here?' Damian looked back to Farringdon, pointing towards what he had just seen, allowing her to follow his finger to Shrewsbury. 'Are you working together?'

'No,' she denied, pulling Damian to the side to keep him out of the way. 'He must have been watching your place and followed us here. Or he had a lookout nearby who called him when we arrived. Maybe you're right, even. Maybe we *do* have a mole.'

Damian chanced another glance down to Shrewsbury, now examining the frontage of the shop. He hadn't found the correct clue in Middle Temple Hall, and because of this had travelled off once more to Deptford, and a church that was nothing more than a red herring.

And even if he had returned to Middle Temple hall, if Mark had been persuaded against his better judgement to give him the correct details, leading him to St Alfege Church, the chances were that Cyrus and Shrewsbury would have either followed the current Unicorn's horn towards the Naval College and the Queen's House, or found himself as equally lost about St Anne's Limehouse as Damian himself had been. After all, the clue they were hunting for in the British Library was completely made up.

Damian still didn't have any idea where the genuine treasure was currently located, or why Hawksmoor had written 'The Wisdom of Solomon' on the side of a forgotten pyramid. And he sure as hell hoped that he hadn't lucked upon the correct answer while sending Farringdon on her wild goose chase.

There was therefore no reason for Shrewsbury to be here unless someone had tipped him of their arrival.

'If he's hunting us, we need to get going,' Katherine said as they turned to the doorway.

Where, standing patiently, was Max.

'Interesting message you sent me,' he said. 'You in trouble?'

'In a way,' Damian replied as he embraced Max warmly. 'Good to see you, man. Thanks for helping.'

'I can't not help the man who's put money into my pocket now, can I?' Max grinned, pulling away. 'And who are your friends?'

'This is Katherine Turner and Professor Farringdon Gales,' Damian introduced each in turn. 'I don't know the names of the others. They're part of some kind of package deal with Professor Gales.'

Max nodded, looking at the agents, all currently trying to 'fit in' with the library's décor.

'Sorry about Andy,' he whispered. 'I'm guessing this is to do with finding the killer?'

'We already know the killer,' Katherine muttered. 'He's downstairs, looking for us.'

'Then we'd better get you inside then,' Max nodded to himself, as if mentally going through a checklist. 'Right, let's get you into the room.'

The group moved forward, but Max stopped.

'Only Damian, Professor Gales and Miss Turner, I'm afraid,' he said.

'What?' Farringdon was obviously trying to keep her temper. 'None of them have pens, or books or whatever bloody silly other things you ban here.'

'Oh, I know that, and I appreciate the gesture,' Max replied. 'However, they don't have reader passes. I know Damian has one and I've also heard of you, Professor Gales, so I know that you're on our records. Miss Turner would be a private guest of Damian's, of which we can waive the rules and allow. I'll waive the requirements for ID and suchlike, as I know you're pressed for time.'

Farringdon's jaw set as she stared at Max.

'Well then, one of these men is my guest.'

Max smiled, although the warmth didn't reach his eyes.

'No guests allowed, I'm afraid.'

'This is stupid,' Farringdon exclaimed. 'You just allowed her in!'

'Did I?' Max shrugged, still not budging as Damian leaned over to Farringdon.

'Look,' he breathed. 'There's no way out of the reading room except for this entrance, right? So keep your guys here. They can go get their jackets back. I know they'll be happier with their guns. Have one follow Shrewsbury, see what he's looking for. He might have a different clue, and not even know we're here. Meanwhile, we'll go in, find the book, check for notes.'

Farringdon shook her head, looking at her agents as she did so.

'This isn't what I agreed,' she grumbled.

'I might have a suggestion,' Max interjected. 'There's a scan of the book on the reader's network, and you can access that from any PC in the British Library. Or there's a microfilm we can order for you.'

'No. It needs to be the original,' Farringdon argued.

Max shrugged.

'Then it's the three of you or nobody,' he replied. 'And remember, I'm doing this as a favour for Damian, not you.'

Farringdon went to speak, and Damian wondered if she was about to throw some serious School of Night weight around, but then her shoulders slumped, and she nodded in agreement.

'Fine,' she hissed as she looked back at the agents with her. 'Grab your jackets, keep guard, and if anything happens, let me know what's going on.'

She pulled out a business card, giving it to the closest agent.

'My number's on that,' she said. 'Any issues, call me.'

It was only a glimpse as the card passed by, but Damian caught the number. It was one he recognised.

'Excellent,' Max said with a smile once more. 'Let's go see that pamphlet then.'

The Rare Books and Music reading room was the same as all the reading rooms within the British Library; an open space filled with row upon row of small tables, with room for readers on either side, ten benches deep, a small wooden barrier upon the back of each desk creating a small 'wall' between facing readers and providing power sockets for laptops. Each table had a light, while some had grey, cushioned book rests for the more important documents.

Half of the tables were already occupied, the readers either writing notes on laptops or taking photos of manuscripts with cameras for examination later in the day, or to be examined elsewhere. Around the walls of the room were ceiling-high shelves of books, mostly leather bound, and to be honest, that was the most 'library' thing that Damian had seen since he arrived.

Across the room was a chest top desk, with the words 'Reservation Enquiries' above it. To Damian's right was a long, similarly high counter with 'Book Returns' above it. A middle-aged lady stood at this one, glaring at the newcomers, but her expression soon brightened as Max walked over to her, speaking a few words into her ear before passing to enter a small room behind her. He returned with a small, leather bound booklet, holding within its pages a pamphlet, no larger than a smartphone in his hands. Looking back at Damian, he nodded towards an empty table across the room. Damian walked towards it, Farringdon and Katherine following him as they met Max at one of the cubicle spaces. He passed the booklet over to them.

'*The curious collection of original pictures, prints, drawings and books of Nicholas Hawksmoor,*' he said as Damian examined the front of the pamphlet. '*To be sold at Auction, at Mister Lambe's April 1740.*' Twenty-seven pages in total, bound into leather at some point for its survival, and last requested by your father almost eleven years ago.'

'Anyone else looked at it since?' Farringdon asked, staring at the booklet as Damian opened the first page carefully.

Max shook his head.

'Funny enough, it's not a popular book,' he replied, looking back to Damian. 'Anyway, if you need me for anything else, just give me a call. I have to go back to my proper job and do some work now.'

'Thanks,' Damian said, embracing Max one more time. 'I owe you.'

'You've done enough for us,' Max replied with a grin. 'This was nothing in return.'

And with that, Max left the reading room, leaving Damian, Farringdon and Katherine to glance down at the booklet.

But Damian wasn't looking at the booklet. He was thinking about the phone number on Farringdon's card. It was the same phone number Andy had texted in Manchester. The same number that Conlan had shown Damian the previous day in a police interview room, highlighted on a list of numbers called from Andy's phone.

Damian replayed in his mind the moment that Cyrus had raised the gun to shoot Damian.

'Wait! I told her I'd only help if there was no killing!'

Her. Andy had been speaking to a her. Not Cyrus, not Shrewsbury, but a female. Could it have been Farringdon Gales? Like a fool, Damian had escaped Shrewsbury and then run straight to her. As he looked back to Farringdon, concentrating on the cover of the booklet, he remembered another moment, back in the Eagle and Child, when she had spoken about Richard Evans.

'I saw him about a week or so back. He'd been in Antwerp for a few weeks.'

Farringdon, the old friend of Richard Evans, saw him only days after he returned, having found the one clue he'd chased after his entire life. Of course Richard would have told her. Maybe not the details, but he would have said he was one step closer, maybe hinted at something more to come. Gullible, misguided Richard could never help himself.

And Farringdon Gales told Martin Shrewsbury. It was the only plausible answer that made sense. Farringdon Gales, and by default the School of Night, had made some kind of arrangement with Martin Shrewsbury. What it was, Damian had no idea, but he could make a calculated guess. A finder's fee perhaps? Even ten or twenty percent of this believed hidden wealth would end up in the billions. Maybe Farringdon was sick of the School of Night's slow bureaucracy and was doing this alone? Either way, she'd sold out Richard Evans, sending him to Shrewsbury and his death, and she'd spoken to Andy, promising him riches and giving him a bullet for his troubles.

There had to be more to this, though. The gauntlet's message wasn't to do with gold, it was more to do with legacies. Whose legacy, though?

'Also remember that the School didn't just hold the gold as its only secret. Look for where Marlowe went.'

Farringdon's last words before Damian and Katherine had left Oxford echoed in his ears. What was Marlowe's connection here? What did Farringdon mean when she said where Marlowe went? Heaven? Hell? Deptford? Abroad, even?

One thing was for certain, though. Farringdon wasn't lying when she said that she wore a lot of hats. The question was, what hat was she wearing right now?

He returned to the moment, realising that Farringdon was talking to him.

'You said there might be a note inside, or something perhaps in the margin,' she said, but then stopped, her face paling. Slowly and carefully, she placed the booklet onto the desk, and with great care, pulled at a small, folded sheet of parchment paper, removing it from the pages on either side, and opening it up to show its true size.

It was smaller than the other pages, but not by much. The paper was of a different stock, a better one, and on it were faintly scratched mysterious symbols around the sketch of a marble head and bust, wearing a Roman toga, placed upon a marble plinth. Under the sketch were small outlines showing a small, spiral staircase.

'This isn't part of the book,' Farringdon whispered. 'They look like designs by Nicholas Hawksmoor.'

Katherine leaned over, examining it carefully.

'The symbols, they're the ones from the Sunne Dial,' she replied, looking up at Damian. 'This must be why your father didn't get any further, as he didn't have the cypher. Nobody had the cypher until you found it two days ago.'

'And now Martin Shrewsbury has it,' Farringdon muttered to herself. Damian smiled, rummaging in his pocket, pulling out his own notebook. Opening it to a set page, the corner of it turned in for ease of finding, he showed Farringdon a page filled with these cryptic symbols, an A to Z written underneath, and only a couple of blank spots.

'I've translated several of these now,' he explained. 'And because of this I know most of the letters.'

'Oh, you clever boy,' Farringdon smiled, patting Damian on the shoulder. 'So you can translate this?'

'I can at least try,' Damian said as he went to take the

paper, but Farringdon stopped him, placing her hand upon his.

'I think we need to check the authenticity of the paper first, don't you?'

'Of course, yes we must,' Damian replied, looking around the room himself. 'But, without an age testing kit around here, I can't see the woman behind the counter being okay with us clipping off parts of the parchment in front of her.'

'Then we need to find a way,' Farringdon muttered. 'I don't know why Robert left this note in a random book, but something doesn't smell right. And until it does? We've got nothing.'

His face expressionless, Damian looked at Katherine. Their exit out of here was reliant on Farringdon believing their lie, but the moment she tested it outside, she'd know something was wrong.

The whole plan was about to collapse, and there was nothing Damian could do about it.

25

CHAOTIC ESCAPE

WATCHING FARRINGDON, DAMIAN NOTICED SHE WAS NERVOUS, looking around the room as if expecting someone, possibly Martin Shrewsbury, to enter at any moment. Katherine had noticed this too, and Damian wondered whether this was because Farringdon was considering the possibility of keeping the treasure for herself.

'Of course we can take it out of the room, idiot,' Katherine faked a smile as she spoke. 'The library has a pamphlet on its records. This one, bound in the booklet Max gave us. We took it out, looked at it, and now we're giving them back the same item. As far as they're concerned, nothing's been taken, as the note was never part of the collection it was placed into.'

Damian made a point of thinking about this.

'But what if Shrewsbury gets it as we leave?' he asked. 'We know his bodyguard's out there with him, but what if he has more men? I don't want to get this far and lose it to chance. Maybe we should at least work out what it means before we leave.'

Farringdon thought for a moment, mulling over the

choices she had to make. Damian knew that in her mind, she was working out the logistics of learning the location before giving the sheet to Shrewsbury. Maybe the thought of taking all the money for herself, of the School of Night finally rediscovering the treasure was finally overriding her loyalty, or even her fear of Shrewsbury and his friends.

'Fine, but let's do it fast,' she urged. Damian was already noting down letters at speed as he read through the symbols.

'It's another poem,' he said, after a couple of minutes of placing letters onto the paper, crossing them out, replacing them, playing the part of the code breaker. '*Seven objects, seven towers, marked to show the key; the eighth however shows the light the penitent man sees.*'

He looked up at Farringdon, watching her carefully for a moment before continuing.

'Inside is death but stands alone the one turned night to day, so turn his head towards the light to show a hidden way.'

There was a moment of silence once Damian had finished. Farringdon leaned forwards and took his notebook, swiftly and deftly tearing the page out of it.

'No offence, but I don't want anyone else knowing this,' she said, almost apologetically. Damian shrugged.

'Go wild,' he said.

Farringdon looked back down at the piece of torn paper in her hand, and the riddle translated on it.

'Seven towers, well that has to be the towers around the Howard Mausoleum that we spoke of this morning,' Farringdon mused. 'And you said back then there were seven magical items described in the Key of Solomon.'

'But there are eight towers,' Damian replied. 'How do we know which one is the eighth?'

'Marked to show the key,' Katherine chimed in on cue.

'Maybe something small, somewhere that only someone who knows the riddle can see, the seven items in the Key of Solomon are marked on each tower. We simply need to find the tower that doesn't have a marking on it.'

'Inside the mausoleum is a statue of William Howard, or at least a bust of him. He has to be the penitent man,' Farringdon was already pacing around the room. 'He was deeply religious, he constantly fought for causes that contradicted his beliefs.'

She paused as a reader *shhhed* her. She went to reply, thought better of it, and returned to the desk, lowering her voice.

'And the bust has him in robes, maybe it's the sackcloth of a man asking for forgiveness?'

She looked at the riddle once more.

'You said earlier that he also brought attention to the School of Night, revealing its identity to people. That could be what's meant here by *bringing night to day*; the School of Night was revealed, and no longer able to hide in the shadows.'

'Of course!' Damian nodded eagerly. 'So turn his head towards the light to show a hidden way. It's a lock! Twist his head, and by that they must mean the bust of Howard to the right angle, aim it at the correct tower outside the pyramid— that's easy enough to do as the towers are at each corner— and there's got to be a lock that opens, a hidden entrance.'

'To Hawksmoor's stolen gold,' Farringdon whispered. 'It's almost too good to be true.'

It *was* too good to be true, mainly as the note had been written only four hours earlier that day, carefully scrawled on a sheet of aged paper with falsified ink by Damian as Katherine attempted to put the riddle together.

'We should go there immediately,' Damian said, looking at Farringdon. 'We could leave now, get out of London before the lunchtime traffic hits and be there by late afternoon.'

This was the moment where Damian knew Farringdon would falter. Of course, she should do just that, as this is what a woman that wanted the treasure would do. But the chances were that she was intending to pass this note and information to Martin Shrewsbury the moment she could lose her agents, just for a instant, possibly within the British Library itself. And, at the same time, there was still the slightest concern this wasn't a genuine sheet, that it was a forgery.

And she was right to think this, because the note had actually been inserted quietly in the pamphlet by Max as he went into the back room, away from sight for moments before he brought the book to them. The note itself, written by Damian that night, had been in his pocket when Farringdon and her men had arrived at the apartment, and Damian had passed it to Max when they had embraced upon meeting. Even the second embrace had served a purpose; Max had secretly slipped Damian the British Library pass of the middle-aged lady at the Returned Books Counter, taken when he leaned in to speak to her while picking up the pamphlet before leaving.

The whole plan had been to show Farringdon that Damian really believed this, so that the moment they escaped, Farringdon's first thought would be that they wanted the gold for themselves, and would therefore race them to Castle Howard, fearing that Damian knew where the clue led, while in reality Damian and Katherine would travel in a completely different direction.

However, before Farringdon could decide on a course of action, noises seeped through from the main entranceway.

What sounded like bullets firing, and then a variety of terri-fied human screams.

As the readers rose from their stations, looking to the reading room entrance in a mixture of concern and fear, Damian could see wisps of smoke appearing in the entranceway.

Downstairs, four men had passed through the security barriers with ease; with no bags or briefcases this was nothing more than a cursory glance, a nod to the guards and then a pass through into the lobby area, and the moment they gained access, they had pulled on rubber masks from their jacket pockets and stopped in the middle of the lobby, each pulling out streams of firecrackers, lighting and throwing them into various corners of the lobby.

At the same time two of the men, one of whom bore a strong physical resemblance to Pietr the Russian, pulled from their pockets two smoke grenades, removing the pins and tossing them up onto the upper level. The sound of bullets firing and smoke billowing through the upper levels not only caused instant chaos among the visitors, now all running for the exit, but also made sure the Library was in lockdown as the four men, using the smoke for cover removed their masks, mingling with the confused visitors.

Damian didn't need to see what was going on to know what was happening, for he had planned this earlier that night, and Mrs Hamilton had passed the message when she had left her apartment, hunting for more coffee. This had been the request he had made to Isabella and the Russian mob, passed on by Max. Damian hadn't been sure whether they would help him, but obviously the thought of a payday now three times the original investment was deemed worthwhile.

Or maybe they felt more of a kinship to Damian now he was a fugitive from the police.

Whatever it was, Damian knew Shrewsbury would now be torn between following Farringdon or leaving the Library as quickly as he could; the last thing he wanted, as the poster boy for the alt-right, was to be found at the site of a suspected terrorist attack on a respected London institution. He would probably run with the other visitors out of the library while Pietr and his Russian friends, now unmasked and in the crowd, would be escorted out through a safe exit by Max, who was waiting for them by the cloakroom.

And now it was time for Damian and Katherine to leave.

Looking at Farringdon, currently watching the tendrils of smoke as if she thought they would attack, Damian spoke softly.

'Did you arrange the accident that killed my dad?' he asked.

Farringdon turned to stare at him, for the first time actually thrown by the situation.

'What? I don't know what you mean,' she replied.

Damian nodded, as if making his mind up about something.

'Or was it Martin Shrewsbury?' he continued. 'Were you working with him back then, or is that a recent addition?'

'Look, I've no idea what this girl has told you—' Farringdon started, but Damian raised a hand, cutting her off.

'The phone number you gave your man at the entrance; it was the same number you spoke to Andy from,' he said. 'Did you know Martin was going to kill him too?'

Farringdon went to reply, but then thought better of it, her body language altering, becoming more aggressive.

'Martin Shrewsbury was the only one who listened to us,' she replied, the words a hiss of anger. 'Richard Evans, your father, they thought us too extremist, that the School had lost its way.'

'How do you mean?' Katherine asked. Farringdon shrugged.

'The true heir to the throne should be English,' she said. 'Not *immigrant*.'

Damian stared at his onetime friend and suddenly everything fell into place.

'You're one of Shrewsbury's supporters,' he said. 'You're hoping he's the true King of England and if not, this is all to help him get there.'

'With the money we find, he can hold the world to ransom,' Farringdon continued. 'No nation will risk that much gold entering the market. It'd kill all currencies.'

'You want more than that,' Katherine said, her own body language now mirroring Farringdon's. 'You want Martin Shrewsbury to be King. But it's really difficult proving he's of Royal line, and even if you could, there's no proof that he's the true heir to the throne.'

'DNA is overrated, and often open to bribery in these sort of cases,' Farringdon smiled. 'Once we find Henry's proclamation, we can prove the line through Elizabeth and Robert Dudley. The *legal* heir to the throne.'

'And this is why you killed my grandfather?' Katherine stepped forward now.

'Richard had a chance to choose the winning side,' Farringdon said, backing away slightly. 'I tried so hard to convince him that it was the right thing to do, but he wouldn't have it. He was only ever interested in the damn gold, never the lost heir.'

Even Damian could see the sudden anger Katherine was exerting. But Farringdon couldn't help herself. She made a mocking sigh as she continued.

'I don't know why you're so concerned about him,' she continued. 'After all, he was a terrible grandfather to you. He took away your childhood, made you follow his quest, inducted you into a society of rejects—'

With a low growl, Katherine swung a vicious roundhouse punch at Farringdon, connecting hard on the jaw and literally taking the elderly academic off her feet, sending her sprawling to the floor. Grabbing her arm, Damian pulled Katherine away.

'I'm not done yet,' she hissed, pulling her arm away from Damian.

'We go now, or we don't go at all,' he replied. Katherine looked to him, her eyes cleared, and she nodded, spitting at the still downed Farringdon.

'We're not done,' she hissed, allowing Damian to lead her to the back of the Reading Room, passing the stunned readers who now watched as Damian and Katherine ran for the locked door.

'You know, we were closer to the front entrance back there,' Katherine whispered as they reached the door, Damian rummaging in his pocket for the ID card Max had given him earlier.

'On any kind of terror threat, no matter how small, security will have locked the main entrance doors,' he exclaimed, pulling the ID card out and swiping it. 'They'll be turning up and unlocking it soon, bringing us all out in a group, and leading all non-staff to the front entrance.'

The door opened with a click.

'Staff, however, have a different exit,' he smiled as he

opened the door, leading Katherine through as he looked back to Farringdon, getting to her feet while clutching her bruised jaw, and glaring at him.

'See you in York!' he exclaimed as he slammed the door behind him, effectively locking Farringdon in with the other academics.

He knew that even with her own security coming to free the room, it'd take Farringdon a good couple of minutes to find a way out of the front entrance; more than enough time for Damian and Katherine to leave the Library via a different route.

Following the corridor to a small flight of stairs, taking these two at a time, he used the stolen ID to open the door at the other end and led Katherine out into the first floor Terrace Restaurant, nestled to the back of the British Museum, and as far away from the main entrance as you could get. Now empty, there was nobody to see Damian and Katherine run past the glass-walled café, pausing only for Damian to lean over the counter and grab his satchel, placed there by Max after retrieving it from the cloakroom, before continuing towards the Fire Exit that led onto the outside patio.

However, before they made it to the doorway, one of Farringdon's agents, performing a search of the floor, walked around the corner and now faced them.

Damian was quicker, though; before the agent could even reach for his gun he moved in fast, chopping up with the edge of his right hand, catching the agent's throat. As the agent staggered back, coughing and gasping for breath, Damian grabbed the lapels of his jacket, yanking them down, and bringing his knee up hard, connecting with the agent's nose. As the agent collapsed to the floor, now unconscious and bleeding from the face, Katherine grabbed Damian and pulled him through the exit.

'I could have done that,' she hissed.

'I know, but I was protecting you.'

'I could have done that quicker.'

In the distance, the sounds of police sirens could be heard, but Damian ignored this, moving across to the right of the patio area, past some tables and over to a black, metal gate to the right. Once there, he tapped his stolen ID against it one last time before opening the gate and tossing the ID aside. After all, the last thing he wanted now was to be found with someone else's ID on his person, friend of Max or not.

The gate led to another flight of stairs that went down two floors, opening out onto a car park at the rear of the Museum. Fifty yards away, there was an entrance, now filled with confused members of staff. Slowing down, Damian and Katherine passed among them and out onto Midland Road beside the Francis Crick Institute. Casually, yet keeping an eye of the melee behind them, Damian and Katherine crossed over towards the large chrome and glass entranceway of St Pancras Station.

'Your plan worked,' Katherine said, breathing out a sigh of relief as they continued across the station towards the platforms. 'It looks like Farringdon really will go straight to York.'

'And as she does, we go the other way,' Damian stopped at a ticket machine, picking up two tickets from it, paying cash to make sure he couldn't be traced. 'We're going back to my family home near Canterbury. You may have forgotten, but we currently still have no idea what *The Wisdom of Solomon* even means,'

Damian passed her a ticket.

'We need to get ahead of the game. We need to go over my dad's notes.'

'I thought you had them?' Katherine pointed at the satchel.

Damian shook his head.

'These are just what Farringdon was given by him over the years, or what they found after he died,' he explained. 'The good stuff is back home. That, and a hopeful solution to this conspiracy.'

He stopped.

'You knew this already, didn't you?' he asked. 'The message Richard gave you. *Take him home.* You were always going to go with me back to my dad's house.'

Katherine shrugged.

'Granddad was always ambiguous with words,' she said. 'Maybe he meant a different home?'

'Or maybe he left something for me there,' Damian commented as he looked up at a screen of timetables. 'The next train's in five minutes. If we can make that, there's no way they'll catch us before it leaves.'

He stopped talking, staring across the station. There, smiling, with Pietr beside her, was Isabella Vladimov.

'Damian, darling,' she said as they walked over, 'so good to see you here.'

Katherine glanced at Damian's expression and wisely kept her mouth shut.

'What are you doing here?' Damian asked. Isabella laughed.

'Why, waiting for you, of course!' she said. 'After all, we are partners in this treasure hunt, yes?'

Damian looked now at Katherine as he replied to

Isabella. 'I didn't say anything about a treasure hunt,' he said cautiously. 'I just said I'd pay you back more.'

'More than you could ever hope to make from a normal scheme of yours,' Isabella replied. 'And after speaking with your friend Max, and learning about your family, I now know you fight with Martin Shrewsbury.'

'Is that an issue?' he asked.

Isabella smiled.

'We have history with him and his companies,' she said. 'After all, I am legitimate businesswoman. And if he is looking for whatever you look for, then it is a treasure hunt, yes?'

'I think you're overestimating the value of what we're looking for here,' Damian suggested. Isabella shrugged.

'You pay me what you owe, that is good business. You pay me what you owe at Martin Shrewsbury's expense? Even better, as it becomes personal.'

She held up a train ticket with a smile. A ticket for the same train that Damian and Katherine were about to catch.

'Come, my friends,' she finished. 'Our train is about to leave.'

26

HOMECOMING

DAMIAN HADN'T GROWN UP IN CANTERBURY; THE HOUSE THAT his family had lived in since he was a small child was seven miles outside of the city, and closer to the coastal town of Whitstable. Canterbury itself was where Marlowe was born, where he was raised, and where there were a dozen different places that Damian could have gone to research a whole variety of issues, but the only place he needed right now was the family house.

What he didn't want to do was bring a Russian Mafioso to it.

At Canterbury, a van had been waiting for them; Isabella's connections had meant that she simply called ahead for some muscle to meet them. The train journey had been difficult, mainly because Isabella kept asking about the gold. Eventually Damian had told her the legend, spending the next half an hour of the journey explaining in great detail the fact that there was probably no money left. This gave Isabella some concerns about Damian's ability to pay her the money he'd promised; but he quickly cleared that up by informing her of his plan. Well, at least the plan of a plan that he had.

Now outside Whitstable, the van pulled up outside the ornate, five bedroomed, detached house at the end of a seemingly nameless narrow country lane. Katherine climbed out and looked up at the building, whistling as she did so.

'You own this? Lucky bugger,' she said. 'This has to be worth close to a million, easy.'

'Yes. No. Probably,' Damian replied, standing by the van, watching the house. 'The problem is that I can't sell it.'

'Why not?' Pietr asked. 'Would solve all problems. You could just give house to us. We give good price.'

'Yeah, I bet you would,' Damian said. 'The problem is that when my parents died, I wasn't in a good place. They wrote a stipulation in the will. I can't sell the house until I'm thirty. Which is a while away.'

'So why don't you live here?' Katherine asked. Damian shrugged.

'I preferred London,' he said darkly. 'That is, until my best friend was murdered and I was under house arrest. Now, I'm liking the countryside a little more.'

Pietr nudged Damian. 'So move in now, yes?'

'I can't because the house is rented out, and I'm currently a wanted man,' Damian explained. 'Dad's notes are in the cellar, held in storage. And if we turn up asking for them, I'll be recognised.'

'So we need to get these people out,' Isabella mused. 'That's simple.'

'No,' Damian replied. 'I don't need that sort of help. I'll get them out my own way.'

Isabella nodded, ignoring the accusation, and waited. Damian thought for a moment.

'Although can I use your phone?' he eventually asked.

Isabella nodded to Pietr, who passed Damian his phone. Using the browser to google a number and then tapping it in, Damian waited for it to answer.

'British Gas? Hi, I'm walking down Mulberry Close, just outside Whitstable—yes, that's the one. Incredibly strong smell of gas coming from somewhere. Can someone come and check it?'

He waited, smiling.

'No worries. Just doing my civic duty and all that.'

He disconnected the line, and then immediately tapped in another, more familiar number.

'Ah, is that Mason's Lettings?' he eventually asked down this line. 'Great. Nigel Parkinson here, British Gas. We have a reported leak on Mulberry Close, and we're asking residents to evacuate the area until we fix it. No, only half an hour, tops. But if one house creates a spark...'

Damian waited.

'Exactly. Anyway, our records state that one of our customers is a Damian Lucas, but the house is rented? Yeah, we're not legally allowed to speak to the tenants. Data protection and all that. Could you call them and let me know if there's anyone in there, and if so, ask them to evacuate the house? Cheers.'

As Damian muted the phone, Isabella clapped her hands. He held a finger up as a faint voice could be heard the other end.

'No, absolutely,' he said. 'Call our head office, and they'll give you the gas leak report number.'

Another wait and then, faintly, over in the house, a phone ringing could be heard. After five rings, it stopped.

'Someone was in,' Katherine muttered. 'Or it hit answer-phone which means they're not.'

Damian had disconnected the phone now; the call had been made, and now they needed to wait. After a couple of minutes, two middle-aged men left the house, got into their car and drove off.

'You okay?' Katherine looked to Damian. He shrugged.

'House is rented by a family,' he replied. 'Neither of those two looked familiar.'

He started towards the house.

'We'll have at least half an hour before British Gas gets here,' he said as he stopped by the gate, pulling over a large stone and taking a small rusty key from underneath.

'Old backup key,' he explained, opening the door and stopping in the entranceway.

The house had been ransacked.

Drawers opened, papers strewn all over the floor. Furniture overturned, pictures hanging at awkward angles as if someone had moved each one to check behind for secret safes. Rugs pulled up, as if hiding secret trap doors in the floorboards. The whole place had been picked through. This wasn't a quick, opportunistic attack, this had been methodical.

Katherine looked at Damian.

'Well, at least we know who those two men were now,' she said. 'The call from the estate agent, saying British Gas were coming probably spooked them.'

'This wasn't a burglary,' Damian muttered as he walked angrily into the living room.

'How do you know?' Katherine looked around again. 'I mean, it bloody well looks like one.' She looked to Isabella accusingly.

'It wasn't me,' Isabella replied. 'For a start, we would have made it look like a burglary. Stolen jewels and moved them somewhere, a rival maybe. This way to aim the police at someone else.'

'Well then, it's a good job it wasn't you, then.' Damian forced a smile, but it was a hollow one.

'What now?' Katherine picked up an overturned coffee table. 'I'm guessing that whatever notes were left in the cellar are probably gone now.'

Damian paid no attention to her, deep in thought as he walked across the hall, opening up a door to an equally ransacked back room, a large, unused fireplace in the middle.

'This used to be dad's office,' he explained as he entered.

Glass statues, broken beyond recognition, were scattered across the carpet, as if whoever had been here had simply given up on niceties, and simply started throwing everything over their shoulder as they hunted for whatever they needed. Making his way carefully across the glass strewn floor to the fireplace, he reached up into it, as if searching by touch.

'Maybe the notes aren't gone,' he replied as he slipped a finger into a small recess in the chimney, picking out a small, golden key with his fingernail, showing it to Katherine.

'A safe?' Isabella asked. Damian shook his head.

'I don't know,' he said, sitting on a chair, staring at the key. 'There's a little cubbyhole in the chimney where dad would put important papers. It's where I found the sheets I stole. I was actually hoping the notes would be there.'

'Dangerous place to put papers,' Pietr muttered.

Damian shook his head.

'The chimney's blocked off,' he replied. 'No fire.'

'Well, a key will always fit a lock,' Katherine took the

golden key, turning it in her hands as she examined it. 'It's a key for a mortice lock.'

Damian rose, taking the key back as he looked at it once more.

'So a door,' he said. 'But which door?'

'Maybe there is more clue up chimney?' Pietr suggested. Nodding, Damian crouched back down, reaching back up.

'There's a piece of paper up here,' he said, pulling a small scrap of notepaper out. Folded, it stated one word.

DAMIAN

Opening the note. Damian grinned ruefully.

'What?' Katherine asked. Damian passed her the note.

'Marlowe named him Little John.'

'What's that supposed to mean?' Isabella, already bored with this, took the paper from Damian, seeing if there was any other message written on it. Damian shrugged.

'It's a last message to me by dad,' he said simply. 'It's probably his way of showing me what it opens.'

'So find the thing it opens.'

'I don't know what it is!' Damian snapped back. 'It might not even be in this house!'

Isabella turned to Pietr.

'I bore of this,' she said. I'll wait in the van outside. You can stay here.'

And with that, she left. Katherine started looking around the room, as if looking for a clue.

'Marlowe named who Little John? And why would he think you'd know this?'

'Because as a kid, I loved the idea that Marlowe was a spy. That a kid from Canterbury could be James Bond.'

'Dee was James Bond,' Katherine said almost unconsciously as she was examining book spines. 'Even signed his work with an '007'.'

'Dee was more Q than Bond, but Marlowe was definitely a spy. He was pulled out of University by Francis Walsingham to spy for him.'

'So who was Little John?' Pietr said. 'Is this like Robin Hood and Little John?'

'You know Robin Hood?' Damian was surprised.

'Of course. He was born in Kiev.'

'Did Farringdon ever visit your father?' Katherine ignored Pietr.

'Occasionally. Why?'

'Because Farringdon, back when we saw her in Oxford, told us to follow Marlowe.'

Damian shook his head at this, pulling out one of his father's notebooks and scanning through it.

'She said to follow where Marlowe went,' he replied. 'Which still makes no sense, unless...' he trailed off as he read a note written in the book.

'Of course.'

Pietr walked over, looking down at the note. 'What is 'of course' meaning?'

Damian pointed at a passage written on the page. 'Marlowe was believed killed in 1593, but before that he was working with Walsingham to capture a Jesuit spy.'

'But which one?' Katherine replied. 'There were loads back then. John Gerard, Nicholas Owen...'

'It's Nicholas Owen,' Damian read the book. 'Listen to my dad's note about him. *'He frequently traveled from one house to another under the name of "Little John" and accepted only the necessities of life as payment before he started off for a new project."*

He looked back up.

'Owen was arrested with John Gerard in 1594, but was under continual surveillance for years before that. It makes sense that Marlowe would have been watching him.'

'Owen was a master builder, but he was better known as the man who made priest holes for Catholics to hide in,' Katherine added.

'That's the clue? The lock is a priest's hole?' Damian looked at the key again. 'This could have been given to me a lot easier.'

'Maybe your father needed you in a state of mind to work this out?' Katherine suggested. Damian shook his head.

'I don't think he ever expected me to return to the house, or even search up there,' he said, looking at the fireplace. 'And ancient as this house is, it's not old enough for a priest hole. Where do we even start?'

'The basement,' Katherine started towards the door. 'You said the notes were kept down there.'

'Yeah, but that said, I'm not sure if the current tenants would have kept them safe.'

'I don't think they even knew they were down there.'

Leaving the study and walking into the hall, Damian gathered his bearings. Across the hall, and under the stairs, was a small white door. Opening it, he revealed not an under stairs cupboard, as most British houses had, but a set of stairs going down.

'Basement,' he explained as he turned on the light at the top of the steps and started down them. Katherine and Pietr followed Damian into what looked like a very basic utility room. The plasterwork was showing signs of age and neglect. Unlike the other rooms in the house, this was a simple space, with no windows, a variety of exposed brickwork, and a single lightbulb hanging on a cord from the ceiling.

To the side, as you left the steps, were a combination of washing and dryer machines and a large, top opening freezer, all plugged into an over-extended plug socket. Across the room was a shelf of power tools, DIY manuals and cooking books, with a variety of old furniture; chairs, stools and small side tables piled up against the wall next to the shelves in case they were ever needed again, a small off-white light switch the only other adornment.

'Looks like they didn't come down here,' she said.

Damian showed a couple of discarded lever arch files that had been pulled from the end of the shelves, household bills and takeaway menus scattered over the floor.

'They looked down here,' he replied. 'They just didn't stay long.'

Damian stood in the middle of the basement, looking around.

'This is off,' he muttered. 'The sizing is wrong.'

Turning to the left, he walked to the wall. Facing the basement, he now paced across the room to the other side. Nodding, he walked to the wall beside him and did the same again, counting each step as he walked.

'The south wall is nearer than it should be,' he stated.

'How can you be sure?' Pietr walked to the wall, examining it.

'Beams on the ceiling,' Damian replied. 'They're spaced apart the same as upstairs, but there's one less.' And with that, walking over to the power tool shelf beside Katherine, Damian tapped the wall, feeling his way along it.

'There's a light switch here,' he said. 'But the switch is on the wall at the top of the stairs. Why would you have one here?'

He flicked the switch; nothing happened. He grabbed the light switch housing, and with a firm, twisting motion, pulled it off. The switch and the moulding were fake, placed into a housing attached to the wall, a small cover to hide a small keyhole. Damian placed the key into the hole, twisting it anti-clockwise with a click. This done, he grasped the metal struts of the shelf and pulled the whole shelf unit away from the wall. The shelf moved easily; small castors were at the bottom of the shelf, unseen until it moved. And nestled behind it and completely invisible when the shelf was against the wall, was a small door.

'A secret room,' Katherine said, impressed.

'Come on then,' Damian said. 'Let's go investigate my dad's secret life.'

27

PRIEST HOLES

THE ROOM ITSELF WAS SPARTAN. THE BRIGHT WHITE WALLS were better prepared than on the other side of the wall, but gave it the overall impression of a hospital waiting room. Three metal filing cabinets stood to one side, and a mahogany bookcase to the back wall stood silently, half filled with musty old leather books. A basic pine desk with drawers, a chair beside it, and a waste bin were the only other items of furniture in the room.

'Cosy,' Katherine said. 'Place has a real '*Silence of the Lambs*' vibe to it.'

Walking to the desk, Damian laughed.

'You have to remember, dad had a study upstairs,' he said. 'That's where he did the bulk of his work. This must have been where he worked on things that couldn't go out there, things that were most likely treasonous, or career suicide for an academic like him.'

He shook his head.

'No, I can't believe he did anything treasonous. He was an academic.'

Pietr, examining the door frame, looked back to them.

'With a secret room,' he grinned. 'You have many academics here with those? Only people with secrets have rooms with doors like this. Look, there is a lock this side, and a rope to pull the shelf back in outside the room. You attach the light switch back over the lock after you open the door, enter, shut and lock the door and pull the cord? Nobody would know you were in here.'

He closed the door to prove his point.

'Secret. I do not think you knew father as well as you think you did.'

Damian looked around again, as if imagining his father in there with him, sitting at the desk.

'I always believed he came down here for a crafty smoke.'

'You couldn't know the truth,' Katherine was examining a filing drawer. 'You were a teenager at best.'

Seeing nothing of interest, she turned back to Damian.

'And when you came back, you were suffering withdrawal. You were otherwise distracted.'

Damian hunted through the bookshelf.

'The problem we have is that I'm far from distracted right now,' he explained. 'There are three things we should be doing. First, hunt down the answer to whatever Hawksmoor was on about, when he said to follow the Wisdom of Solomon. Whatever that leads us to will hopefully be the last resting place of the lost gold. Getting there before Shrewsbury or Farringdon is key. We all have the same clue.'

'Do we?' Pietr looked uncomfortable at the door.

Damian nodded. 'Pretty much. I'm guessing that Farringdon passed it on. So it's a race. And the only advantage we have is we sent them the wrong answers.'

'And what are things two and three?' Pietr was still

looking unhappy. Damian shrugged as he continued rifling through the books.

'Two, we know Martin Shrewsbury wants to find a proclamation that Henry the Eighth was an illegitimate ruler and the Plantagenet line was the true line of Divine Right. But even with that, it doesn't help him with his own legitimacy, unless he has the line of descent, so we're onto number three, where there's a very strong possibility that Arthur Dudley's son was raised by Christopher Marlowe under a fake name, and that his children, and his children's children, and on and on down to the modern day, whoever is the current eldest son or daughter will be the true Plantagenet heir, and true ruler of England.'

He paused, looking at the now pale Pietr.

'You okay?'

'Shutting door to your father's treason room was mistake,' Pietr explained. 'I do not like being confined. It feels like Federal Government Institution. Prison.'

'You can wait outside if you want,' Damian suggested.

'Isabella—'

'Said to stay in the study, not come down here,' Katherine interrupted. 'Go wait on the stairs, it's a little more open there.'

With a relieved smile, Pietr nodded and, opening the secret door once more, left.

'If it wasn't for the fact he can be a vicious bastard, I could start liking him,' Damian said, pulling a leather-bound notebook from the shelf. 'If we can find the proof that Arthur lived, we find the line. The line shows who the ruler is. The proclamation proves that they have a valid argument for the throne. And the gold gives them more money than God to force the issue.'

He tapped the leather book.

'Luckily dad was an expert on Christopher Marlowe. Had it all written down. That said, dad kept saying it was in the realms of make believe and conspiracies. You can make everything seem believable; just look at what we did last night.'

Placing the book on the desk, Damian flicked through the pages, quickly scanning each one as he ran his finger down the page. Finished, he went to close it but paused as he glanced at a flyer on the desk. Picking it up, Damian looked at it further as he spoke.

'This is a flyer for the event my dad went to the night he died,' he said. 'Recognise anything?'

He passed the flyer across to Katherine, who examined it.

'Looks like a book launch in Oxford. That's a hell of a drive from Canterbury.'

Damian turned the flyer over.

'Farringdon,' he placed the flyer into the leather book. 'It has to be. My father only ever went to the library there, or drove up to meet with her.'

'She never said he'd been to the event?'

'It never came up.'

Damian stopped as quickly as he had started. The flyer had been covering a laptop, the power lead still plugged into the side. A small, slim one, it had a post-it on the top, one word on it, written in the same handwriting as the note they had found hidden behind the painting.

DAMIAN

Attached to the side of the laptop was a small USB flash drive. On it, in silver sharpie, were the words

PLAY ME

Damian fell into the chair, staring at it.

'We need to see what your father has to say,' Katherine said softly, opening the laptop and pressing the power button. The file window of the USB stick came up on the screen. There was only one file, an mp4 video file. Nervously, Damian pressed on the icon to play it.

A window appeared. In it was a question.

WHAT WAS MARLOWE'S NEW NAME

Under it was a space to type a word in, seven letters long. Damian stared at the window in a mixture of horror and shock.

'I don't bloody believe it!' he said. 'All this way and it's another bloody riddle!'

'Well, it's one we need to work out anyway,' Katherine tried to reassure Damian, picking up the leather book and opening it. Damian leaned back.

'Marlowe was killed during a staged Deptford brawl on the thirtieth of May, 1593. He then goes to Spain, finds Arthur's son, and apparently brings him back.'

'So Marlowe would have brought him back when, though? A year later? More?' Katherine thought for a moment. 'It'd take a while to get new, fake papers. Say 1594, maybe 1595.'

'Too soon,' Damian replied. 'He'd need a good couple of years to help people forget him. Especially with Gerard being arrested in 1594. Also, he would have to change his appearance. Say three years. That makes it 1596.'

'He'd need to find a place to keep low.'

Damian shook his head. 'Marlowe could never keep his head down. The whole reason for his faked death in the first place was because he was too much of a showman, couldn't hold his tongue.'

'Marlowe was liked, right?' Katherine was walking around the study now. 'So, it makes sense that he'd go back to people he knew, that he trusted. Thomas Walsingham, for example, would have been able to ferret out a couple of solid identities. And the plague was around then. Plenty of deaths, new identities to take.'

'Okay then,' Damian leaned over the leather book once more, scanning through the pages, looking for someone, a name that could assist him. 'Someone who turned up in London around 1596, hung out with Marlowe's old friends and re-entered society…'

He paused, his finger now on a name.

Thomas Heywood.

'He was an Elizabethan playwright and actor,' Katherine nodded. 'To be honest, I'm surprised I didn't think of him earlier. Granddad went on about him all the time. He was convinced that he was connected to the School somehow but could never prove it.'

'I don't know his work,' Damian thought for a moment. 'No, wait. He edited a couple of Marlowe's plays, that's as far as I know. That, and it was a page of his I sold to fuel my drug habit.'

'He did more than that, and he's perfect,' Katherine exclaimed. 'First off, no one knows when he was born. According to granddad, it was between 1570 and 1575. When was Marlowe born?'

'1564, so at best there's only a six years' difference, and Marlowe looked younger than his age,' Damian added, reading from the page. 'Also, it says here that Thomas was 'robust and ruddy faced', which pretty much means fat and tanned. Three years hiding in the Spanish sun, or even travelling across Europe, would do that. Okay, what else?'

Katherine thought for a moment. 'Heywood claimed that he'd been to Cambridge University, but there was no proof. All that was confirmed was that he had a working knowledge of the place. Which Marlowe, as a graduate, would have known.'

'So currently we have a man with an incredibly sketchy past.'

'It gets better,' Katherine replied, warming to the task. 'Granddad had a copy of a playbill from October 1596, when Philip Henslowe, who ran half the theatres in London, commissioned a play from Heywood for the Admiral's Men to perform.'

'Definitely one from Heywood?'

'Debut commission.'

Damian whistled as he looked to the ceiling, as if imagining the scene in his head.

'It's almost unheard of for an unknown,' he said. 'Usually the playwright is an actor who has earned that spot.'

He looked back at Katherine as a thought crossed his mind.

'Henslowe was a good friend of Marlowe,' he said. 'He paid Marlowe's gambling debts in the past, and after Marlowe's death, the Admiral's Men pretty much continually performed all of his work, something they'd done also in the years leading up to his death.'

Katherine nodded, pointing at a line in the book. 'And by 1598, less than two years after his arrival in London, Henslowe's diary had Heywood written in the ledger as a player in The Admiral's Men but given no wage.'

'He did it for free?'

Katherine shook her head. 'He'd have received shares in the company, something that only important company members could achieve.'

Damian nodded to himself. 'Not within two years of arrival, they wouldn't. Anything else out of the ordinary?'

'Oh, yes. In fact, it's something that nobody's been able to explain,' Katherine replied. 'You mentioned he edited a couple of plays, but it went further. Heywood was a prolific author and playwright, but never courted royalty. And within a few years of his arrival there was a new King in town in James the First. Heywood lived in Clerkenwell until around 1641 when he died. However, in 1633, he sponsored a new version of Marlowe's *The Jew Of Malta*, adding a new prologue and epilogue to the play; effectively re-writing Marlowe's work. It was said that people couldn't tell which lines were written by Heywood, and which was the original Marlowe.'

'Ballsy, rewriting someone's play like that. Although perhaps not as ballsy if it's your own, I suppose.'

He pulled open one of his father's notebooks, a line niggling at the back of his mind.

'Dad wrote something about Heywood,' he said, flipping through the pages. 'I saw it when I was in Mister Sun's car—'

He stopped, reading out a piece of text written in a corner of a page.

'Heywood wrote a line about Marlowe in his 1635 *Hier-*

achie of Angels. He said that *Marlowe was renowned for his rare art and wit, but could never attain beyond the name of Kit.'*

'Words written by a friend, but Heywood never met Marlowe,' Katherine smiled. 'And odd he talks about 'Marlowe' never attaining anything while *named* as such.'

'Did Heywood have children?' Damian wondered. Katherine considered this at length but then shook her head.

'Nothing I recall saying he had a wife, but then a lot of the stage folk back then weren't that big into women.'

She thought for a moment.

'That said, I remember granddad talking about Heywood once, saying that when the Admiral's Men became Prince Henry's Men in 1604, there was a note in Henslowe's diary saying that Thomas's son Robert was cast as *Ebea, the maid* in a production of Marlowe's *Tamburlaine the Great.* It was common for teenage boys to play the smaller female parts. So, Robert would have had to be no older than fourteen or fifteen. Any older, and his voice would have broken.'

'If we say that Dee saw Arthur's baby in late 1589, then that would fit perfectly.' Damian smiled. 'And Robert is a fitting family tradition name. I think we know now why Richard wanted you here with me at this moment.'

He leaned over to the computer and, in the space for the answer, typed in seven letters.

H - E - Y - W - O - O - D

This done, he pressed return.

There was a moment when nothing happened, and then a video started playing. It was recorded in the very room in which they sat in. A lone man, speaking some of his last ever words into a camera, possibly hours before he died.

But it wasn't the man Damian had expected.

'Hello Damian,' said the visual ghost of Richard Evans, looking out of the laptop screen at Damian and Katherine. 'If you're watching this, it means that I'm dead.'

28

MESSAGE FROM THE DEAD

KATHERINE STARED AT THE LAPTOP SCREEN, TEARS STREAMING down her face as she watched the recording of her late grandfather.

'I know, I know, it sounds a tad dramatic, but it's true,' Richard Evans said. 'If I'm still alive, the chances are I'd already have told you not to listen to this, but such is life. I hope you don't mind me sneaking in while your tenants were out. And sorry about the clue to find the room, Damian, but I know your father never told you about this place. I think he was probably ashamed of it, a shrine to his dirty little hobby, his secret.'

On the screen, Richard paused, as if realising he was rambling.

'I'm not staying long though, as I think I'm being followed. I'm going back into London tomorrow, I need to see Temple Inn Church again, so hopefully they'll have given up by then.'

'He recorded this the day before he died,' Katherine whispered.

Damian stared at the man on the screen. Richard looked more tired since the last time they had seen each other. But then he had been running all over Europe in the intervening time. And even after a couple of days, Damian knew he looked a state.

On the screen, Richard held up a piece of paper.

'I'm not sure if I'll be able to pass this message to you, so I thought I'd give it here, just in case,' he said. 'Found it in Antwerp. I'd gone there after finding a clue to the location in Middle Temple, of all places. Did you know that Robert Dudley has a suit of armour made of etched steel that was bought from there? Anyway, after a few clues and one-way streets, I found myself in an unmarked crypt in The Cathedral of Our Lady in Antwerp, and a line of text that was most likely placed there by John Dee before his death.'

Richard smiled.

'Did you know he had connections in Antwerp? He printed his Monas Hieroglyphica there. And he transcribed Johannes Trithemius's Steganographica there in the 1560s.'

'He never knew how close he truly was to finishing this,' Katherine muttered to herself as the ghost of Richard Evans continued.

'So anyway, the text was in Enochian, the old language of John Dee, but reads 'Among books, pirate treasure leads to Satan's step'. And I really believe that it leads you to Chetham's Library in Manchester. I don't think I'll be able to check this though, as Shrewsbury's people will follow me. I think it's Shrewsbury, at least.'

Damian leaned forward, pressing a key and pausing the video.

'He knew that Martin Shrewsbury was hunting him. Even back then.'

Katherine leaned back, wiping a tear from her cheek.

'Bloody fool should have called me earlier,' she replied. 'I could have helped him.'

'I think in his own way, he was trying to keep you safe,' Damian replied, pressing 'play' once more. 'But you're right. He was a bloody fool to go it alone.'

On the screen, Richard Evans shifted uncomfortably in his chair.

'Yes, Shrewsbury,' he started. 'If I die, he'll come looking for you. Fascist dickhead of the highest order. Spent ten years trying to prove that he was the last true Plantagenet, convinced that with this proof he could topple the Royal Family, as if they need anything else to topple them, what with princes leaving for the States and others being accused of... Anyway. He had your father looking into it for him for a long time, paid him handsomely for it, too. But Robert never found the proof that Shrewsbury was from Plantagenet descent. Not from Richard, of course, but from Perkin Warbeck himself.'

He coughed, took a mouthful of water, and continued.

'Marlowe was Heywood, but he had no child. He adopted a Spanish boy, the son of Arthur Dudley. Now why give a damn about a bastard? Well, your father was convinced that there was a rather important secret wedding, and that paperwork still exists to prove it. Maybe. I don't know.'

'St Alfege,' Damian muttered.

'Of course, there's more to this,' Richard continued, not hearing Damian's reply. 'Your father did further research, and learnt that there was a real strong chance that Arthur Dudley's great-grandfather was a bastard himself, that of Perkin Warbeck and Elizabeth Grey. But there's a belief that before she married Edmund Dudley in 1503, she secretly married Perkin. If this could ever be proven, it'd mean the second marriage was bigamous and unlawful, and that her son with Perkin, John Dudley, was a legitimate Plantagenet. As you can imagine, having both marriage certificates would make anyone's claim valid. And, if you believe the story that Wolsey and Bonner possessed the proclamation from King Henry giving Warbeck the crown, well then there's a damned good court case there.'

'Looks like we were bang on the money,' Damian said. 'Apart from Perkin and Grey being married.'

'Now here's the thing,' the video continued. 'Shrewsbury wanted the proof and the money. He's swayed Farringdon to his cause, so don't trust her, she's become a bit of a bitch recently, but more importantly, and this is the main reason for this video, he's also the one that killed your father.'

Damian almost fell over as he stood up quickly, staring down at the screen.

'I didn't know until recently, when I realised just how deep Farringdon was with him,' on the screen, Richard leaned closer, as if scared that someone would overhear his last words to Damian. 'Arthur Dudley's line now goes through Robert Heywood. And for years we've hunted proof of this. The day of your father's death, he received a call confirming the name of the last surviving descendant of Robert Heywood, and by default Arthur Dudley, through Robert Dudley and Queen Elizabeth. It was him, boy. Your father. And, by default of his death, it's now you.'

'Jesus,' Katherine paused the recording. 'I swear, I didn't know this.'

'It has to be a joke,' Damian shook his head. 'I can't believe this.'

'Your dad spent years looking into this. You said this yourself. What if he suspected, but needed to find out for himself?'

'Shrewsbury pays my dad to prove he's the legitimate King. My dad then learns that *he's* actually the proper heir.'

He picked up the flyer for the book launch off the table.

'He goes back to the library in Oxford, maybe to check this clue. He knows he's being watched, so he uses this as an excuse, makes out he's there to see Farringdon. Maybe Martin Shrewsbury is around, too. He tells them his findings, probably thinks he's saving Shrewsbury a ton of hassle, doing him a favour. On the way home there's car trouble. Maybe the brake's been cut. After the crash there was no way to see if there was any foul play, and to be honest the police, as I did, just accepted Farringdon's word, that my dad had been angry about something and had driven off in a rage.'

'That could still be true,' Katherine replied. 'If he gave his findings, it wouldn't have gone well with either Shrewsbury or Farringdon. He rows with Shrewsbury, goes to leave, doesn't realise that someone fixed his car. Taking him out of the equation means that Shrewsbury can still make the claim. They didn't know he'd written this down, and you were pretty much a lost cause at this point. They probably thought they could buy you off with some smack.'

Damian went to reply, angry at the accusation, but stopped, nodding.

'You're probably not wrong there,' he said. 'But now he knows it's a false claim. He looks for the money. Trillions now in gold that, if put into the market, could destabilise everything. He's going to *buy* his way in.'

Sitting back down, Damian pressed play once more, and Richard Evans sprung back into life.

'I know, it's probably a lot to take in. You're the true Plantagenet heir, and through a vague technicality, the true King of England, God knows if you want such a bloody thing these days. But there's no paperwork, so there's nothing to prove this. All I know is that Farringdon Gales and Martin Shrewsbury caused your father's death. I'm sure of it.'

Richard Evans leaned back, rubbing his face with his hands before leaning back in.

'Find the gold before Shrewsbury and Gales do, Damian. Don't let them bastardise everything your father had done,' he smiled. 'Of course, I might do it myself, and this is all pointless. And we'll watch this at Christmas and laugh about it. But to be honest, Martin Shrewsbury is a brutal, Nazi bastard and I don't think I have long to plan my next move. That and the fact that I have stage four cancer. Surprise! So, if I die of that first? Take it as read that I still want you to beat that bastard.'

Damian noted Katherine was now crying, and he put his arm around her, allowing her to sob quietly into his shoulder. Richard was winding up his message, already gathering up his items on the screen.

'One more thing, I'm hoping you've found my grand-daughter, Katherine,' Richard finished. 'You used to play with her when you were a kid and if I remember correctly, you had a bit of a crush on her.'

Katherine looked at Damian at this.

'She can help you a lot with this, probably even opened this file for you, and she'll keep you alive better than anyone else would. I'm hoping she's right there with you.'

He paused, his voice cracking with emotion.

'Katie, I'm sorry for dragging you down with me on this damn fool crusade. When this is all done, you need to get on with your life, to think of the future rather than looking to the past. And know that even though I never really told you, I love you dearly. And I've never been prouder of you.'

Katherine kissed her fingers and held them to the screen as Richard finished his message.

'I don't think Henry Tudor knew the crap he'd have to deal with when he did his tour around England. That centuries later, his proclamation would cause such misery and death. Maybe if he did, he'd have dispensed with the theatrics and just got on with stuff. Talking of which, I need to get on with things. Off to London, couple of places to revisit before my own clock runs out. I wonder if my shadows will return?'

With that, Richard leaned forward, taking the camera—and the message stopped.

Katherine rose, moving away from Damian as she attempted to wipe her eyes with her hand.

'You okay?' Damian asked. Nodding, Katherine looked back at him.

'Ghosts from the past,' she whispered. 'Hurt more when you never expect them. Let's get on with this.'

Katherine wiped a last tear.

'Okay, what do we now know that we didn't before that?' Damian asked.

'You're King of England,' Katherine smiled. 'And if I'd played my cards right when we were kids, I could be Queen now.'

'And what a kingdom you'd have,' Damian chuckled. 'Apart from the lack of anything and the Neo Nazis wanting our toys. What else is there?'

'Possible marriage certificate for Perkin. Probably locked away with the other documents.'

Damian nodded and then stopped.

'Henry Tudor's tour,' he muttered. 'I'm a bloody fool.'

'What do you mean?' Katherine stared after him as Damian ransacked the shelves, hunting through old leather-bound books, discarding them as quickly as he picked them up, constantly searching through them.

'I mean that your grandfather just solved the last puzzle without realising it,' Damian explained, tossing aside another book before picking up another. 'I might not be an expert at history, but there's one thing I know about Henry Tudor. After he defeated Richard the Third at Bosworth, he went on a triumphant tour of England, visiting his new subjects and ending in York, in 1486.'

'You know this because?'

'We almost forged something to do with it once,' Damian smiled. 'Andy kept going on about it for days before we gave up.'

He opened a book, flicking to a page and reading it.

'Listen,' he said, reading from the page. 'Henry arrived at the York boundary, where he was met by York's aldermen and sheriffs. They took him to the mayor, who led him to Mickle-gate Bar, the royal entrance to the city. On the route towards Stonegate, he passed York citizens dressed as all six previous King Henrys, and a woman dressed as the Virgin Mary blessed him. William Poteman, the Provost of Beverley Minster and dressed as King Solomon, greeted Henry, stating that Henry 'governed by righteous providence', and gave him an ornate sceptre, stating that Henry now had 'the wisdom of Solomon'.

'*The Wisdom of Solomon,*' Katherine repeated the line. 'It could be a coincidence.'

Damian pulled another book out of the shelf, flipping

quickly through the pages until finishing at a particular page, pointing at a sketch of a choir screen.

'In 1716, Nicholas Hawksmoor was hired by Beverley Minster to help with restoration of the north wall, which was close to collapsing. His work took weeks to complete, and in doing so required extensive excavations.'

'He worked on the crypt?'

'No. Unlike every other church, minster and cathedral around at this time, according to the parish records Beverley Minster never had a crypt.'

'Hawksmoor hid the crypt then?'

'Quite possibly. Officially, the north wall was collapsing partly because of the Chapterhouse next to it having been demolished in 1548.'

'So Hawksmoor worked on the north wall?'

'And in other areas.'

'St Anne's Limehouse was finished a decade later. It would have been easy to leave the clue. And Hawksmoor went rogue in late 1714 after Queen Anne's death, so doing this a year or two later would make sense, too. And if there was a crypt, perhaps also leading under the Chapterhouse, one that was lost when the building was demolished...'

'There's a good chance that Hawksmoor hid the gold there and then blocked it up.'

Katherine looked back at Damian, her eyes wide.

'We might have just found the last resting place of the Plantagenet Gold,' she whispered, frowning as she saw Damian's face. 'What's wrong?'

'Beverley Minster is thirty miles west of York,' Damian replied. 'And it's also about thirty-five miles southwest of Castle Howard. Of all the places we could have sent our enemies, we've picked a location that is positioned almost next to the bloody place. And once they realise they're in the wrong location, it won't take them long to learn the truth, especially with York connected to Henry Tudor and the pageants.'

'Then we just have to get there first,' Katherine replied. 'A train can have us there by this evening. And I don't think that they'll have given up on Howard that quickly.'

'I might have an idea,' Damian mused as he looked back at the laptop. 'But it's one you might not like. The gold is important. We need to find a way so Shrewsbury and Farringdon don't get it. But at the same time, I'm still wanted for murder, and I want Martin Shrewsbury and his bald buddy Cyrus to go down for both Andy and Richard. And maybe even my parents.'

'How are you going to manage that?'

Damian smiled.

'I was thinking that once we get to Beverley, we invite everyone to come and play,' he said. 'I think we need to end it right there.'

Walking out of the room and sealing it back up behind them, they walked to the stairs where, at the top by the door, sat Pietr.

'So?' he asked.

'We need to go to York,' Damian said as they made their way out of the house, wiping down any surface they touched. After all, when the real tenants came home, they were likely to call the police about the attempted burglary.

'Isn't that where you sent everyone?' Pietr asked as they left the house.

Damian nodded.

'Yeah, kinda hoped you wouldn't remember that,' he said.

Pietr looked to the van, where Isabella waited in the front passenger seat.

'She won't like that,' he muttered. 'Long drive.'

'She doesn't have to come,' Katherine replied. 'I don't recall asking her in the first bloody place.'

'We need her. And Pietr,' Damian said as he walked to the van, tapping on the window. Isabella looked at him for a moment and then let the window lower.

'I owe you a hundred grand, right?' he asked.

Isabella nodded.

'But we have helped you too,' she replied. 'Cost will go up.'

'As it should,' Damian said, holding a hand up to stop Katherine from replying. 'So, let me make you an offer. One I think you'll like.'

Isabella nodded, allowing him to continue.

'You help me get to York, you help me finish this, and I guarantee you that by the end of today, you'll get a quarter of a million pounds,' Damian said. Katherine grabbed him, turning him around.

'Are you insane?' she exclaimed.

Damian smiled.

'Probably,' he replied, 'but I have a plan.'

'You have problems paying us one hundred, but you find more than double in a day?' Pietr looked from Isabella to Damian. 'This sounds like another scam.'

'No scam,' Damian turned back to face the Russians. 'In fact, I'll tell you right now where it'll come from. Martin Shrewsbury himself.'

Isabella opened the door, climbing out of the van and facing Damian.

'And why would he give us this?' she asked.

'Because he'll think he'll be getting much, much more,' Damian replied, holding out a hand. 'What do you say?'

'What will he get?' Isabella didn't take the offered hand. Damian left it there.

'Public humiliation, prison and probably the loss of everything,' he suggested.

Isabella smiled. 'Then we have a deal,' she said, finally shaking the hand. 'When do you need to be in York?'

'As soon as we can,' Damian replied. 'After I set up a couple of things, that is.'

Isabella looked at the driver of the van.

'Call ahead,' she said. 'We need the helicopter prepped and ready to fly.'

'You have a helicopter?' Damian was stunned. Isabella smiled.

'I have a man with one who owes me almost as much as you do,' she replied. 'He lets me use it, or he finds himself leaving it one day, while in the air.'

And with that chilling reminder of his debt, Damian looked one last time at his family home before climbing into a van owned by Russian gangsters and heading to a country airport, passing a *British Gas* van hurtling in the other direction.

29

CHOICES MADE

DETECTIVE INSPECTOR CONLAN WASN'T HAVING THE BEST OF days. Yesterday, she'd captured the believed murderer of Andrew Holdman, but within a matter of hours they had forced her to pass both him and the girl who had been arrested with him over to Domestic Counter-Terrorism for 'special duties'. She didn't know what this entailed, but there was one thing that she knew for sure. As far as Domestic Counter-Terrorism was concerned, the police were surplus to requirements here. Within an hour of Lucas being freed, they had already moved Conlan off the case and onto something else. Damian Lucas was not their jurisdiction or concern anymore. And that pissed her off immensely.

Leaving New Scotland Yard, Conlan emerged onto the Embankment and, with a huff of annoyance, crossed the road, walking over to the riverside pavement so she was staring across the Thames at the London Eye as she lit up a cigarette. Memories of the conversation that Conlan and Briggs had with Damian Lucas kept returning as she looked out across the water. The self-assured conviction that he had, when stating what he honestly believed to be truths. And then there was the statement that he had made, the statement that had shaken Conlan as she looked into it;

'You have me at the scene of Andy's murder, but as a witness, not a suspect. There's no CCTV showing me killing Andy, nor is there a murder weapon. You won't believe that Martin Shrewsbury is the actual killer, even though I'm sure if you checked thoroughly, you'll see that his car was in Manchester at the time, and coincidentally he was at Middle Temple today when we were. He's chasing me, I'm in fear for my life and Katherine Turner, who I honestly assumed was a genuine police officer, was assisting me in proving my story. Show me a scrap of actual evidence that proves that I'm the killer or release me.'

After Damian was taken by Domestic Counter-Terrorism, Conlan had travelled to Middle Temple, where she had spoken with one of the security guards there, his story confirming what Damian had said. And then there was the issue with Chetham's Library. Security footage of the building had unaccountably vanished five minutes leading to and from the murder, yet nobody there could explain how this happened.

However, after checking, Conlan had also learned Martin Shrewsbury's car was seen by traffic CCTV in Manchester, driving up earlier in the day, and then travelling back down to London within minutes of Damian's arrest. And more than that, Shrewsbury's mobile phone had also pinged in the Manchester cell towers. She'd taken this information to her superiors, hoping for an opportunity to look further into the case but within minutes of applying for a warrant, she'd been given other duties.

And then there was the phone call she had just received. A Detective Inspector from Deptford named Warren, who'd seen Damian Lucas the day of the murder, and who had CCTV footage from Greenwich showing Richard Evans being forced by a tall, bald man into a limousine, the same limousine that a variety of witnesses had seen Richard Evans leave in Deptford, mere minutes before he died at St Nicholas's church. Weirdly, the location that Evans had entered the limousine, a car registered to Martin Shrewsbury, was close to a small bistro where the police had received a tip off from the waitress stating Damian Lucas was sitting outside in a baseball cap and sunglasses a few days later.

Of course, she'd made the request for information while still on the case, and now she couldn't do anything with this. Nothing made sense anymore. Indeed, there was a very strong chance Damian Lucas was telling the truth, that he was indeed innocent, and there wasn't a hope in hell, bar a confession from Shrewsbury himself that Conlan, Briggs or anyone else could bring him in for it.

'That'll kill you.'

The voice was warm, conversational, but had a purpose. This wasn't some tourist having a chat. Conlan turned to face a young man, a pair of black Levis under a checked shirt, a pinstripe blazer trying to give him an air of professionalism while his brown curly hair roamed freely, giving him the appearance of a slightly confused academic. The man pointed at the cigarette.

'You should quit, Detective Inspector Conlan.'

'Is that a comment about the cigarette, or about something else?' she asked. 'For example, a prominent right-wing millionaire?'

'Shrewsbury? He's a dick and deserves everything that's coming to him,' the man said, holding out his hand, offering it in a handshake. 'I'm Max Larridge. From the British Library.'

Conlan shook the hand, still unsure what the hell was going on here. 'I hear you had a bit of a scare this morning,' she replied. Max shrugged.

'We occasionally get things like that. Of course, it was an interesting morning all around, what with Damian Lucas and Martin Shrewsbury both there as well.'

This caught Conlan's attention.

'Together?'

'Oh, hell no. Shrewsbury came in shortly after Damian did. But it was obvious he knew Damian was around.'

'Did Damian enter alone?'

'He had a pretty young friend, and a ton of what I think were government types. Oh, and Farringdon Gales. Nut-job professor.'

The name that was written on the request for Damian's release.

"Gales is Domestic Counter-Terrorism,' she said.

Max's eyes lit up, as if a piece of a puzzle had just been placed into position.

'And where are they now?' she continued.

'Ah, that's the sixty-four-thousand-dollar question now, isn't it?' Max smiled. 'Shrewsbury went outside when the madness began, followed shortly by Farringdon, but Damian escaped out the back door.'

'Why would he leave Farringdon?'

'Because Farringdon works for Shrewsbury,' Max said. 'Although if you've seen the texts that Andy Holdman sent, you'd know that already.'

'I would? How so?'

'Because he sent them to a phone owned by Farringdon

Gales, and she passed them straight on to Martin Shrewsbury. I'm guessing you can't check the validity of that, though, because they've probably taken you off the case. How am I doing?'

Conlan shrugged.

'Very well, although I'm unsure how a worker at the British Library knows about all of this, or even my involvement in this.'

Max looked back at Conlan, the smile now gone.

'Because I was told about it an hour ago, and asked to find you,' he said. 'Reception said you'd come out here for a smoke, and I'd been given your description.'

'You had? Who by?' Conlan knew the answer before she even asked the question. 'You've spoken to Damian Lucas, haven't you?'

Max nodded.

'He's a friend, and I don't enjoy seeing my friends in trouble.'

'He asked you to speak to me?'

'He wants you to clear his name,' Max explained. 'He's got a plan that will, he believes, get both Farringdon Gales and Martin Shrewsbury to admit their actions to him. He intends to record this, or at least find a way for you and your men to also hear it. Would that be enough for you to do something for him?'

Conlan thought for a moment. She knew that this would go against everything her superiors had said, that she'd be returning to a case that she'd been taken off, and she'd be gunning for a millionaire who could most likely destroy her career in one swift motion.

But on the other hand, if Shrewsbury had indeed caused

the murder of two people, then some time in prison would be exactly what was required.

'What does he want me to do?' she asked.

Max smiled, pulling out a flash drive.

'Well, first off, you should watch this,' he said. 'The password is 'Heywood', all capitals, and it might just explain what's going on a little. I'd suggest, however, that you don't show it to anyone else. It's kind of treason, in a way. After that? I'd get on a train to York.'

Conlan stared down at the flash drive in her hand. 'How do I—'

But Max Larridge was gone.

And Detective Inspector Conlan of New Scotland Yard had a decision to make.

30

THE YORKISTS

I<small>T WAS ALMOST FIVE IN THE AFTERNOON WHEN</small> D<small>AMIAN AND</small> Katherine finally arrived in York. Isabella had been true to her word and after Damian had made sure through a borrowed iPad that Max could both download and transfer Richard's message to his own flash drive, they had climbed back into the van and after a short drive Pietr had taken them to a remote airfield in North Kent, where a twin engine helicopter was chartered in her name. From there it had been an hour and a half's worth of flight time, with Pietr and Isabella joining Damian and Katherine as they sat in the back seats.

To be honest, Damian hadn't really paid that much attention to the flight, as he'd been going over his father's notes, still thrown by the video message that he'd seen hours earlier. Katherine however was worried; there was every chance that Martin Shrewsbury would have chartered his own helicopter to York; hell, he probably owned a fleet of them, and there was every possibility that either he or Cyrus might be at the heliport when they landed.

They needn't have been concerned; by the time they

arrived, Isabella made sure her people (or at least people loaned to her by someone else who owed a debt) had locked the location down. And once off the helicopter, they were quickly separated into two cars, each going a different direction.

This was part of Damian's plan, one he'd explained while heading through Kent. Isabella and Pietr would have their moment in the spotlight, but it wasn't yet; and for the plan to work, Shrewsbury couldn't know that Russian gangsters were helping Damian. If anything, Shrewsbury, and Farringdon for that matter, had to believe that Damian and Katherine were desperate and against a wall.

The car drove to the outskirts of York, dropping them off on Station Road, where they now peered across to the grey stone wall, atop a steep bank of grass, that surrounded York.

'I take it we don't have to climb the wall to get in?' Katherine asked. Damian looked around, as if trying to gain his bearings.

'Wouldn't be my first time,' he replied, turning left, the wall to the city now on his right. 'Yours?'

'Actually, no.'

'Come on, it's a bit of a walk from here.'

As they crossed over the road, Katherine pulled out a phone, a cheap and simple iPhone rip-off 'burner phone' that Isabella had given them on the helicopter.

'Should we call him now?' she asked.

Damian thought for a moment.

'Nah, let's make him wait,' he replied. 'I'm sure he's busy right now, anyway.'

'Helping Farringdon or watching her?' Katherine said. 'Do you think she went for it herself? Or did she run to him with the clue, hoping he'll give the School of Night some kind of finder's fee?'

'Which would you do?' Damian asked. 'If it was you?'

'Take the whole damn thing and to hell with the lot of you,' Katherine replied with a smile. 'Although with you being my King and such, I'd need to pay a tithe, I'm sure—'

She ducked, laughing as Damian threw a light punch at her arm.

'Hey!' she exclaimed. 'That's not kingly behaviour!'

By now they had walked through one of the large, pointed arches that allowed the road to pass through York's walls, turning left, crossing Lendal Bridge, and the River Ouse. Passing Lendal Tower, a small, thirteenth century stone tower that seemed more used as an advertising billboard for city cruises now, Damian and Katherine turned right, the buildings either side now more modern, red brick in design, with popular coffee stores and restaurants lining the sides, gradually changing into a variety of expensive clothing and jewellery stores as they moved out into the expanse of St Helen's Square, a grey slabbed, pedestrian quarter filled with Georgian townhouses now turned into expensive restaurants.

Looking around, Damian nodded.

'This'll do,' he said. 'We're almost there.'

He pointed along the Square to the left. 'That's—'

'Stonegate. I know,' Katherine said. 'Leads all the way into York Minster.'

She paused.

'Would Henry have come this way? When he came to York?'

Damian nodded down Coney Street.

'That's the quickest route to Micklegate,' he said. 'Makes

sense that he'd come this way, up Stonegate and into the Cathedral.'

Katherine concentrated on the square, as if trying to imagine the pageantry that would have greeted the victorious Henry Tudor.

'He could have met Solomon right here.'

Damian shrugged.

'If he ever did,' he replied. 'I mean, it could be a story, made up.'

'As long as Hawksmoor believed it, that's all that matters,' Katherine said.

Taking the phone in one hand, Damian used the other to pull a small business card out of his jeans pocket. It was the one Shrewsbury had given Damian when they last met at Middle Temple. Although that was only yesterday, it felt like a week had gone by. Damian dialled the number and waited.

It was answered on the third ring.

'Who is this?' the voice of Shrewsbury was unmistakable.

'It's the true King of England,' Damian replied.

There was a chuckle down the phone.

'Damian! You're still alive. How wonderful. And you're now just as deranged, it seems, as everyone else on his treasure hunt,' there was a pause, and Damian could imagine Shrewsbury waving to someone, possibly Cyrus, as he continued the call. 'What do I owe this pleasure to? I assumed you were with Miss Gales?'

Interesting. He doesn't know we're not with her.

'Why would you think that?' he made his voice calm as he replied, oh, so conversationally back down the phone.

'Because you were with her in the British Library, and you both left so quickly when all that nasty business with the fire-crackers and the smoke started.'

'Oh, I assumed you'd spoken to Farringdon since then,' Damian looked at Katherine, listening in on the phone beside him. Now was the point where they'd see if Farringdon was the loyal drone or the opportunist.

'Why would you think that?'

Damian sighed.

'I'll tell you what, Martin,' he started. 'Let's cut through all this pleasant-sounding crap. I know Andy was texting her and I know she contacted you. I know she was the one who gave Richard Evans to you when he found the clue in Antwerp, and she's been working for you since my dad was alive.'

He tried to hold back the anger in his voice, but he couldn't quite manage it.

'I'm not sure yet whether she was involved with you in my parents' murder, or whether you took that one alone, but I now know that after she found her clue in the British Library, instead of running to you like a good little sycophant, she's gone her own merry way north, with you following. How close am I?'

'Very,' Shrewsbury's tone was colder now. 'In fact, we're watching them outside Castle Howard as we speak. They're having a gay old time running around a mausoleum. I'm assuming it's a lie?'

'Why would you think that?'

'Because you're in the centre of York right now.'

Damian looked to Katherine, who shrugged. They knew Shrewsbury would try to pinpoint their location as quickly as possible, and there were enough background sounds to give that—even if Shrewsbury wasn't using high-grade tracking software—away.

'I know the correct location,' Damian replied. 'I sent Farringdon to Castle Howard to give me some time at home.'

'Your Hackney flat?'

'Parent's house in Kent.'

'Ah. Well, I hope you cleaned up.'

Katherine nodded at this. It *was* Shrewsbury's men who trashed the house.

'Oh, I didn't need to,' Damian forced a smile as he spoke. 'I found what I needed elsewhere. You didn't find the priest hole.'

There was a pause on the line, and Damian knew that he'd scored a strike. For the first time, Shrewsbury wasn't in control.

'The basement.' A statement, not a question. Damian kept quiet. He knew that on the other end of the phone, Martin Shrewsbury was silently kicking himself for not looking harder down there. Eventually, the voice continued.

'So, what is this then, some gloating?'

'Actually, I'm doing what you told me to do,' Damian said, walking across the square towards Stonegate. 'You said to consider you an option if I was arrested. Well, I was arrested, I'm still under suspicion for Andy's murder, and once Farringdon realises I've lied to her and sent her on a wild goose chase, I don't think either her or the School of Night are going to be helping me anytime soon with that problem.'

'This is a negotiation?' Shrewsbury sounded suspicious.

'In a way, I suppose. You see, I want my life back,' Damian stated. 'You can have the gold, I couldn't really give a damn about that. Although I'd appreciate it if you paid some Russians I owe money to, and give Katherine Turner the share that you were going to give to Farringdon.'

'Turner. I'm guessing she's the girl we saw in Middle Temple? The one that you claimed was the tour guide?'

'That's the one. She's part of a Hawksmoor-related rival of Farringdon's. She's been assisting me, and I thought it'd be a gracious gesture.'

'But you don't want the gold.'

'I just want this murder charge gone.'

'And the fact that you're the true King?'

Damian laughed at the lunacy of the call.

'Does anyone really want to be part of the Monarchy right now?' he said. 'Show me someone who can prove it, and I'll even let you buy me a crown.'

'You're telling me you can live with the fact that the murderer of your friend—'

'And Richard Evans. And maybe my parents.'

'—will go free?'

Damian paused. This was the moment where he really needed to sell this.

'Well, yes, that's an issue here,' he replied. 'You poisoned Richard and your goon shot Andy, and I can't prove it was you that fixed the brakes on my parents' car. But it was Farringdon who led them all to you. In a way, she...'

He let the sentence trail off. On the other end of the line, Shrewsbury chuckled as he connected the dots to Damian's implied comment.

'You know, Mister Lucas, I believe that I've seriously underestimated you,' he replied. 'Perhaps I should have worked with you from the start.'

'If you had, you wouldn't have had to kill so many people.'

'Okay, so what's your offer?' Shrewsbury had given up playing. 'I know you're in York, I'm assuming you want to meet with me?'

'Yes,' Damian agreed. 'Seven pm, St Helen's Square. Once you're there, I'll text you a location only a five-minute walk away. Come alone. No bald-headed enforcers, and no tricks.'

'How do I know you're not trying to lure me away from Castle Howard, so you can find the treasure yourself?'

'Because if I had suspected the treasure was there, do you seriously think that I would have sent Farringdon ahead of me?'

'Fair point. And if I refuse this deal? If I flood the town with people loyal to me, find you before this agreed time?'

'York is a town of very narrow streets and alleyways,' Damian continued. 'If I see one person out of place before I see you? I'm gone. And believe me, I've become very good over the last couple of days of being *gone*.'

'Why seven? That's two hours from now. I can be there far earlier.'

'My rules, my decisions.' Damian looked around the square as he spoke, seeing the end of day commuters already on their way to the station. 'Besides, it's rush hour and you're thirty miles away. It's going to take you a good hour to get here, anyway.'

'I don't know exactly what game you are playing, but seven it is,' Martin Shrewsbury sounded relaxed, as if organising a simple dinner date. 'I look forward to it. I might even honour the deal.'

Damian didn't bother to reply, disconnecting the call and taking a deep breath, exhaling as he bent over, forcing himself not to throw up right there in the square. Katherine watched him silently for a moment.

'Want me to make the next call?' she asked.

Damian shook his head.

'No, this is my stupid bloody plan, so I'll do it,' he replied, once more dialling a telephone number. After a moment, the phone answered.

'Who's this?' Farringdon's voice was terse, as if she was holding back her own frustration at the situation that she currently faced. 'Martin? Is that you?'

'How's the mausoleum?' Damian asked, keeping his voice light. 'I'm guessing you're having a ball right now with all those towers.'

'You little shit,' Farringdon spat the words out as she replied. 'How did you manage it?'

'You left me alone in my apartment with your biggest rival and Richard's granddaughter,' Damian replied. 'What did you honestly think we were going to do?'

'Well, I'm impressed,' Farringdon stated. 'And it takes a lot to do that. I underestimated you, still thought you were the drug-addled teenager who stole cash from daddy's wallet. What do you want?'

Damian looked at Katherine, her fists tightly balled as she held her own emotions in check. He knew very well what she wanted right now; and Farringdon wouldn't enter a room with that on the table.

'A deal.'

'Are you conning me, Damian? That's always your thing, isn't it?'

Damian held his breath, saying nothing. He knew Farringdon had to make the next move here.

And she did.

'Go on then,' she hissed down the phone. 'What's your plan?'

And so Damian told her about it.

31

BONNER'S RECTORY

'You said something in the British Library today,' Damian said. 'I wanted to ask you what it meant.'

'Before or after I was sucker punched?'

'Come on, Farringdon. We can both agree you deserved that,' Damian replied. 'I was talking about when you discussed the possibility of Shrewsbury being King.'

'What of it?'

'You said the true heir to the throne should be English, not immigrant.'

'And what of it?' Farringdon's voice took on a frosty edge. 'They call themselves Windsor, but they're not English. They're the house of Saxe-Coburg and Gotha. Germans; one's even defected to America. And Philip was a Greek who took the name Mountbatten to keep the British public happy.'

"That's not what I meant,' Damian persisted. 'You know damn well that Shrewsbury isn't the proper heir to the Plantagenet throne, because on the day he died, my dad told you *he* was, didn't he?'

There was a moment of silence.

'Yes,' Farringdon replied. 'But he told me he hadn't mentioned it to anyone, even your mother.'

'And so, when he died, you assumed that nobody else knew?'

'True.'

'Well then, it must suck to be so continually wrong,' Damian snapped. 'And I don't think your current poster boy for royalty is very happy with you for sneaking off and trying to gain the money for yourself. Or are you still claiming it's for the School of Night?'

'You've spoken to him?'

'Yeah,' Damian continued. 'And I think we all need to have a little chat, before I tell you the actual location of the gold.'

'You worked out... Of course you did,' Farringdon's voice was softer now, more resigned. 'So where and when?'

'Outside York Minster,' Damian said. 'Seven pm. I'll text you where to go. Come alone, and leave your friends, including the nice Mister Sun, somewhere far away from you.'

'Will Martin be there?'

'Yes.'

'Will he be armed?'

'I don't think killing is the sort of thing he likes to do personally,' Damian said, already walking towards Stonegate. 'I think we should all have a very jolly conversation, don't you?'

'I could tell the police you ran,' Farringdon countered. 'That you're no longer under my jurisdiction. They'd arrest you. You'd go to jail for murder.'

'And you'd be broke and hunted for the rest of your life by

either white supremacists or your own people,' Damian laughed. 'You've got no move to play, Farringdon. Seven pm. Minster. Be there.'

And with that, he disconnected the phone for a second time.

'So now what?' Katherine asked as they entered Stonegate, walking down the narrow, stone-flagged street, the shops now a mixture of up market clothing stores, expensive food and drink emporiums and ancient pubs, all built within a higgledy piggledy patchwork of buildings that lined the sides of the road, the styles ranging from pre-Tudor to modern day in design.

'I thought a spot of food,' Damian replied.

'Sounds like a plan,' Katherine smiled as she checked her watch. It was approaching five-thirty in the evening. 'What time will *she* turn up?'

'No idea,' Damian shrugged. 'All I hope is that it's before seven.'

He turned left, passing through a small doorway to an enclosed alleyway, eventually opening out into the courtyard of The Olde Starre Inne. The day was ending, so the beer garden was already filling with tourists and workers toasting the end of their working days, as Damian and Katherine entered the bar itself.

The Olde Starr Inne boasted the title of one of the most haunted locations in York, but you wouldn't guess that by entering the bar, decorated with a mixture of mahogany panelling and blue walls, long, dark wooden benches placed alongside them,.

Standing high-tables, made from upturned barrels with a circle of wood on top to act as a surface were scattered around the room, and long, red leather benches or rooms wallpapered with yellowing postcards, each one written on in spidery, scrawled hand.

If there wasn't a stained glass window, specially designed with '*Star Inn*' written in glass leading through to another area beside you, then it was most likely to be a wall, either covered with a print, map or picture connected to York; all in glass frames and hanging from long used picture hooks, or hidden behind modern day fruit machines, their sounds and flashing lights completely at odds with the rest of the décor.

It was unashamedly a bar for tourists.

Grabbing two drinks and finding a secluded corner table as they waited for their food to arrive, Katherine leaned against the bench, looking up at the ceiling.

'Shrewsbury thinks the proclamation is going to be with the treasures,' she said. 'Farringdon as good as said so when she spoke to us back in the British Library.'

'Makes sense,' Damian replied. 'Especially if Bonner gave it to the School of Night to save his life.'

'Or he brought it here,' Katherine offered. 'When you told me about the whole Perkin Warbeck situation, I had a look at your father's notes when you were forging the Hawksmoor.'

'What did you find?' Damian had seen Katherine reading the notebooks but hadn't realised she found anything. In response, Katherine motioned for him to pass her the satchel and, once on her lap, she rummaged through it, pulling out one of Robert Lucas' notebooks, flipping it open at a particular page.

'So, before he died, Wolsey was Archbishop of York, and Bonner was his faithful servant and Cardinal, right?' she said, showing Damian the page. 'Look. End of 1530, Wolsey travels to London, knowing that he's likely to be imprisoned, even executed by his petulant king. We thought that Bonner might have been given the scroll, the proclamation for safekeeping, but if that was the case he wouldn't have brought it with them to London either.'

'Because if Wolsey was arrested, there was every chance Bonner would be arrested too,' Damian replied. 'They would have had to place it somewhere safe before coming to London, knowing that if needed, they could get it.'

He thought for a moment.

'Somewhere in York Minster?' he proposed. Katherine tapped the page again to get his attention.

'Read the page,' she said. 'Your father found a list of Rectors for Beverley, and more importantly Beverley Minster. In 1530, mere months before Wolsey's death, Edmund Bonner was made a Rector in Beverley for eleven years.'

'Bonner knew the area,' Damian re-read the list again. 'He must have visited Beverley Minster often. He'd know where to hide something.'

'And there were a lot of places to hide things,' Katherine replied. 'Yorkshire was a major location for the *Harrowing*, the complete destruction of cities that fought against Norman rule. Beverley was mostly saved because of its connection to Saint John of Beverley, the onetime Bishop of York, but many Minsters and churches in the North of England had underground tunnels and exit ways for the hunted to be hidden away and then taken to safety. William the Conqueror spent the winter of 1069 in York, and over the next year sent his men out to destroy entire villages and slaughter inhabitants, all to bring the rebels out of hiding.'

'But Beverley was saved?' Damian frowned.

'Seemingly so. And if that was the case, it'd make sense that people would make their way here for safety. The old monastery built where Beverley Minster is now would have been a beacon for help. Especially as it was one of the few locations in England that still gave sanctuary.'

'Surely William would have just seen these people? Hundreds, thousands of extra villagers are a bit obvious.'

'Not if they're underground,' Katherine replied. 'Think. Beverley claims to have no crypt under the Minster, but what if that was because the crypt was used for something else? If there were tunnels under Beverley, possibly even from when the Vikings first attacked, they could go all the way to the river Hull, a mile or two to the East. You could get a small boat and sail south, even come out at the Humber. Or north, to what was a wilder, more barren Yorkshire than we know today.'

Damian thought about this for a moment. 'An underground railway, before they even existed, so to speak. Smack bang under Beverley itself.'

'It's a possibility,' Katherine admitted.

'There might be more than gold under the Minster,' Damian thought to himself. 'Makes sense why Hawksmoor took the stolen treasure to Beverley. After all, if he'd found out where Bonner had hidden the proclamation, he'd know there was likely a location he could use. And if he excavated the North Wall, he might have accidentally found the tunnel system under the Minster.'

Damian sighed, putting the notebooks away as their food arrived. Tucking into a cod and chips, he carried on speaking, his mouth half filled with food as he spoke, eager to comment before he lost the thread of the conversation.

'I should call my friends,' he said.

'By friends, do you mean the Russians you owe money to?'

'Well, when you say it like that... What other options do we have?'

'We've got each other,' Katherine replied. Damian smiled.

'Yeah, that works.'

He didn't know if it was the way he said it, or whether it was the fact that they had both acknowledged it, but Katherine paused at this, looking at him, her gaze as intense as it had been the previous night, when they had forged the Hawksmoor document.

'What does that mean?' she asked.

'I was agreeing with you,' Damian replied, confused what she meant.

'Yeah, but the *way* you said it,' Katherine continued.

Damian shrugged, taking a mouthful of fish as he tried to work out what to say next.

'I dunno,' he eventually replied. 'I meant it was nice to have someone I could properly trust, you know?'

He saw Katherine visibly relax at that.

'Yeah, that is nice,' she replied.

Damian paused. He knew what he was about to do was stupid, but he had to say something. Within a couple of hours, they could be dead, or worse.

'Look,' he started. 'Neither of us knows what's going to happen tonight, and I don't want to go into this with any regrets or unspoken truths.'

'Okay...' Katherine stopped eating, her guard rising again.

'I lied to you earlier,' Damian continued. 'Richard was right. I had a crush on you when we were kids. Into my teens, in fact.'

'You did?' Katherine seemed surprised at this. 'I didn't know I'd bumped into you when I was a teenager.'

'There was a wedding. I was fifteen, and you were about

six months, or maybe a year older than me,' Damian thought for a moment. 'I remember seeing you in a pale blue dress.'

'Yeah, mum bought it for me,' Katherine remembered the dress well. She had hated it. 'I was just sixteen. I didn't know you were there.'

'Briefly,' Damian admitted. 'Dad was ill during the reception. He was allergic to seafood, but at the same time, he was addicted to crab cakes. We didn't stay long, I can't even remember whose wedding it was, just you in the blue dress.'

Katherine blushed a little.

'Thank you,' she said.

'I'm just saying this because, well, I think there's a bloody good chance I'm not seeing tomorrow outside of a jail cell or a shallow grave, but, well, I kinda wish I'd got to know you better back then,' Damian garbled out the words quickly and then looked away, eating his food as if he'd never spoken.

Katherine smiled wider now.

'Damn right,' she said. 'You should have. I could have been a queen.'

Damian smiled at this, staring at his plate as if scared to look at the woman beside him.

'Maybe if we get out of this, perhaps—'

Damian stopped as the shadow of a figure moved across in front of them, blocking the light from above, playing across his dinner. Looking up, he saw Detective Inspector Conlan, in the same grey suit that she'd been wearing the previous day, standing in front of them, hands on her hips and a wicked smile on her face.

'Damian Lucas,' she said with a sense of enormous glee as she stared at him. 'You're bloody well *nicked*, mate.'

32

THE MEETING

Cyrus hadn't meant to be in York when Shrewsbury called him; he'd been sent ahead to find a suitable five-star hotel and book the biggest suite for the night. So when his employer called, telling him to snoop around the centre of town looking for Damian Lucas, he'd taken the task with relish.

In fact, he'd made his way to Stonegate when he heard shattering glass, and saw Damian and the woman run from a pub as if for their very lives. Which possibly was true, as a moment later a suited man, tall and slim, ran out after them.

'Police!' he yelled, but it was too late. Damian and Katherine had already run into the narrow alleyways around the street, and so finding them would be even harder now.

Cyrus muttered a curse to himself as he texted Martin Shrewsbury with the news. He considered entering the bar from which Damian had run from, maybe seeing who was with the tall slim detective who even now swore into a phone, but he wasn't a fool. There was still a chance that he could be recognised from when he hunted Richard Evans, or even from Middle Temple the previous day. And the last thing Cyrus wanted was to be hunted himself.

The detective ran off into the alleys, and so Cyrus strolled the direction that Damian had. Half an hour earlier, Damian had probably felt in control, but now everything was falling apart. And Cyrus was happy about that. Shrewsbury might be grateful Damian hadn't been killed in Chetham's Library, and that clues he had since found were helpful, but Cyrus still felt a personal insult and Damian still breathing was proof Cyrus had failed in his own job.

And Cyrus never failed.

His phone beeped to show another message. Shrewsbury wanted Cyrus to keep on the police officer, to see where he led. As Cyrus turned to return to the pub, he saw the detective leave, walking off towards the main square.

Torn between his job and his need, Cyrus sighed and followed the detective down the road. Damian would have to wait, but not for much longer.

He didn't see the second female detective leave, already on the phone as she left the pub, heading off towards a waiting car at the end of the road.

———

It was still light in York at seven in the evening. The August sun remained warm, and Shrewsbury had been standing in St Helen's Square for five minutes, hating every second. He understood now how clever Damian had been with this location; for the last three minutes, he'd already had six people ask for selfies, three people shout insults at him and at least a dozen more had taken surreptitious photos of him, all probably hitting social media.

Damian couldn't have found a better army of informants if he'd tried, and right now could see exactly where his enemy was, while Shrewsbury had no idea where to even start his own search. Shrewsbury was again impressed by the man. It was just a shame that within a few hours, Cyrus would most likely be finishing the job that he had failed to do over forty-eight hours earlier.

His phone beeped at the stroke of seven—at least Damian was punctual—and Shrewsbury read the message, starting east towards York's Shambles Market.

They still took photos of him as he left.

OUTSIDE YORK MINSTER, FARRINGDON GALES RECEIVED THE same message. At the other end of Stonegate, there had been little chance of her accidentally bumping into Martin Shrewsbury, but that didn't stop her looking around. Paranoia was only paranoia when they *weren't* out to get you, and Farringdon Gales had run out on Martin Shrewsbury.

Looking at Mister Sun, standing five feet away from her, she nodded.

'I've got the address,' she said, showing the phone. 'Keep me on GPS and follow from a discrete distance.'

Mister Sun nodded, walking off into the crowds, disappearing from view as quickly as he had arrived. Satisfied all arrangements that could be made had been made, Farringdon started off towards York Shambles Market.

Unlike Martin Shrewsbury though, she didn't notice the

Russians taking photos of her before walking off towards a large blue van parked to the left of York Minster.

———

AT THREE MINUTES PAST SEVEN, MARTIN SHREWSBURY ENTERED York's Shambles Market. An open air thoroughfare, the Market had closed two hours earlier; now it was just lines of empty tables with white tarpaulin roofs above them. At the side, beside the frontage of a Travel Agent, Damian and Katherine emerged, Damian nodding to him.

'I heard you had trouble,' Shrewsbury said as he walked over. 'Police get close, did they?'

'Interrupted our dinner,' Damian replied cautiously. 'How did you know?'

'Eye witness account. Saw you run like startled hares as the police chased after you.'

Damian shrugged. 'They're here. So what? They've been hunting me for days.'

'Well then, let's sort this out before they find you again,' Shrewsbury snapped. 'I've had a long bloody day and I've had it with clues and quests and other such bollocks.'

'You need to calm down more,' Damian smiled. 'The way I see it, I found the clue in Chethams and then translated it, I found the message in Middle Temple and I invited you to York.'

'True,' Shrewsbury reluctantly replied. 'Take your bloody time, then.'

'I'm curious,' Damian asked, watching Shrewsbury carefully. 'How long were you in Deptford before you realised you were in the wrong place?'

'Until we heard that you'd been arrested outside St Alfege church,' Shrewsbury admitted. 'I was this close to pulling a digger into the churchyard, too. How did you figure out the actual message?'

'Did you go to St Alfege?' Katherine asked coldly, ignoring the question. 'Maybe poisoned Dermot until he told you what he told us?'

Shrewsbury looked back at Damian.

'Who's Dermot?'

'The guide at St Alfege,' Damian replied. 'We're assuming you went there after the police left.'

'We did,' Shrewsbury admitted. 'And we learnt all about your little Unicorn clue in the Middle Temple. The guide, Dermot? He told us all about it.'

'What did you do to him?' Damian straightened in his seat, but Shrewsbury waved him back down.

'I paid him ten thousand pounds,' he replied. 'Cash. There and then. He explained you said the unicorn's horn pointed to the next clue. We thought he meant the Naval College until Farringdon called from New Scotland Yard, saying it actually led to a pyramid and another bloody clue.'

'Yeah. The unicorn was moved.'

'I guessed that,' Shrewsbury snapped. 'I also know that your buddy Dermot didn't bother telling me that part, even though we'd paid him handsomely.'

'He was a friend of my dad. Probably sensed that you were a wrong'un.'

Shrewsbury went to reply, but Farringdon, out of breath and red faced, walked through the now closed market stalls towards them.

'I've a good mind to have you both put in prison again,'

she snapped. Damian smiled before looking back at Shrewsbury.

'You see, it could have been worse. We never lied to *you* like Farringdon here, sending you on a completely pointless wild goose chase.'

Shrewsbury shrugged an acknowledgement to this as Farringdon looked to Katherine.

'So were the firecrackers from friends of yours?'

'Let's just say interested parties,' Damian smiled. 'Passed the message under your darling Mister Sun's very nose.'

Farringdon nodded to herself.

'The neighbour. Bloody Hawksmoor. Bloody renegades.'

'Bloody *murderers*,' Katherine retorted. 'And that goes for both of you.'

'My hands have never touched blood,' Farringdon was indignant.

'That's because you always got your buddy there to do it,' Katherine snapped, pointing at Shrewsbury. She looked to continue, but Damian placed a hand on her shoulder.

'Rein your dog in,' Farringdon muttered.

Damian *tsked*.

'And there we were, about to tell you both the location of the missing treasure,' he said, looking to Shrewsbury. 'And the proclamation. But now I think we'll just go hand ourselves to the police, because as you said, you know they almost caught us, and they'll find us again...'

'No,' Shrewsbury said, his face almost pleading. 'I agree with the terms you gave on the phone. Just don't leave. I need to finish this.'

'What terms?' Farringdon asked.

'You just lost your cut of the gold,' Katherine smiled.

Farringdon, a betrayed look on her face, looked at Shrewsbury.

'Oh, you'll get a cut,' he muttered. 'Just not as large. And be grateful I've done that, after all this hassle, and the fact you didn't tell me personally of your jaunt up north.'

'I knew you'd follow me,' Farringdon almost sulked. 'We saw you at the Library.'

'Now how about you tell us where the hell we're going tonight?' Shrewsbury asked.

Damian pulled out a flyer from the satchel. It was one of those thin, coloured tourist flyers that you often found laid out in rows on stands in train stations and hotel lobbies.

'Beverley Minster,' he replied. 'Edmund Bonner was Rector of the local parish when given the proclamation by Wolsey. The Provost of Beverley Minster, William Poteman dressed as King Solomon and greeted Henry during his pageant, bestowing on him a sceptre named as 'Solomon's Wisdom'.'

'The Wisdom of Solomon,' Farringdon sighed. 'I should have got that. The scene is in a window at Cambridge college refectory.'

'Anyway, a year after stealing the treasures, Hawksmoor helped rebuild the Minster. Apparently, the whole place was in great disrepair, and the north wall was collapsing.'

'Why do we care about this?' Shrewsbury muttered. 'If he's hidden it in a church, people would have known. This isn't exactly something you could leave hidden in a tomb.'

'But you could in a crypt.'

'Beverley Minster doesn't have a crypt, it's common knowledge,' Farringdon argued. 'And your story dies right there, doesn't it?'

'The Minster doesn't, that's true,' Damian turned to face

Farringdon now. 'But maybe there was one, once. Perhaps under the old monastery they built the Minster *on*.'

Katherine smiled darkly at Farringdon, as if scoring a point, which, in a way, she was.

'A crypt hidden during the Harrowing, and with an entranceway lost when the Chapterhouse was destroyed during the dissolution of monasteries.'

There was silence as Farringdon and Martin Shrewsbury both took this in.

Eventually, it was the latter who spoke.

'And you reckon it's still there?' he asked.

Damian shrugged.

'The Chapterhouse steps remain, going nowhere,' he replied. 'Hawksmoor was given the opportunity to remove them but didn't. Why? And they only hired him to fix the wall, but he took great interest in the renovation of an ornate wooden choir screen, out of the goodness of his own heart. Again, why?'

'All of this is based on a guess,' Farringdon muttered.

'Every step of the journey has been based on guesses,' Damian replied. 'Every single path we've taken has been with a leap of faith. What's so different about this one?'

'That you're telling us about it, rather than making up some old bollocks to throw us off?' Farringdon folded her arms as she glared at Damian, who sighed, rubbing the bridge of his nose.

'I'm tired, Farringdon,' he said. 'I've seen my best friend die and I've been chased all over the country. I've been shot at, arrested and learnt things about my family I never wanted to know. But like Martin there, I just want this to end. So, we thought it would be easier if we all went and looked together.'

'I'm in,' Shrewsbury nodded. 'I've got nothing to lose and everything to gain.'

'Well, there's no way in hell I'm letting the three of you do anything without me,' Farringdon muttered. 'Let's go.'

Damian smiled at Martin Shrewsbury.

'Can we cadge a lift from you?' he asked with a smile.

33

THE MINSTER

Even with the rush hour now over, the thirty-mile trip to Beverley Minster still took almost an hour for the two cars, one driven by Shrewsbury himself and one by Farringdon, in close convoy to arrive at Beverley.

The logistics of this had been difficult from the start; Shrewsbury called Cyrus, telling him to secure the church at all costs, to make sure it closed early for the day. Farringdon, meanwhile, was calling Mister Sun and telling him to get there first and stop Cyrus from setting up any little surprises for when they arrived. The whole thing had become a game of one-upmanship. And, as far as Damian was concerned, this suited him just fine.

Damian had agreed to sit in the back of Shrewsbury's Jaguar, while Farringdon followed them with a silent Katherine beside her; a two-car convoy out of York, through the wall at Monkgate and then east down the A1079, a single lane A-road that cut its way through lush fields and into the Yorkshire countryside. Soon however the road led into the suburban houses of Beverley and then into Beverley town centre itself, down the cobbled street of Highgate, pulling to a stop as the majestic Beverley Minster loomed up in front of them, parking beside the gate that led to the North entrance.

Getting out of the Jaguar and looking up at the Minster, the first thing that struck Damian was the sheer size of it. Any city would have been proud to call this a cathedral rather than a parish church—but that had never been the case here. The Gothic style and stone structure of the walls reminded him of Westminster Abbey, which wasn't really that surprising, as Nicholas Hawksmoor had designed the West Towers of the abbey shortly before he died in 1736, likely inspired by his time spent at this same church.

'Fun drive?' Damian asked Katherine as she approached with Farringdon.

'Next time, I'll drive with the fascist,' Katherine muttered. 'All I had was an hour of why I needed to join the right School of Night.'

'She tried to recruit you?' Damian was amused by this.

'I've done more with pennies than they have with millions,' Katherine smirked. 'They probably want me to lead them.'

The path through the churchyard formed a small semicircle, then a cobbled pathway leading to two double doors, and signage indicating the times of services for the church, as well as a map of the Minster on a fashionable black background. Shrewsbury didn't pay it a second glance, already walking towards the North Porch's main entrance, where the familiar bald form of Cyrus could be seen waiting for them.

'They wouldn't close up shop for me, but I explained who you were and the moment they heard your name, their eyes widened,' he said.

'Of course they did,' Shrewsbury replied with a sigh.

'They probably realised they were about to make their yearly donation quota in one day.'

Passing his bodyguard, and with Damian, Katherine, and Farringdon following in close behind him, Shrewsbury entered through the glass doors into the large, open Nave of Beverley Minster.

The church was over three hundred feet long, longer than most British cathedrals, and split into several parts. Across the Nave in front of them, and placed against the south wall between two pillars, was a large Norman font, with an elaborate wooden lid on top. To the right was the Great West Door, made of the same dark oak and covered in early Georgian carvings, matching the font cover, with the stairs that led up to the South-West Tower to the right of it, mirroring the stairs to the North-West Tower across the Nave.

Wide stone pillars went along the entire length of the Nave on both sides, leading to the middle of the Minster, where there was a large wooden Chancel, the floor within created by Hawksmoor, and a wooden screen holding the enormous, five-hundred pipe organ above the choir seating beside the tomb of St John of Beverley.

Because the Minster had taken many centuries to build, and had spent decades in stages of incredible disrepair, the entire building was a mixture of various Gothic styles; Early English limestone butted up against Decorated, while further on into the church Perpendicular Gothic architecture rose above them all to a spectacular white painted roof way above everything else.

The whole place was empty, bar one woman; a short, brown-haired lady in a grey suit, who currently walked towards them impatiently, fiddling with her cheap glasses as she spoke.

'I don't care how famous you are, Mister Shrewsbury, you can't just turn up and close my church!' she exclaimed. 'I have parishioners, they need their spiritual guidance, and the Vergers need to set out the chairs for a harp recital tomorrow!'

Shrewsbury nodded, walking towards her, meeting her midway.

'I completely understand, and I'll be a matter of minutes, an hour total,' he said, pulling out his phone. 'And to recompense you for this, how about I transfer, I don't know, say, ten thousand pounds into whatever bank account you see fit?'

He opened an app on the phone, showing it to the woman.

'Just tap the account details in here and I'll do it right now.'

The woman stared at the phone in utter shock, as if weighing up the needs of her parishioners against the sudden windfall that was being offered here.

'An hour?' she confirmed.

'Maybe more, maybe less,' Martin replied. 'We're on a treasure hunt and might need to have a real good look around. We might need to move a few pieces of stone, so it might be a little noisy.'

The woman looked around, still torn.

'Moving stone sounds like vandalism,' she muttered, almost to herself.

'How about I up the donation to fifteen thousand instead?' Martin offered. 'I'm sure you can fix anything we break with less than five thousand extra pounds and some contractors...' He trailed off as the woman looked back to him, an indignant expression on her face.

'Are you bribing me?' she asked.

Shrewsbury simply shrugged.

'It depends on whether the money goes to the church, or into your pockets,' he said.

The woman thought about this for a moment before snatching it quickly and typing in a number. Passing it back to Shrewsbury, she was suddenly all smiles.

'Well, I can't see why a man like you, with such a public profile, shouldn't be allowed to worship God without being interrupted,' she said, waving towards the Northern Transept. 'I'll just be over there, in the gift shop.'

As she walked away, Shrewsbury looked back at Damian.

'If you're wrong, you owe me fifteen grand,' he hissed.

'Oh, I'll be owing you way more than that by the end of this,' Damian replied. Before Shrewsbury could reply to this, Farringdon looked back to the Northern door, where Mister Sun was entering.

'I thought we said no additionals?' Katherine muttered as she saw the agent approaching.

Farringdon pointed at Cyrus.

'If he's here, then I'm allowed mine. And with the best will in the world, *child*, you're nothing but an additional, too.'

Damian shrugged. 'I don't care either way, to be honest,' he said, walking towards the wooden Chancel in the middle of the Nave. 'Bring as many as you want.'

Farringdon crossed over to Mister Sun and spoke briefly to him, nodding at the gift shop to the north of the Nave. As Mister Sun walked off towards it, Katherine walked over to her.

'If Mister Sun does anything to that woman...' she started.

'Oh grow up,' Farringdon snapped back. 'He's just making sure if we do make a noise or something, the lady remembers she's just been paid an enormous sum of money and is now technically an accomplice.'

'Basically, you're going to scare her into keeping quiet,' Damian replied. 'I can't believe that I used to respect you.'

Farringdon glared back at Damian as he continued down the Nave.

'This from the drug addict who sold the very paperwork that started this, all for a quick hit,' she hissed.

Damian went to speak, but forced himself to calm his voice, looking instead at Martin Shrewsbury.

'There's a Saxon Frith Stool in the Minster, I think down by the Altar,' he said conversationally.

'Is it connected to the treasure?' Cyrus asked.

'Not really,' Damian happily replied. 'It's possibly one of the oldest in the country, definitely one of perhaps two that survive, and from before 1066.'

'So what is a Frith Stool?' Shrewsbury couldn't help himself.

Katherine, walking up beside him, now answered.

'It's a stone chair that was part of Beverley's Sanctuary,' she explained. 'King Athelstan gave the right of sanctuary to the church after the battle of Brunanburh, back in 973. He claimed that the church's dead saint, St John of Beverley provided spiritual help when he spent the night praying here before the battle, causing Athelstan's win against his rivals.'

'You should know all about this,' Damian turned and smiled at Shrewsbury. 'The battle was between Athelstan and a group of foreign kings including Constantine the Second, Olaf Guthfrithson and Owen of Strathclyde.'

'Why should I know of this?' Shrewsbury was almost bored in his reply, as if expecting a joke at his expense.

'Because Athelstan's win is cited as the point of origin for

English Nationalism,' Farringdon answered before Damian could.

'And we all know how much you *love* Nationalism,' Damian finished, his voice hard and cold.

Before Shrewsbury could reply to this, Damian changed tone, now light-hearted again, as if he was a history teacher educating his class.

'Anyway, because of that win, he granted a square mile of sanctuary around the Minster. Anyone accused of a crime could come within four stone markers placed around the town and claim asylum.'

'Not the asylum that you and your friends hate, of course,' Katherine chipped in. Damian could see that Shrewsbury was slowly reddening with anger.

'Yes, not the *brown* people,' Damian continued, 'more the unjustly accused. And people charged with greater crimes had to come to the Minster itself and sit on the Frith Stool itself, not only to ask the church for sanctuary but also to ask God himself for forgiveness.'

'So why should I care about this stool?' Shrewsbury finally replied, gathering his composure.

Damian paused, turning to face Shrewsbury, Farringdon, and Cyrus.

'Richard Evans. Andy Holdman. My parents. The list, I'm sure, is longer than that. All three of you should take the time to sit on that stool and beg God for forgiveness for what you all did.'

There was a moment of silence. And then Shrewsbury chuckled.

'God loves me, Mister Lucas,' he simply replied. 'I don't need a stool to learn that. Now, can we get on with this? As amusing and informative as your history lecture is, I'm simply not feeling it today.'

Damian shrugged and nodded, as if his comments hadn't really been all that important to him, and turned back into the Nave, walking once more towards the Altar at the East end of the Minster.

'Hawksmoor loved his sacred geometry,' he explained as they entered the Chancel in the middle of the Nave, the small screened off area of ornate carved magnificence under the pipe organ. Along the sides were eighteen carved figures; popes, cardinals, martyrs, angels, soldiers, all varied in appearance as you walked along the chancel, watching down from above two rows of choir seating; a mixture of dark wood and red velvet lit by two sets of lights on either side. Damian paused in the middle of the chancel, facing the altar, the others now standing with him between the two sets of wooden stalls, facing each other across a small floor made of geometric cubes.

'And when he was brought in to make certain the north wall didn't fall down, he also made architectural suggestions to the supervisors of the project, one of which was the designing of a different flooring here.'

He pointed down at the pattern, a series of three-sided, three-dimensional cubes in black, grey, marble and white, giving the impression of a cubic mountain, leading towards the altar, white-topped stepping stones towards God.

'The cube is what's called a platonic solid,' he continued. 'It symbolises the duality of nature, as by looking the other direction the cubes change as you stare at them, and now look as if they travel away from the altar instead.'

He pointed back away from them, back the way they had

come. The geometric squares stopped at the arched entrance to the Chancel.

'Like a magic eye painting,' Farringdon muttered.

'But Hawksmoor wasn't paid to create flooring. They paid him to fix a building's walls. The Chancel, however, was something he took a great interest in.'

'The Chancel is a mirror,' Farringdon spoke up now. 'Two sides, leading to a path that travels both ways.'

'Sacred Geometry,' Damian replied, walking towards the altar at the end of the flooring. As the others followed, Damian moved from the Chancel, turning north, through the pillars to the west of the North-East Transept, now finally facing the north wall that Nicholas Hawksmoor was believed to have fixed all those centuries earlier.

Another entrance to the Minster faced him, now closed to the public; two ornate gold and black metal railings reaching out into the Nave from either side of a large, arched wooden door.

'What's through there?' Cyrus asked.

'Couple of small offices, a disabled toilet,' Damian replied. 'But the door isn't why we're here. Think bigger.'

Either side of the wooden door were stone steps, only around a dozen on both sides, flanked by thin stone pillars bridging a thin stone banister and leading to nothing; just a narrow platform above the door, where a plaque was placed. Showing a man caring for a child, it was inscribed 'John of Beverley Medal 685AD'.

'That's where the Chapterhouse entrance would have been,' Katherine said. 'Two sides leading up to a door that was walled up when the building was destroyed. Sacred duality again.'

'If the door no longer exists, and the wall is external, the crypt is what, outside?' Shrewsbury walked up to the wall beside the door, tapping at the stones under the steps.

'Or under,' Damian suggested.

Farringdon hissed, a release of frustration that turned all attention to her.

'There's no 'under',' she said. 'As I've said before, there's no crypt. And if there is a crypt in the Chapterhouse, its entrance is long gone.'

'Hawksmoor would have left a clue,' Damian replied. 'He has at every stage. He would have done so here.'

There was an audible click of a gun being cocked, and Damian turned to see Cyrus, gun in hand; the gun that killed Andy now aimed at him.

'The professor has been with us for years,' he hissed. 'We've known you less than a week. Your dad was flaky as shit and maybe you are, too. So show us this 'Hawksmoor clue' right now, or you'll be joining your parents, the old geezer and your traitor mate very soon.'

Damian swallowed and nodded, suddenly unable to speak. Which was a good thing because currently, he had nothing to say...

Because he had literally no idea where the next clue could be.

34

TURBULENT PRIESTS

'So where do we look then?' Shrewsbury was already examining the wall, ignoring the fact that Cyrus had a gun trained on the man he was speaking to. Damian looked around the Minster, as if looking for divine guidance.

'Anything that Hawksmoor touched, or had a part in designing, is likely to be a clue,' he said, already walking back into the Chancel. Reluctantly, the others followed.

Standing back in the middle of the Chancel, Damian turned in a slow circle as he tried to look for something, anything, that was out of order. The ornate choir seating that mirrored each other weren't created by Hawksmoor's hand, but had been carved in the sixteenth century. That said, Hawksmoor would have spent a lot of time within the Chancel while creating the flooring, and Damian knew the architect wasn't averse to a little vandalism, as the glass in Drake's lantern and the etched letters in the table at Middle Temple proved.

Along each side were eighteen figures, mainly religious. There were more at the end of the Chancel, but that had been built after Hawksmoor's death, created to hold the pipe organ and matching the look of the Chancel. As Katherine examined the benches, Damian moved closer to one figure. There was something on the base...

'The figures,' Farringdon said as she examined a different figure across the Chancel, excitedly pointing at the base. 'There are markings scratched into the bases.'

Examining the next one, Damian realised Farringdon was indeed correct, and that upon the base of each of these figures, eighteen on each side, were very familiar cypher markings. He made his way along the choir bench, marking down each cypher. As before, he didn't need the Sunne Dial; and as he walked to the end of the row, he already knew what the message on this side of the chancel said.

watches over the find

Looking back to Farringdon, working out her own eighteen cyphers on her side of the Chancel, he waited until she finished.

'What do you have?' He asked. Farringdon smiled.

'*The turbulent priest,*' she replied.

'*The turbulent priest watches over the find,*' Damian said.

'Turbulent priest, that's Thomas Becket, right?' Shrewsbury looked up at the Frith Stool and the altar. 'The Archbishop of Canterbury?'

'That's right,' Damian said, walking towards him. 'Named so after a command that Henry the Second gave. He was furious that Becket had excommunicated the Archbishop of York, and the Bishops of London and Salisbury after they crowned Henry's son as heir apparent without using Canterbury Cathedral. He's reported to have said in anger, 'will no one rid me of this turbulent priest."

'Let me guess, someone took that as an order,' Shrewsbury sat down on the Frith Stool, using it as a chair as Katherine spoke. 'Sounds like my kind of people.'

'Four knights did and killed Becket at Canterbury in 1170. He's buried there still.'

'*Bloody hellfire!*' Shrewsbury shouted. 'So we need to go back to *Canterbury* now?'

Damian shook his head. 'That's where he's buried, not where he watches over.'

He left the Chancel, once more walking over to the Chapterhouse steps, the others following him now as he looked away from the steps and to a wooden board split into four rows of gold names against the opposite wall. On the first two boards were lists of Abbots and Provosts of Beverley from 700AD until 1543. The following boards were a list of Incumbents of Beverley from 1548 until 2009.

There, listed as Provost from 1154 was Thomas Becket.

Damian pointed directly across the floor, now pointing to the wooden donation box, placed on top of a black metal double grating to the left of the entrance, and embedded into the stone.

'*The turbulent priest watches over the find,*' he whispered.

'The donation box?' Cyrus looked questioningly at Shrewsbury.

'No, not the bloody donation box,' Farringdon hissed. 'The grating under it.'

Shrewsbury nodded to Cyrus, who was already moving the donation box off the grating.

'Pull that up, will you?' he asked. Cyrus nodded, pulling what looked to be a crowbar out of his inside jacket pocket. With Cyrus's help, Shrewsbury prised the grating on the left-hand side of the entranceway out of the floor, flipping it over and slamming it to the stone beside it with an echoing clang.

'Someone's going to hear that,' Farringdon chided, looking back towards the gift shop.

'For fifteen grand, they can film it,' Shrewsbury replied as he helped Cyrus remove the other half of the grating with a similarly loud clang, before laying down on the floor beside the hole, and rapping on the stone within with his knuckles. 'And besides, if your guy doesn't stop her from talking, my guy certainly will.'

'This isn't what I signed up for,' Farringdon complained. 'You said no more deaths.'

'No King has ever gained power without a little bloodshed,' Shrewsbury replied, knocking once more on the stone, a two-foot drop under the now removed grating.

He paused, a smile on his lips.

'It sounds hollow,' he said before walking over to the red ropes that blocked entrance to the steps, taking one of the massively heavy, metal stands that they were clipped onto. Then, using the large, round base as a sledgehammer, he slammed the stand into the now exposed stone.

Damian winced as the echo clattered around the Minster, but before he could say anything Cyrus had picked up another of the stands and was joining his employer in the effort of smashing the stone, repeatedly slamming the metal stand into the ground, breaking up the dark flagstone underneath.

After three more strikes, the stone shattered into three parts and fell away, revealing a hole into the depths beneath Beverley Minster.

Farringdon leaned closer to the hole, pulling out her smartphone and turning the flash on, shining it down into the abyss beneath the stairs.

'There are steps!' she exclaimed, looking back at the

others. 'There's a drop of about four, maybe five feet, but then there are steps, heading down and to the north.'

Damian looked at Shrewsbury, and before anyone could say anything he grabbed the stand from him, hammering down onto the remaining stone, breaking it away, enabling the hole to be easily fitted through.

It was dark, deep, and incredibly narrow. Even the thought of climbing down into it made Damian shudder.

'I'm going first,' he said, staring down into the hole.

'You want the ceiling to fall on you? Be my guest,' Shrewsbury said. 'But just know, I'll be directly behind you.'

'There might be a queue before you,' a voice spoke from down the Nave, and Damian looked around to see Isabella and Pietr walking towards them, Pietr with his own gun aimed at Cyrus.

'Who the hell are you?' Shrewsbury asked, turning to face the newcomers.

Isabella indicated Damian.

'We are, shall we say, silent partners of this one,' she said. 'We funded his escape. We will take over from here.'

'The hell you will—' Cyrus moved to pull his gun back out, but Pietr turned the gun on him, as Isabella smiled.

'Martin Shrewsbury. You are rich man, and about to become richer, I think. Perhaps we can come to some agreement?'

'Go to hell,' Shrewsbury's face was tight. 'I'm not being shaken down.'

'Fine,' Isabella replied. 'We take over, and gain whatever is down tunnel.'

Damian could see the conflict in Shrewsbury's face.

'This is what you meant?' he asked Damian without looking.

'Yeah, sorry, I promised them a cut,' Damian replied. 'Two hundred and fifty grand.'

'*A quarter of a million?*' Shrewsbury almost screamed the number in anger.

'Well, there's supposed to be way more than that down there, right?' Damian shrugged. 'And they helped me out when others—that's you—set me up.'

Shrewsbury looked to the hole in the floor. To Isabella. To the hole again.

'Fine,' he sighed. 'A banker's draft do?'

'We took liberty of connecting to your bank,' Isabella replied, passing a phone over. 'You can put your bank details in. Transfer now would be better.'

His mouth fixed in a snarl, Shrewsbury connected to his personal account, and with a small yet audible groan tapped in a number, pressing return. He passed the phone back to Isabella, who checked the screen. She looked at Damian, nodding.

'Your debt is clear,' she said.

'Thanks,' Damian replied. 'And you...?'

'We will keep the deal,' Isabella said.

'What deal?' Farringdon now asked.

Damian looked at her.

'These lovely people are outside,' he explained. 'They're stopping any more of your men—' he looked to Shrewsbury '—and your men from coming in.'

'There are many,' Pietr smiled. 'all furious.'

At this, Farringdon deflated a little and Damian realised this must have been her plan all along; to keep her agents outside until the gold was found and then take it by force. Now, however, it was an even playing field. He nodded to

Pietr, and both Isabella and Pietr backed their way out of the Minster.

Now alone again, Shrewsbury turned to face Damian.

'When this is done, I'm going to kill you personally,' he hissed.

'When this is done, you'll be richer than God,' Damian replied. 'So shut up and let me get on with this.'

Damian slung his satchel over his head, allowing it to cross his body rather than just hanging from his shoulder. This done, he pulled out the burner phone and, turning on the flash, sat down on the edge of the hole, allowing his feet to dangle into the darkness.

'Shall we?' he asked.

35

CHAPTERHOUSE BLUES

Using the torch to check the floor beneath him, Damian saw Farringdon was correct, and the floor was only four, maybe five feet beneath him.

Passing his phone to Katherine, he used his arms for support as he lowered himself slowly into the hole, reaching up and taking it back from her once he stood on solid ground, with only his head able to poke out into the church now.

As he turned to light the way down the steps, the musty, ancient smell hit him first. Like a mildewed bathroom suffering from damp, it was harsh and unpleasant. But then there was every chance that this air was last breathed over three hundred years ago, so Damian expected it would probably be stale and rotten.

What it did mean was that with no fresh air, this was possibly an airtight location. There were likely to be no other entrances or exits. Which meant, if the ceiling fell down, or if the doorway did collapse, there was absolutely no way out of this.

Calm down, he thought to himself. *Slow, deep breaths. It's just a crypt. You've done these before.*

Heading north and downward were another dozen steps; all within a narrow passageway, roughly hewn out of the ground with an arched roof, and shored up with bricks. At the bottom was a brief passage that led to a doorway, the room behind it barred from view by a wooden door, built in the same style as the ones above, leading into the Minster.

Big and heavy, Damian thought to himself as he trudged down to it, examining the wood, the metal ring embedded into the side. Twisting it, he carefully opened the door, revealing a room—

There was a thump from behind him, and Damian turned to see Shrewsbury in the tunnel, a break-and-shake handful of glow sticks in his hand. Breaking, and shaking, Shrewsbury threw the green and orange sticks past Damian, through the door and into the now revealed corridor on the other side of it; which seemed to lead to another set of stairs to the east.

As Damian pushed the door completely open and followed the lights, he realised the twelve steps he had already taken brought him twenty feet below the church, and the steps to the right took him down to another passage that wound around to the left.

Now possibly thirty feet underground, and in a dank smelling corridor, Damian checked his phone, seeing that there was no signal down here. Another couple of glow sticks clattered past him as he arrived at another closed door. This one was older, heavier. There were no etchings or ornate designs on it, and it looked pre-Norman in design.

'What is it?' Shrewsbury asked, walking up behind him. Damian ignored him, continuing to examine the door.

'I think this was part of the original church or monastery,' he replied. 'The door looks pre-Norman, maybe ninth century.'

'Can it be opened?' Shrewsbury didn't seem to care for architecture or history. All he wanted was the door pushed aside. Taking the ring and turning it, raising the latch on the other side of it, Damian pushed against the door.

It wouldn't budge.

'Is it locked?' Shrewsbury moved closer now, pushing at the door beside Damian, who shook his head.

'No, just incredibly stiff,' he replied as together, the two of them pushed the ancient door open with a loud and screeching groan as hinges, rusted over centuries, were finally forced back into life.

Taking a deep breath to again calm his nerves, Damian moved through the doorway as Shrewsbury tossed more glow sticks ahead of him, walking into a large, eight-sided crypt from the west entrance, easily fifty feet in diameter, with four wide limestone pillars supporting the ceiling.

To the left, heading southwards, was a tunnel, a roughly cut hole into the depths that was mirrored on the north side of the crypt.

To the east side, opposite them, was another tunnel, but this looked more modern, with limestone bricks supporting the archway.

Between each tunnel was a door, wooden and closed; and in the middle of the crypt, placed onto a carved limestone base, was an ornate gold sceptre.

As Damian approached it, Shrewsbury followed him into the crypt, with Katherine, Farringdon and Cyrus following in quick succession.

'Is this it?' Shrewsbury asked.

Damian nodded, his voice unable to speak as he tried to find the words. Eventually he managed, indicating the walls.

'Chapterhouses were eight sided,' he whispered. 'This is the crypt, lost for three hundred years.'

He pointed at the sceptre. It was slim, maybe an inch in diameter and over three feet long, made of gold with two rubies embedded into it—the first was near the base, above a jewel encrusted handle, but the second was at the top of the sceptre, encased within a golden bracket. It was simple, yet elegant.

And it was incredibly old.

'That, I believe, is the 'wisdom of Solomon' that Beverley Minster offered Henry Tudor,' he said, almost too scared to touch it.

'Why would it be here?' Shrewsbury looked around the crypt, his face frowning as he tried to work out whether this was truly the end of his search, or another trick by Damian.

'A marker, perhaps,' Damian motioned to the doors. 'Either way, there's a very strong chance that behind one of these doors lies the hidden treasure of the School of Night. Gold, jewels, ancient papers, the whole thing. The quest that people have been on for hundreds of years has finally ended.'

'And the tunnels?'

'I don't know,' Damian admitted. 'The one to the east is more modern and might lead somewhere else in the Minster. A second entrance, perhaps. The other two are older, rougher too. They were probably made when the Vikings raided, or during the Norman Harrowing. One probably heads towards the river Hull, the other out to God knows where.'

Shrewsbury smiled, looking at Cyrus.

'Pass me the gun,' he said simply.

Cyrus looked confused for a moment, as if he hadn't

really understood what Shrewsbury was asking for, before pulling out his weapon; the same gun that he had tried to shoot Damian with in Manchester, the same gun that had killed Andy in Chetham's Library, the same weapon that only minutes earlier he had aimed himself at Damian, passing it over to his employer.

Shrewsbury took the weapon, examining it for a single moment before turning it on Damian.

'You've cost me a lot of money,' he said.

'I think I've given you equivalent value,' Damian replied, waving an arm around. 'Without me, you'd never have found this.'

Shrewsbury thought for a moment.

'True,' he said. 'But you've still cost me a lot of money. And that's a debt you won't be able to pay.'

'But that was part of the deal we made,' Damian replied, suddenly realising that the plan he had was now unravelling. 'You agreed to pay the Russians the debt I owed.'

'You didn't mention it was so high,' Shrewsbury said, cocking the gun.

'You never asked,' Damian looked around, as if searching for a way out. All he saw were Farringdon and Katherine staring at the scene in shock and Cyrus licking his lips, eager to see Damian killed. 'And hell, Martin. If you have to ask the price, then you can't afford it. Isn't that what you rich pricks say?'

Shrewsbury looked around the room, to the doors, to the people standing within.

'True, I made a deal. That your friend would get money, and I would repay your debt. The latter of which I've now done.'

He raised the gun, aiming it at Damian.

'Your services have been invaluable, but unfortunately, like you, they aren't needed anymore.'

36

TREASURE HUNTING

'W*AIT!*'

Shrewsbury lowered the gun as Farringdon Gales stood between it and Damian.

'I'm happy to shoot you as well,' he said.

'You still need him,' Farringdon replied, showing the doors. 'He didn't say all of these doors, he said *one* of these doors. Hawksmoor would have set it up that only the right door will lead to treasure. The others?'

She looked up at the crypt's ceiling.

'They're probably booby trapped. Open the wrong door, and the whole thing collapses on us.'

Damian looked at Katherine in surprise. The last thing he expected was Farringdon to step in on his behalf. In fact, he'd been expecting a different end to this.

She was making sure another person wasn't killed on her watch.

'Eight doorways and exits,' Farringdon looked at Damian as she spoke. 'This is your Key of Solomon again, isn't it?'

'What does she mean?' Shrewsbury asked.

Damian shrugged.

'I don't know,' he replied, a smile on his face. 'Go open a door. See what happens.'

'What's the Key of Solomon?' This time Shrewsbury turned to Farringdon, who simply shrugged.

'It a name for a book known as King Solomon's Grimoire, but in reality a book of renaissance magic written in the fifteenth century and owned by John Dee,' she explained. 'In it, there's a line about created magical items. The knife, sword, poniard, dagger, lance, wand and staff.'

'That's only seven items,' Shrewsbury was angering again.

'There's only seven choices,' Farringdon replied, pointing at the eighth wall, the entrance that they had entered through. 'The eighth item was always to be left open. And we know that it only leads out of here.'

Shrewsbury looked back to the open doorway.

'Which of the doors is it?' he asked, already bought into Farringdon's statement about the doors being booby trapped.

Damian shook his head.

'No, you're going to have to kill me,' he said. 'Like you did the others.'

Shrewsbury carefully looked around the crypt, staring in turn at the possibly booby-trapped doors.

'If you won't help me, I'll kill the girl,' he hissed, turning the gun to Katherine.

'No change there,' Damian replied calmly. 'Not the first time you've threatened to kill someone to make me do your bidding. Or had you forgotten Manchester?'

Shrewsbury was pacing now, the anger rising. Watching this, waiting for the perfect moment, Damian spoke, his voice calm and measured.

'Just answer me three things,' he said. 'Do that, and I'll tell you.'

Shrewsbury paused. Without even looking at Damian, he nodded agreement.

'Ask them,' he muttered.

'First, you didn't need to kill Andy, so why order the death?' Damian started. 'You could have promised us riches galore. The treasure was worth trillions, you could have offered us millions, just like you did Farringdon there, and still done everything you needed. Second, why kill Richard? He was dying of cancer, anyway. You could have promised him something, offered to look after his family, but you poisoned him? Why?'

Before Shrewsbury could reply to either of the first two questions, Damian calmly walked over to him.

'And third, tell me how you killed my parents, and why you did it.'

Shrewsbury looked down at the gun, as if deciding whether one more wave of it in Damian's general direction might finally work.

Deciding against it, he looked up.

'Your friend was a business choice,' he said simply. 'Both of you were. I didn't know how much you knew, and I didn't want a rival hunting the same things that I was. The plan was to shoot you both and plant the gun in your hands. Two treasure hunters fight and kill each other. Nobody would know that the clue had been solved. And it would have worked, if you hadn't run.'

'You should have done it yourself if you wanted it done,' Damian snapped. 'Your dog here has constantly failed you.'

Cyrus moved in on this, but Shrewsbury waved him back.

'Telling Cyrus to kill you was as good as doing it myself,'

he replied coldly. 'but once you escaped, I knew it was a matter of time before you hunted down a friend who could help you. And as the only living friend of yours who could do that worked for me, I knew I could keep an eye on you.'

Damian looked at Farringdon, who looked at the floor.

'Tell me about Richard,' he said without looking at Shrewsbury. 'Tell me why.'

'I've already told you.'

'Tell me again.'

'Honestly, it was simply bad luck,' Shrewsbury sighed. 'After Robert died, I went on alone for a while, but didn't get anywhere. I turned to Miss Gales here, as you know, but even with her talents, I couldn't decipher any more of the clues without the Sunne Dial. When I heard Richard had it, I knew I had to get it. To use it. So, I tried to negotiate with him. And to gain a position of power in the negotiations, I poisoned his whisky.'

He walked around the crypt as he spoke, gesticulating with the gun as he did so.

'I had an antidote,' he admitted, 'and I had every intention of using it. I just wanted the line of text that he'd found in Antwerp.'

'Which Farringdon told you he'd found.'

'Yes. But he jumped out of the car before I could give him the antidote. And by the time we'd found him, his heart had simply given out.'

Shrewsbury chuckled as he looked back at Damian.

'The funny part is that Andy told Farringdon later that Richard had written you a postcard and sent it from Deptford before he died. All that time he was in my car, and he had the bloody thing written on a card inside his jacket pocket.'

'And my parents?'

Shrewsbury's face darkened.

'Your father confronted me at a book launch in Oxford,' he explained. 'I'd paid him a King's ransom to find me proof I was linked to the Plantagenet line. And then he has the cheek to storm up to me, demanding whether I'd known all along, if this was all a joke.'

'This was after he'd learnt that he was the true heir?' Damian looked to Farringdon, who quietly nodded.

'*I* was supposed to be the heir,' Shrewsbury snapped. 'I was supposed to be king! Not some nobody academic from some shit village in Kent!'

'How did you kill him?' Damian kept his voice calm.

'I spiked his drink with some amphetamines, and Cyrus went outside, found his car and loosened his brakes,' Shrewsbury replied. 'Once your father left, he was already in an agitated state. Add a frayed break line to the mix and he was always going to drive fast and brake late. Eventually, the stress on the line would break it, and then...'

Shrewsbury shrugged.

'Boom.'

'My mum was in that car,' Damian whispered icily.

'Omelettes and eggs, I'm afraid,' Shrewsbury turned the gun back on Damian. 'And now I've had enough of parlour games, and I'd very much like what's owed to me. Behind one of these doors is trillions of pounds' worth of gold bullion. I'm going to buy the world. And we will remake it in my image.'

'What, a racist, xenophobic dickhead?' Katherine spat. 'Good luck with that.'

The crypt echoed with the sound of a gunshot as Martin Shrewsbury fired his gun into the roof. Katherine ducked as Damian moved towards Shrewsbury again.

'Are you an idiot? You could bring the whole thing down on us!'

'*Open the door!*' Shrewsbury screamed.

There was a silence as Damian and Shrewsbury stared at each other. Then, nodding, Damian walked back to the centre of the room, picking up the sceptre and examining it.

'I'd say it's that one,' he eventually said, pointing at the door across from the entranceway.

'You sure?' Shrewsbury walked to the door, looking back, gun aimed at Damian, who shrugged, holding up the sceptre.

'The sceptre was pointing at it. Apart from that, I haven't got a clue.'

'But what about all that Key of Solomon rubbish?'

Damian smiled, a dark, vicious one. 'That was all made up,' he admitted.

'You think I'm scared to kill you?' Shrewsbury asked. Damian shook his head.

'No, I think you're just fine with that. As long as it's poison, or your bodyguard, or a gun from a distance.'

He moved forward.

'You just don't like to get your hands dirty.'

'At least let us see the treasure before you kill us,' Katherine intervened as the two men faced each other. 'We've come all this way. One look, please.'

Shrewsbury paused, nodded, and then grabbed the handle of the door. Flinching as he did so in case there was some kind of booby trap behind it, he opened it—

Revealing an empty room.

'Where's the gold?' He asked, looking back at Damian, who shrugged.

'Well,' he smiled. 'I had a one in four chance of being right.'

Damian walked over to the first door and grabbed the handle. Before anyone could stop him, he pulled it open.

There was nothing in it.

'Two down, two to go,' he said.

'No!' Farringdon ran to the door to the right of the entranceway and pulled it open; there was nothing there.

Katherine moved to the last door, the one that led to the southwest of the crypt and opened it.

The reflection of gold, illuminated by glow sticks hit her face as she stared in shock into the room.

'I think I found it,' she whispered.

Shrewsbury pushed past her. It was large, roughly hewn, and inside it were four large, wooden chests, four feet wide by three deep, and three feet high, each ending in a curved lid.

Running over to the closest chest, Shrewsbury opened it up to reveal a mound of gold coins, spilling out onto the stone floor of the room as the lid clicked open. Without waiting, he moved to the other wooden chests, opening them, revealing them to be filled with a variety of gold coins, heavy gold chains, and ornate jewellery.

Riches from around the world, stolen during the Crusades, brought back to England by Richard the Lionheart and the Knights Templar were there for the taking.

The Plantagenet Gold existed after all.

37

GUNSHOTS

'Richard the Lionheart's gold!' Farringdon exclaimed.

'It's not enough!' Shrewsbury shouted back, searching the walls, in case there were more chests hidden somewhere. 'It's not what I was promised!'

'You wanted gold, here's the gold,' Damian looked through one chest, passing the sceptre to Katherine and picking up a small, ornate leather tube that had been placed on the top of the chest. Examining the tube, he saw that there were no jewels, no opulence whatsoever placed upon it. Amongst the other treasures in the room, even with the markings etched into the leather, it was ugly, plain even.

'I don't understand,' Shrewsbury said, still working through the chests, as if still looking for more. 'The legends said that there would be trillions worth of gold here! They used several ships to bring them back from the crusades! There should have been rooms upon rooms, filled with treasures; not four manky boxes!'

'The Knights Templar must have taken a larger share than people realised,' Katherine suggested.

'It's not like there's nothing to see here. There's still several millions' worth of antique coins in these chests,' Farringdon replied, holding up a small golden coin. 'This is a Byzantine Imperial gold coin, minted in Jerusalem in the mid eleven hundreds. Alone, and in this condition, it's worth a couple of thousand pounds, easy. And there're hundreds, thousands of these even to be found in this chest alone!'

'I've *spent* several million finding this!' Shrewsbury snapped. 'And where are the papers! The marriage certificates? The proof that Richard Shrewsbury was Henry's heir? These are what I needed! Not a few boxes of baubles!'

Damian looked at the leather tube, suddenly feeling the weight of history pulling at it.

'The School of Night must have withdrawn some of the gold to keep the line of Elizabeth safe,' Farringdon said, walking over to another chest and examining a gold necklace in the glow stick-hued light. 'They obviously used more of it doing this than we realised.'

'As well as every King from Richard the Lionheart to Edward the Fifth,' Damian continued. 'Over the centuries, the myth of the gold became bigger than the gold itself.'

Shrewsbury went to reply, but looked at Damian, the scroll case in his hand.

'What's that?' he asked.

'It looks like a Tudor scroll case,' Farringdon smiled as she snatched the leather tube. Opening the top, she peered inside it, slowly and gently pulling out a rolled-up piece of parchment with a small wax seal melted into the bottom.

'Well?' Shrewsbury was getting irritated again. Katherine kept looking at the entrance, as if considering escaping.

Farringdon didn't open the scroll fully; instead, she

started reading gently from the top, only opening the page up as she moved down.

'It's the proclamation,' she whispered. 'From Henry the Seventh himself, that Perkin Warbeck was Richard of Shrewsbury. That the Plantagenet line continued.'

Dropping the gun, Shrewsbury fell to his knees, rummaging in the treasure chest beside him.

'The others must be here!' he exclaimed. 'The marriage certificates!'

'No,' Damian replied softly. 'This was placed on the top, not hidden within. We would have seen them if they were here.'

He moved casually to the side of the room, where something placed behind one chest had caught his eye.

A sword, maybe even from the time of Richard the Lionheart.

But Cyrus, seeing this, moved in faster, picking the sword from the floor before Damian could reach it.

'Rusty old piece of crap,' he muttered, looking at it. 'Doesn't even have any jewels on it. I wonder what it's worth?'

Farringdon looked up from the scroll as she carefully replaced it in the tube, turning to the others.

'What now?' she asked. 'I mean, proclamation aside, there's still maybe ten, twenty million's worth here. Maybe we can still make a deal?'

'Still hoping for your cut?' Shrewsbury sneered, snatching the leather tube. 'Christ, you're a parasite! Just looking for what you can suck from me! A barnacle stuck to a boat!'

'Yeah,' Damian smiled. 'didn't they teach you at brown shirt school? You need to stand real straight, and not slouch when you say 'Heil Hitler.'

Shrewsbury picked up the gun from the floor, turning it to Damian who, as if using it as a shield, pulled the leather satchel around to his front.

'Heil Hitler,' Shrewsbury said as he pulled the trigger.

As the bullet hit Damian square in the chest, he went flying across the room, crumpling onto the floor. Shrewsbury looked at Katherine, the gun aimed at her—

Katherine swung the sceptre viciously at Martin's hand, connecting hard, and sending the gun sprawling into the corner before he could fire it. Cyrus, seeing this, raised the antique sword to strike her down, but Katherine was already on a roll, charging into Cyrus in a mid-section rugby tackle, the two of them crashing into the wall. There was a sickening *crunch* as Cyrus' head connected hard against the limestone brickwork. Reaching for the gun, Shrewsbury stopped as he heard the noise from outside the room.

Booted feet, running down the stairs.

'Armed police! Put down your weapons!'

Shrewsbury ran into the eight-sided crypt, running to the door as, along the roughhewn corridor, he could see the reflections of torches. The police were edging their way down, unsure of what would wait for them.

Struggling as he pushed the heavy wooden door to the crypt closed, he eventually slammed down a wooden bar, sealing the inhabitants of the crypt inside with him.

Grabbing the fallen gun, Katherine ran over to Damian, now rising groggily to his feet.

'You're alive!' she exclaimed as he examined his leather satchel, noting the bullet hole that had pierced through it, burrowing into several of Robert Lucas' notebooks.

'Calculated risk,' Damian croaked, rubbing at his bruised

chest. 'Handgun from fifteen feet, several inches of protection...'

He opened the satchel, reaching inside, pulling out an ornate, wooden cross, now splintered in the middle by the appearance of a bullet embedded into its centre.

It was the cross from Chetham's Library, the cross that started the whole quest.

'And someone up there looking after me,' he finished.

'You could have been killed,' she whispered.

Damian looked over to Cyrus, unconscious against the door, blood splattered on the wall behind his head.

'I hoped to give you time to escape,' he whispered.

'You sacrificed your life for me?' Katherine's eyebrows raised in shock. 'You're a man of many surprises, Damian Lucas.'

'Indeed, not to mention the one that's now trying to get into the crypt,' Shrewsbury said, walking back into the treasure room. Behind him, the police, pounding on the door could be heard. 'I'm guessing this surprise is all thanks to you?'

Damian rose now, pulling up his shirt as he did so.

'I bet you wish you'd sat on the Frith Stool and asked for sanctuary now, eh?' he asked as he revealed a small wire taped to his now bruised chest. 'The police have heard every word that we said down here. They've been waiting for you to screw up since we arrived. The woman at the shop you gave the bribe to? That was Detective Inspector Conlan of New Scotland Yard.'

'My men—' Shrewsbury started, but Damian raised a hand.

'If they weren't taken by the police, then my Russian

friends will have kept them busy,' he said. 'After all, you paid them to do so.'

'I what?' Shrewsbury realised as he spoke. 'The debt you owed.'

Damian nodded. 'Thanks for paying them for me. If you hadn't, none of this would have probably happened.'

'How?' Farringdon asked, her voice more impressed than surprised. Damian turned to face her across the empty room.

'I'm a con man,' he said simply. 'It's all about the story.'

EARLIER

Damian leaned back in the seat as he looked up at Detective Inspector Conlan, standing in front of them in the saloon bar of The Olde Starre Inne, with her partner, Detective Constable Briggs behind her.

'No, seriously,' she continued. 'You're under arrest.'

Damian watched Conlan for a moment, seeing that she wasn't moving towards her handcuffs. This was a power play, a simple act of establishing dominance.

'That's one option,' he said. 'But, I have a better one for you.'

'What's better than taking in a known murderer?'

'That we both know that the moment you walk me into Scotland Yard, someone will just walk me back out of it?' Damian replied.

'He's right,' Katherine added, still eating her dinner. 'And after all, we did ask you to come to York.'

'And I'd say by now you're wondering if I am the murderer at all?' Damian finished.

Conlan sat across the table from Damian and Katherine.

'You remember what I said the last time we sat across a table?' Damian asked.

'Yes. And your friend with the floppy hair reminded me earlier today,' she replied. 'If you're screwing me around, I'll have your spleen. So what's the deal here then? I mean, I watched the video of Richard Evans. Apparently, you're some long-lost King or something?'

'I'm just a man trying to clear his name,' Damian replied. 'And I could do with some help with that. Someone who wants the same thing I want.'

'And that's me? Why?'

'Because I think you're the type of copper that wants justice served,' Damian continued, nodding to Briggs as well. 'You won't take the easy option. That you're both here proves this.'

He looked out of the window.

'I intend to bring Farringdon Gales, Martin Shrewsbury and his goon Cyrus whatever-his-surname-is to Beverley Minster around eight o'clock tonight,' he explained. 'While there, I'll get them to admit to the murders of Andrew Holdman, Richard Evans, and Robert and Louise Lucas. And, also while there, I might be able to find you a lost historical treasure that'll have you both on the police lecture circuit for years.'

'So what do you want us to do?' Briggs folded his arms as he considered this. Katherine passed a sheet of paper across to Conlan, with handwritten names on it.

'I'm betting you were taken off the case the moment they took us out the door,' she said. 'That's because Farringdon Gales has some big names on her side. The moment this all hits the fan? Those names I gave you will rapidly distance themselves from her. In fact, if you call them in the next hour, they might even give you what you need to take her down in the first place.'

'Clear the Minster, play the part of the tour guide if you want, but give me time to do what needs to be done,' Damian finished. 'Oh, let any Russians in the area pass freely, and make sure you get hold of Cyrus's gun when you do arrest everyone. That's the one that killed Andy.'

Conlan stared long and hard at Damian.

'And if they don't confess?' she asked. 'If this doesn't go the way you think it will?'

'Then you can arrest me for whichever murders you want,' Damian replied. 'Either way, you get a win.'

'What's supposed to be under Beverley Minster then?' Briggs asked.

'A shit ton of gold,' Katherine smiled.

Conlan nodded, as if this was the sort of thing that she heard all the time.

'You wear a wire,' she said. 'You wear a wire and the moment I hear the confession, we take everyone down.'

Damian nodded. 'That's fine by me,' he said. Conlan rose from the chair, looking to Briggs, who nodded agreement.

'Then we have some calls to make,' she said, walking towards the entrance of the bar once more. 'Stay here, and I'll get someone to you with a wire to tape on.'

'They need to be here before seven. That's when the others turn up.'

Conlan checked her watch. 'Then let's hope the names on this list are quick workers,' she said. 'Either way, I'll see you in a couple of hours.'

'You know you're being watched though, right?' Briggs added.

'What do you mean?' Katherine rose from the table as Briggs looked towards the front entrance.

'Out on the street. Couldn't miss the bugger as we came in. Same guy who owned the phone that called in the tip in Temple Inn. The bodyguard you reckoned killed your mate.'

'You checked into that?' Damian was surprised.

'Of course we did,' Briggs sniffed. 'We're police.'

'Then we need to deal with this,' Damian replied, grabbing a last mouthful of food. 'Which of you is the better runner?'

Conlan looked to Briggs. 'He is. Why?'

'Because he needs to sell something,' Damian looked at Katherine as he grabbed his things. 'A quick jog down Stonegate's alleys should do it.'

Then, with a quick drain of his now empty pint glass, he hurled it at the pub window, grabbing Katherine by the arm and pulling her out of the main door at a sprint.

Conlan looked to Briggs.

'Off you go,' she said.

NOW

Katherine rose, the gun in her hand now pointing directly at Shrewsbury.

'Give me one damned reason I shouldn't kill this piece of shit right now,' she asked as her finger tightened on the trigger. 'Give me one reason why I shouldn't avenge my granddad.'

Shrewsbury ignored Katherine, walking over to Cyrus, examining him.

'He's not dead,' he replied. 'Not that you care, anyway.'

Rising, he now held the leather tube in one hand, and the antique sword in the other.

'Oh, come on!' Damian exclaimed. 'Give it up! You lost!'

He started towards the door, but Shrewsbury raised the blade of the sword.

'This might not be razor sharp, but it sure as hell isn't blunt,' he warned. 'Let the police wait for a moment.'

Katherine moved forward, gun still aimed at Shrewsbury's head.

'You don't get to make the rules anymore,' she whispered. 'You get to beg for your life.'

'Yeah, that's not going to happen with the safety on,' Shrewsbury crowed.

All it took was a moment; Katherine looked away for a split second to check the gun—but it was enough. As Katherine realised she'd been conned, Shrewsbury bolted for safety, sprinting out through the more recent of the doors in the crypt, running westwards, back towards the Minster.

'Dammit!' Katherine cried out, turning to Farringdon; but Farringdon too had disappeared, the faintest light of a glow stick seen up the eastern tunnel.

Damian, cursing, walked to the door to open it.

'Wait,' Katherine said, stopping him in his tracks. 'If the police come through, the first thing they'll do is arrest everyone they see.'

Damian looked down the west passage. He knew what Katherine meant; the minutes that Damian and Katherine spent proving their innocence would give Shrewsbury and Farringdon more time to escape. After all, nobody knew where the passages went.

'You go after Farringdon, I'll take Shrewsbury,' he said,

throwing his satchel to the floor and picking up the sceptre, holding it like a weapon. 'But don't kill her.'

'Unless it's self-defence,' Katherine replied, running east into the rough tunnel.

Damian looked back at the door, torn whether he should open it.

They'll get through eventually, he thought to himself before turning west and running after Martin Shrewsbury.

38

TUNNEL RATS

THE TUNNEL THAT DAMIAN RAN DOWN WAS MADE FROM A mixture of limestone and brick, was very narrow and had a low roof. Even with the smartphone torch in his hand, Damian couldn't see more than four feet in front of or behind him.

From the darkness, he caught the faintest shadow of light; the distant form of Shrewsbury's orange glow stick. Eventually the corridor curved to the left, but around fifty feet in front of him he could see a faint luminance, although it seemed to come from higher up. Entering a small clearing, only four feet square, he found long metal bars jutting out of the wall. Looking upwards, he could faintly make Shrewsbury out, using the bars as a ladder.

'Give up!' he shouted up, but Shrewsbury continued on, ignoring him.

Tucking the sceptre through his belt to secure it, Damian held his smartphone between his teeth and started after him.

THE TUNNEL THAT KATHERINE RAN INTO WASN'T AS WELL
designed as Damian's one; this looked like someone had pick-
axed it out of the very stone under Beverley, hacked at with
axes and swords; an act of desperation rather than of architectural planning.

She followed the twists and turns of the passage, counting
the steps as she ran, with each step just under a yard, and
basing the entrance to the tunnel about fifty yards north of
Beverley Minster, she reckoned the path was now running
almost directly under Friarsgate, the road that led towards
the modern Flemingate shopping centre.

Katherine wondered whether the foundations of the
centre would have blocked the path, or whether Farringdon
was going to keep running until she reached the River Hull,
but she didn't need to worry, because as she turned another
corner, she found Farringdon Gales leaning against the wall,
hands on her knees, taking in great, gasping gulps of breath.

She rose slowly as she saw Katherine appear.

'I'm not as fit as I used to be,' she said morosely. 'I used to
be a whiz at cross country. Now, I collapse at the slightest
thought of running, and my knees seem to have gone on
strike.'

Katherine raised the gun, aiming it at Farringdon, who
placed her hands in the air.

'Master race indeed,' Katherine snapped.

'You have me, my dear,' Farringdon said. 'Take me in,
gather your reward.'

Katherine didn't move.

'I'm not here to take you in,' she said. 'I'm here to avenge
Richard Evans.'

Farringdon paused as Katherine reached into her jacket
pocket, pulling out some small gold pieces.

'I couldn't find thirty silver pieces for you, *Judas*, so have some gold instead,' she said, tossing the handful of coins at Farringdon.

'I didn't kill Richard,' Farringdon stared down at the fallen coins. 'I loved him like a brother.'

'You didn't need to kill him,' Katherine hissed. 'You just needed to let Shrewsbury know what you'd found out. Then, with that done, you could leave it for him to sort out.'

Her teeth snarled.

'Just like Damian's parents.'

Farringdon's face darkened at that.

'So you're just going to shoot me?' she seemed almost disappointed as she asked. 'I thought better of someone like you, Katherine.'

'Really? Well then you need to lower your expectations,' Katherine said as she pulled the trigger.

———

As the gunshot echoed through the tunnels, Damian glanced back down from his current position, twenty feet into the air and hanging from a metal bar. The light from his smartphone torch only showed a few feet above and below, and Damian felt as if he was stuck on Jacob's ladder between Heaven and Purgatory.

In truth, he believed he must be in a crawl space between the inner and outer walls of Beverley Minster, possibly created when Nicholas Hawksmoor rebuilt the north side. Or it was a natural gap created during the various rebuilding; perhaps a shift in the foundations to fit an architect's style, or something deliberately built to hide Catholics during Henry the Eighth's reformation, the ghost of Nicholas Owen mocking him once more. Whatever the reason for this incredibly narrow chimney, with the thin metals bars that doubled as a ladder was, Damian cursed whomever had created it.

He had been climbing consistently for a while now; his arms were tiring, and he was glad he couldn't see down more than a couple of feet, as he believed he must have been over a hundred feet in the air now.

About forty feet further above him, there was the fading light of Shrewsbury's dying glow stick. Soon he too would be in darkness as it spluttered out. Damian wondered exactly how he was going to bring Shrewsbury back; after all, if this ladder went nowhere, the trip downwards could be speedy— and fatal.

There was a cracking sound above, like wood splintering, and a thin shaft of momentary light shone into the chimney above him. Damian had to shut his eyes for a second at the sudden brightness, as his eyes had become accustomed to the semi-darkness. When he opened them, the light was gone, and so was Shrewsbury. Willing his tired muscles to continue upwards that little bit more, Damian pushed onwards, clambering quickly to where he had seen the light.

There was a thin piece of wood now beside him, across the chimney from the metal bar ladder. On this was a dusty footprint, from where Martin Shrewsbury had obviously kicked at it. Taking a deep breath, Damian did the same, almost falling off the makeshift ladder when the wood gave way, and light from outside shone into the chimney. Carefully stepping across, Damian clambered through the thin wooden entrance to find himself in a dusty room three quarters of the way up the tower. Looking around, he could see gutters sloping down from the roof, leading to plastic pipes against the wall; this had to be the roof of the tower above him, and that the pipes were the intricate drainage system that Beverley Minster had built to stop the rain falling directly into the Belfry.

There was a small door to the side; beside it was a discarded and almost dead glow stick. Putting his smartphone away, pulling his sceptre out from his belt and once more wielding it as a weapon, Damian opened the door to find himself on an incredibly narrow winding staircase, with limestone steps heading both upwards and downwards.

The logical route for Shrewsbury would have been to go down, to outrun the police and escape through the North entrance, but through a very thin window just up from him, Damian could see the reflection of blue flashing lights. It looked like all the police in Yorkshire were outside.

Shrewsbury wouldn't have gone down to that, he thought to himself as he turned left out of the room, grabbing the blue rope that served as a handrail up the middle stone pillar and starting towards the roof. He was at a massive disadvantage here; there was a longstanding urban myth that castle steps always rotated to the right as defenders, fighting downwards against an ascending force, would have their right hand free, while the middle pillar would hinder the attackers. And myth or not, with a sword in his hand, Shrewsbury could cause Damian great trouble if he so wanted. Steeling himself in case, Damian continued upwards, recalling the gunshot that he had heard moments earlier. He hoped Katherine hadn't killed Farringdon. And that he even considered she would, worried him.

FARRINGDON OPENED HER EYES AND STARED AT KATHERINE, THE gun still in her hand. Two inches to the right was a chipped hole in the stone where the bullet had struck; a small shard of stone had clipped Farringdon's ear, which now dripped blood.

'I thought I was dead.' Farringdon exclaimed softly, her eyes wide.

'You should be,' Katherine admitted. 'And a week ago, if I'd been in this situation, I wouldn't have hesitated.'

'What changed?'

'Damian,' Katherine shrugged. 'Imagine the disappointment on his face the moment he heard that I shot an unarmed academic, even one like you.'

Farringdon nodded.

'Well, thank God for Damian,' she said.

Katherine shook her head.

'Don't think this means you're getting away with anything,' she continued. 'The moment Conlan comes through, you're heading to jail.'

Farringdon nodded.

'I can deal with that,' she replied. 'I held my part of the bargain until the end.'

'What bargain?' Katherine lowered the gun. In the distance, down the tunnel behind them, she could hear boots approaching. The police would soon be upon them.

Farringdon shrugged.

'The School of Night,' she replied with a smile, reaching for her jacket, pausing as Katherine raised the gun again, and then continuing to reach in as Katherine nodded agreement. Slowly and carefully, she pulled out a sheet of parchment.

'Shrewsbury thinks he has the proclamation in his

possession,' she explained, the sheet of ancient paper now in her hand. 'But all he has is an empty leather tube.'

'Why would you do that?' Katherine asked. Farringdon simply rolled the parchment carefully into a tube, ensuring that the wax seal was secure, and passed it across.

'Our remit was always to keep the line of Elizabeth safe,' she said. 'Damian is the line.'

'You're kidding me!' Katherine exclaimed. 'He's almost died a dozen times!'

'Becoming a King is something that needs to be earned, I suppose,' Farringdon shrugged.

Katherine took the offered parchment.

'You surprise me,' she whispered. 'At the very end, you do the right thing.'

Farringdon laughed.

'Oh, my dear child, I'm not doing anything for you or Damian,' she said. 'I know that by doing this, I'll be of use to you.'

'For what?'

'You have the proclamation, but not the wedding certificates,' Farringdon smiled. 'Eventually, Damian will have to ask me for my help in finding them. The moment he does, I'll have him.'

The smile disappeared.

'Not *your* School of Night, but mine,' she hissed. '*I'll* be the one who creates a King.'

Katherine went to speak, but the light of torches suddenly lit the tunnel, as armed police ran towards them.

'Put down the gun!' the lead officer said. 'Hands on your head!'

Detective Inspector Conlan moved her way to the front.

'Don't worry about her,' she said, waving at Katherine. 'She's SO14.'

Katherine almost laughed at this, as the police passed her, taking Farringdon into custody. Conlan looked around the tunnel.

'We found the bodyguard in the crypt,' she said. 'Your work?'

Katherine nodded.

'And Shrewsbury and Lucas?'

'They went down the west tunnel,' Katherine replied. Conlan nodded again, as if she had been expecting this answer.

'Briggs went down there. We'll get them shortly,' she replied. 'Until then, shall we get out of these bloody silly tunnels?'

'Don't mind if I do,' Katherine said before passing the gun to Conlan. 'You might need this. It's had a lot of fingerprints on it, but it's the gun that killed Andy Holdman.'

And with that Katherine turned and walked back down the tunnel, towards Beverley Minster, fresh air and daylight.

39

CROWNED BY BLOOD

DAMIAN HAD ALSO FOUND FRESH AIR AND DAYLIGHT AS HE MADE his way down a narrow corridor at the top of the stairs, emerging onto the top of the North-West Tower.

The floor was arched, the lead-lined roof of the tower now beneath his feet, a white flagpole bolted into a piece of wood attached to the middle of it. Limestone blocks, stacked four high, created the battlements of the tower, with stone finials and carved crockets above them. Every four feet there was a space in the battlement, a waist high, foot-wide viewing port that gave incredible vistas of the Yorkshire countryside and the rest of the Minster below, depending on which direction you looked.

And, standing on the other side of the roof, with a sword in one hand and a leather scroll tube on the other, was a wide-eyed Martin Shrewsbury.

'It's over, Martin,' Damian said as he moved towards him. 'The police have surrounded the whole church. You can't escape.'

He hefted the sceptre, feeling its weight.

'But I *really* want you to try to get past me,' he said. 'For Andy. For Richard. And, more importantly, for my parents.'

Shrewsbury looked at his own sword and chuckled.

'Sword fights on a Minster roof?' he said, his tone amused. 'Well, I suppose if there was any way to gain a kingship, it's in a one-on-one battle.'

Before Damian could reply, Shrewsbury charged at him, swinging the sword down in a killing blow. Damian only just dodged out of the way, the sceptre deflecting the blow into the flagpole with a loud, metallic *clang*. As Damian regained his footing on the lead roof, Shrewsbury attacked again; this time in small, stabbing, thrusting motions, the aim to push Damian back down the stairs, where one moment of lost balance could be fatal.

Damian ducked to the side and swung his sceptre up hard, connecting with Shrewsbury's midsection, a *whuff* of air expelling out of the millionaire's mouth as, grasping his gut, Shrewsbury spun fast, swinging the sword weakly at Damian, who batted it away with the sceptre.

Damian backed away from Shrewsbury, edging to the stone battlements. He knew the sceptre was getting a pounding and being made of a far softer gold wouldn't last much longer against the heavier sword. All he could do was keep the flagpole between Shrewsbury and himself and hope to keep his opponent busy until the police arrived.

Shrewsbury, however, had other plans and immediately charged at Damian, knocking the sceptre aside and pushing Damian against the battlement, sword blade horizontal, as if trying to push the blade through Damian's neck. Damian had got his arm up to block the blade—but even though the sword was blunt, it wasn't *that* blunt—and slowly, Damian could feel the blood trickling down his forearm as the edge of the ancient sword bit through his jacket sleeve and into it.

'You're going to die, Lucas!' Shrewsbury exclaimed with psychotic glee. 'I'm finally going to do what I should have done in Manchester!'

And Damian knew without a doubt that Martin Shrewsbury was correct.

There was only one way he might get out of this; Shrewsbury, in his desperation to end Damian, had dropped the leather tube onto the roof. And, with a well-placed knee to the groin that sent Shrewsbury staggering back momentarily, Damian reached down quickly and grabbed it, holding it in the air, the blood now trickling down his arm as he did so.

'Come closer and I drop this,' Damian said, waving the tube over the edge of the battlements. 'You need this way more than I do.'

'You wouldn't dare,' Shrewsbury hissed.

Damian looked up at the tube.

This was the proclamation that stated Perkin Warbeck was Richard Shrewsbury, the younger of the Princes of the Tower. It was one of the biggest historical finds in years, even bigger than Richard the Third in a Leicester car park. And, if it *was* thrown off the top of this Minster, there was every chance that it would be destroyed for all time.

But it also caused the deaths of Andy, Richard and his parents, among many others over centuries of conflict.

As far as Damian was concerned, it was cursed.

'Try me,' he hissed.

'Fine,' Shrewsbury replied, lowering the sword. 'let's go downstairs, see the police. I'll guarantee you I'll be out of custody before midnight tonight. Because that's the thing about being rich. Everyone is for sale.'

Damian knew Shrewsbury was right. There was no chance in hell that he'd be left in jail overnight. And before the police could get their act together and charge him with the murders of Damian's friends and family, Martin Shrewsbury would be on a private plane to somewhere that didn't have extradition laws, still fighting to prove he was a legitimate ruler, still leading thousands of racist followers, all of whom would now see him as a martyr to their cause.

He'd probably make even more money from it.

'Nah, screw that,' Damian said, tossing the tube up in the air, watching it as it turned in a lazy arc, falling over the battlements of Beverley Minster.

'No!' Shrewsbury cried, dropping the sword as he ran towards the edge of the tower, his eyes fixed upon the leather tube as he vaulted the waist high battlement to reach up and grab it. His fingers brushed the edge of the leather as he grasped out, catching it, but he was overbalancing, too far over the edge...

Damian grabbed his hand, holding Shrewsbury steady as he stared at him, eyes cold.

'You saved me,' Shrewsbury said in surprise, his hand now gripping Damian's for dear life. Damian, however, shook his head.

'All I did was delay the inevitable,' he said. 'I didn't want you jumping off the Minster and falling to your death like some accident. I wanted you to know *it was because of me.*'

With a look of horror, Shrewsbury stared at Damian, his eyes cold as he pulled his hand away, leaving Shrewsbury to once more overbalance. Damian stood still, not moving forward to save him as, his momentum carrying him over the edge, Martin Shrewsbury found himself slipping, now in open air, empty space, floating for the briefest moment before gravity took charge again, and he fell the hundred and seventy feet to the stone-clad pavement below.

'That's for you, Andy,' Damian muttered, before picking up the sceptre and the sword from the lead roof, tucking the latter into his belt and walking down the narrow steps back to the Nave of Beverley Minster.

'I THOUGHT YOU WERE SUPPOSED TO COME IN THE MOMENT they made the confession?'

Damian faced Detective Inspector Conlan in the Nave of Beverley Minster, opening his shirt and tearing off the wire with his right hand, as a medic tended to the gash on his left forearm.

'We lost your signal once you went under,' Conlan replied apologetically. 'We didn't even realise that things had gone pear-shaped until we heard the first gunshot. And we couldn't go running in, as we didn't know what was down there.'

She looked at the sceptre in Damian's hand.

'Nice stick. Little bent though.'

'Saved my life,' Damian said, looking out of the door to the north of the Minster, where currently police forensic officers were placing a blue tent over the fallen body of Martin Shrewsbury. 'So you didn't get any of it?'

'Don't worry, everything else that happened today and my own testimony will go a long way in proving your innocence, and the late Mister Shrewsbury's guilt.'

Conlan looked Damian in the eye.

'And there was no way you could have saved him?'

'No,' Damian lied. 'I grabbed at his arm, but he was too far over the battlement to be saved.'

'Right. Oh well,' Conlan mused.

'And Farringdon? I heard a gunshot.'

'I missed,' Katherine, walking over to them, smiled, looking down at Damian's now bandaged arm. 'that looks painful.'

'Well, she's definitely still alive, and down as an accessory to murder, but it'll depend on what happens once Briggs gets her to the station,' Conlan explained. 'Those people you gave me on the list? Half of them hated her. The other half loved her. She still has a lot of friends in very high places.'

'What about us?' Katherine asked. 'I mean, are we to be arrested too?'

'Last I heard, you were under the jurisdiction of Counter Terrorism,' Conlan flashed a rare smile as they walked back across the Nave of the Minster, towards the cordoned off hole leading to the Chapterhouse crypt. 'They can decide what to do with you. Of course, by the time they do, we'll have dropped all charges.'

She looked at the hole in the ground.

'Several million in gold?' she whispered. Damian nodded.

'Go have a look,' he suggested. 'It's not audited, nobody would know if a couple of coins disappeared.'

Conlan laughed.

'We've already had fifteen grand placed in the police pension fund tonight,' she replied. 'I think there's been enough bribing of officials since you arrived.'

'The church is gonna be pissed that we damaged the floor,' Damian muttered.

'They can buy a whole new church with that gold,' Katherine replied. 'After all, there's no legal challenge to it, and it's been on, or at least *under* their land for the last three hundred years.'

'If you believe your grandfather, then it's Mister Lucas' gold,' Conlan said. 'I mean, if it was held for the Plantagenets...'

'No proof, no gold,' Damian said ruefully. 'The documents that we expected to see weren't there, and the proclamation was thrown off the top of the Minster.'

'Not quite,' Katherine smiled. 'The tube was empty. Farringdon snaffled the proclamation.'

'Shrewsbury died jumping for an empty tube?' Damian shook his head. 'I almost wish he'd survived, just to learn that.'

He paused, looking around.

'My dad's notes!' he exclaimed. 'I had a satchel, dad's notes were in it. In the confusion, I must have left it down in the crypt.'

'I'll get them,' Katherine said, nodding to Conlan. 'Before the York forensics put them in with everything else.'

And with that, she ran back to the hole, jumping quickly in and disappearing from view.

'They should at least give you a finder's fee,' Conlan muttered.

'I'm just happy having my freedom back,' Damian admitted. 'Thanks for your help.'

Conlan nodded at the sceptre.

'We'll need that as evidence,' she said. Damian sighed.

'Can I have a quick look at it first?' he asked. 'It saved my life, and I think Henry Tudor once held it. The historian in me wants to give it a closer examination before I pass it on and never see it again.'

He nodded to the ornate wooden Chancel in the middle of the Nave.

'I'll just be by that,' he suggested.

With a nod from Conlan, Damian walked over to the pews beside the Chancel, sitting down and carefully inspecting the sceptre.

It was true he wanted to look at it, but not because it was a simple item of history. When he had fought on the roof of the west tower, he'd noticed something on the side of the sceptre, something that he wanted to confirm before giving it away. Turning it over in the light, he saw what he had suspected. Along the length of the sceptre were faint markings, as if carved into the gold itself. Roughly etched, but markings that were likely to have been made in the early eighteen hundreds by a rogue architect with a thing for treasure hunts; and these were a series of symbols that Damian knew all too well.

There was a polite cough behind him, and Damian turned to see Pietr standing patiently at the entrance to the Chancel.

'You lead interesting life, Mister Lucas,' he said, entering. 'I am sorry your fat friend is dead.'

'Me too, Pietr,' Damian said. 'We... We're square now?'

'All fine and dandy, as you say,' the Russian nodded. 'We go home now. Until the next time we speak.'

'We'll speak again?' Damian asked. Pietr chuckled.

'Your life? It is filled with danger. You'll need help. And today you paid us on... How you say? Ah yes. *Retainer*.'

Damian smiled. 'Hopefully I won't need to, but it's appreciated.'

As Pietr left, Damian saw Katherine climb out of the hole with the help of some officers, his satchel on her shoulder as she nodded over to Damian.

'I'll see if your Russians can sort us out a lift to York,' she said, continuing towards the North entrance. Damian waved to her in agreement, already turning back to the sceptre and the translation. He no longer needed a dial or a sheet of paper with the symbols on. This cypher was an old friend now, reading the words that the markings created almost as easily as if he was reading a book written in English.

And the riddle that appeared was one that fitted the same rhythm and cadence as the others that he had decoded.

Two roses torn asunder, picked to choose a cause; A great bard's scrawl upon the wall, beneath fair England's laws.

Damian leaned back as he looked at the rhyme, scribbled down on the back of the food receipt from The Old Starre Inne. For the first time, he didn't need to research this, check this or even search through notes about this. He knew what this rhyme meant. And, looking up, he saw Farringdon, about to be led away, watching him with the hint of a smile.

'You found another clue!' she shouted. 'Good for you! Find it!'

Looking at the piece of paper, reading the clue once more, Damian chuckled to himself. He was becoming his father, whether he liked it or not. Another quest, another clue. What would happen when he found the next one? Would there be another level to climb? Had Hawksmoor never tired of this? Was this why his father and Richard, even Farringdon, spent their lives hunting ghosts?

Damian took the receipt and, with quick, even strokes, tore it into small pieces. Then, walking to a bank of small candles, he burned the little pieces, one by one. Nobody would ever learn the last location. And Damian was done with conspiracies.

The Minster was emptying now, as the forensic science

officers, free to start their jobs began examining the hole in the floor, checking the stands that had been used to open it. One of the officers, however, walked over to Damian.

'Sorry,' he said apologetically. 'We need the sceptre.'

'Oh, right. Of course,' Damian handed it over, finding that this was actually harder than he expected it to be. 'Any idea what'll happen to the money?'

'Looking for a finder's fee?' The officer grinned. 'Unlikely, mate. They'll lock this up in court for years.'

'Yeah, I thought as much,' Damian nodded, turning and walking towards the North entrance. By now, Katherine would have found someone to take them to York. Maybe they could have that drink they'd talked about.

Maybe, maybe, maybe.

'What do you want done with the books?' the officer shouted after him.

'What books?' Damian turned back to the officer, who pointed into the crypt.

'The pile of notebooks down there,' the officer said. 'Apparently, they were your dad's books or something? All dumped by the wall beside a splintered wooden cross?'

Damian looked to the North door again, where only minutes earlier Katherine had walked out with his bulging satchel; one filled with books and a splintered wooden cross.

Or so he'd thought.

Running out into the courtyard, Damian looked around. The location was a hive of activity, with police vans leaving and cars making three-point turns, trying to avoid the crowds of Beverley locals, all trying to find out what was going on, to see who it was that had jumped from the tower of Beverley Minster.

Of Katherine Turner, though, there was no sign.

Damian laughed.

He couldn't help it, he just began laughing, right there in the courtyard. A satchel, filled to the brim with gold coins and jewels, just walked out of the Minster under the noses of the police. Money that would never be missed; after all, nobody had audited the money, and there was no way to accurately state the amount that was supposed to be there.

A satchel of antique gold and jewels, with more probably in her pockets? With the coins worth thousands each, let alone what the jewels were worth? Katherine Turner had most likely walked out of Beverley Minster, past the police and past the crowds of people with several million pounds' worth in her possession, if not more.

Damian bent over, still laughing. At the end of the day, the School of Night—or at least a singular branch of the School of Night still had Plantagenet gold to look after.

And that, as far as Damian was concerned, was exactly as it should be.

EPILOGUE

Detective Inspector Conlan was as good as her word; by the time Damian reached York police station, all charges had been dropped, and he was free to leave. He agreed to stay in York for a few more days, however; there were many shadowy, suited people with a large amount of questions, and they wanted answers to every single one of them.

There was also the circumstance of Martin Shrewsbury's death; whether he had fallen to his fate or whether Damian had pushed him. Luckily for Damian, almost a hundred witnesses below the Minster's towers had seen Martin Shrewsbury jump to his death as he tried to grab hold of a leather tube, and it was later deemed *death by misadventure.*

Beverley Minster hadn't been too happy to learn of the vandalism to their floor; however, this changed when they realised that, as they had been unaware custodians of the gold for over three hundred years, they had a very strong case for keeping a large part of it, as well as securing a fund to have the tunnel opened up so that people could visit the Chapterhouse crypt.

Damian had joked about a finder's fee, but several days after returning to his flat in Hackney, he was visited by Governmental men in suits, shadowy figures who worked within the Palace of Westminster who, after explaining to Damian that repeating anything that they said during this conversation could be taken as an act of treason, discussed their recent findings.

The audit of the lost Plantagenet Treasure was an estimated twenty-three million pounds in monetary value, but the academic and historical value was priceless. And, as a gesture of goodwill, the British Government were happy to credit Damian with the find, as well as providing him with a finder's fee, which came to roughly six hundred grand.

Besides this, they offered him the sceptre that had saved his life and the proclamation to do with as he wished. Damian didn't really trust the people offering this; he felt like this was the Taymaster deal again, however he was on the other side of the table, and there was a definite unspoken suggestion given here that it would be preferred if Damian didn't tell anyone about it—after all, a written decree by Henry the Seventh, claiming that Perkin Warbeck wasn't dead, was indeed Richard of Shrewsbury, the younger of the Princes in the Tower and was his legal heir over Henry the Eighth was something that could cause riots in academia— and, after making very sure Damian understood what they meant, they left him in peace.

Damian knew the moment they left he wasn't going to follow their advice.

A week later, Damian learnt that Farringdon Gales had worked out her own deal with the British Government, most likely brokered through her remaining contacts. She was a free woman again, but excommunicated from the School of

Night, and with her reputation and career in tatters, Damian didn't know what the future could really hold for her.

Damian spent the next week ensuring that the proclamation and the sceptre went to the right places; the sceptre returned to Beverley Minster, where the trustees were overjoyed to gain back such a historical item, before being horrified at the damage to it, while the proclamation was given to the British Library through Max Larridge to exhibit in the Ritblat Gallery, under the names of Robert Lucas and Richard Evans.

The proclamation's revelation had caused a divisive split amongst the historical community, with one side claiming this to be the greatest historical find since Richard the Third, while the other constantly expressed doubts about its validity, pointing out that Damian was an unreliable witness with a known history of art forgery. Damian, meanwhile became a minor celebrity in the weeks that followed, with three separate Universities offering him his completed degree if he agreed to lecture there twice a year, leading the charge of a dozen international institutions who wanted him to talk about his experiences. A high six-figure advance was offered for him to write his story. Everyone wanted a part of Damian Lucas.

Of course, there were people who *hated* him. His post now had to be checked by an external source, as Martin Shrewsbury's racist and alt-right allies saw Damian as a figurehead of the enemy, and the man who caused the death of their leader. And in the end Damian had used the finder's fee money to buy his flat outright, renting it out and, after his Canterbury house's tenants moved out because of the 'high state of burglaries' and 'unsafe gas levels' in the area, he moved back to the family home.

He hadn't gone to Andy's funeral.

He'd considered it, but he felt at the time the media circus that his life had become wasn't something that he wanted to put Andy's family through. So, he'd sent flowers and a message of sympathy.

Six months on from the events at Beverley Minster, Damian Lucas had been largely forgotten from public memory. And if he was honest with himself, it was exactly how he wanted it.

Returning to the family home, Damian had found that it felt different. The ghosts and echoes in every room became familiar, and soothed rather than unsettled him.

He'd started to renovate the house; it was his now, and he wanted to place his own imprint on the property. And it felt good to actually do some work on the building; painting walls, laying new carpet down, choosing new furniture. The secret room in the basement was removed; instead, the entire basement was refurbished out to become a small home gym. Damian didn't need to hide from people anymore.

He was at peace with himself; the King who would never be. The academic with a family history crazier than anyone else he knew.

He had almost forgotten about her when Katherine Turner knocked on his door one late March morning.

'I LIKE WHAT YOU'VE DONE TO THE PLACE,' SHE SAID AS SHE entered the living room. Wearing a pair of jeans and a hooded top, her long brown hair cascading over the top of it, she looked nothing like the suited woman that Damian first met all those months earlier.

'Coffee?' Damian shouted from the kitchen as Katherine sat on the sofa.

'Please,' she replied as Damian returned to the room, mugs of coffee in his hands. Passing one to her, he sat in an armchair to her right, watching her.

'I never thought I'd see you again,' he admitted.

'You can't get rid of me that easily,' she replied. 'I thought it'd be best to keep away while you sorted your life out.'

'And it took a while to fence a ton of stolen gold coins, right?' Damian smiled. Katherine shrugged.

'It was there, and nobody was paying any attention to it,' she replied. 'And I knew the government would take it as soon as they got any of their civil servants near it.'

'How much did you make?' Damian sipped at his coffee.

'Just over three million, give or take.'

'You did well.'

'I didn't keep any of it,' Katherine replied. 'It went to the School of Night. I used the money to regain trust, to forge new alliances and to restore the School into one solid entity.'

Damian raised his eyebrows in surprise.

'You didn't keep any of it?'

'Well, a few coins might have fallen down the back of the sofa,' Katherine laughed, finally relaxing.

'So, did they make you their leader?' Damian asked. 'I know Farringdon isn't part of the School anymore.'

'I left, too,' Katherine shook her head. 'I'd only joined because of my granddad. It's time for me to find my own way.'

There was a pause.

'So,' she said.

'So,' Damian replied.

'I was in York this week,' Katherine continued. 'Saw the

sceptre. They've restored it to how it was before you started repeatedly hitting a fascist with it.'

'You were hitting guns with it first.'

'Touché,' Katherine nodded. 'Anyway, there were some scratches along the side. Looked like at some point, they were a message. Now, of course, half of them are all buffed away.'

'That's a shame,' said Damian, straight faced.

'What did the message say?'

'Why do you think I'd know?'

'Because you were writing it down on a piece of paper when I last saw you,' Katherine smiled. 'What did it say?'

Damian thought for a moment. It'd been months since he'd last thought about the sceptre's last clue.

'Two roses torn asunder, picked to choose a cause; A great bard's scrawl upon the wall, beneath fair England's laws.'

Katherine considered the words.

'And have you been to find out what it led to?' she asked.

'I'm not sure if I want to,' he replied.

Katherine rose from the sofa, holding out her hand.

'Then it's a good job I'm here then,' she said. 'Come on, let's go finish this damn thing together.'

Rising, Damian took the offered hand.

'I suppose we'd better go to London then,' he said.

MARK WAS ON SHIFT WHEN DAMIAN AND KATHERINE ENTERED the main doors of Middle Temple Hall.

'Oh no,' he said as they stood in front of the security desk. 'You almost cost me my job last time.'

'True,' Damian replied. 'But you did help stop a terrible man become King.'

'I did?' Mark smiled. 'I'm a Kingmaker now? I like that.'

He pointed a finger accusingly at Damian.

'You promised to come tell me what happened,' he said. 'It's been months.'

'Story's not over,' Damian replied. 'One last thing, and then I'll tell you everything.'

'Where do you need to go now?' Mark sighed. Damian looked to Katherine.

'The garden outside the lower door, the one we escaped from last time,' she said. 'We need to go to the place where the Wars of the Roses began.'

'That's just a made-up story,' Mark was already walking into the great hall, indicating to another guard to take over in the security room. The hall was set up for lunch, with long tables covering the length of it as Mark led Damian and Katherine towards Drake's cupboard and the hidden door. As they walked, Damian could hear whispered comments, as people in the hall realised who Mark was leading past them.

'We'd better hurry,' he said softly. 'Last thing we need is an audience.'

'Come on, it feels good to be nervous again, doesn't it?' Katherine grinned.

Opening the door and taking the stairs to the lower west exit, Mark used his security pass to open the door, emerging out into the Middle Temple Gardens.

'Now what?' he asked.

Damian looked around. The last time he'd been here, he was running from the police, and hadn't really taken the time to truly examine the location. The walls of the hall were made of brick, with white stone edging on the corners, all laid upon larger, white stone slabs. The paving stones were a duller, darker grey and followed the hall to the left, the grass leading on the right to a series of ornate, square low hedges.

'*Two roses torn asunder, picked to choose a cause,*' Katherine said as she looked around. '*Henry the Sixth Part One*, where the Wars of the Roses were decided, with each side picking either a white or red rose.'

'Yeah, but even if that was true, those rose bushes went centuries ago,' Mark replied. 'They redesigned the entire garden at the turn of the eighteenth century.'

'Exactly,' Katherine examined the patio. 'And if you recall, you said that Drake's lantern was broken during the redesign of the gardens, likely by an architect helping with the outer walls of the building.'

'Bloody hell,' Mark looked back at the walls of the Hall. 'Hawksmoor was working on this?'

'Probably briefly, and only to do what needed to be done,' Katherine replied, now moving over to the wall to the left of the entrance. 'He wouldn't have wanted to risk being recognised.'

'*A great bard's scrawl upon the wall, beneath fair England's laws,*' Damian brushed at one stone. 'To me, that says that one of these stones has something on it.'

'Great Bard... So Shakespeare then?' Mark examined the higher bricks in the wall.

Damian crouched, looking down at a brick two rows up from the white stone base.

'Or maybe not,' he said, indicating two letters etched into the brick itself. Small and almost invisible because of the years of negligence, they were undeniably a C and an M.

'*A* great bard, not *the* great bard,' he replied. 'C.M. Christopher Marlowe.'

He pulled out a penknife, scratching at the mortar around the brick.

'Now hang on!' Mark said, looking around in horror. 'You can't go scraping around our bricks like that!'

'Come close and look, you can see that the mortar's different,' Damian whispered as Katherine knelt down beside him, scratching at the other side. 'And to be honest, I don't think this is going to take long to check out—'

He stopped as the brick fell out of the wall. Or, rather, a half-inch deep fake frontage of brick fell out, revealing a roughly hewn hole behind it, in which was a familiar looking, slim leather tube. Mark couldn't help himself, and knelt down beside Damian, helping him carefully remove the tube from the hole in the wall. This done, he placed the fake frontage back in place.

'I'll get that fixed later,' he said, looking at the slightly damaged wall with an almost parental concern as Damian rose, opening the tube and carefully removing the contents.

There were three documents. The first two were wedding certificates; one from 1502, announcing the marriage of Richard Shrewsbury and Elizabeth Grey, a union that legitimised their son, John Dudley, as a true Plantagenet. The second was from St Alfege, dated Easter 1561; the secret marriage of Queen Elizabeth and Robert Dudley in a ceremony witnessed by only three people; William Cecil, John Dee and Thomas Tallis, all of whom had signed the document.

'Jesus,' Katherine said, examining the documents. 'There you go, then. The full Plantagenet line, all the way to Arthur.'

Damian looked at the third and final paper, a note from John Dee, telling Christopher Marlowe to travel to Spain, locate Arthur Dee or his newborn son, and bring them back to England, a command that Marlowe had faked his death to obey, returning years later as Thomas Heywood.

Everything that his father had hunted for, that Richard Evans had searched for, these forlorn quests had led to this one moment. With these documents and the one that was now in the Ritblat Gallery, Damian Lucas had a powerful argument to claim he was the legitimate heir to the throne of England.

'What will you do?' Katherine asked.

Taking the documents and placing them back into the leather case that they had hidden in for over three hundred years, Damian shrugged.

'I think I'll hang them up in my study,' he eventually said. 'Have you seen the Royal Family lately? I'd be causing myself more hassle if I made these public. Besides, we owe Mark a drink and the whole damn story.'

Katherine pulled Damian around to face her.

'You could have everything with these!' she said earnestly.

Damian nodded.

'Possibly,' he replied. 'Have dinner with me.'

'What?'

'Months ago, I said I wanted to take you to dinner,' Damian's voice softened as he spoke the words he'd wanted to say for so long. 'I like you, Katherine. A lot. I've missed you. So come to dinner with me. Tonight.'

Katherine smiled.

'I'd love to have dinner.'

'Then I already have everything I want,' Damian smiled. 'Who needs the pressures of kingship, anyway?'

With this, he took Katherine's hand in his own, leaning forward as he finally kissed her, feeling her lean into the kiss as she pulled him tight to her.

There was a polite cough, and Damian reluctantly pulled away, looking to Mark, now standing by the door.

'I like you, Damian,' Mark said, 'but King or no King, I'm not really up for doing that sort of thing, just so you know. I just want the story.'

And, with the last part of the puzzle completed and a tube containing priceless historical secrets now in his possession and a lunchtime story to tell a family friend, Damian Lucas, the true King of England laughed as he left Middle Temple Hall with Katherine Turner and Mark beside him, leaving the ornate side garden empty once more, a garden where, hundreds of years earlier, the future of another Kingship was said to have been debated.

ACKNOWLEDGEMENTS

When you write a series of books, you find that there are a ton of people out there who help you, sometimes without even realising, and so I wanted to do a little acknowledgement to some of them.

There are many out there I need to thank, and they know who they are. People like Andy Briggs, who started me on this path, first by suggesting repeatedly I write this book over four years ago now, but more importantly for a discussion over a coffee during a pandemic in September 2020, convincing me that Jack was a good idea. Which, my friends, he was.

I need to thank others, though; the staff of Chetham Library, including Sue McLoughlin, who back in June 2017 was the Heritage Manager of the library and, on short notice took me on a private tour of John Dee's rooms, the volunteers of Beverley Minster for allowing me to wander around as I tried to work out clues in 2019, Stephen Saleh, who brought me in to work on a John Dee-related graphic novel, allowing me to research my own book while doing his, but more importantly Orla and Mark, my guides in Middle Temple; Mark was genuinely a Security Guard of forty years employment, and his revelations and stories while we walked around, including down the 'secret stairs', helped me create most of the Middle Temple section, and warranted his actual arrival in the story.

Then there are people like Barry Hutchinson, who patiently zoom-called and gave advice back in 2020, the people on various Facebook groups who encouraged me when I didn't know if I could even do this, the designers who gave advice on cover design and on book formatting all the way to my friends and family, who saw what I was doing not as mad folly, but as something good, including my brother Chris Lee, who I truly believe could make a fortune as a post-retirement copy editor, if not a solid writing career of his own, and Jacqueline Beard MBE, who has copyedited all of my Declan Walsh books, line by line for me, and deserves *way more* than our agreed fee for this one. Both of these people shaped the book you read. Also, thanks to Maureen Webb and Edwina Townsend, my last line of editing defence, who picked up the erroneous end mistakes.

And finally, I owe a lot of this to James Wills, who for years worked as my literary agent and even before the pandemic was suggesting how to make this story better, faster and shorter!

But mainly, I tip my hat and thank you. *The reader.* Who, five books ago took a chance on an unknown author in a pile of Kindle books, and thought you'd give them a go, and who has carried on this far with them.

I write my novels for you. And with luck, I'll keep writing them for a very long time.

Jack Gatland / Tony Lee,
    London, January 2022

ABOUT THE AUTHOR

Jack Gatland is the pen name of *#1 New York Times Bestselling Author* Tony Lee, who has been writing in all media for almost thirty-five years, including comics, graphic novels, middle grade books, audio drama, TV and film for *DC Comics, Marvel, BBC, ITV, Random House, Penguin USA, Hachette* and a ton of other publishers and broadcasters.

These have included licenses such as *Doctor Who, Spider Man, X-Men, Star Trek, Battlestar Galactica, MacGyver,* BBC's *Doctors, Wallace and Gromit* and *Shrek,* as well as work created with musicians such as *Ozzy Osbourne, Joe Satriani* and *Megadeth.*

As Tony, he's toured the world talking to reluctant readers with his 'Change The Channel' school tours, and lectures on screenwriting and comic scripting for *Raindance* in London. As Jack, he's written the *Detective Inspector Declan Walsh* series of crime procedural novels, of which, at the time of writing, he has eight books released.

An introvert West Londoner by heart, he lives with his wife Tracy and dog Fosco, just outside London.

In fact, feel free to follow him on all his social media by clicking on the links below. Over time these can be places where we can engage, discuss Declan, Damian and others, and put the world to rights.

www.jackgatland.com

Subscribe to Jack's Readers List:
www.subscribepage.com/jackgatland

www.facebook.com/jackgatlandbooks
www.twitter.com/jackgatlandbook
ww.instagram.com/jackgatland

Want more books by Jack Gatland? Turn the page...

LETTER FROM THE DEAD

"BY THE TIME YOU READ THIS, I WILL BE DEAD..."

A TWENTY YEAR OLD MURDER...
A PRIME MINISTER LEADERSHIP BATTLE...
A PARANOID, HOMELESS EX-MINISTER...
AN EVANGELICAL PREACHER WITH A SECRET...

DI DECLAN WALSH HAS HAD BETTER FIRST DAYS...

AVAILABLE ON AMAZON / KINDLEUNLIMITED

EIGHT PEOPLE. EIGHT SECRETS.
ONE SNIPER.

THE
BOARD
ROOM

HOW FAR WOULD YOU GO TO GAIN JUSTICE?

NEW YORK TIMES #1 BESTSELLER TONY LEE WRITING AS

JACK GATLAND

A NEW STANDALONE THRILLER WITH
A TWIST - FROM THE CREATOR OF THE
BESTSELLING 'DI DECLAN WALSH' SERIES

AVAILABLE ON AMAZON / KINDLE UNLIMITED

THE THEFT OF A **PRICELESS** PAINTING...
A GANGSTER WITH A **CRIPPLING DEBT**...
A **BODY COUNT** RISING BY THE HOUR...

AND ELLIE RECKLESS IS CAUGHT IN THE MIDDLE.

JACK GATLAND

PAINT
— THE —
DEAD

A 'COP FOR CRIMINALS' ELLIE RECKLESS NOVEL

A NEW PROCEDURAL CRIME SERIES WITH
A TWIST - FROM THE CREATOR OF THE
BESTSELLING 'DI DECLAN WALSH' SERIES

AVAILABLE ON AMAZON / KINDLE UNLIMITED

THEY TRIED TO KILL HIM...
NOW HE'S OUT FOR **REVENGE.**

NEW YORK TIMES #1 BESTSELLER **TONY LEE** WRITING AS

JACK GATLAND

THE MURDER OF AN **MI5 AGENT**...
A BURNED SPY **ON THE RUN** FROM HIS OWN PEOPLE...
AN ENEMY OUT TO **STOP HIM** AT ANY COST...
AND A **PRESIDENT** ABOUT TO BE **ASSASSINATED**...

SLEEPING SOLDIERS

A **TOM MARLOWE** THRILLER

BOOK 1 IN A NEW SERIES OF THRILLERS IN THE STYLE OF
JASON BOURNE, JOHN MILTON OR **BURN NOTICE,** AND
SPINNING OUT OF THE **DECLAN WALSH** SERIES OF BOOKS

AVAILABLE ON AMAZON / KINDLE UNLIMITED

Printed in Great Britain
by Amazon